A FORBIDDEN LOVE MAFIA ROMANCE

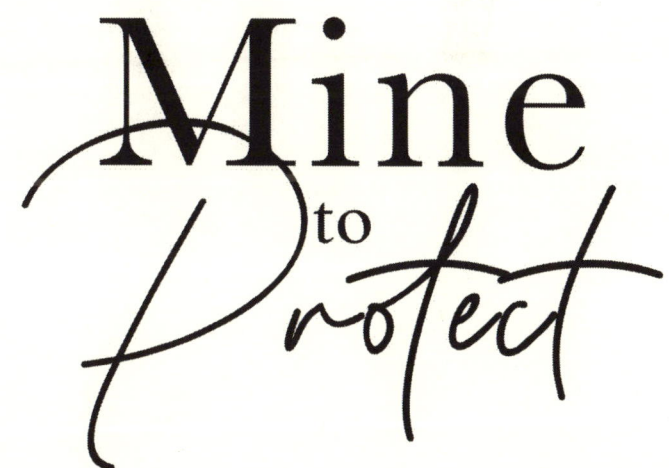

AWARD-WINNING AUTHOR
EMILY A. MYERS

Mine to Protect

Copyright © 2022 by Emily A. Myers

All rights reserved. This book or any portion thereof may not be reproduced or used in any manner whatsoever without the express written permission of the publisher, except for the use of brief quotations in an article or book review.

This is a work of fiction. Any references to historical events, real people, or real places are used fictitiously. Other names, characters, places, and events are the products of the author's imagination or used in a fictitious manner, and any resemblance to actual persons, living or dead, or actual events and locales is entirely coincidental.

Edited by Beth Attwood

Cover Design by Vanessa Mendozzi

eBook ISBN 979-8-9850282-9-4

Paperback ISBN 979-8-9866970-1-7

Hardcover ISBN 979-8-9866970-0-0

www.emilyamyers.com

❦ Created with Vellum

To all the women still searching for their friend group, their partner, or even themselves. One day, you will everything you've ever dreamed of.

A FORBIDDEN LOVE MAFIA ROMANCE

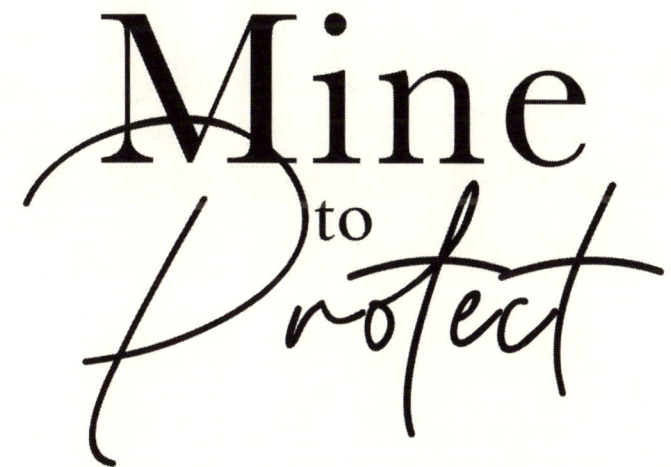

AWARD-WINNING AUTHOR
EMILY A. MYERS

I

Alister

THE NIGHT THE BROTHERHOOD SUPERIORS FELL TO THEIR knees before me is a night I can never forget, no matter how badly I want to. After a year of searching for my sister Cara, first for her, then only for her abductors, I finally found myself face-to-face with the men responsible for her death. They kneeled before the Blood King of New Orleans as I and my associates ripped the skin from their bones. As their cries filled my ears and their blood covered my hands, there was a brief moment when I felt justice had been served. My sister had been avenged. But the moment evaded me as quickly as it came when I found my sister, dressed in a tattered, bloodstained nightgown, standing among the tortured corpses left in my wake. It was the first time I saw my sister's ghost. It's as if she wanted to tell me this war for vengeance isn't over. Or perhaps she just wanted to see for herself what her abduction and murder had created—a monster. She has haunted me ever since.

My eyes shift from the golden-brown liquid in my cup to the photograph at the edge of my wooden desk. I guess I like to torture myself as much as others, because every time I see it, the pit in my stomach grows. It was taken when my family was whole. Myself, my sisters, Sophia and Cara, stand with our parents along the white spiral staircase leading into the grand ballroom of our home. It was the last Christmas we shared together before my mother was killed, in these ancient walls no less. New Orleans hasn't felt like home since, let alone the grand French-inspired estate that's been in my family since my ancestors immigrated from Sicily in the late 1800s.

With each passing year, my family loses a member. My mother was killed when I was sixteen during a botched hit meant to take out my entire family. My father died last year, nearly twenty years after my mother. Unlike the bullet that took her from me, cancer was his poison. And my sister Cara, she was taken in the night from her dorm room shortly after my father passed and I came to power. The rest you already know. Except, perhaps, one thing, the most important thing. *Why?*

Why would someone put a hit on my family? Why would my eighteen-year-old sister be ripped from her bed, sold into sex slavery, and killed? It's because of our blood. We are the Amatos, the gatekeepers of the criminal underworld stretching from the Texas border all the way to the Florida Keys. For the innocent, we are the only thing standing between them and full-on anarchy. Though, they wouldn't know it. For those privy to this world of darkness to which I unfortunately belong, we are royalty. And like the kings and queens of the past, we are flush with wealth and connections carefully attained by our ancestors and modern-day business deals that help keep our illegal drug trade secret. Our wealth and reputation accompanied by our unique network of connections in Mexico, the Caribbean, Chicago, and New York City make us targets of those looking to make a name for themselves among the world's most dangerous and vile. But what was once a powerful and untouchable dynasty is now only a brother and sister desperately trying to survive.

I failed Cara. I carry my failure every day. It feels like one hundred cuts split my skin. This photo, her bedroom just down the hall from mine, the memories of her playing repeatedly in my head, even the sound of her name crossing another's lips sets my skin ablaze like salt rubbed into my one hundred cuts. It's almost unbearable, and yet, unlike the night I lost myself in the blood of my enemies, I cling to the pain. I cling to it so that I never forget what my enemies are capable of and to justify to myself the horrendous things I must do to maintain control of the throne I never wanted. This throne is my burden, but it is also my lifeline. Because for me and my sister Sophia, there is only one way out of this Hell. And I'll be damned if I allow Sophia to suffer the same fate as Cara.

As the door to my study squeaks open, I move my hand from my glass of bourbon to the gun holstered beneath my desk. "Alister?" I close my eyes, allowing my racing heart to slow, and remove my finger from the trigger.

"Come in, Sophia." Sophia enters my wood-paneled office wearing pajamas and a lifeless expression I've become too accustomed to. Her raven hair lies limp against her button-down as she places my dinner tray in front of me. "Sorry I missed supper. I guess I lost track of time," I say as I unbutton the top two buttons of my white dress shirt. She only nods before taking a seat in one of the chairs across from me. I watch as she moves slowly. She, like everyone else, believed the lies I told about Cara's whereabouts while I searched for her and her abductors. I only told Sophia the truth when I had to. She hasn't had as much time as I have to make peace with our sister's death. Though, even after a year, peace is the last thing I feel.

"How was your day?" I ask as I pluck the lid from atop my plate.

"Busy with preparations for tomorrow. The press conference is scheduled for ten a.m. All the requested media has RSVP'd."

At that, I nod and down the rest of my drink. "Yeah, I might need one of those too." As my eyes meet hers, she presses her lips firmly into a flat line, as if to keep them from quivering. I oblige her request and pour her a glass of the smooth, subtly sweet alcohol. After over a year of lies, there is some relief in the version of events we plan to tell the media tomorrow about Cara's death. And yet, the burden of the truth weighs heavier than ever.

As the words of the speech I've prepared come to me, a chill dances across my tan skin, letting me know she's here. I look up to find Cara standing behind Sophia. She's dressed in the same ragged nightgown. Though, for the first time, I find small droplets of tears trickling down her gray-blue skin. I can look at her for only a second before I'm forced to turn away. I wouldn't mind being haunted by her if she looked like herself. But every time I see her, rather her ghost, I'm reminded of the horror she faced and the pain she endured. I'm reminded that I couldn't save her. She's dead because I couldn't—

"Alister? Are you okay?" Sophia asks.

"Yes, um..." I clear my throat and search my mind for a way to get back to the mundane. "How about the Halloween party? Is there anything left to do for it?" It's one of the many charitable functions we host to keep up appearances with the New Orleans elite. When I was growing up, it was the most fun of all the parties my mother hosted. Since her passing, I've learned it's nothing more than a cover for a meeting even more elite than the partygoers.

"The party is taken care of. How about you? Have you finished preparing for the annual meeting of the capos?" At that, I lower my fork, returning it to the tray before me. My dark eyes find hers. She isn't supposed to know about that. "You know, I can't believe I didn't figure it out sooner. Grandma always said October 15 is an important day in our family history."

Sophia has always been the smartest woman in the room, but I highly doubt her intelligence is what alerted her to the centuries-old ritual taking place tomorrow night. "Sophia, I've got enough to worry about. I shouldn't have to add you snooping through my office to the list."

"Don't worry. I didn't invade your sanctum. You forgot to remove their names from the guest list you emailed me." I nod, annoyed by my mistake but pleased with the small burst of color flushed across Sophia's cheeks. Though, as her defensiveness leaves her, she is left once more with sallow skin and dim eyes. "You should've told me," she says then.

I take a deep breath and another bite of my dinner before saying the words sure to start an argument. "There's nothing to tell."

"Like Hell there isn't!" Sophia yells, prompting me to massage my temples and pour myself another bourbon. "You may be king, but I am just as much a part of this family, this *business* as you."

"Family, yes. Business, no. You know this, Sophia."

"What I know is that they are one in the same," she says, leaning forward with a fire in her eyes. "All you do is work, Alister. You're never here and when you are, you're in this office, staring into space, studying the security cameras, and doing God only knows what else."

"And what else would you have me do, Sophia? I'm doing everything I can to keep this family together, to keep us safe. And the only way I know how to do that is to make sure we are strong on all fronts. You handle the legitimate businesses and I handle the other. That's the arrangement we established after Dad passed and it works—*sort of*."

"It doesn't matter because everything is different now. Cara's dead, Alister, and—"

"Do you think I need reminding?" At that, my lethal grip

shatters my cup. Sharp fragments of glass crush into my palm. The initial sting is followed by a prolonged ache as amber liquid invades the cut. I shake the shards from my hand as Sophia stands and makes her way to the cabinet where I keep the first aid supplies. "Forget it, Soph. It's just a scratch."

"Just let me make myself useful," she bites out. I press my lips together, silencing myself. I hate to fight with my sister, but in times like this, it's better than the silence otherwise found between us. She has every right to be upset with me, and she is. I kept the truth of our sister's disappearance and murder from her for a full year before telling her the truth three months ago. There was a part of me that didn't know if I would tell her, if I'd tell anyone. Not only did I not know how to tell her, I also didn't want her to have to live with the burden of knowing and yet not knowing.

It took me months to discover who had purchased Cara. And when I finally tracked down the sick bastard, he'd already gotten his fill of her and had disposed of her body. How do you explain that to your little sister? Granted, Sophia is in her late twenties. But, still, how do you say the words? Even now, I can barely get through it. And yet, knowing and not knowing the full truth is only part of why I didn't tell Sophia what happened to Cara.

Sophia pulls her chair across the red-and-cream-colored rug to sit closer to me while doctoring my hand. My throat aches as I work up the courage to say the words she deserves to hear. She isn't a kid anymore. In fact, despite my best efforts to keep her safe, she's the one who saved me when my plan to take down the brotherhood was thwarted. I know I don't have to protect her from every little thing, even though that very mentality has been engrained in me ever since the night my mother, *our mother*, was killed. And yet, I can't help myself. She's all I have left, and protecting her is the only part of my life that makes sense. It's the only honorable part of me left.

"Listen, Sophia—"

"Let me go first," she says, cutting me off. I nod. She exhales as she returns her attention to my hand. "I know you think I'm upset that you didn't tell me the truth about Cara, and you're right. I am upset. But the past couple of months have shown me my being upset with you has less to do with the past and more to do with the present."

"What do you mean?" I wince as Sophia tightens the gauze. She stands and returns the supplies to the cabinet before facing me again.

"When Dad died, it was hard on all of us. Most of all, it was hard on you. Your entire life changed the moment he took his last breath." My eyes return to the photograph on my desk as she speaks. "So, I was willing to do whatever you needed me to to make the transition to power easier for you. I happily took over the legitimate businesses while you figured out what the Hell it even means to be the Blood King."

Sophia sits next to me once more, pulling my attention back to her. "But now, after losing Dad *and* Cara, it's clear the toll the past year has taken on you." She reaches out and presses her hand against my cheek, running her fingers across my stubble. The ache in my throat only intensifies as I see the pain in her features. "You need my help, and not just in the sun, but in the shadows too. And yet, you refuse to ask for it."

"Sophia." I take her hand in mine, brushing my thumb over her knuckles. "I already lost one sister. I won't survive losing you too. And I'm not saying you can't handle yourself, because, deep down, I know you can. After all, I trained you myself. But...*I* can't handle you being a part of this world. And it's not just because it's dangerous. What we do is illegal, Sophia. Whether or not we like to admit it, our family's reign has an expiration date. It will either end in death or in jail." That's a lie. Not even jail time can end a reign like ours. But it can make us easier targets for a competing family to take us out. I bite my lip as the image of Sophia's dead body flashes behind my eyes.

"My secrets are mine. My burdens are mine. So that when it all comes to an end, you can walk away." Another lie. There is no walking away for either of us. "I'm sorry if that means I'm oppressive and harsh and more of a bodyguard than a brother. But right now, I don't know how to be anything else." Finally, the truth.

I release Sophia's hand and turn away from her, moving my eyes to the security monitor. I search each screen, giving myself enough time to fight off the tears threatening to reveal themselves. In my peripheral vision I see Sophia bury her face in her hands as she rests her elbows on her lap. This is what it means to be the Blood King. Over a century of Amato men have sacrificed love, friendship, honor, everything including their humanity for a greater cause now muddled by greed.

There was a time when illegal work was the only work available to Italian immigrants looking to earn a livable wage. But, more than money, the American Mafia was formed to protect Italian immigrants who were persecuted because they were different than their white counterparts. This racism and elitism was never more prominent than on October 15, 1890, the day my family and our respective organization holds in reverence. On this day, the New Orleans police chief was murdered, execution-style, and eleven Italian men were arrested, one of whom was an Amato. Of all the attention the New York City families receive, this occurrence in our own New Orleans is actually the first event of suspected Mafia activity in the Americas to gain national and international attention. And it's because of this that when the men accused were acquitted of all charges, a slaughter ensued in which all eleven Italian men were killed.

No one wanted to believe the Italians were innocent. And Hell, maybe they weren't. But what was meant as a deterrence only cemented the bond of the families who lost loved ones that day. Upon a vote, the Amatos took charge of a new Mafia syndicate in New Orleans and quickly adopted the pseudonym Blood King along with the vow that no more Italian blood would be spilled in the streets of New Orleans under their rule. The Amatos were already a wealthy lot before their sudden rise to royal status shortly after their stateside arrival. Still, what would become of the Amato family, *my* family, was forever changed on that fateful day.

Tapestries of the Amato family crest, once purple and gold, were changed to red and gold to symbolize the blood that had been spilled and the blood all Amato kings swear to protect. One of several custom tapestries hangs on the wood-paneled wall of my office just to my right. Gold-set family jewels from Italy made of rubies and diamonds were embossed with the Amato family crest for all members of the royal household to wear as a symbol of their status and alliance, while a special piece was gifted to the new king, a piece passed down to every king thereafter. The gold-set ring on my right hand is large, heavy, and impossible to miss. In the center of a gold casing that looks like a crown there is a large deep red ruby. Atop it is the Amato crest etched in gold. More pavé rubies cover the sides, working their way between gold plates on which one is the letter *A* and on the other is the symbol of a crown. This ring represents my power, my position as king. And now, I, like my father and the others before him, must make the ultimate sacrifice to provide for and protect the people under our charge. What no one admits, but I've painfully learned, is that anyone who loves the king must also make the ultimate sacrifice.

I know Sophia needs me, me Alister, not me the Blood King. But I don't know how to be there for her without breaking. And, now more than ever, I have to stay strong and vigilant. This is the second year in a row I will hold the annual meeting of the capos without Cara in attendance. The last thing I can allow is for an ambitious capo to smell blood in the water. If the truth of Cara's murder gets out, it will mean war—war with our enemies and, possibly, war within our own ranks. That's why I hesitated to tell Sophia the truth, why I haven't told anyone else, and why the world believes my sister is studying abroad in Europe. This secret is a burden to all whom carry it, but the truth? The truth will be the death of us.

Sophia stands, drawing my attention. "Wait, Soph..." I reach out, taking hold of her wrist before she can leave. "I..." She's right. I am struggling, struggling to carry the weight of a one-hundred-year reign, struggling to accept that my sister is gone, that I failed her. But, most of all, I'm suffocating, drowning in hopelessness because there is no escaping this world, this throne, this thing known as the Mafia. I know I should set aside my worry, even if just for a day, and hold her, cry with her, be her brother. But I've been caught off guard too many times. I've lost too many people to pretend to be normal. Because all it takes is three seconds and one bullet to shatter what's left of my black heart.

"I love you and I'm sorry I'm not the brother you need right now. I...I hope I find my way back to him one day."

Sophia pulls her wrist from my grasp. Disappointment flattens her lips and drains the color from her cheeks. "Me too." At that, she turns and leaves me be with a plate of cold food, a deafening silence, and our sister's ghost.

2

Ariana

"Gotta keep up, Ray!" I yell as my feet pound against the gravel jogging path through Audubon Park. It's a crisp October morning in the Crescent City, free from the humidity I loathe. Slivers of sunlight work their way through the tangled branches of the oaks above me. It warms my skin as I inhale the earthy scent drifting down from the Spanish moss. This is my happy place, my *me time*, which is why I don't feel bad about leaving Ray in the dust.

My long brown hair slaps against my back as I run as if a rider's crop is propelling me farther and faster. Though, as I cross the stone bridge, I slow to take in the green, murky waters below. Birds swoop down, skimming the top of the water for their breakfast, while fathers set up lawn chairs on the bank for a day of teaching their sons how to fish. Every morning it's the same. The people of the city get away from the brick and mortar in exchange for something simpler, quieter. I guess you could say I'm here for the same reason, to block out all the noise and stress that follows my every move as a member of the Organized

Crime Task Force for FBI New Orleans. But, truly, I'm here for something more. I'm here to remember.

Once I make my way to the bottom of the bridge, I hook a left and sprint down the oak-lined alley parallel to the pond. I run as fast as I can, pushing past the ache in my chest and the burn in my legs, until I reach the grassy meadow. My chest heaves as my heart pounds. I lean forward and rest my hands on my knees as the memories return to me.

I can see her with her curly dark hair standing close to the bank. She fluffs a blanket for us to sit on and pulls two sandwiches from her purse. She looks at me with a smile on her face, a smile so beautiful I wonder why I don't see it more often. Or, at least, I did. *Come here, Ariana. It's time to eat.* My mom reaches out to me. The simple motion creates an ache in my chest greater than any run ever could. As a younger version of myself races past me with a bushel of wildflowers in tow, I look away. And like yesterday and the day before that, I lose my mom all over again.

"Thought I'd find you here," Ray says through ragged breaths. I turn to find him walking the last few steps. His pale face is now bloodshot red, and his blond hair is damp with sweat. "What is it about this spot, huh? I tell you there's a lot better trails than this one."

"Yeah, well, it was your choice to tag along."

"Hey, I'm not complaining. I'm just curious. Five years we've worked together, and I feel like I barely know you. You love to run, and you love this spot. So, tell me, what's the story?"

Ray's blue eyes search mine as I consider how to respond. This is why I don't have any friends. Why, in the five years I've worked for the FBI, I've rejected every invite to every party and rebuffed every advance by every coworker, including Ray. I don't allow people to get close to me, because then they start asking questions. Most of which I don't have the answers to. And for the ones I do, the answers are too painful to share.

"There's no story," I finally say. "And, if there were, I certainly wouldn't offer it to someone who can't even beat me in a race."

"Oh, is that what this was?" Ray asks, eyebrows raised. "Because you see, I was thinking we could call this something else."

"Let me guess." A small smirk works its way across my lips as I stretch out my muscles.

"*A date*. I mean, you are my Valentine after all." I roll my eyes as Ray, for the millionth time, shoots his shot. When I agreed to let him tag along for my morning runs, I expected him to last one week tops before he finally lost interest. It's been two months of mornings just like this one and, to my surprise, he hasn't let up in the slightest. I suppose I don't mind the company. But the questions and the flirty comments, that I could do without.

"Nice play on words, but you know where I stand. I don't date coworkers. And besides, why ruin a good thing with a relationship?" I punch his arm as I move past him. It's not his fault, really. He's perfectly handsome in that golden boy, wholesome kind of way. And he's nice, thoughtful, and smart. He's the kind of guy any girl would be lucky to date or even just be friends with. *A friend*—I guess he's the closest I have to one, which makes turning him down a delicate dance.

"Fine. I'll quit," he jokes as he jogs to catch up with me.

"Perfect! You know, I've been thinking. The world really could use one less intelligence analyst." I can't help but smile as Ray takes my sarcasm in stride. Though, his next question steals the easy energy between us.

"You know it's not the same at the office without you. Any idea when your leave will end?"

"No." I sigh. "Bilieux made it clear my suspension is indefinite." I drop my gaze to the gravel as memories of my meltdown flash behind my eyes.

> *"Are you kidding me? You're just going to let him go? Give him a year to cover their tracks and rework their entire criminal organization?" I stand with such force my chair tips over. My team watches with wide eyes and parted lips. In five years, they've barely seen me smile let alone raise my voice. I take a deep breath and steady myself by pressing my finger into the manila folder sitting on the table before me.*
>
> *"We've got them, sir. We've got the names of their associates, transaction records detailing the sale of illegal drugs, schematics of their compound, and a witness testimony to back it all up. And, with all due respect, we didn't work for any of it. Alister Amato and his organization was handed to us on a silver platter by Emma Marshall. Imagine what else we could find if we only looked for ourselves. Imagine the connections they must have to other syndicates."*
>
> *"Valentine!" I jump as my boss's voice roars through the room. I know I've crossed a line. No. I've obliterated the line between passion and obsession. But I can't help myself, not after what I saw. "We don't have a choice. The Amato organization is at the top of our list, but there is one organization that is even more of a priority."*
>
> *"The brotherhood," I mumble.*
>
> *As SSA Bilieux speaks, my heartbeat slows. "Our witness didn't only provide information on Amato. She provided intel on the brotherhood. And now we have a chance to take them down, to save hundreds, if not thousands of women from their captors and keep many more from ever being victimized. But, in order to do that, we need information that only Alister Amato has."*
>
> *My cheeks burn as the truth lands heavy on me. I'm not a monster. I want to help those women. And, any other day of the week, I'd prioritize taking down a sex trafficking syndicate over a drug kingpin. But not today. No, no, I can't. Slowly, my arms begin to tremble, and my eyes fill with tears.*

"Ariana?" Ray reaches for me, but I pull my hand away. I turn in his direction, but my vision is too blurry to make out his features.

"You have to ask him. You have t—"

"Ariana, you can ask Alister Amato anything you want—one year from today." As Bilieux, the agent in charge, gives his order, I break.

I blacked out and went on a rampage that ended with me facedown on the floor of the bureau in handcuffs. The aftermath comes to me only in snippets. The flipped desk, the torn papers. The broken glass surrounding me and the blood trickling down my arm. As we walk, I catch a glimpse of the scar just beneath my thumb. It's a constant reminder of the day a facade eighteen years in the making came crumbling to the ground.

"It's a wonder I didn't get fired. Still, it wouldn't surprise me if they wait to bring me back until after the Amato investigation is complete. After how I acted, there's no way they could put me on the case. The Amatos no doubt have top attorneys. If they caught wind of my outburst, any evidence I discovered would be deemed inadmissible."

"But we've still got nine months before we can even open an investigation into the Amatos. And, like you said, they know we're coming. They've got plenty of time to alert their contacts and change up their operations. It could be a year or more before we're able to close the books on them."

I nod. "Don't remind me."

"Hey." Ray stops, forcing me to stop with him. "It's going to be okay. We're going to bring them to justice, and you will have your position back in no time." The sincerity in his eyes warms my heart, so much so there's a part of me that wishes things could be different, that wants to let him get to know the real me, even the parts I hide from myself. But that part of me is squashed by the screams, the blood, and the eerie chill of death that reminds me I'm broken. And nothing but the truth will fix me, if even that.

"Thanks, um, everything in due time, right?" Ray nods, though as he drops his eyes to his feet, I can tell there's something more he wishes to ask me. I bite my lip, not wanting to encourage him, but I can't help it. "Ray? Is there something else?"

"Yeah, um, that day at the bureau, you never finished telling me what you wanted me to ask Amato. You said, '*You have to ask him.*' Ask him what?" My chest tightens as I remember back, my brows furrowing as I feign confusion. There's only one benefit to the blackout rage I experienced that day. No one questions me when I tell them I don't remember what happened or why I was so adamant we investigate Alister Amato as soon as possible. But that couldn't be further from the truth.

"That day is such a blur, Ray." I shake my head. "If I said something along those lines, I don't remember why. And what I do remember, I try not to. It, um, it wasn't my finest moment." *Understatement of the year.*

Emotion fills Ray's baby blue eyes as I refuse to open up. I can't be sure if he pities me or if he can tell I'm lying. The only thing I'm certain of is that he doesn't judge me, which only makes lying to him that much harder.

"Come on. I don't want to make you late for work. Bilieux might decide to extend my sentence."

Ray lets out a chuckle, shifting back into his lighthearted self. "You really are the Queen of Mystery, you know that?"

"Oh, you know. It's all part of my charm." And yet, *charming* is the last word I'd use to describe myself and my life.

When I was ten years old, I was placed into the foster care system, which made for an uncertain and traumatic adolescence as I bounced from house to house. The scar on my hand isn't my first nor the most memorably earned. But no matter what happened between those four walls during those eight years, it never compared to what happened before I entered the system.

I close my eyes as if to blink away the memories that never leave me, but it's no use. Instead of the warm, tree-filled park, I'm right back at that old, drafty apartment. The one with the loose floorboards, roaches crawling on the walls, and mold growing in the corner. Moans and screams fill my ears just as they did all those years ago. After what feels like forever, a man adjusts his pants as he leaves the room my mother and I shared. And then it's quiet, so quiet I feel like I'm the only person left on the planet. That is, until my mother appears, adjusts her apron, and offers to make me a sandwich. Her face is damp with tears as she does. There are bruises on her arms and around her throat. And yet, all of this, this Hell that my mother endured, for God only knows what reason, is not the thing I remember most. Not by a long shot.

"Hey, Bilieux, twelve o'clock." Ray gives me a nudge, alerting me to our boss just up ahead. I welcome the distraction from my own personal Hell. Though, I can't help but find my boss's presence strange. I've run this trail enough to know it can't mean anything good. Ray and I pick up the pace, meeting Bilieux among a group of media trucks and workers setting up a makeshift stage.

"Agent Bilieux."

"Agent Valentine." My boss gives me a once-over as Ray and I approach. The last time I saw him he pressed his knee into the center of my back as he pinned me to the floor. Our exchange is quick and to the point, which only makes me feel more uneasy, both about my future with the FBI and his reason for being here this morning.

"What's up, Boss?" Ray asks, oblivious to the tension I feel. He offers his hand to Bilieux while I do my best to avoid eye contact.

"I'm on an assignment. There's an important press conference about to take place, and I want to personally see that it goes as planned." I feel Bilieux's eyes shift to me as he speaks, though I keep mine focused on scanning the park.

"Press conference? What's it about?" Ray asks.

Bilieux clears his throat, and thinking me preoccupied, pulls Ray a few steps away. That's when I notice them. Amato soldiers dressed in black suits, no doubt strapped with nines, create a secure perimeter around the stage. I'd recognize their faces in my sleep, though I can't let Bilieux know. Because, despite orders to use my time off to relax and seek psychological help, I've been conducting an investigation of my own into the Amato outfit, expanding on the original intel provided by our civilian informant. The presence of Amato soldiers can mean only one thing. Their boss is on his way. This press conference is for him. And Bilieux isn't here to make sure it goes smoothly. He's here to make sure I don't do something stupid.

3

Alister

I adjust my cuff links as Sophia, Gio, my head of security and underboss, and I walk from our SUV to the stage. The simple movement gives me an excuse to lower my head so that no one notices the raw agony smeared across my features. Today, I'm going to tell a lie. Not unlike most days. Though, today, the lie hurts just as much as the truth. I'm going to tell the world that my sister Cara was killed in a car accident in Europe while studying abroad. A car accident. No one will question it. Not the police nor those looking for any excuse to challenge my rule. Though, just in case, I staged a crash in Italy to help sell the story. And yet, my body is still riddled with anxiety and heartache as I prepare to say the words. Because no matter how true or untrue they are, one tragic fact remains—my sister is dead and now there is no more pretending otherwise.

"Alister!" As Gio enters my office, pale and breathless, all oxygen leaves my lungs. My pen falls from between my fingers as the large wooden door slams shut behind him. Gio hesitates. Slowly, I stand, though the look on Gio's face lets me know I'll wish I was sitting when he shares

his news. He takes a step forward with his head lowered. His actions force me to lean forward and brace myself against the edge of my desk.

"What's happened?" The words scrape through me as a million scenarios run through my mind.

Gio bites the inside of his cheek as he struggles to collect himself. Finally, he says, "Cara's guards aren't answering. After the brotherhood's threats—"

"Let's go."

Of all the scenarios I imagined, nothing prepared me for what I found when I finally made it to my sister's dorm room or what followed in the months afterward. Her room had been tossed, furniture flipped. There were papers, books, and clothes all over the floor. The brotherhood's calling card, a note etched with gold calligraphy, rested on her pillow. The moment I saw it, I knew she was gone, and it was all my fault.

"Alister? Alister, are you okay?" As Sophia's voice pulls me back to the present, I realize I've stopped walking and find myself standing still among the swaying branches of the oaks above. Spanish moss catches in the breeze, filling the air with the scent of the earth. It's quiet, despite all the media outlets in New Orleans on the other side of the stage just up ahead.

"Alister?" Sophia moves closer to me. Concern furrows her brows as she places her hand on my cheek. She's freezing, despite the warmth of the sun streaming down on us.

"I'm fine," I tell her. "Just ready to get this over with."

Sophia shakes her head, prompting Gio to distance himself as he monitors our perimeter. "It'll never be over, Alister. No matter what we do or say today, this pain will never end." I wish I could tell her she's wrong, that it'll get better. But, as more memories flood me, I can only nod.

Our bullets rip through the dark night, muffled by the sounds of the ocean waves. Lifeless bodies fall around me as Gio and I make our way onto the black-painted sea vessel in search of my sister and the man who stole her from me. I've been anticipating this moment ever since the night I lost her. And yet, it has done nothing to prepare my heart, which pounds desperately in my chest. Desperation—that is what I've felt for months now as I've followed up on every possible lead to find Cara. I thought it would've left me by now and been replaced by something else, something that makes me feel powerful. And yet, as Gio and I pummel our way through the lower deck, I've never felt weaker.

Inside every room there is a girl restrained in some fashion. Some are tied to the bed. Others are bound in other positions. They've been beaten and branded with tattoos of their captor's mark. Despite this, their faces have been left untouched. I suppose only at the request of this monster's clientele. But their eyes—their eyes say it all. They are empty, and not just because they've been drugged to keep them obedient, but because the horror they've endured, the degradation, has stolen their souls and their will to live.

As I reach the last of the girls' rooms, I hesitate. I've yet to find Cara, which means she's either in this room or she's with him. Either way, I'm afraid of what I will find. Gio comes up behind me and places his hand on my shoulder. Sweat drips down both of our faces as sadness fills our eyes. Gio knew coming here was a suicide mission. Either we'd both die or what we'd find would make us wish we were dead. And yet, without hesitation, he followed my every move. He's the only one who knows the truth about Cara. He's the only one I can trust.

"I've got your back, Boss," Gio says. I nod as my hand moves to the doorknob.

"And I've got yours." At that, I open the door to an empty room, the sight of which nearly brings me to my knees. Blood and other bodily fluids stain the sheets of the twin bed and the leather of the cuffs still attached to the wall. Unlike the other girls' rooms, there are signs of a struggle or, perhaps, even more. There's a broken mirror to my left. It

looks as if someone, someone meaning my sister, was thrown into it. I manage to take another step into the room only to find a wooden X to my right. I look away, unwilling to examine the torture devices sitting on a table nearby.

My throat burns with the cries and screams I refuse to let out. Instead, I press my lips together and ball my fists in an effort to maintain control. I do so until I taste blood and until the skin stretched across my knuckles feels as if it may split open.

"There's one more room to check," Gio says. Despite his determination, I note the hopelessness in his voice. There's only one place left on this ship Cara could be. If she isn't there...

The silencers on our weapons, accompanied by the roar of the ocean, has kept our presence a secret from the man who owns this ship, the man who believes he owns these women. The element of surprise is to our advantage. Though as I exit Cara's room and assess the lock on the door of the captain's quarters, I realize there is no way to enter quietly.

"If she's in there, he could use her as a shield or a hostage," Gio says, putting his tactical knowledge to good use. Despite the sense he makes, I can only home in on the word *if*. Because the fact is, if Cara isn't in this room, then she's either dead or she's been sold to another who will surely kill her once he learns of the fate that will befall him.

"Then I go in alone."

"What? Boss, no. You shouldn't see your sister like—"

"If I go in alone, he'll think there's only one of us," I say, fighting through the mental images of Cara and this man, the same images that've haunted me ever since the night she was taken. "If he demands I put down my weapon, you'll still have yours. Wait until he lets his guard down and then disarm him. Just be careful not to hit anything vital. I want to take my time with him."

Gio's dark eyes scan mine, searching for any hesitation. He finds none, because despite everything I feel inside, the thought of finally seeing my sister again, holding her, saving her, breaks through and leaves only clarity. Gio nods and backs away. At that, I take my *shotgun and blow through the only thing standing between me and the man who will soon die the slowest of deaths. The metal blackens as the gunpowder connects. Though, not nearly as much as my heart as—*

She wasn't there. My lips part as I reach the steps to the stage. I move up them slowly, almost as slowly as I exacted my revenge against the overweight, balding bastard who thought himself a god among men. Or rather, among women. I made sure he knew his real place though, before sending him to meet his maker. Though, it wouldn't surprise me if God skipped the whole judgment thing and sent his wretched ass straight to Hell. Perhaps I'll meet him there one day and we can continue our session. It would almost make burning for eternity worth it.

Where is she? Where is she!? As I reach the mic stand, I keep my eyes plastered to my shoes as, for the millionth time, memories of my cries rip through me. My throat still aches as I mouth the words. My eyes widen and glisten with unspeakable emotion as they did that night, the night I was told I was too late.

By the time we reached the ship, Cara had already been killed. Apparently, she'd outlived her usefulness. Only days before Gio's and my arrival, her body was disposed of in a barrel filled with lye. When I said before that there was nothing left of her to find, I meant it. When we finally tracked down the location of the barrel, the chemical had done its job. Inside the stainless-steel cylinder was nothing more than a brown syrup-like liquid.

At that, I pinch my eyes closed as emotion roils through me. I never got to see my sister again—her dark hair, her hopeful eyes, her tan skin. She never got the chance to grow up, to fall in love, to have a life all her own. As a member of our family, she never would've had a normal life. But it didn't have to be torturous and far too short.

The man who bought my sister from the brotherhood had no

idea she was a Mafia princess, no idea she was my sister, the sister of the Blood King. No doubt the brotherhood kept those details to themselves, knowing no one would dare touch Cara for fear of my retribution. When they sold her, they thought they were saving themselves. They thought I'd be so focused on finding her I'd forget about them and the fact that they were the ones who started all of this. But I didn't. Just like the slow and sinister revenge I took upon the man who raped and tortured Cara, I had my way with the members of the brotherhood who had abducted and sold her. It's been three months since their fall, three months since I thought this Hell would finally come to an end. But Sophia is right. Cara's death has filled us both with unceasing pain that rattles us to our cores.

I can't. I can't lose it here, not in front of all these cameras. In my world, weakness gets you killed. Which is why I didn't tell anyone about Cara or bring backup on my quest to save her. It's why I didn't tell Sophia, because the burden of the truth is unbearable. It's why, even now, on the day I reveal this heartbreaking news to the world, I still can't tell the whole truth. I can't cry. I can't yell. I can't break. Because then, they'll come for me. They'll come for her. At that, I turn to Sophia.

Sophia stands behind me to my right, while Gio stands behind me on my left dressed in his typical navy blue suit. Her face is damp with tears, though her expression is vacant. She's trying to be strong, even though she's broken inside, tortured even. She's like me. And like me, she needs this to be over, even if only for a moment.

"Thank you all for taking the time to be with us today," I begin, still refusing to look at the crowd. "As you know, my family and I aren't the biggest fans of the press. The last time we spoke was at my father's funeral. An unfortunate day, just like this one." I clear my throat, finally lifting my eyes to take in the crowd. My lips part as I plan to continue with my prepared speech. Though I am quickly silenced by what I find before me, or rather, *who* I find.

Cara's ghost stands among the crowd. Like so many times before, the chill of death accompanies her, pricking at my skin. Only, unlike before, she opens her mouth and, for the first time in over a year, I hear my sister's voice. *I wish I died that way, in a car crash while having the time of my life in Europe. The sun would've felt so good on my skin. It's the last thing I would remember.*

She pauses, as if reliving the last moment of her life. I can't tell you how many times I've wondered what she experienced, what her final moments were like. I pray endlessly that she knew how much Sophia and I love her, how we, *I*, never stopped searching for her. But being haunted by her makes me think my prayers went unanswered.

As my heart threatens to rip out of my chest, Cara's eyes find me once more. And despite her ghoulish disposition, in her gaze I find glimmers of the girl I once knew, the sister I swore to protect. Which only makes what she says next that much more gut-wrenching.

No fear. No pain. My death would've been instant. But that's not what happened, and you know it. As the words cross her lips, tears fall from her sunken eyes. The sight is too much for me to bear. Not only does she haunt me, but she is haunted by the horror she was forced to endure.

I grip the mic stand for support as my knees threaten to give out. I sense Gio inch closer, though he doesn't make any obvious moves to steady me. Once more, I lower my head as I collect myself. That's when I feel Sophia's hand on my back. I turn to her to find her tears have dried, and instead of the lifeless expression I saw before, her cheeks glow with a strength I envy.

"It's okay," she whispers. "You don't have to do this alone."

I nod, somehow finding it in me to turn away from the crowd. Sophia and Gio exchange a glance of concern as the crowd begins to whisper. "I don't want to lie about what happened. I..." I shake my head. "Cara would want us to tell the truth."

"But, Boss, you know what that means. Everything we've done to keep Cara's abduction and murder a secret, everything we've done to avoid a war will be for nothing."

As Gio states what I know to be fact, understanding washes over Sophia. Her lips part as she realizes the morbid reality I've been protecting her from. Finally, she says, "I'm prepared for the consequences."

"No, you aren't," I tell her.

"Maybe not," Sophia admits. "But I'm prepared to die. Isn't it all the same in the end?"

My golden eyes search hers just as Gio searched mine the night we attempted to save Cara. In them I find no hesitation, not even fear. Though she should be afraid. We all should be. Because if I do this, we will face the greatest threat of our lives, a war so bloody it could very well end the Amato line. Yet, after everything that's happened, losing our parents and now our sister, like Sophia, I don't hesitate when I consider if I'm ready to leave this world. So much of me is already dead. At that, I turn. Hand in hand with Sophia, I face the crowd once more and prepare to deliver the words I never expected to say.

"Over a year ago, we learned of a criminal organization operating in our city. Known only as the brotherhood, they preyed on innocent young women, mostly those attending universities here in New Orleans. Through various tactics they tricked these women into attending parties where they were drugged and assaulted." As I speak, the members of the media lean in, forcing their microphones closer to the stage as they hold their breath.

"It was a dark day for our city when the FBI finally succeeded in taking down this despicable, heinous organization. Because it was on this day that we learned the brotherhood was more than what we originally thought. As if a domestic group of sex predators wasn't enough, we learned the brotherhood was a front for a global sex trafficking syndicate that had been operating for over a decade. Over that time, thousands of women were abducted, trafficked, and once sold, experienced unthinkable abuse."

I pause, once again searching the crowd for Cara. As I say these next words, I want her to know I'm doing it for her. I'm risking everything for her, because her memory deserves to be honored, not painted over with so much rose gold tomorrow's news reads *"New Orleans Heiress Dead in Italy in High-Speed Crash."* She deserves more than that. She deserves for the truth to be told. Finally, I find her. She looks at me with the same sad expression as always. I take her in, knowing that if my words grant her peace, this will be the last time I see her. I clear my throat and—

"Though the men responsible for these crimes are either dead or in jail, their victims and the families of their victims are forever scarred by the trauma they inflicted. Today, along with my sister Sophia, I want to extend my deepest condolences to the survivors of this atrocity. We share your pain."

At that, whispers swarm among the media while Sophia releases her hand from mine and lifts it to her mouth, fresh emotion overtaking her. I look over my shoulder and motion for Gio to take Sophia to the car. Thankfully, she doesn't protest. Though, without her next to me, a heaviness returns, the same heaviness I've felt ever since my father took his last breath. I am the Blood King, and this burden is mine, no matter how badly I wish it wasn't.

"Our sister, Cara Amato, was one of the brotherhood's victims." The words cut through me like jagged glass. "She was taken from her dorm room in the middle of the night, right here in New Orleans. And she was never seen or heard from again."

The truth is met with gasps, wide eyes, and a slew of questions being shouted in my direction. Feeling the weight of the moment taking its toll, I end my remarks with both a prayer and a warning. "Today we honor my sister's memory and all those who've suffered at the hands of the brotherhood and similar syndicates. May the suffering of evil men be eternal. And may the souls of their victims find peace."

I blink the emotion from my eyes just long enough to see Cara disappear before me. I hope she finds the peace she deserves. I hope the truth will set her free, even if it means the death of me.

4

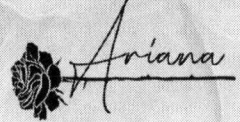

FRESHLY SHOWERED, DRESSED IN A CREAM-COLORED OVERSIZE T-shirt and pale blue cotton shorts, I wrap my damp hair in a towel and make my way through my French Quarter apartment. Sunlight beams in through the glass of my double French doors, illuminating the small, shotgun-style space. Bouncing off my white walls and onto my bare arms, the sunlight dries the few water droplets remaining.

I make my way to the living room, grab the remote from the coffee table, and turn on the TV for background noise before plopping down on my gray couch. With all the thoughts constantly running through my mind and the foot traffic just outside my door, silence isn't my friend. And yet, the moment the red light flips off and the TV clicks on, I regret my decision. Because staring back at me is none other than the dark-haired, square-jawed Alister Amato—the Blood King himself.

I take a deep breath and debate changing the channel from my usual news broadcast. I bite my lip. Rather than test my self-control in front of Bilieux and the rest of the world, I left the park before the Amatos arrived. Still, I'd be lying if I said I wasn't curious about what they had to say. One reason the Amatos have gotten away with their illegal operation for so long is because they stay out of the public eye. Well, as much as the wealthiest and most influential family in New Orleans can.

To be honest, I was shocked when we received a witness testimony against them. I thought for sure that Emma girl was lying. But then, I looked into her track record. She was the one who broke the case against the brotherhood over a year ago. A credible source, to say the least. Her testimony accompanied by the evidence she gathered during her time at the Amato estate was enough to pique my interest and make me question everything I thought I knew about the Amatos. But it wasn't until the night of the brotherhood takedown that I truly accepted her word as truth.

"Valentine, I want you to photograph every inch of this place. The evidence we gather tonight will help us take down two syndicates. We can't afford to miss anything."

"Yes, sir." I grab the camera from the back of the SUV as Agent Bilieux addresses the rest of the team. I approach the boat, formerly used by the brotherhood, photographing the entrance and the rails of the boarding ramp seeing as they've already been dusted for fingerprints. But once inside, I follow the voices and the frenzy of agents to the primary crime scene—the porcelain white room now drenched in blood and spattered with bullet holes. Biological evidence degrades the fastest, and from what I'm told, there's a lot here that needs to be captured.

As I reach the double doors leading into the grand ballroom aboard the luxury yacht, I lift my camera. I'm prepared for the blood, guts, exposed bones, and the stench of human excrement that usually accompanies a mass murder scene such as this one. And yet, what I find through the lens of my camera is nothing short of the stuff of nightmares. My nightmares to be exact. At the sight of it, the camera slips through my fingers. The only thing keeping it from falling to the floor is the strap hung around my neck.

"Agent, are you okay?" I turn to my right to find a man I don't know looking at me with concern. Perhaps he's CIA, given his lack of visible credentials and the international implications of this investigation. As my eyes meet his, my tongue swells in my mouth, inhibiting my speech. I nod and manage to take a step forward. I don't want him to see the sweat budding on my lip and forehead nor my trembling fingers.

Bodies of armed guards peppered with bullets lie around the room. But they aren't what have my attention. I move to the center of the room, dazed, and yet aware enough not to step in the blood or disrupt the evidence. My eyes widen in horror, as does my mouth, as without blinking, I take in the bodies of the brotherhood superiors. Unsurprisingly, they've been tortured. I knew Alister Amato had a personal reason for going after them. I expected this much. So, it's not the chunks of human flesh, scattered fingernails, and teeth that make me quiver. It's the X carved across their chests and torsos that pulls me in and takes me back to the night I lost everything, back to the night I lost her.

Before the memories can take over, I peel my eyes from the tortured corpses and rush out of the room. I lift my hand to my mouth, pretending like I have to vomit. It's a normal response to such a scene and yet it isn't the reason for my reaction. But no one can know that.

I make my way through the boat and out onto the deck overlooking the water. "It can't, it can't be..." Once I'm sure I'm alone, I drop to the floor and pull my knees to my chest. Despite the sultry summer heat, I feel cold as fresh tears drip down my cheeks. "All this time, all this time and he was right here." I bury my face in my hands as more tears fall. I gave up on discovering the truth of what happened to my mother long ago. But after the way those bodies were mutilated, the same way my mother's body was, I can't ignore the commonality.

"Ariana? Hey, are you okay?" Ray's voice soaks up my tears like a sponge. I quickly wipe any dampness from my cheeks and move my hand to my stomach, once more feigning nausea.

"Hey, yeah. Just queasy." I stand as Ray reaches me.

"Yeah, I get it. That in there... It's unlike anything I've ever seen."

I nod, wishing I could say the same. *"Yeah, I... It's not something I'll ever forget."* At that, I move past him and get back to work.

After eighteen years of pretending like I was okay not knowing the truth, telling myself my mother wouldn't want me stuck in the past, that one night and that stupid X brought everything back, as if it ever left me. And I haven't been able to sleep a solid night since. Every night, I go to sleep with the memories of my mother's murder playing behind my closed eyes. Every morning, I wake to either the sounds of her screams or of my cries, the ones that ripped from a ten-year-old me as I sat stuck in the air vent she hid me in. I must've cried for days before the stench of my mother's rotting flesh got the neighbors' attention.

As anger replaces the sadness inside me, I grit my teeth and turn up the volume. Alister Amato and his sadistic family don't deserve a minute of my time. And yet, as I sit down on my couch, my eyes and ears refuse to leave him. Because, after all this time, I deserve the truth, and my mother deserves justice. And Alister Amato, he's the only one who can give it to me, to *us*.

As Alister opens with a spill on the brotherhood, I settle in, tossing a blanket over my legs. Maybe I should've stayed. I could've confronted him afterward and finally, this anticipation, this Hell would be over. But that's exactly what Bilieux was afraid of. I may not have gotten fired for my previous outburst, but if I went after Amato today, that would've been the end of my time with the bureau. Of course, that's a risk I continue to take as I plan the perfect moment for a confrontation with the Blood King.

I know he didn't kill my mother. He was only a child when

she was murdered, just as I was. But with his father no longer with us and Alister's position as the head of the Amato criminal organization, he, no doubt, has access to records of the hits issued by previous heads of his family, especially those ordered by his father, Domenico. After seeing the way the brotherhood members' bodies were mutilated, there's no denying the attack against my mother was orchestrated by the same group, or rather, *family*. The question is why? In my experience, hits are power plays, either to maintain or gain power. That means my mother must've posed a threat to the Amatos. But how?

After all this time, I need to know who partook in the killing of my mother, and I need to know why. It's a simple request, really. Though one I doubt Alister will oblige. Kingpins such as him are bred to obey a code of silence and loyalty. Despite the fact that his loyalty is to murderers, drug dealers, and potentially people of worse character, Alister won't easily turn against them. He can't without risking his own safety and the safety of those he loves. Which, in fact, is the only reason I haven't confronted him in the three months I've been on leave from the bureau.

My approach must be calculated. I need to find a way to get to him when his guard is down, and his security is light. Which is why I've opted for an indirect approach into his world. It took only a few weeks of yoga classes before his sister, Sophia, and I started getting coffee and then lunch. We've become friends, well, friendly enough to use her to get an introduction to her brother. Three months in the making, tonight is the night I will come face-to-face with Alister Amato.

The plan is simple. Seduce him so I can get him alone, where I'll either question him directly or use my powers of persuasion to get him to trust me. I'm prepared for the long con, though I hope it doesn't come to that. Despite her belonging to a family whose history is drenched in blood, I don't like lying to Sophia. She's a nice person. At least she seems to be. Maybe it's just a front she puts on for outsiders like me. Then again, I can't exactly judge her considering I do the same thing only for a different reason.

And yet, as I watch Alister's chiseled face etch with pain as he recounts the horrific way he lost his sister, Sophia isn't the only one I feel guilty for using. The loss of his sister is still fresh, and given the horrific nature of her death, I can only imagine Alister is still hurting. Taking advantage of him during this vulnerable time makes me sick to my stomach because I know what it's like to lose someone so violently and suddenly you are haunted by their death. And yet, my sympathy for him quickly evaporates as the images of the bodies left in his wake flash through my mind.

My cheeks burn with a cocktail of fear and anticipation as I stare into Alister's golden-brown eyes. His dark brows crinkle as he speaks, making him look even more wicked, dangerous than I know him to be. I'm confident in my abilities, but I'd be stupid to think this is going to be easy. From experience, both my own and with the FBI, I know that people respond to vulnerability in one of two drastically different ways. Either they give in to their emotions and circumstances, allowing themselves to be crippled by them, or they become paranoid and obsessive, hell-bent on overcoming their trauma. I'd like to think Alister will be an easy target given his emotional state. But, as I watch him now and notice the slight curl to his lip, the glint in his eye as he stares down the camera, it's as if he knows a war of sorts is coming. And he's ready for it, which makes him more dangerous than ever.

At that, I pause the program and pull my eyes away from him. My muscles tense as I anticipate what the night will bring. For the con to work, he can't know that I'm FBI, even though my position with the bureau might be the only thing to save me if he learns the real reason why I'm inserting myself into his life.

Then again, knowing what I know of him, something tells me even my badge won't save me from his wrath. And yet, the fear of being captured, tortured, murdered even is not the greatest fear catapulting inside me. The truth is, as much as I want, *need* to know why my mother was killed, I'm afraid of what the answers will reveal.

I stand and make my way from the living room, through the kitchen, and down the hallway toward my bedroom. This isn't the first time I've searched for answers regarding the night I lost my mother. When I turned eighteen and finally got out on my own, the first thing I did was search for the truth. But I was so young when my mother died and our life so unusual, I didn't have much to go on. There were no family photos or knick-knacks let alone relatives who could answer my questions. I didn't even know our last name because we never used it. My mother didn't have credit cards, at least from what I saw. Now that I think of it, I never even saw a bill sitting on the dining room table. But the unusual nature of my upbringing doesn't end there.

Before entering the foster care system, I can't remember ever attending a school. The only time we left our apartment was when my mother took me to the park once a week for a cheap picnic by the river. That or when I stayed with our neighbor while my mother presumably went to work. At that, I wince. I didn't know back then what kind of work my mother did nor did I make any headway in that area until recently—a painful discovery to say the least.

Inside my bedroom, the sunlight streams in through two sets of French doors, much like my living room. It glints off the crystal chandelier hanging from the tall ceilings of the ancient building I call home. Despite its age, my current home is a far cry from the small, dark, and drafty apartment my mother and I lived in. I move across the room and yank my curtains closed, blocking out the light and any prying eyes. Like I said, crippled or paranoid. Can you guess which one I am?

With the room shrouded in darkness, I move through the familiar space to my armoire and, like I have a thousand times before, I find the Polaroid taped to the back. When I began my search for my mother, the only connection I had to her was the building we lived in and a single name, a name I'd never heard spoken until the night I witnessed her murder—Valentina. I bite my lip as I drop to the floor. The building got me nowhere. There was no record of anyone named Valentina ever living there. I even searched public records, but without a last name to input, my search didn't get very far. It wasn't until the night of the brotherhood investigation, the night I realized my mother's connection to the Amatos, that I finally made some investigative headway.

I flip the Polaroid over and see my mother wearing high heels and bits of lingerie. I found it on a wall covered in photos just like this one inside one of the strip clubs owned by the Amatos, despite the fact that there is no record of a woman named Valentina ever working there. There's no writing on the photo revealing her name or the year it was taken. But it's her. Another unexplainable connection to the Amatos and the New Orleans underbelly.

I remember her curls and her eyes clear as day. And yet, as I look at her, I know nothing of her but the stories I've told myself over the years, some to help me sleep at night, others to help me move on with my life. I told myself that everything my mother did, everything she sacrificed, even her death was for me, so that I could have a better life. It's why I stopped looking, why I got a degree and earned a position with the FBI. I wanted, *want*, to help people like my mother, people who are forgotten, alone, and desperate. And it's been an adequate Band-Aid. But now, the truth is bleeding through.

The Amatos took away my chance at knowing my mother. Based on the way we lived before her death and the frequent male visitors with bulges between their legs, I have a feeling they took a lot more than her life. They made her a ghost, a woman without a family, without hope, without a name. So much so that when Child Protective Services finally found a placement for me, they asked me what I wanted my last name to be.

"Valentine," I whisper.

I fight through the tears threatening to fall and set my mother's picture to the side. Emotion roiling through me, I stand, searching for an outfit worthy of drawing a king's attention. As my fingers smooth over the black fabric of my dress, my fear eases, giving way to my determination. To Hell with Bilieux and his orders. To Hell with Alister Amato and his guards. Tonight, I will have my answers. Tonight, I will have my justice.

5

My mother's screams wake me, though not quickly enough. I roll out of bed, groggy with sleep. But when I open my bedroom door to find my parents' guard lying on the floor in a puddle of blood, adrenaline takes over. I run down the hallway as I hear my father say, "Please. Please, don't."

No! My mind makes sense of what's happening just as the gunshot rings through the hollow halls of Laroux House. It stops me dead in my tracks as do the sounds of my father's cries and of my mother's body falling to the floor. My heart races, urging me forward, and yet I hesitate, not ready to see what I know waits for me.

"It hurts, doesn't it? Losing the woman you love. But what about your children? My guess is that'll hurt more."

"Alister? What's happening?" I turn to find Sophia standing just down the hallway, which now echoes with Cara's cries. Confusion washes over her, sleep still present in her eyes.

"Get back in your room and hide," I whisper, waving at her to move.

"Alister?"

"Now!"

Sophia's lip quivers, and she runs back into her room and locks the door. Knowing I have to protect her and Cara is the only thing that allows me to push through my own fear and emotions and close the distance to my parents' room.

"Shoot him in the leg. I want him to watch while I destroy what's left of the Amato line."

My fists ball and my dark eyes shift into slits as I quietly step over the body of my parents' guard. More will be here soon, unless these men have already taken them out. But, from the looks of it, I don't have time to wait and neither does my dad.

As if propelled by sheer rage, I lunge forward and tackle the man who killed my mother, knocking the gun from him. We land on a pile of glass left in the wake of the two men's invasion. As I wrestle the second intruder, my body becomes damp, though I'm not sure why, and my arms and legs sting as shards of glass break my skin. Despite this, I keep my eyes on the man within my grasp, knowing that if I allow myself a moment to assess the irreparable damage he's done, I'll break. I'm so focused, I barely hear the gunshot coming from the other side of the room. And yet, I twitch, wanting to check on my dad. But as the life begins to drain from the man beneath me, I'm unable to pull away from him. That is, until I realize the source of the liquid wetting my clothes and skin—blood. My mother's blood, to be exact.

I can't help myself. My eyes shift from the man to the dark curls sprawled next to us. Among the broken glass and pool of blood lies my mother's lifeless body. She stares back at me with frightened eyes and parted lips. Reality hits and images of a life without my mother race through my mind, and my body begins to shake, and tears flood my face. My fingers loosen around the man's neck, though only for a moment. As thoughts of Sophia and Cara come to me, I am reinvigorated with a fury so lethal my skin burns. I've already lost my mother. I can't lose them too. Once more, I tighten my grip with the intent of crushing *every bone in the assailant's neck. His limbs go limp and his face turns blue, and I look at him with a certainty even the Devil wouldn't question. "You will die for this," I say through gritted teeth. At that, I increase the pressure until—*

"Alister, no!" My father's hand on my shoulder sends a shock through my body, one of relief and regret. Slowly, I turn to find his face etched with sadness. And yet, just as much as his pain is evident, so is his lust for revenge. "Death would be too kind for him."

"Excuse me, sir. I didn't mean to disturb you," Gio says, pulling me from my thoughts. As I blink, the stone walls of my family's underground Blood Cellar come into view. This place always triggers memories of the past. Most of all, it reminds me of that night, the night I made my first kill, the night I learned what it means to be an Amato and the Blood Prince of New Orleans. As horrific as losing Cara was, *is*, hers is not the only death I've been forced to endure. I can only hope it was the last.

"A welcome interruption," I say, adjusting myself in my chair. Gio nods, knowing the darkness this place holds.

"I need to gather the supplies for tonight's ritual, but I can come back later if you—"

"No, go ahead," I say, motioning for him to approach the wooden cabinet to my left. It holds more things than even I'm aware of—family photos from the old country, discarded purple and gold tapestries, extra jewels engraved or embossed with the family crest, and, of course, records upon records dating back a century.

As Gio reaches the cabinet, I stand, moving from my place at the head of the table to the wall of blood. It, though only one form of record keeping, serves as an account of every notable kill of every Blood King, including mine. Among the thousands of tiny glass bottles I find the vial of blood belonging to the man who killed my mother, the man whose name I never knew, the man whose boss was never divulged. My father was right. Death was too kind for him. But eventually, there is nothing left to do but die. And yet, on nights like tonight, he is more alive than ever. I think of him and everything about that night that never made sense.

My father took his time with him, both for his sake and mine. He tortured the man in ways even I have never replicated, teaching me, while trying to discover who the man worked for. He didn't have any familial allegiance. That would've been easy enough for us to figure out. But no. He was a ghost, a hired gun.

Whoever tried to kill me and my family that night didn't want the hit tracing back to them if it wasn't a success. Which, for some reason, makes me believe it was ordered by someone familiar, a friend of my father's, someone who would know which bedroom was my parents'. It makes me sick we never learned the truth. And, as I prepare to welcome my organization's capos into my home, I can't help but wonder if one of them was involved. And now that the truth of Cara's murder has been revealed, I can't help but wonder if they will try again.

I place the vial back on the shelf as Gio finds the silver box containing the supplies for the Blood Oath ritual. In most organizations, the Blood Oath is recited only once upon one's initiation. But after my mother was killed, my father began conducting the ritual annually, to remind his followers of their loyalty. With war looming in the shadows, tonight's recitation is more important than ever.

"Copy," Gio says with his hand on his earpiece.

"What is it?"

"Guests are starting to arrive. The partygoers are being escorted straight to the gardens. And your personal guests are gathering in your parlor."

I nod, reaching for my ring. As I twist it around my finger, it weighs heavy on me, just like my task tonight. I must rally the capos and make sure they are ready for war. Most of all, I must make sure they are still loyal to me. Without their support, I won't have enough men to defend against my outside enemies. Not to mention, if their allegiances shift, my own men will join the ranks of those who plot against me.

"Boss, are you okay?"

I can't help but smile at Gio's remark. Only he would dare ask me that question. Well, aside from Sophia, though I know he only asks out of courtesy. He knows as well as I do that I haven't been okay in a very long time.

"I'm not going to tell the capos about the deal with the FBI, not yet at least. After today's press conference, they'll already be on edge. I need to ensure I have their support before I tell them our entire organization is changing. Even with the new cruise line, our legitimate earnings are less than what we bring in through the drug trade. From a financial standpoint, I doubt they'll be pleased with the idea of legitimizing. And, the truth is, I'm not sure I can afford their displeasure. As word of Cara's death spreads... Well, it's no doubt earned me a war with our enemies. I'll need my capos' support if I'm to win it, survive it."

"Well, I pity the man who picks a war with you, sir."

At that, I nod, once more taking in the large, ornate ring that once belonged to my father. Nights like tonight are not only a test of loyalty for my followers but also a test of my own. I am the Blood King, and yet the Blood King is so much more than me. After what happened to Cara, I questioned if I could do it, if I could uphold the century-long reign of the Amato line. I allowed myself to believe, if only for a moment, that I had a choice, that I could walk away if I felt inadequate. This ring reminds me I can't, that I have no choice but to rise up or endure the consequences. Every day is a sacrifice. Now, I must ask my men to make the same sacrifice. If they won't...

"As do I, Gio. As do I."

GIO and I enter the room off the parlor, and my shoulders instantly slump at the sight of Sophia. She stands, dressed in her silver 1920s flapper costume, staring down the capos through the video monitors streaming from the inside of the parlor.

"No," I groan, though she hasn't even asked the question I expect her to.

"*No, what?*" As she turns to face me, confusion quickly shifts to disappointment. She raises her brow and crosses her arms over her chest. "You must not have seen the costume I left out for you."

I smirk, closing the distance between us. "I saw it. I just chose to ignore it. Why pretend to be a gangster when I already am one?" When I reach her, my eyes instantly move to the security monitors.

"How very discreet of you?"

"Discretion would be wearing a pirate or firefighter costume. Neither of which am I doing. Besides, you and I both know you aren't here to assess my wardrobe." At that, my eyes shift from the cameras to her. Upon my look, the light leaves her as she lowers her chin. "You know I can't let you go in with me," I say, lifting her chin so she can meet my gaze.

"I know. I just wanted to be here in case you need me."

I nod. "Well, I appreciate it." She offers me a small smile and then proceeds to adjust my bow tie and the lapels of my suit jacket.

"If anyone asks, tell them you're James Bond. You can't host a Halloween party and not show up in a costume."

"Fine. Speaking of the party, you should get out there. Your absence will be more noticeable than my lack of costume." Sophia nods, though she doesn't make any moves to leave. My eyes narrow as I take in her features. As if reading my mind, Gio makes an excuse to leave the room, giving us a moment. "Hey, Soph, what's going on?"

She shakes her head as she fights off tears. "I just...I'm not ready to face them, to answer a million questions. I may not have to pretend to be okay anymore, but, in a way, having everyone know the truth is worse."

I nod, pulling her into my chest. "I know. I know." And I do. I carry the same fear and insecurity with me as I prepare to face my men, the ones cackling and boasting in between draws of their cigars. Their laughter is almost loud enough to escape the soundproof walls of the parlor. Clearly, the death of my sister hasn't put a damper on their mood. Very sympathetic, gentlemen. Sophia pulls away from me then as my body tenses beneath her.

"Alister—?"

"Listen, if you...if you don't want to go to the party, you don't have to. Everyone will understand—"

"No. No, I'm going. It's the least I can do." She studies me for a second, searching my eyes for any sign that she should stay. I do my best to relax and allow the tension to leave me. Finally, she shifts her attention to the smudge of makeup on my shoulder. She wipes it away and plucks a few pieces of lint from my suit. Good. If I can fool her, then the capos should be a cakewalk. "Weakness gets us killed. I may be sad, but I am not weak. And neither are you."

I nod, and, despite my initial thought, I'm glad she's here. Her words give me the strength to stand up tall and prepare to put on the show of my life. Like her, I carry the weight of my sister's death on my shoulders, and my mother's, for that matter. But I can't let my men sense it.

"Are you ready, sir?" Gio asks, rejoining us.

"Yes."

As Gio and I walk into the parlor, silence befalls it. My men stand in reverence as I take my place among them. Cigar smoke fills the air along with the sharp stench of cologne. It mixes with the usual hint of leather and wood to create a sickening aroma that reeks of testosterone, greed, and power.

As I make my way through the room, I size up the men, *my* men. It still feels strange thinking of them in this way, seeing as every single one of them is older than I am. Vitale, Parisi, and Gagliano are my New Orleans capos in addition to Gio, who runs my personal operation. Gabriel Parisi is the closest to my age. As such, we've become friends. Well, as friendly as I can be with a subordinate. I give him a quick nod, noting he stands in the center of the group while Vitale and Gagliano couldn't have more space between them. That's strange. All the capos from Texas and Florida stand together, but not those of my own city.

I motion for Gio to begin the Blood Oath ritual, which he proceeds to set up by removing from the box the knife, goblet, and photo of St. John, the saint of loyalty among other things. Gio's uncle watches him with pride as he moves. Seeing the glint in the old man's eye eases some of the tension in my muscles as I suspect I can count on Moretti's support, even if it's grounded in nothing more than love for his nephew. Parisi is another I can count on. But the rest of them? I fear they are more loyal to the money than anything else. War threatens our business, as does the deal I was forced to make with the FBI, which is why I can't tell them of it. Not yet at least.

Gio finishes preparations for the ritual and returns to my side, and I step forward to recite the Blood Oath. "For over one hundred years, we, and our ancestors alike, have recited the sacred Blood Oath. With these words, we renew our vow of loyalty to each other and to our cause. We remind ourselves of our obligations and the importance of unity."

As I speak, my words feel empty. They are the same words spoken by every Blood King before me, and yet the challenges my organization faces today are nothing like the challenges of our ancestors. We aren't persecuted and robbed of opportunity. We aren't weak and in need of protection. We don't even stand for all Italians as is the honorable way. We stand for ourselves and each other in the name of greed. And the only thing other than money uniting the men in this room is fear, fear of prosecution and fear of death.

At that, I pause and look from my men to the table before us. My father knew how I felt, *feel*. I think, at times, he felt the same. But, like him, and like the men in this room, I'm in too deep to walk away. Everyone who bears my name is.

"Blood is my beginning. My blood I will defend. Or, so help me, I will burn. By blood, I will meet my end."

As I speak, I grab the knife and prick my finger. My blood drips into the goblet, which is passed around the group for their own blood offering. When the goblet reaches me again, I set it back on the table and place the photograph of the saint in the cup. The ritual is simple, really. By blood you are born into this life. If you fail to live up to your oath, you are sentenced to death, a sentence dealt out by the ones who you've betrayed. All I have to do is light the saint on fire and I'm done. I can turn the meeting over to the capos to discuss business. And yet, I can't stop myself from adding one thing to the ancient ritual.

"War is coming, gentlemen." Surprise washes over my men's faces as I speak. It's not because they are surprised at my assumption, but my break from tradition. "As it does, let me make one thing abundantly clear. Despite what our ancestors would prefer, the oath you are reciting tonight is not of your loyalty to one another. It is of your loyalty to me. The Blood King protects those loyal to him and sentences his enemies and the enemies of his allies to death. For those who betray their king, those who betray me, it is your blood I'll collect next."

6

Ariana

I EXPECTED EXTRAVAGANCE, BUT WHAT WAITS FOR ME IN THE gardens of the Amato estate is nothing short of a haunted fairy tale. After a carriage ride from the front gate through the foggy forest surrounding Laroux House, I find myself greeted by glitter and glamour, black roses, fog, a dance floor lit by crystal chandeliers hanging from invisible strings, and even more towering decorations that convey both spookiness and sophistication. "Wow," I whisper. And that's just the start of it.

As I make my way through the party of influential Southerners, party lights illuminate the night sky and the guests' elaborate costumes with shades of purple and red. And I thought I would be overdressed. I glance down at my black ensemble. The strapless corseted gown is left over from an undercover assignment I had a few years ago. I had to infiltrate a high-stakes poker game to clone a suspect's phone. The dress has a sheer bodice with delicate lace feathers offering me minimal covering. That accompanied by the slits showing off both of my legs was enough to entice my former target, allowing me to complete my mission. I was hoping the same visual tactic would work tonight. But now, I'm not so sure my exposed skin and angel wings will stand out enough to keep Alister's attention. That is, if I can even find him.

When I reach the pool area, now lit to make the water look like blood, I grab a champagne flute from a serving tray to help me blend in. As if that's even possible. Everyone around me is in deep conversation with one another and I know literally no one here. I sip my drink and offer the passing gentleman an awkward smile. *Focus, Ari.*

I continue through the party, keeping my eyes peeled for Alister, Sophia, and their guards. I'm sure this entire place is under surveillance given the intense security check at the gate and the shadowy figures of the Amato guards I spotted throughout the forest. But Alister and Sophia's personal protection won't put that much distance between them and their charge. I find the guards, I find the boss.

I loop the party twice without any sight of them. That is, until the DJ cuts his set to introduce them.

"Alright, alright, alright. Let's give a warm welcome to our hosts, Alister and Sophia Amato, our King and Queen of Halloween." Yeah, they're the king and queen of something. Just not Halloween. Nevertheless, I join in with the rest in applauding their entrance. But within a matter of seconds, the applause shifts to whispers and sideways glances as the crowd discusses what's on everyone's minds—Cara.

"I feel so terrible for them."

"I'm surprised they didn't cancel."

"Oh no, they couldn't cancel even if they wanted to. This event is cohosted by the Historical Preservation Society and has been planned for a year."

"You know, as awful as what happened to their sister is, why did they choose to reveal the truth today, knowing that we would all be here? Now no one knows what to say to them. It's just awkward."

Geez. Make it about you much?

"Well, maybe that's why. They didn't want to lie to us."

"Poor things."

As Alister and Sophia make their way down the steps from their mansion with a capital *M*, they look fabulous. Sophia wears a formfitting silver flapper dress. Jewels and beads adorn the bodice while silver fringe shimmies from her hips down to the ground as she walks. Alister, on the other hand, doesn't look much different in his typical three-piece black suit. Though he, along with his sister, still look every bit the business moguls and royalty they are. And yet, I find myself pitying them as I overhear the chatter of the vipers waiting for them at the bottom of the stairs. The same woman who's upset at them for putting *her* in an awkward position is one of the first to gather to greet the siblings.

Sophia's eyes move from the party to the ambush that awaits her. Her lips part as worry furrows her dark brows. As they near the group, she turns to her brother. Alister gives her an empathetic look and takes her hand in his. The simple gesture brings a small smile to my lips and makes me feel even more guilty for what I'm about to do. Nevertheless, I down the rest of my drink and proceed to join the vipers.

As I approach the group, Sophia instantly finds me among the crowd of partygoers. Good to know our coffee dates made an impression. "Mr. and Ms. Amato, I'm sorry to interrupt. But there's an urgent matter requiring your attention." As I deliver the Amato siblings a life raft, the crowd's attention shifts from Alister and Sophia to our surroundings as they try to find the urgent matter that doesn't exist. With the guests briefly distracted, Alister's personal guard makes his move.

The tall, brooding man with perfectly groomed facial hair

and slicked back hair that nearly reaches his shoulders leans toward me, taking my wrist in his hand, and I jump. "Turn around and walk," he bites out as he presses the barrel of his handgun into my back. But before I can even muster up fake fear, Sophia steps in.

"Gio, no. She's my friend," Sophia whispers, looking between me and the gun with frantic eyes. The man named Gio immediately follows orders, concealing the gun within his suit jacket before anyone notices. Despite this, his dark eyes, now shifted into suspicious slits, don't leave me, nor do Alister's.

Alister—he stands only two feet away. I've never been this close to him before, close enough to see the golden hue of his brown eyes, the wide bridge of his nose, the precise shave of his facial hair, and the way his muscles threaten to rip the sleeves of his black tux. As Sophia approaches me, pulling me in for a hug, I find myself entranced by him. I'm not sure if it's my desperate need for the truth, my desire to see him brought to justice, or something else, but my legs feel frozen in place in his presence, as if we are being forced together by a magnetic field.

"I am so sorry," Sophia says, pulling away from me. When she takes a step back, blocking Alister from view, the trance is broken. "I'm not sure if you saw the news today, but we, um, we're kind of on edge around here."

"Yeah, no, it's okay, really. That's actually why I brought the *urgent matter* to your attention, so you'd have an excuse to leave these vultures in the dust." She smiles, both surprised and pleased with my plan. "You both would," I say, nodding in the direction of her stern older brother.

At that, Sophia steps aside and reaches for Alister's hand. He reluctantly gives it to her and closes the distance between us. "Let's go," she says, dragging her brother away from the steps with Gio following closely behind him.

Sophia leads the four of us away from the party toward a

gravel trail that winds through the forest. Alister and Gio keep close while within view of the party guests. I suppose they don't want to risk getting sucked back in by the busybodies. But, once we make it to the enchanted forest's edge, they fall back a few steps to have a hushed conversation. No doubt it's about me. I try to hear what they're saying, but the chirping crickets, moaning frogs, and whoosh of the fog machine drown out their voices. Speaking of fog—

"Whoa!" I extend my arms to balance myself as I nearly fall on the dimly lit path.

"Careful," Sophia says, instinctively reaching out to steady me.

"Thanks. Note to self, gravel and high heels, not the best combination." Sophia laughs. "You seem to handle it pretty well though."

"Yeah, well, I've had a lot of practice in heels. And, besides, I could walk these paths in my sleep." She looks up then, taking in the beauty of the night. I do the same. Even without the floating chandeliers, black roses, and twinkle lights draped through the oak trees, I imagine this place is beautiful. Tonight, it's even more so. "Thanks for saving us," Sophia says then.

"No problem." I offer her a smile, which she returns, though it quickly leaves her. "Listen, we don't have to talk about it if you don't want to, but I do want to say I'm sorry." I don't say for Cara or what happened to her sister, because I know this night is painful enough. Hearing her sister's name would only make it more so.

"Thank you. And you're right, I don't want to talk about it."

"Alright, that's far enough." Sophia and I turn to find Alister and Gio closing in on us. When they reach us, Gio moves his hand to his pistol, ready to draw it if I try anything. Talk about on edge. If they knew I'm FBI, then I'd understand the reaction. But, to them, I'm just a normal girl with no weapons who can barely walk in these heels let alone fight and run in these angel wings. I get that Cara's abduction has probably made them hypervigilant when it comes to protecting Sophia, but I have a feeling there is something else prompting this over-the-top response.

"Gio, again with the gun," Sophia says, crossing her arms over her chest. She sighs, letting me know this is only a taste of the overprotectiveness she's forced to endure. "Alister, Gio, this is my friend Ariana. She is my guest tonight and should be treated as such."

"Ms. Sophia, with all due respect, when someone unfamiliar approaches you at a party with a made-up excuse to get you away from the safety of the crowd, it's my job to take precautions," Gio says.

"I understand, Gio. And I appreciate your vigilance. But Ariana was only helping me, helping *us*."

Sophia turns to Alister then, but his attention is solely on me as he studies my every movement, my every breath. His eyes graze my body all the way from my aching feet to my slightly parted lips. His gaze gives me chills. Or, perhaps, it's just the wind lifting my hair and sending most of my dress billowing behind me. As I stand before him, I feel naked. So naked, I begin to wonder if he knows the truth, if he somehow figured out who I am and why I'm here. No. How could he? And yet—

"Clever," he says then, finally moving his eyes from me to the trees surrounding us.

"Excuse me?" I ask.

"You're clever," he says, returning his gaze to me. Only this time, for the first time, he isn't assessing me or studying me. He looks at me without flat lips and tension in his stance. He looks at me like a normal person, allowing some of my own tension to ease. "Dealing with the crowd is always the most difficult part of these events, even more so tonight for obvious reasons. I apologize on behalf of my head of security for the misunderstanding."

"No apology is necessary."

Alister gives me a gentle nod before turning to Sophia. "You and your friend should take some time in the gardens. I'd say the *urgent matter* has earned you an hour. But I really must get back."

Alister turns and heads back to the party with Gio in tow, though my peripheral vision tells me Sophia and I are anything but alone. Alister is keeping an eye on me, *us*. Though I can't help but wonder, if he's so certain Sophia needs protecting, either from me or someone else, why would he risk her safety by returning to a party even the dead can tell he loathes? There's something else going on here. Yet, despite my careful planning, I'm no closer to figuring it out or getting Alister alone. And with Gio and every other guard here on high alert, I'm starting to wonder if getting him alone is even possible.

"Is your brother always so intense?" I ask once Alister and Gio are out of earshot.

"Only on days that end in *Y*." At that, Sophia and I laugh and continue our stroll through the gardens.

❦

"THERE YOU ARE! I've been looking for you." As Sophia and I arrive back at the party after our walk through the gardens, a blond-haired man with an accent calls out to us, well, Sophia. He finishes off his glass of champagne, and based on his swaggering walk, bright eyes, and playful grin, I'd say it wasn't his first.

"I'm sure you have," Sophia says. She gives me a look filled with annoyance as the man approaches. Whomever this guy is, she doesn't want anything to do with him.

"Now, now, darling. Let's not fight," he says, registering the tension in Sophia's voice and the way she stands. "Dance with me." He offers Sophia his hand, which she doesn't even glance at.

"What are you doing here, Caleb? When we broke up, I made it clear it was for the last time." Oh, he's her ex. Got it.

"Hey, do you want anything to drink? I think I'm going to go get something," I ask. I'd rather not stick around for the conversation or rather, argument that's about to take place.

"Sure, thanks."

I excuse myself just as Sophia puts her hands on her hips. I get that Alister worries for her, but, from the looks of it, she can handle herself. Still, I wonder what all the fuss is about. It's a party. Why would Alister and his security detail be so on edge?

That's when I see him. In the opposite direction of the party, Alister, Gio, and another man whom I don't know sneak away from the crowd and into Laroux House. For someone who was adamant he needed to get back to the party, he doesn't seem to be spending much time socializing. So, what is he doing? Whatever it is, I need to know. I've got to find a way inside that house. And yet, just as I go to take a step toward it, I'm reminded of the Amatos' security and the fact that tonight of all nights, they've got their bases covered. Without Sophia, I'll never make it in there. Even with the schematics of their compound, I won't be able to bypass the security cameras *and* the Amatos' armed guards without blowing my cover. No. Sophia is still my best way to Alister.

Sticking with my original plan, I hightail it to the nearest food station in search of the drinks I promised Sophia. I grab two bloodred cocktails from the table and—

"For me? You shouldn't have." As I turn, I'm faced with a man I don't know, as if I know anyone here. He towers over me by at least a foot. Like Alister, he hasn't bothered to wear a costume, which I find a bit odd given the setting. Unlike Alister, he has bright green eyes and a buzz cut so short he almost appears bald in the poor lighting.

"For my friend. Excuse me," I say, moving past him. Though, as I do, he repositions himself, stepping in front of me. *Great.* He's one of those who don't know how to take a hint. Deciding it best not to draw attention to myself, I handle him more delicately than I would if the setting were different. At least I try to. "Listen, I'm flattered. But I really need to get back to my friend. She's having a rough go of it and could really use a cocktail."

"Well, how about you?" he asks, moving his hand to my arm. He caresses me from my forearm to my shoulder, sending chills through my body. And not the good kind. "Would you like to have a rough go of it?" He moves his fingers through my silky, straight hair and brushes it over my shoulder, exposing my neck and chest. I flinch. I have half a mind to let the drinks fall to the ground and show him how rough I can be right here, right now. But before I can, he removes his hand and takes a step back. "I'm just giving you a hard time. Enjoy the party."

As he leaves me, I watch him with narrowed eyes and begin to follow him at a distance. He was smart to leave me alone, but that doesn't mean he won't find someone else to give a hard time. Though, as I follow him through the crowd, condensation on my fingers reminds me of the glasses I hold and of Sophia, whom I find nowhere, not even with her drunk, sloppy ex, Caleb. I make a beeline to the British blond just as he sits down next to another brunette he hopes to charm.

"Hey, where is Sophia?" I ask. The bite in my voice is obvious, but I don't care. Not only am I on edge because of my encounter with the buzz cut bastard, but in less than five minutes of knowing Caleb, I'm already certain I don't like him.

"Hey...Sophia's friend. Are you going to drink those?" As he spots the drinks in my hands, his eyes are even glassier than before. Deciding it better he passes out sooner rather than later, I hand him the drinks, which he then uses to woo his new girl.

"Hey!" I snap to regain his attention. "Sophia? You know, the girl you were begging to take you back no more than ten minutes ago. Where is she?" At that, the brunette sitting next to him stands, thanks me, and leaves with her drink in tow. Caleb rolls his eyes and exhales. "The quicker you answer, the quicker I leave." I raise a brow and cross my arms over my chest. He nods and struggles to stand.

"Look, some guy came up and asked her to dance. She left with him and that was that. And for the record, I wasn't cheating on her. At least not this time. We're broken up. She made that pretty clear no more than ten minutes ago, as you said."

I nod as Caleb walks away in search of his next replacement girl. Though, as I turn to the dance floor in search of Sophia, once more she is nowhere to be found. Even under the night sky, her silver bejeweled flapper dress would stand out like the moon.

"Hey!" I call after Caleb, but the music is too loud for him to hear me.

It could be nothing. Maybe she did get asked to dance by a handsome stranger. Or maybe he wasn't a stranger at all. Maybe she knew him. Maybe they left to talk or whatever. After today's press conference, I'm sure she has a ton of friends who'd like to offer their condolences, just like me. Well, not exactly like me. And yet, the more I tell myself Sophia is fine, the more my insides tighten. I don't know why Alister and his guards are on high alert tonight, but they clearly are. And, whatever Alister is doing in that house, it's certainly not connected to his party hosting responsibilities.

7

Alister

As Gio and Gabriel Parisi take a seat on the brown leather couch in my office, I pour us each a glass of bourbon from the bottle I keep in my desk. Ever since the meeting with the capos, I've been bothered by the interaction between Vitale and Gagliano. Or rather, the lack of. But, as my father always said, certain matters must be handled delicately. Knowing I'll eventually have to tell them of the deal I struck with the FBI to make the family business legitimate, I can't risk pissing them off with a direct confrontation. At least not now. But that doesn't mean I have to ignore their behavior. And if I'm being honest, I'd take any excuse to skip out on the party early. Well, *almost* any.

At that, thoughts of Sophia's friend come to mind, thoughts I quickly shove out of my system as I sit in one of the red upholstered chairs across from Gio and Gabriel. I can't do anything about her now. But the second I'm done with this meeting, I'm directing my attention to her. If she's as close to my sister as I think she is, I need to know everything about her. The fact that I don't and she's alone with Sophia now makes me itch.

"Thanks, Boss," Gio says, taking his glass.

"Yes, thank you." Gabriel takes his as well, though neither of the men bring the cup to their lips until I do.

"Cheers," I say, lifting my glass and then taking my first sip.

"Cheers."

The three of us sit in silence for a moment while I think of the best way to broach the subject. Gabriel isn't like the others. He isn't old and entitled. He doesn't look at me like I'm a child playing dress-up with his father's crown like the others do. Well, I suppose I should say Vitale. I only see my out-of-state capos once a year, which isn't enough for them to form an opinion of me or get underneath my skin. But Vitale? He's the oldest of the capos and based in New Orleans, which means he has the hardest time following my commands and he's around enough to make his distaste for me known. Gagliano is in his mid to late forties. He doesn't say much, which makes it hard for me to get a read on him. I'm still trying to figure out which of them I trust the least.

"It's a Hell of a party, sir," Gabriel says, breaking the silence.

"Yes, thank you. It's all Sophia's doing," I say, taking another sip of my bourbon before setting my glass to the side.

"I'm sure she was thankful for the distraction given recent events."

I nod, leaning back in my chair. Even though I like and trust Gabriel, I'm sure to keep my face void of emotion when it comes to Cara, or *recent events*, as he put it.

"I guess that's one way of looking at it. But, speaking of recent events, is there something going on with Vitale and Gagliano I should know about?"

Gabriel's brows furrow at my question. He leans forward and places his empty glass on the table between us. "Not that I'm aware of. Why?"

"Well, I couldn't help but notice at the meeting that they

didn't say two words to one another. They stood on opposite sides of the room and never exchanged one glance. Normally, I wouldn't think anything of it, but given everything's that happened this past year, I need to make sure my men are united, now more than ever."

Gabriel nods. Once more, he relaxes into the sofa. "I understand. I guess I didn't notice anything about their behavior today as strange because they've always been distant toward one another." *Always* meaning for at least ten years. That's how long Gabriel has been a capo. He took over after his father passed, as is the way in our circle.

"Do you have any idea why?" Not that it matters. If they've managed to coexist for that long without incident, then I shouldn't have anything to worry about, at least when it comes to them fulfilling their duties.

"No. Whatever happened between them, it was before my time."

And mine. I nod.

"Well, I've got enough problems of my own to concern myself with theirs. But, moving forward, I'd like my New Orleans capos to present a more united front. Do you think you can convey that to them?"

"Of course, Boss," Gabriel says. "I'll speak with them and remind them of your request for more men to be stationed here and at the warehouse. We all know how Vitale likes to pretend he's hard of hearing when it comes to certain things."

"Yeah." I smile. "Well, if he keeps it up, he won't have to pretend anymore."

At that, Gio stands with his finger pressed to his earpiece. "Excuse me for a moment." My eyes narrow as Gio moves to the other side of the wood-paneled room. Whatever's happening, he doesn't want Gabriel to know. Or perhaps, he doesn't want to put me in a position to lose my shit in front of Gabriel.

Reading the room, Gabriel stands. "It was a pleasure, sir." He offers me his hand. "Call me anytime."

"Thanks, Gabriel," I say, standing to shake his hand. Gabriel leaves and Gio turns to me with a look on his face I've only ever seen once before. Instantly, the color leaves my cheeks and my throat aches with the same words I spoke the night I learned of Cara's abduction. "What's happened?"

Gio balls his fists and says, "Sophia's guards missed their twenty-minute check-in and they're not responding to comms. Neither are the men posted on the southeast side of the property."

At that, a million scenarios race through my mind in a matter of seconds. Every single one of them makes my heart beat faster and my fists ache with the need to punch, stab, and kill. I shrug out of my suit jacket, unbutton the top three buttons of my dress shirt, roll up my sleeves, and grab the gun holstered to my desk. Not again. I push past the déjà vu pricking at my insides as I cock my pistol.

"Let's go."

―⋆―

Music from the party blares through the trees as Gio and I race to find Sophia. Per the estate's surveillance cameras, she was last seen entering the woods at the southeast corner of the property with a man whom I don't know. Maybe she does. Why else would she leave with him? She was raised to be cautious and trained to prepare for threats. Even more so now she knows the importance of being careful. But, if everything was alright, her guards wouldn't be MIA nor the men patrolling the southeast corner of the property, the same corner that fronts Lake Pontchartrain. I push myself to run faster, knowing that if this is an abduction attempt, they could be planning to make their escape by using a boat to cross the lake.

"Boss, I see something," Gio says from a few steps ahead. "No." He stops. "No, don't—" Gio turns and tries to stop me, but I push past him. That is, until I see what he sees.

My legs go numb as Sophia's dark hair and sparkling dress come into view. I nearly trip at the sight of her lying on the gravel path just up ahead. She isn't moving. She—

"*Sophia!*" I yell and sprint the last few steps to her. I drop to my knees and immediately pull her into my arms. Her body is limp. "Sophia! Sophia, wake up. Wake up!" Sophia remains still in my arms, and my heart beats so quickly in my chest it feels as if it might rip out any second now. I shake her, my eyes wide with horror. As I do, I manage to fight through my fear long enough to realize she's still warm. "Gio, check for a pulse," I say as he drops down beside me. He brings his fingers to her neck as I hold her, unable to let her go.

Gio exhales in relief before saying, "She's still with us."

"Then why isn't she moving, Gio? Why isn't she waking up?"

Gio leans down and sniffs around Sophia's nose and mouth. My brows furrow. "She was drugged. I'm picking up hints of chloroform. Dr. Ramirez is a guest tonight. I can have him check her out once we get her back inside." As Gio speaks, I pinch my eyes closed and pull Sophia tighter against me as my body adjusts to the news. Everything in me goes from cold to hot, terrified to infuriated. My heartbeat slows and my trembling fingers stiffen with the need to kill, the need to protect. Someone did this. Someone *here* did this. I open my eyes and when I do, I don't recognize myself. Not the deadly force blazing through my bones nor my tone of voice.

"Whoever did this, I will mount their heads on my wall like the animals they are." I turn to Gio as more of my men arrive behind us. "Find them."

Gio nods and motions for the newly arrived guards to take Sophia. They move slowly as they approach me. Smart. They won't take her from me until I'm ready to let her go. I brush a brunette curl from her face as images of my mother come to me and then of Cara. Sophia is my weakness, and the entire world knows it. Whoever did this won't stop until she's dead. Which means, I can't stop until they are. At that, I loosen my arms and allow the men to take Sophia from me.

"Gentle," I order as I stand. "Let us know as soon as you get her inside. Move quickly and cautiously. Whoever did this is likely still on the premises."

"Yes, sir." I watch as a group of four guards take Sophia back toward the house, unwilling to take my eyes off her.

"Boss, I've got something over here. Boss?" Finally, I turn and make my way to where Gio stands just a few feet away from where we found Sophia. Gio kneels and points to the blood splatter on the rocks.

"Sophia wasn't injured." I state the obvious while wondering whose blood it could be.

"She also wasn't wearing angel wings." Gio hands me a single white feather, now coated in blood. The rest of the wings lay discarded just off the path. At the sight of them, my fists clench.

"I knew it."

"Sir?"

"There's a reason why I don't trust anyone, Gio." I hold up the feather. "*This*. That girl, that so-called friend of my sister's, is part of the team who tried to abduct Sophia. Sophia always has a knife on her. She must've cut her before she was chloroformed."

"Maybe, but we don't know for sure."

"Within two hours of her trying to get Sophia away from the party, my sister was almost abducted. I don't believe in coincidences, Gio. You know that."

"Yes, sir, I do. But Sophia seemed to know her. Ariana, I think."

"It wouldn't be the first time someone close to my sister betrayed her. Besides, how many friends does my sister have, Gio?" He pauses to think. "Not many. A million acquaintances, but not a lot of friends, as is the Amato curse. Now, don't you find it strange that if those two were so close, Sophia never mentioned her?"

"I'm not following," Gio says. I shake my head in frustration and use all my restraint to keep from barreling into the nearest tree.

"What I'm saying is, they must've been new friends, which means Sophia couldn't have known the girl that well. What if she, Ariana, was playing her to get an invite to this party? To catch Sophia with her guard down and—"

"Okay," Gio says. "But, with all due respect, if her plan was to abduct Sophia, why would she draw you and me away from the party too? And again, why not abduct Sophia as soon as we left the forest? It wasn't until over an hour later that Sophia left the party with a man, not a woman." Gio shakes his head as he tries to make sense of this mess. But it doesn't. None of this makes sense.

"I expected a war, Gio. I anticipated attacks like this in response to Cara's murder, but not tonight. The press conference went live this morning. None of our enemies would've been able to make it to New Orleans, infiltrate the party, and execute an abduction plan this thought out in between this morning and now."

"Whoever did this had time to plan," Gio says.

"Enough time to place someone like Ariana into my sister's life."

Gio turns away from me, examining the area again. I know

he doesn't fully buy into my theory. Hell, maybe I don't either. But, right now, it's all I've got.

"If she wasn't a part of it, then why else would she be here, Gio? And where is she now? We know Sophia didn't leave the party with her. So, she would've had no other reason for being here, at the site of my sister's abduction. And, even if she was an innocent bystander in the wrong place at the wrong time, there's no way the men would've abandoned their mission because of her."

Gio nods. The more I think about it, the more my theory starts to make sense. "Well, whatever happened, you'll know soon enough. The blood on that feather is fresh. With most of our men redirected to this area, she couldn't have gotten far." At that, Gio lifts his finger to his earpiece. I take a step closer to him, knowing my other men haven't had enough time to get Sophia back to Laroux House.

"What is it?" I ask.

"Shots fired down by the lake. Our men interrupted their escape."

Gio and I run as fast as we can toward the lake, following a trail of blood and disheveled gravel. It looks like the men who tried to abduct Sophia were running as fast as we are during their attempted escape. When we reach the ridge overlooking the lake, Gio and I pull our weapons and take cover among the trees.

"Malik, status update," Gio says over his comms, while I peek my head out from my position to examine the waterfront. As Gio gets a report from his head soldier, I stand and watch as the boat speeds away into the night.

"They got away."

"All but one," Gio says. "Malik is taking her to the house for questioning."

"*Her?*"

Gio nods. "Looks like you were right. Ariana was working with the men who tried to abduct Sophia. Our men spotted her trying to flee with the others, but the gunfire separated her from the rest. We'll find them, Alister. I'll break her. I'll get her to tell me everything."

"No. I will." Gio watches me, making sure I'm certain. Given what the torture does to me, I usually let Gio handle it. But, tonight, I'll make an exception, just like I did the night I came face-to-face with Cara's captor and, eventually, her abductors.

8

Ariana

IRONY IS A BITCH. I KNEW SOPHIA WOULD BE MY ONLY WAY into the Amato home. I just didn't realize my faux friendship with her would have me engage in hand-to-hand combat with two trained men twice my size. In an attempt to save her life, I almost lost mine. I wince as my adrenaline wanes and the sting of my injuries takes over. I can't see anything from where I lie, which makes it hard for me to assess the damage my dance with death left me with. I try to push myself up from the cold, rocky floor, but sharp pain courses through my chest. It feels like I may have a cracked rib. Yet, that's just the start of it.

Blood drenches the sheer mesh of my dress's bodice. I move my hand slowly to my chest, and as I do, it throbs, letting me know my arm is badly bruised and probably fractured. Finally, my fingers find my damp skin, and I move them in the darkness to try to assess the severity of my wounds. The men who I fought had knives. They got a few cuts in before they heard the Amato guards headed our way. When they did, one of them sucker punched me and then they both ran.

Honestly, I don't know why I chased them. I could've just

lain there and pretended to be a victim of the same attack that almost cost Sophia her life. But as I watched them run, something in me clicked. Maybe it was instinct, my FBI training kicking in. Even with the Amato guards closing in, these men clearly had a calculated plan of attack. I knew they'd escape if I didn't stop them. And I just couldn't let them go. I guess because as much as I view Sophia as a means to an end, collateral damage in my investigation into my mother's murder, maybe I'm also starting to view her as a friend, maybe I'm starting to care. I close my eyes and lower my arm slowly to my side.

"No. No, I can't care," I say through labored breaths.

It's FBI 101—when you get emotionally attached to your mission, you make mistakes, sometimes life-threatening ones. As I rest my aching head against the damp, jagged wall behind me, I realize I'm feeling the consequences of my mistake. And yet, it could've been so much worse. Even still, it can be.

Based on the stench of mold and mildew, the poor air condition, the pitch-black darkness, and the sounds of scurrying rats in the distance, I can only assume I'm in the Amato dungeon. Emma mentioned this place in her testimony. It's three stories underneath the Amato manor, part of the first iteration of Laroux House built in the 1800s during the South's dark days. The home has been added on to over the decades to make up the grand estate we see today. But, back then, Laroux House was more modest, though not without its secret penchant for evil. Today, evil still lurks within the confines of Alister's personal den of torture. And my being here can only mean one thing. He thinks I had something to do with Sophia's near abduction or else he wouldn't risk exposing himself by bringing me down here.

As I consider how I will explain my actions, the screech of metal draws my attention to my right. The door to the dungeon opens, and I spot the silhouette of a man—about six foot three inches and chiseled to perfection as if he's made of marble. But he isn't. He's made of flesh and bone. He's the Blood King and he's here for me.

I pinch my eyes closed and try to use my hand to shield my face as Alister turns on the lights. My arm aches as I move. Though, in this moment, the pain coursing through my head rivals it. The sound of footsteps lets me know Alister is walking toward my cell, though I don't see him. My prolonged period in the dark has made my eyes sensitive to the light. Slowly, I open them as Alister enters my steel cage, before locking us both inside. *That's not good.*

As Alister turns to me, towering over me like I'm nothing more than a bug he's ready to squash, my eyes finally acclimate, and I take him in. His dark locks and facial hair stand out against his white button-down and tan skin, though not nearly as much as the death glare he casts upon me. His wicked eyes don't leave mine. Just like when we first met, he studies me, wondering how I could've fooled him. Perhaps he feels betrayed. However, my guess is he feels more disappointed in himself that he almost let another sister die on his watch. The thought makes me drop my gaze as a small dose of sympathy works its way into my veins. What happened tonight was not his fault, and yet, he'll think it was. It will trigger all the old feelings he has regarding Cara's death, though I'm not sure those feelings ever go away.

I move my eyes to take in not only my surroundings but the magnitude of this moment. The walls of the dungeon are stained with blood. Just past my cell, there is a chair with wrist and ankle restraints. More blood covers the floor surrounding it. Most morbid of all, there is a stainless-steel table with a black cloth draped over it next to the chair. From my time with the FBI, I've seen my fair share of torture devices. I imagine they are what rest beneath the cloth, waiting for me and anyone who dares cross the Blood King. After what happened to Cara and now Sophia, if Alister feels like the failure I suspect he does, he will stop at nothing to make that feeling go away, to put his enemies down. And, as far as he knows, I'm his best chance to do just that.

"Alister—"

"Don't speak to me as if you know me," he says through gritted teeth. Instinctively, I go to nod, but the throbbing in my head makes me regret it.

"Okay," I whisper. I expect him to lunge at me or slap me. I brace myself against the rough wall behind me in anticipation. But he makes no moves toward me. You'd think the staring competition would give me time to come up with an excuse to explain my whereabouts, something that doesn't have me divulge I'm a member of the FBI. Yet, I've got nothing. I was never planning to lie to Alister. Once I had him alone, I was going to confront him and tell him everything. But now that I'm his prisoner, if he learns I'm with the FBI, he may get rid of me out of fear that I've seen too much.

He takes a step toward me then, prompting me to sit up straighter. "Ah!" I move my hand to my side as sharp pain courses through me. Alister kneels, bringing himself eye level with me. I do my best to control my breathing as he moves closer. I'm not afraid of much. Why would I be? Unlike Alister, I have nothing and no one to lose. But with my injuries, there's no way I'll be able to fight him off if...

It's then that Alister brings his hand to my cheek. He barely touches me and yet I feel his strength. He forces me to look at him, pressing ever so slightly onto the sore place where one of Sophia's abductors landed a punch.

"You're a fighter, aren't you? Tell me, how much fight do you have left in you?" At that, he brushes my brown locks over my shoulder, exposing the cut on my chest. I'm tempted to look at it to gauge how much time I have left before I lose consciousness from blood loss. Yet, I can't take my eyes off Alister. The way he looks at me, it's almost like he's commanding me not to turn away from him. Just as quickly as Alister approached me, he stands, backing away.

"You're going to tell me everything—who sent you, what they want with my sister, where you were planning on taking her, and any other question I may think of. If you don't—"

"You'll kill me," I say. Alister cocks a brow at my matter-of-fact response.

"For some people, death is not enough," he says, pacing the cell as if pondering what methods of torture are best suited for my alleged crime. "For some people, death is the end of their punishment, not the punishment itself."

I have no doubt he's a man of his word. He comes to stand before me once more, and I know what I must do. I must tell him the truth, the whole truth, because if I don't, I'm as good as dead. At least, if I tell the truth, I've got a fifty percent chance of survival. Maybe sixty.

"Do you understand?" he asks me.

"I understand and I will tell you everything. It's just, I'm not who you think I am. And what I'm about to tell you won't answer the questions I know you have."

Alister crosses his arms over his chest. His facial features shift and his shoulders slump ever so slightly. There's a chance he won't believe me, but I'm not the first girl he's been wrong about and he knows it.

"I'm listening."

At that, I take a deep breath to calm my nerves. Though, again, my cracked rib makes me regret it. As the pain rips through me, I can't help but smile.

"Is something funny?" Alister asks. Clearly, his patience is wearing thin.

"No. I just…I've been anticipating this moment for a while

now and I certainly never thought it would go down like this. It kind of hurts to breathe."

"Yeah, that won't be the only thing that hurts if you don't get on with it." Alister drops his arms to his sides. The veins in his neck throb. Okay, it's now or never.

I bring my hand to my side to keep pressure on my ribs as I speak. One more breath and—

"My name is Ariana Valentine and I work for the FBI, a member of the Organized Crime Task Force to be exact. And before you remind me of your grace period, which still has nine months remaining, let me assure you—I'm not here to take you down or hurt your sister. I'm...I'm here for your help."

At that, Alister laughs and shakes his head. "*My help?*" He jabs his finger into his chest. "This is rich. You're on the task force set to investigate me and *you're* here asking for *my* help." He begins to pace the small space again. "I'm inclined to believe you are who you say are, considering no one outside of my inner circle even knows about the deal I have with the FBI. But what I don't understand is why you would come to me and, even more so, why you think I would agree to help you knowing that you will lead the charge against me in just a few months' time."

"I've come to you because I'm pretty sure your father had my mother killed eighteen years ago. Now that he's gone, you're the only one with enough access to help me learn the truth. And since he was your father, you kind of owe me."

Alister shakes his head and backs away from me, resting against the steel bars of the cell. "You come into my house, use my sister to get close to me, and then you accuse my late father of murder." He speaks so softly I can barely hear him. And yet, every word slices through me just like the knives of the men I fought.

"I realize the timing is terrible, given what happened to—"

"Stop!" Alister yells, pushing himself off the bars. He kneels in front of me again. With his face only inches from mine, I'm able to see past his anger and even fear at the thought of losing Sophia. I see past all of it to something new, something almost undetectable—defeat. "My father was an honorable businessman."

"You and I both know he was more than that and so are you." As the words cross my lips, I surprise myself. It's probably not smart to antagonize my captor when I not only need his help but am at his mercy. Alister lowers his head then as he attempts to steady his breathing.

"Look, I'm not trying to disrespect you or antagonize you. It's just...I know who you are, Alister, and what you do as the Blood King. You can't pretend with me."

Alister lifts his head, meeting my eyes once more. As he does, all emotion leaves him. He is numb and monotone. "Perhaps you know of my business, but you know nothing of me." He looks down, taking in my cuts and bruises. "If you weren't part of the team who tried to abduct Sophia, then I suppose you got these injuries trying to save her."

"Yes."

Alister nods. "That and that alone has earned you ten minutes of my time, during which I want you to answer one question." I need more than ten minutes, but, right now, I'm in no position to argue.

"Okay," I agree.

Alister looks at me again, though he hesitates to speak. Perhaps he doesn't want to know what I think. He doesn't want to believe his father could've ordered a hit against an innocent, defenseless woman, endangering not only her but her ten-year-old child. Then again, there's also the possibility my mother wasn't innocent. But did she deserve to die? No. No. I refuse to believe that.

Finally, after assessing the consequences of his question,

much like I have my actions, he asks, "Why do you think my father was the one who had your mother killed?"

Now it is my turn to look away from him, my throat raw as the words prepare to make their escape. I've never told anyone what I'm about to tell him, Alister Amato, the Blood King of New Orleans, my target, and my captor. I've never even spoken the words to myself. For eighteen years, I've held this secret inside, avoiding every question and even relationship that could lead to this painful memory coming out. I bite my lip as my eyes glaze over with tears I work every single day not to cry.

"For eighteen years, I told myself lie after lie. I'd make up stories about who my mother was and why she was killed. I even looked into her once, tried to make sense of her death, but I didn't get very far. It's kind of hard to investigate a ghost, someone without a last name, or a credit card, or even a place of work. After she died, it was like she never existed. Eventually, I accepted that I'd never know the truth. I'd never know her. But...that all changed the night I was called to investigate the massacre aboard the ship named *Kratos*."

Alister takes a deep breath, realization dawning on him. He sinks back on his bottom and rests his elbows on his knees. "Well, since we're being honest, I wouldn't call what I did to the brotherhood superiors a massacre."

"I know. You'd call it justice." At that, he smiles, and there's a shift in the energy between us. No longer is he towering over me, threatening to end me. He's down on my level, meeting my gaze eye to eye. He's listening to me. And somehow in the middle of it all, he's cracked a joke and made me forget about my pain and where I am. I'm thankful for it, for this brief moment of normalcy. It makes it easier for me to say what comes next, the words I fear will change everything between us once again.

"When the FBI arrived on scene, we already knew what had gone down. Per Emma's testimony, we knew you and your men were the ones who murdered the brotherhood superiors. We weren't there to investigate their deaths. Rather, we were there to gather intel that would allow us to take down the rest of their organization."

"And mine," Alister says.

I nod. "Yes. But...when I saw how their bodies were mutilated, with an X carved across their chest and torso, it took me back to the night a group of men broke into my mother's and my apartment, beat her, and then killed her in the same way you killed the brotherhood superiors."

As I speak, Alister's eyes darken, and his lips press into a flat line. I haven't even told him about finding my mother's photograph taped to the wall of one of his strip clubs, but the look in his eyes tells me I don't have to. He knows as well as I do my mother was killed in a hit, one that his father ordered. At that, I twitch. It's as if I'm back there, desperately wanting to fight them off her, help her, save her, but I can't. I can't do anything.

"Ariana, we're going to play hide and seek, okay?"

"Okay, Mommy."

"I remember my mom running from the kitchen to the windows that overlooked the street. She must've heard something. Whatever it was, I didn't. I was at the table drawing. Knowing now what happened next, I guess she heard the men drive up because immediately, she grabbed me and told me we were going to play hide and seek. She said, *'Don't make a sound and don't come out for anyone except me.'*"

As the memories flood my mind, tears drench my cheeks. My lip quivers. I do my best to control myself, but I can't. When I finish telling Alister what his father did to my mother, I don't see his face. I don't gauge his reaction. My tears have blocked him from my view. Perhaps it's for the best.

"And I didn't. I didn't come out. Not that I even could've. She put me inside an air vent and moved a piece of furniture in front of it to hide me. She moved so quickly that she must've known they would come for her. She must've prepared to hide me. But…if she knew, why didn't she run? Why didn't she have a gun or some other way of protecting herself?"

This is why I've never told anyone this before. Because with the memory of my mother's murder comes questions. The pain of not knowing why my mother was killed is almost as great as the pain of her absence. I cover my face with my hands, allowing all the emotion I've kept inside me to escape.

She didn't save herself. She saved me. No matter what she did to get involved with the Amatos, no matter how bad, she always protected me. Though her efforts that night didn't stop me from witnessing her murder. They only hid the faces of the men who beat and killed her and kept me alive to remember it in all its horror.

I jump as Alister moves his hand to my knee. His unexpected touch sends electricity coursing through me. I quickly wipe the tears from my eyes and place my hands at my sides. "What are you doing?"

"I'm…I'm sorry," he says. And I can tell he is. His golden-brown eyes are now dark like honey as empathy shines through them. But I don't need him to be sorry for a crime he didn't commit. I need him to help me understand why it was committed. And I need him to help me find the men who took part in it.

"Do you see now why I need your help?" I ask him. "I've waited eighteen years to understand the truth. I can't wait anymore, Alister. I won't."

9

Alister

As Ariana speaks, a million thoughts race through my mind. I'm pissed that she clearly used Sophia to get close to me. Thoughts of Sophia make me feel helpless and like the last place I should be right now is this dungeon. And yet, I feel Ariana's pain. I've suffered my own share of tragedy, even witnessed my mother's murder like Ariana. But she was so young when tragedy struck her. I can't imagine what it must've been like and what the past eighteen years have felt like not knowing the truth. And yet, if I believe her and what she said about her mother being killed in the Amato style, then I also must believe my father was involved. Only victims of the Blood King himself or of a hit ordered by the Blood King are executed in this way.

I don't want to believe it's possible my father ordered a hit like this—an entire group of men to kill one woman—but as I look into Ariana's eyes, there's no glimmer of deception. There is only heartbreak and a desperation to know the truth. And yet, I have my own truth to uncover.

The men who came after Sophia tonight were organized. They knew enough about my property to sneak in and off the compound using a boat. And whether it was dumb luck or they're just that good, they managed to dock in a location without surveillance. To top it off, they were skilled fighters, as is evident from the wounds on Ariana's body. From the looks of it, she's lucky to be alive. And yet, as much as I empathize with her and appreciate her for saving my sister, I can't turn my back on the threat facing my family now. For these men to be as organized and skilled as they were, it lets me know their abduction attempt was a hit from a powerful enemy. They didn't get what they came for, which means they'll try again. They can't afford to fail if they plan to live, as is the way of our world. I have to find them before they make another move against Sophia.

"Do you see now why I need your help?" Ariana asks. "I've waited eighteen years to understand the truth. I can't wait anymore, Alister. I won't."

Ariana looks at me with pleading eyes, her lips parted as she awaits my response. The simple movement draws my attention to the bruising on her cheek. From there, my eyes drift until I find the cut across her collarbone. Even lower, I find another cut above her left breast. Through the sheer fabric of her dress, I find more bruising and redness, especially around the area where she keeps her hand positioned. No doubt she's got a broken rib, or at least a fracture. I remove my hand from her knee and stand, putting distance between us as if it'll make what I have to do easier.

How can I turn my back on her? The woman who saved the most important person in the world to me. On any other day, I'd pledge my life to her in gratitude. But...

"Please, I'm begging you," Ariana says as if she knows I will deny her request. "It wasn't that long ago that you went to someone asking for their help. Now it's your turn to return the favor."

At the mention of Emma, the hairs on my arms rise. She's

right. When I learned it was the brotherhood who took Cara, I went to Emma and made a deal with her. Because we had a shared enemy, our arrangement worked in both of our favors. Sort of. Turns out Emma didn't trust me as much as I thought she did, as much as I trusted her. I guess after what I did in pretending to hand her over to the brotherhood I can't blame her. She turned on me and started working with the FBI behind my back. Even though I managed to make a deal with them to avoid immediate prosecution, I didn't come away from our arrangement completely unscathed. Exhibit A—Ariana.

When I look at Ariana, I see Emma. Not physically, but emotionally. They are both innocent women who by some tragic twist of fate got mixed up in this world of darkness to which I unfortunately belong. The only difference—Emma was in deeper than Ariana from the start. She had no choice but to face off with the brotherhood to earn her freedom. But Ariana? She's only gotten a glimpse of the pain that waits for her if she keeps digging into her mother's past—a past no doubt filled with secrets and trauma that will rock her to her core.

My father wouldn't have ordered her mother dead if she was innocent. Ariana knows enough about my world to know this must be the case. Though I don't think she's accepted it, that her mother could've done something to deserve—

I stop myself and take a deep breath. I'm losing it. I've been the Blood King for only a year, and I've buried more bodies than I can count. But it wasn't the day my father died that my life became tainted with an unshakable darkness. No. It was the day my mother was killed. For sixteen years, I've been so consumed by revenge and the need for control that I've actually convinced myself some people deserve to be tortured and killed for their crimes. Even as the logical, humane part of me realizes how ridiculous that sounds, there's another part of me that knows I don't regret a single life I've taken. Which is why Ariana can't get anywhere near the truth, whatever the truth is. She can still walk away without any more bloodshed, without any more hurt, without losing herself to her quest for revenge. She can still save herself from this world. At least, that's what I tell myself to justify my turning her away.

At that, I turn to Ariana. It's clear exhaustion is weighing on her as she struggles to keep her head upright. "You're not going to help me, are you?" Her voice is shallow. I have to move closer just to hear her. Though, before I can respond, unconsciousness consumes her. Her body slips and—

I lunge forward and place my hands beneath her head as she collapses onto the floor. As my hands caress her delicate yet damaged body, I feel an unwelcome chill.

"Ariana." I brush her dark hair from where it covers her face. "Ariana, wake up." I shake her but she doesn't move. Like my mother and Sophia, Ariana lies cold and still in my arms in the wake of an attack waged on my home. She isn't family, but in my home, she is my responsibility. And like Hell am I letting her die on my watch.

I move my hands from underneath Ariana's head and slowly back away from her. "Gio," I say into my comms.

"Yes, Boss?"

"How is Sophia?"

"She's stable, resting now." I close my eyes and exhale in relief.

"Thank God. Listen, let Dr. Ramirez know I'm coming up with another patient. She's currently unconscious and will need immediate attention." Gio hesitates as I unlock the cell holding me and Ariana. "Gio?"

"Yes, Boss. I'll let him know. Should I set up a guest room for the examination and treatment?"

"Yes. And Gio?"

"Yeah, Boss?"

"She's not one of them. She's...she's FBI. And she saved Sophia's life."

"Well, that is, um...interesting," Gio says. *Interesting.* He doesn't even know the half of it. Ariana's spent her life taking down men like me, and yet tonight she saved the life of the person most important to me and asked me for my help. A series of events I never saw coming.

"Interesting. Yeah, I'd say so." I exit my comms with Gio, swing the cell door open, and return to Ariana. She doesn't move or moan as I scoop her into my arms, which makes me wonder if her injuries are worse than they appear. I need to get her to Dr. R ASAP. Yet, up close, I can't help but take a moment to look at her, to see past the dried blood and bruising. She looks so young and innocent from her silky, dark hair to her plush, round lips to her taut yet baby-soft skin. She doesn't look like a woman who has lived through the Hell she has, and yet, as the skirt of her dress falls away from her body, revealing the skin of her upper thighs, I find scars that let me know I've gotten only a glimpse of the pain she's endured.

"A fallen angel," I whisper. "We've got to get you back up in the sky so you can fly far, far away from here and never come back."

ARIANA REMAINS unconscious while Dr. Ramirez performs his exam and tends to her wounds. I had a couple of my maids undress her and wipe away the dried blood and dirt before he entered. Now she wears nothing but her underwear and one of my T-shirts. It hangs loose on her, nearly reaching her knees, that is, until Dr. R is forced to lift it to continue his treatment. I stand at the foot of the bed in the third-floor bedroom as he does, revealing Ariana's toned, slender figure. Though, that isn't the only thing that's revealed. The small scars, some narrow slits, and some round, begin on her upper thighs and continue onto her hips where they disappear, perhaps continuing onto her back. While most of them could be self-inflicted or perhaps even a consequence of working for the FBI, some of them are in places I know she couldn't reach herself. It's as if someone...

"She's waking up," Dr. R says, forcing me to redirect my attention from Ariana's body to her face. I move to the opposite side of the bed from Dr. R and sit just as Ariana starts to stir.

"Ariana. It's Alister. Can you hear me?" I say her name and mine, as if we've known each forever, and the words feel strange as they cross my lips.

"Cold," she whispers.

"Oh, sorry. I was in the middle of—" The sound of Dr. Ramirez's voice fully awakens Ariana, and her eyes flash open as he reaches for the hem of her shirt. At his touch, she forces herself up and out of his grasp, despite the pain I know she must feel. A fighter.

"Ariana, it's okay," I say, moving closer to her. "This is Dr. Ramirez. He's here to help you." Ariana's fists ball as her eyes move between the two of us. It's as if she's asking herself which of us should she lunge at first. Realizing she probably trusts me even less than the good doctor, I stand and move back to the foot of the bed.

"Ariana, you with me?" Dr. R asks. "Like Mr. Amato said, I'm here to help."

Ariana takes stock of her surroundings, including the stethoscope hanging around Dr. R's neck, and she finally relaxes. I'm not sure if it's the pain becoming too much for her to bear or if she actually trusts us not to hurt her. Either way, she unballs her fists and lies down once more instead of pressing herself against the bed frame. She pinches her eyes closed as her pain-stricken face reveals the discomfort I know she must feel.

Once she's settled, Dr. R continues. "I've ruled out internal bleeding, but you do have a cracked rib. I can wrap your torso for you and give you some medicine to help with the pain. I'll also take a look at the cuts on your chest and see if they need stitches. Is that alright with you?"

Ariana is quiet for a moment before shifting her attention from the doctor to me. "Why?" she asks. "Why are you doing this?"

"Dr. Ramirez, will you give us a minute?" I ask.

"Of course, sir."

It's not that I don't trust him. I trust Dr. R with my life and Sophia's, not only because of his skill but because of his discretion. But I have no idea where this conversation will go, and I can't have Ariana revealing she's FBI or any other sensitive details in front of him. No one can know the extent of the attack against Sophia, especially not until I figure out who's behind it.

As Dr. R leaves, I take his place beside Ariana on the bed. To my surprise, she doesn't move away from me. "Dr. Ramirez was tending to Sophia when you lost consciousness. I brought you here so you can be treated, because I'm pretty sure my deal with the FBI would be voided if you die on my property. And, for saving Sophia, it's the least I can do."

"*The least*," Ariana scoffs. "Yes, in fact, it is the least. You never answered my question. Or should I accept your silence as all the answer I get?" At her comment, I can't help but smile. She's been conscious for only two minutes and she hasn't missed a beat.

"Right now you need to let Dr. Ramirez tend to your injuries, and then you need to rest."

"You're avoiding answering me. And since when do doctors make house calls?"

"Well, there are certain perks to being rich. Not to mention he was a guest at the party tonight." Ariana nods, though annoyance still consumes her as she moves her eyes to the ceiling. "I'll, um, step out so that Dr. R can finish his treatment, unless you want me to stay."

It's then that Ariana returns her slanted gaze to me. Her cheeks blush with fury as she bites out her response. "I'd love nothing more."

I laugh. Ariana's sarcasm both stings and intrigues me. She's got a spunkiness to her that reminds me of Cara, the more rebellious of my two sisters.

"Got it." I stand, though as I make my way out of the room, something stops me and I turn back to her. "Thank you."

"For what?" Ariana asks.

I take another step toward her. "For saving Sophia. Seeing what those men did to you, I can't imagine what they would've done to my sister. I'm sorry you got caught in their crosshairs, but I am grateful that you were there and didn't just stand by and let them take her."

"Sitting on the sidelines isn't in my nature, and you're welcome. Is she—?"

"She's fine. Listen, if you need anything, you can press this button." I move to the nightstand and point to the button built into the backside of it. "My maids can bring you food or whatever else you need. Dr. R will give you enough medication to ease the pain and help you sleep, but if you wake up, you can buzz down and request more." As I speak, Ariana's brows furrow. "What?" I ask.

"You're just...not what I expected."

"Oh yeah?" I cross my arms over my chest. "And what did you expect?"

Ariana smiles and shrugs her shoulders, though the grimace that follows lets me know she regrets it.

"I don't know." She brushes off the pain. "I guess I expected you to be emotionless, ruthless, cruel, and vindictive. Basically, I imagined you'd have a tail and horns, even if just figurative."

I smile, unable to tell her that she'd be right. I'm all those things and more. I'm the Devil to those who threaten my family. Until she becomes a threat, she has no need to see that side of me, at least any more than she already has.

Before the conversation shifts back to her request for help, I take my leave. "Feel better, Ariana."

"Thanks. Wait, my phone. Where's my phone?" Ariana asks, searching the surrounding covers.

"That you will get in the morning when I take you home." Disappointment returns to Ariana's features as I exit the room, leaving her in the care of Dr. R. Though as I walk away, thoughts of her and what I will do if she doesn't take *no* for an answer stay with me. If she becomes the threat I know she's capable of being, I'll have no choice but to prove her right and reveal to her the side of myself I hate the most. When the Devil comes out, it won't matter that she's FBI. It can't. Let's just hope it doesn't come to that.

10

Alister

With over two hundred guests, it's hard to find my suspects in the camera footage of the party. So, instead I focus on tracking Ariana. With her white angel wings, she stands out. And since she's with Sophia most of the time, I'm able to spot them as they return to the party from their walk.

"Caleb. That son of a bitch."

I fast-forward through Sophia's interaction with her lying, cheating asshole of an ex. He must've been someone's plus-one, because Sophia oversaw the guest list, and despite his family's wealth and connections, there's no way she would've included him after what he did to her. It's Caleb who separates Ariana from Sophia, making her an easy target for the men who tried to abduct her.

I pause the feed as a man I don't recognize approaches the two of them. I shake my head and pour myself another glass of bourbon. Sophia said the man asked her to dance to get her away from Caleb. A simple but effective tactic. Who wouldn't want to escape that entitled prick? It was after he got her away from

Caleb that things got complicated. According to Sophia, he told her his men had eyes on me and that if she didn't go with him, they'd kill me. She knew he could've been lying, but just as much as she is my weakness, I'm hers. So, she left with him without putting up a fight. She didn't mention anything about Ariana showing up, because once the men got her out of sight of the party guests, they drugged her. I decided it best not to mention Ariana's involvement, since that would lead to more questions regarding Ariana's job and reason for befriending my sister. After such a traumatic night, I don't want to add to Sophia's stress by revealing her friend isn't who she says she is. Though, all things considered, I couldn't be happier that Ariana was there.

I down the rest of my bourbon and nearly break the glass as I slam it against my desk. Deep breaths. I must stay in control if I'm going to find out who's behind this attack. At that thought, I zoom in on the camera footage to take a closer look at the man in question. The best visuals I have of him is a side shot from when he first approaches Sophia and Caleb, and then, as he and Sophia make their way to the forest's edge, a tree camera picks up a frontal image. I take screenshots of both images, doing my best to focus on the perp and not the sadness etched across Sophia's face nor the tight grip the animal has around my sister's arm.

He's tall, well over six feet, perhaps even taller than me. Though, he's got more of a medium build compared to my stockiness. I grab a sticky note and write down my assessment of him to hand off to Gio. He's got a buzz cut, which makes it hard to know what his hair color is, though his fair skin and eyebrows suggest he's probably a blond, meaning he's more than likely associated with a competing criminal organization rather than someone from within the Mafia. All capos and soldiers are Italian, per tradition.

At first, I thought the hit was ordered by someone closer to home, someone who would've known about this party. But the party is advertised as one of the most exclusive events in New Orleans each year since it's sponsored by the Historical Preservation Society. A simple internet search on my family or upcoming New Orleans events would've let the world know when and where the event would take place and that Sophia and I both would be there, which means proximity to New Orleans isn't necessarily a factor for tonight's assailants. No. This could've been anyone and for any reason. News of Cara's death hasn't had time to travel. Even my own capos who may secretly envy the throne wouldn't have had time to plan an attack that organized between the press conference and now. Whoever did this clearly has a vendetta against my family that began long before the public knew anything of Cara.

After pouring myself another glass of bourbon, I search the suspect's visible skin for tattoos and notable markings but find none from either angle. He's wearing a black suit with matching black gloves and a high-neck sweater that covers most of his skin. The gloves let me know I won't find any DNA evidence on Sophia or Ariana—another detail that tells me I'm dealing with professionals.

"Found anything?" Gio asks as he enters my office.

"Maybe," I say, pouring him a drink. "You?"

Gio shakes his head. "None of the party guests left early or around the time of the attack, which would suggest guilt. We scoured the woods and found nothing—no listening devices, no hidden weapons. The dock is clear too. Our men did catch a glimpse of the boat as the assailants made their escape. They described it as a white cabin cruiser. Super typical. Nothing unique of note under the cover of night."

I nod. "That's not surprising. Everything about this attack was perfectly planned."

"The only thing they didn't account for was an undercover FBI agent," Gio says.

"Yeah, that was something none of us saw coming, though I guess that's becoming the norm lately." Anger courses through me as I think about all the ways my home has been invaded—the night my mother was killed, the morning the brotherhood abducted Julian and Mason by posing as police officers, and now. After three months of upgrading my home security and weapons stock, I thought for sure I was prepared. I swore to Sophia that she was safe here, that no one would ever breach the walls of our home again. But I was wrong. I'm always wrong.

Cara's abduction and death triggered a fear in me that I first felt after my mother's death, a fear absorbed from my father. In the weeks, months, even years after my mother was taken from us, my father evolved into a hypervigilant, paranoid man. Effectively, his evolution was the end of Sophia's and my childhood as we knew it. Weekends were spent training in hand-to-hand and weapons combat. For me, more so than Sophia, but even she was tasked with learning certain skills. It was my father's way of coping, and I don't blame him. But his desire for us to be able to protect ourselves isn't the only thing he taught us, well, me.

Everything my father did since my mother's death was out of fear—fear of losing us the same way he lost her. He felt he had to be perfect, and so I grew to feel the same way. I adopted his fear, his desire to protect, and his need for perfection, not from others but for himself. The day he died, those feelings inside me only amplified, because I knew I'm all my sisters have. I'm the one tasked with protecting them. And yet, I've failed them, time and time again. First Cara. Now Sophia. Well, not anymore.

I shake my head and scroll back through the camera footage to keep myself from getting lost in my own wicked mind. That's when it occurs to me. I check the timestamp of when the man gets Sophia to the forest's edge. Eleven p.m.

"Hey, do you know when our men apprehended Ariana by the docks? What time was it?"

Gio pulls out his phone. "Eleven twenty-five p.m. is when Malik texted me."

I nod. "Okay. On the run, in the middle of the night, when no one else is out on the water, it probably took them an hour to an hour and a half to cross Lake Ponchartrain. I want you to look into the places they could've docked on the other side of the lake between midnight and two a.m. My guess is they docked somewhere and then left New Orleans by car. If we can find where they docked, we can get our contacts in the police department to tap into the video camera feeds throughout the city to see which direction they went. And, if we can find the boat, we may luck out and find who it was registered to and maybe even some DNA."

"Sounds like a plan. Is there anything else?" Gio asks.

"Yeah." I hand him the sticky note. "Here's a description of the man who approached Sophia based on the security camera coverage. I've also emailed you two images of him. Send them to our contacts ASAP so we can get an ID. My thoughts are Irish mob or Bratva based on appearance."

"Wow. Why would they want to wage war against you? Did your father ever have any dealings with them that went south?"

"Aside from the generations-long feud between the Irish and the Italians, I don't know." I shake my head. "But, unlike with Cara's abduction, not every attack is personal. Sometimes people are just greedy. And with our connections with the Mexican cartels and imports and exports with the Caribbean factions, our organization is a top target for anyone looking to expand their criminal empire." Gio nods. "Gio?"

"Yes, Boss?"

"Nothing like this can ever happen again. Our enemies only attack when they sense weakness. And I hate to say it, but we are weak and unprepared. This attack proves it. This place is supposed to be a fortress after the fortune I spent upgrading our security. And yet, these men bypassed every camera, every sensor, and I have no idea how."

"Do you think we have a mole?"

I hesitate. I hate to think we have a traitor in our midst. But how else could these men have been so prepared? "Either we do, or Cassio does. I'll call him and make another order, one that we keep between us, and I'll tell him to do the same. We keep this close to the vest, and we keep an eye on our men. We need to find out who we can trust and not just the people in our organizations. We need to investigate everyone in our lives, including Caleb Townsend."

"Sophia's ex?" Gio asks as he sips his bourbon.

"Yeah. It's probably nothing, but he wasn't on the guest list and yet he was the last person to see Sophia before she was abducted. No matter how unlikely it is that he was involved, he's a lead we need to follow up on."

"Will do." Gio drops my gaze, though his tone indicates there's something he isn't telling me.

"What is it?" I ask.

Gio finishes off his bourbon and leans forward in his chair. "What about the girl, Ariana?"

"What about her?"

"Do you truly trust that she had nothing to do with this? Just because she's FBI doesn't mean she isn't playing both sides. We know that from experience."

"I know," I admit. "But, um, there's something about her that makes me believe her. I mean, you know me, I don't trust anyone. So, I can't say that I trust she won't turn on us. But I do believe her when she says she isn't here to hurt me or Sophia. She wasn't a part of this."

"Then why is she here? You don't expect me to believe her friendship with Sophia is just a coincidence."

"No." I smile. "But that is a story for tomorrow."

"Understood, sir. I'll get started on these leads and will have a report for you midday tomorrow."

"Thanks, Gio."

As Gio leaves, I exit out of the surveillance footage and, in desperate need of a shower, prepare to turn in. That is, until thoughts of Ariana return to me. "Impeccable timing," I groan as I sit once more. I know I won't sleep until I do a little digging into my houseguest. It's not that Gio's mistrust has made me question Ariana. It's just, I can't turn her away without giving her something, some small bit of intel that will keep her occupied while I prepare for the war that is no doubt on its way.

I grab the black book from the center drawer of my desk and flip back to the year 2003, which, if my math is correct, is the year Ariana's mother was killed. My father kept a detailed record of all his hits, as do all bosses. It includes the victim's name, casualty count, date, and reason for the hit. There are three from that year, which means it was a relatively peaceful time for our business. None of the hits are women or have a casualty count of only one. This gives me a sense of relief. Maybe Ariana is wrong. It's been eighteen years and she was just a little girl when her mother was murdered. It's possible her memories are distorted. It's possible my family had nothing to do with— Though there are no other names written on the hit list for the year in question, there is something on the page that steals my hope just as quickly as it came. On the fourth line of the page, there is an ink blot and the beginnings of a letter. It's as if my father went to write something but stopped before he could finish.

I close the book and place it back inside my desk drawer, before locking it. My eyes drift from my desk to the photograph on the edge. My father stares back at me with a smile I miss. There are only two reasons my father wouldn't document a hit. One, because it didn't happen. And two, because it was wrongfully executed, an unjustifiable murder of an innocent based on poor intel.

"What did you do, Dad?"

11

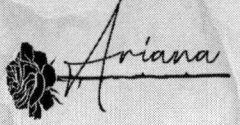

THE HALLS OF THE AMATO MANSION ARE DARK AS I MAKE MY way across the creaky wooden floors from the third floor to the second. Alister may not have denied my request for help officially, but I could see his response all over his face. He has no intention of helping me. Now that he knows who I am and what I look like, I'll never have an opportunity like tonight to get the answers I need. So, with enough painkillers in my system to make my cracked rib bearable, I tiptoe through the halls to where schematics say Alister's office is. I have no idea what I'm looking for or where it may be hidden, but his office is the place to start.

As I move, I cross my arms over my chest and shove my hands underneath my armpits to help keep warm. My oversize T-shirt can hardly compete with the draftiness of the 1800s-era home. From creaky floorboards to wallpapered and wood-paneled walls to the flickering brass wall sconces casting creepy shadows throughout the halls, the place looks nothing short of haunted. And yet, as I round the corner to the corridor of Alister's office, it isn't a ghost that nearly draws a gasp from me. It's the guard posted halfway down the hall. No doubt, he stands in front of the very door I need to open. Quickly and quietly, I take a step back into the darkness from which I came. My simple movement is met with a touch of warmth I welcome and the shocking sound of breaking glass, which I do not.

"Oh my God!" I say as I turn face-first into Alister's bare chest. As my body presses into his, our eyes lock, though only for a moment. Cereal, milk, and broken glass land at our feet, and the sounds of his guards' footsteps fill the silence between us. I take a step back, unable to read Alister in the dim lighting of the hallway. The longer he goes without speaking the more my nerves take over. I ball my fists, readying myself for a fight.

Finally, he says, "I guess that's what I get for trying to sneak up on you sneaking up on me." The hint of humor in Alister's voice allows the air to leave my lungs. I hadn't even realized I was holding my breath. "It's okay, gentlemen. I've got this," Alister says, waving off his guards as they reach us. His movement draws my attention to the massive ring on his finger, which somehow seems out of place given his topless, gray sweatpants ensemble. Though, it only claims my attention for a mere moment before I'm drawn back to his chiseled frame. *So, that's what abs look like.* The men leave as quickly as they approached, which allows the last bit of tension in my bones to dissipate. Still, as I anticipate what will happen next, I'm left speechless in Alister's presence. He leans forward then and shoves his hands into the pockets of his sweatpants. "Why aren't you saying anything?" he asks.

"I'm, um..." I look from him to the milk-soaked floor, allowing my hands to relax. I take a step back, avoiding the shards of glass next to my bare feet, and stand up straight as I find my resolve. "I wasn't sneaking. I was snooping," I clarify, though I'm not sure it helps my case. But, considering Alister hasn't beat me or sent me back down to the dungeon, maybe I stand a better chance of getting the information I came for than I thought.

Alister nods. "Which is why you're coming with me. Careful of the glass." At that, Alister grabs me by the forearm and proceeds to escort me back the way I came. *No!* I thought too soon.

"Wait, please," I beg, though I make no moves to escape him as the quick pace reminds me of my injuries. "Please don't send me back to the dungeon. It stinks and it's cold. I'll die down there." Okay, I'm being dramatic, which Alister clearly recognizes. Perhaps having two sisters has conditioned him to recognize a tantrum or ploy. "I'm sorry," I finally say as Alister and I reach the end of the hallway.

"No, you're not," Alister says, stopping just before we reach the stairwell to the third floor. "But don't worry. You're not going to the dungeon. Although, I guess that's a matter of opinion."

"What do you mean?" I ask, confusion washing over me.

There's a glint in Alister's dark eyes as he tightens his grip around my arm once more. He hooks a left and drags me along with him. We pass several doors until we reach the one in the center of the massive windowless corridor. Alister opens the door and shoves me in. As I steady myself using a black velvet chair just inside the room, I notice marks on my arm in the shape of Alister's fingers. *Not cool.* Though, as Alister follows in behind me, fresh fear lifts the hairs on my arms, and I know a few bruises may be the least of my worries. Alister closes the large wooden door behind him, pulls out his phone, and texts someone.

"Now, try getting out of this one," Alister says. He flips his phone so I can see, revealing video footage of the hallway from which we came. Guards now stand in front of every door. And, as I turn to find a massive bed just a few feet away, I realize what

Alister meant by *a matter of opinion*. He's right. I may prefer the dungeon three stories into the earth than this one. Sweat dampens my body and my heartbeat quickens in anticipation of what will happen next. This must be the residential wing for his family. Well, him and Sophia. And, seeing as he's dressed in pajamas, or rather, barely dressed at all, this must be his room. *His room.*

As realization dawns on me, memories of my past threaten to resurface as the T-shirt I'm wearing doesn't seem to give me as much coverage as I once thought it did. I turn to Alister to find him watching me from a few feet away. He stands relaxed with his hands still in his pockets. Though, I know in a matter of seconds he could be over here and—

As if sensing my worry, he says, "Do you really think so low of me?" His dark eyes narrow. I open my mouth, but no words come out. Alister's jaw clenches as he looks away from me. "You take the bed. I'll take the settee." Alister moves toward the small piece of furniture pressed against the black painted wall while my fear begins to settle and my reality sinks in.

I'm in nothing but a T-shirt in Alister Amato's bedroom, a T-shirt which, given its size, is likely his. And now, I'm expected to sleep in *his* bed. I make no moves toward it, even as Alister tries in vain to find a comfortable position on the too small, too rigid mini couch. Rather, I take in my surroundings, assess a potential exit, and take note of things that can be used as a weapon if Alister decides to lose his manners.

Alister's room is the perfect blend of classic and contemporary. It's large, including a sitting area separate from the bed, which sits up on a pedestal of sorts. Illuminated by soft overhead lighting, the mahogany bed is a commanding piece of furniture. So commanding, it makes my insides quiver. I move my eyes from it quickly to take in the other elements of the space. The walls are painted black, which, along with the dark wood floors, gives the room a masculine feel. Yet, the brass wall sconces, crystal chandelier hanging above us, and silky charcoal linens adds the same touch of glamour and sophistication found elsewhere in the home. His room is gorgeous, a blend of the old and the new just like the large floor-to-ceiling windows on either side of his bed. There. That's my exit. Though, given the two-story drop and my current injuries, I hope I don't have to take it.

"You going to stand there all night? Because if that's the case, I'll happily take the bed." I jump as Alister's voice pulls me back to him. I bring my hand to my chest as my heart beats rapidly. I pinch my eyes closed and open them to find Alister's body language has softened. Instead of anger or even impatience, he looks at me with gentle understanding, a look that reminds me of his sister and what happened to her. It lets me know he isn't going to—

"I'm not going to hurt you, Ariana. You don't have to worry," he says, reaching for the iPad on the small coffee table between us.

I nod. "Sorry. I...I know. I'm just taking it all in." Alister only nods and then directs his attention to his device. "I wasn't expecting this," I say as I move toward him.

"Which part?" Alister mumbles.

"All of it. When I left my apartment this evening, well, I guess yesterday evening, I had a plan. It involved me ending up in your bedroom, but not in this capacity."

At that, Alister's lips lift into a grin. He sets his iPad on the coffee table in front of us as I take a seat next to him on the black velvet settee. With talk of my plan, I find my bearings. We're getting back to normal—he the target and me the tracker. Though the moment of normalcy is shattered when he asks, "And in what capacity did you plan to end up in my bedroom?"

As Alister studies my face, I blush and turn away from him, focusing my attention on the dresser across the room rather than his shirtless frame or mystery-filled eyes. It's not that I'm embarrassed or ashamed that I was willing to seduce him to get the answers I need. It's just, now that we're alone in his bedroom, both of us half-naked, the thought of being with him feels different than it did when I was planning my seduction from the comfort and safety of my apartment. Now he knows who I am and what I want. Me pretending to be someone else, just a random, nameless hookup, is no longer an option.

"I planned to seduce you," I admit, keeping my eyes focused on the dresser. "And then, once I had you alone, I planned to question you regarding my mother's murder. Two steps. No fuss."

Thinking of my mother brings me back to my place of comfort, the place in my mind that, though horrible, is where I can exist without distraction. I close my eyes and take a deep breath, allowing the unfamiliar nerves and awkwardness brought on by Alister's presence to leave me. Once calm, I turn back to him to find, in light of my admission, his smile has grown to reach his eyes. His pearly-white teeth shine bright in the dim lighting of the room while his tan skin glistens in the glow of the flickering candles on the table before us. He's... I stop myself before mentally finishing my sentence. As Alister watches me with intrigue, I fill in the blank with other words—*evil, murderer*—all true and yet not my first choice for describing the man sitting just inches from me.

"Very efficient," he says then. "At least it would be if I were easy to seduce."

"Oh, come on. Don't even try to play hard to get. With the stress of your *lifestyle*..."

"*Lifestyle?* As if this existence is a choice?" Alister's brows furrow. I roll my eyes.

"You're probably constantly looking for a release. A fancy party like tonight where all the women are dressed to impress, or rather, dressed for sex, you were ending up with someone in your bed tonight. And I was...I was hoping it would be me." Alister raises a brow. "For interrogation purposes only," I assure him. "I knew I'd never be able to force my way to you, especially with your guards."

"And how would you overpower me once you had me alone? How could you guarantee I'd answer your questions? You think me a monster. After what you've seen of my special skillset in torture, how could you not? So, I doubt you were planning on me agreeing to help you based on the goodness in my heart."

"You make good points. But, for the record, those men deserved what you gave them. And, as far as you being a monster, well, I haven't made up my mind yet."

I shift in my seat and lean back against the settee. It's true. Alister could've beat me and killed me in that dungeon, and no one would've known. He could've raped me upon forcing me into his bedroom. But, again, he hasn't laid a hand on me. Maybe it's only because I'm FBI and he doesn't know I've been suspended. Maybe he fears the FBI will break their unprecedented arrangement with him if he hurts me or if I die under suspicious circumstances on his property. But there's something about him that makes me think the kindness he's shown me is more than that. It comes natural to him. Though, even as I think it, I wish I didn't. I can't have this getting complicated.

Alister knows as much when he says, "Well, I guess I should thank you for that. But, given our circumstances, it's best you think the worst of me. It'll be easier when—"

"When you turn down my request for help or when I'm forced to investigate you for your illegal acts?" He's right. It is best I think the worst of him. But how can I when I've seen his worst and his treatment of me is the complete opposite? Well, minus my short stint in his dungeon.

Alister hesitates, clearly not ready to kill my hope of finding my mother's killers. I, not yet ready to accept his denial, allow him to avoid my question.

"I survived those men. They were trained, armed. I was outnumbered and outweighed, and I survived with nothing more than my fists. Do you really think I couldn't take you in a room full of potential weapons?" I ask. "The books on the shelves, the lamp next to your bed, even the sheet could be used to create a noose. All I'd need is the element of surprise and—"

"And when my men heard sounds of a struggle, they'd just think we were having rough sex," Alister says.

"Exactly. But it doesn't matter. I much prefer this turn of events."

"You mean the one that resulted in you being beaten by two grown men, locked in a dungeon, and now held prisoner in my bedroom? You prefer that than a simple seduction?"

"Well, according to you, it wouldn't have been so simple."

Alister nods and moves his eyes from me to the table before us. As he does, I take note of a new feeling, one not grounded in attraction, awkwardness, or fear. One that I can't remember the last time I felt, and yet one I do recognize. Sitting here with Alister, talking, it feels...normal. Not normal in that it's what I'm used to. Normal in that it's what relationships should be—honest. I don't have to keep the truth of my mother's murder from him like I do Ray. Or the truth of my job from him like I would a random encounter. I don't have to lie to him, which relieves me of the heaviness of my past. It feels...easy with him. And yet, the ease and honesty between us makes me want to put my guard back up higher than it ever was before. Not because I can't allow him to know me. But because I'm scared he will get to know me. Maybe I'm even scared I'll get to know him. I'll get distracted by his mystery, manners, and, let's be honest, his physique, and I'll never get what I came here for. Maybe that's what this impromptu slumber party is all about. He wants me to get comfortable with him. And yet, I can't. I can't lose focus. Just as I plan to redirect the conversation to my mother, Alister surprises me with an admission of his own.

"You said my lifestyle must make me desperate for a release. Kudos, by the way, for finding a polite way to call me a man whore. That took skill."

"Wait. Did you just crack a joke? Did I detect actual humor? My, my, you keep surprising me, Mr. Amato. Here I was thinking you were all doom and gloom, death glares, and bulging muscles."

"More like I keep surprising myself." *Yeah, maybe I do too.* "The truth is…" Alister shakes his head and crosses his arms over his chest, the laughter between us now followed by thick silence. "My life isn't suitable for any kind of relationship, not even a casual one or a friendship." I nod, knowing exactly how he feels. "It's too dangerous."

"You and Gio seem pretty close. Or is that just when you're planning the demise of your enemies?"

"Gio is family. He may not be blood, but he's my brother. The structure of our world doesn't allow us to cross certain lines. He is and forever will be my subordinate. But I'd die for him, just like I would Sophia, just like I would any of my family. It's just…Sophia is the only one left."

"I get it," I say. "It's hard to let people get to know you when you don't know your own self. Or, in your case, maybe you do know who you are. You just can't let anyone see it."

"You mean the Blood King."

I shrug my shoulders. "In my short time with you, Alister, I've seen a man capable of more than torture and mass murder. You're more than the Blood King. Just like I'm more than an FBI agent or even a girl who lost her mom in the most horrific way. And yet, like you, I keep myself closed off, all of me, because I can't, *we* can't segment out the parts of ourselves that we don't understand or like or want."

I shake my head. I shouldn't have said that. The lines between us are too blurry. It's just— I tug my T-shirt over my knees as my honesty leaves me feeling exposed.

"Are you cold?" Alister asks.

"Um, yeah, kind of," I mumble. Alister stands and grabs me a spare blanket from the foot of his bed. "Thanks."

"You're welcome."

I wrap the blanket around my legs as Alister settles back in beside me. Despite his relaxed position, tension keeps his facial features tight. Clearly, our topic of conversation still weighs heavy on him, though he doesn't say anything more on the matter. Perhaps he's feeling the lines between us blur as well.

I know I shouldn't say anything more, and yet, as I look at him, I can't help but see the worry etched in the wrinkles on his forehead, the sadness in his eyes, the exhaustion in the way his lips droop. It's a feeling I know all too well so I can't stop myself from—

"Alister," I say.

"Yeah?" he asks, turning back to me.

"I, um…I can imagine trust is hard to come by in your line of work. Hell, it's hard for everyone. But for you? Me sitting here tonight is proof that you have reasons to be paranoid, to keep people at arm's length. But, if you found a way to trust Gio, someone who isn't your blood, maybe that means you can learn to trust someone else too, someday. I just…I know I don't know you. In fact, I'm pretty sure we're mortal enemies in more ways than one." At that, we both smile. "But I know as well as anyone how it feels to be alone—to feel like you are the only person in the entire world you can count on."

I lower my eyes to the blanket in my lap and brush my fingers over the tufts of softness, giving myself time to fight off my emotions and the memories of my past. Finally, I say, "No one should be alone forever. Not even you."

As the words cross my lips, Alister's eyes don't leave mine. His brows furrow as if he's wondering if I'm telling him the truth. Or perhaps, it's not the truth of my words he questions. Rather, he wonders why I've chosen to say them to him. Maybe he thinks I'm playing him. Still trying to seduce him or worse, manipulate his emotions to get the information I want from him. But I'm not. I'm—

"Ariana, you should know, I looked into my father's records for the year you said your mother was killed."

"You did?" My eyes widen with surprise. Hope rushes through my veins like heroin as I sit up straight, waiting for what he'll say next. And yet, as the wrinkles on his forehead deepen, my heart sinks.

"There was no record of a hit matching the details of your mother's murder for that year. I didn't even plan on looking, but your persistence was evident. I knew you wouldn't stop pestering me if I didn't give you something. So, I...I hoped I'd find enough to get you off my tail and onto someone else's. But..."

"You found nothing." I shrug the blanket off my legs and stand. Is he only telling me this because he fears I'm getting too close to him? I'm starting to see the real him, so he wants to push me away? But, as I turn to him and search his eyes for deception, I find none. "*Nothing*," I repeat. "No, no, no! This doesn't make sense." I run my fingers through my hair as I shake my head.

"Ariana, I'm sorry. I—" Alister says, standing.

"No, you're not sorry! You're lying to me!" I yell, shoving my finger into his chest. "You're lying to me." As the words cross my lips for the second time, they're barely audible despite the volume I demonstrated just moments before. My chest heaves. My hands begin to shake.

Whether Alister is lying or not, one thing is certain. He plans on being no help to me. I've known it for hours now. I saw it in his eyes while we were still in the dungeon. Dr. Ramirez, offering me his bed, our entire conversation, it was all out of guilt because he knew he would turn me away in the end. Though, maybe I'm giving him too much credit by assuming he feels guilty. He probably couldn't care less. He's got his own wars to win, his own secrets to uncover. I'm just the girl who lied to him, who used his sister to get close to him, who he owes nothing to. And that's exactly what he's given me—*nothing*. At that, I break.

I bring my hand to my side as my emotion works through the last of my medication. "Ah!" I cry out in pain, tears flooding my face. Though the pain of my injuries is nothing compared to the pain of Alister's admission coursing through my veins like ice. I turn away from him, but he pulls me back to him. I'm too emotional to protest when he swoops me up into my arms and carries me to the large bed with sheets the color of a foggy night. As Alister holds me, his warmth chases away the chill of hopelessness I've become accustomed to, but only for a moment. When he lowers me to the bed, his warmth leaves me and so does any chance of me finding out the truth of what happened to my mother.

"Nothing," I say once more. Alister places me among the pillows, drapes the comforter over my body, and kneels beside me. His face is only inches from mine when I turn to him.

"Ariana, I know you don't want to be alone anymore, but your answer to that isn't here. It's not with me. And it's not with your mom either. Even if I had found something, it only would've led to more bloodshed, more death. Is that what you want? Is that what your mother would want? As hard as it is to hear, it's time for you to move on."

I watch him in disbelief, knowing that if anyone had the balls to tell him that when his sister went missing, he would've killed them. Why can't he understand how important this is? Why can't he help me? Is he afraid I'll get too close? To him or to his operation?

Honestly, I don't even care anymore. I don't care that he's a mob boss, a drug dealer, a murderer, or that my team will investigate him in a matter of months. I don't care about any of it. All I want is to know what happened to—

I turn away from him and fight through my heartache enough to speak without breaking.

"You know nothing about me. If you did, you'd know that I've already tried moving on. For ten years!" The words scrape through me. "For ten years I tried to pretend to be normal. But normal is the last thing that my life has been, Alister. It's isolated and filled with anxiety, secrets, nightmares. It's not living. It's Hell! I told myself I didn't need to know the truth, that my mother wouldn't want me to know. But, when you lose someone like that, my mom, your sister, moving on without knowing exactly what happened to them isn't an option." I turn back to him. "But you were right about one thing. I'm not giving up on this. I'm going to be the biggest thorn in your side until you agree to help me, because if you think that a five-second glance at your father's records is enough to convince me you're useless when it comes to this, you're wrong."

At that, Alister nods. "Get some sleep. We have to get up early so I can get you home before Sophia wakes up."

Alister stands and makes his way back to the rigid settee while I fight the urge to roll over onto my side. The only thing keeping more tears from falling is the fresh rage igniting every nerve in my body. I didn't come this far to give up now. And yet, as Alister switches off the light, blows out the candles, and returns his attention to his iPad, I know my rage is caused by more than his lack of news regarding my mother.

Alister is the only person I know who can help me learn the truth once and for all. But working with him was, *is* more than a necessity for me. I *want* Alister to help me because I know he understands what I'm feeling. For once in my life, I don't have to pretend or lie. He gets what I've gone through, which only makes his unwillingness to help me hurt more. He understands my pain, and yet he's doing nothing to take it away.

As I finally admit the truth to myself, I feel weak and ashamed. I've always wanted someone to be there for me, to help me. When my mother died, when I was bullied at school for being so behind, when the other kids in my foster homes ganged up on me and took their own frustration out on my body, when my foster dad came into my room and—

But, just like then, all I have is myself. I was a fool to think that would change because of Alister Amato of all people. No. It's on me to discover the truth. If Alister won't help me out of the goodness of his heart, as he so kindly put it, I'll have to find another way to convince him to help me.

I close my eyes and pray that morning comes quickly. I need to get out of this house before I let the poison inside of it infect me and turn me into one of them—a monster, a selfish, emotionless, bloodthirsty monster. My lip quivers as I try to convince myself I was right about Alister and that the past few hours were all a lie. But as tears seep out of my closed eyes and down my cheeks, I know the only liar here is me.

12

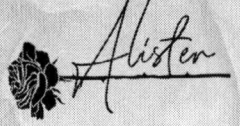

It's been six weeks since I dropped Ariana off at her apartment and crushed any chance she has of learning the truth of her mother's murder. Of course, that hasn't stopped her from stalking me and half begging, half blackmailing me to change my mind. I haven't, though I'd be lying if I said her pleas haven't worn me down. Her constant efforts over the past several weeks have proven to me she's admirably relentless and, equally so, desperate.

While I've come to enjoy our brief run-ins filled with her rare breed of humor, every encounter ends the same. Her dark eyes melt beneath my stern gaze as disappointment drains her, just like the night we shared together all those weeks prior. It's that night that lets me know she's not only desperate to discover the truth surrounding her mother's murder, she's also desperate to make sense of her pain. I pinch my eyes closed as images of her crying herself to sleep dance through my head. She tossed and turned all night, writhing against the sheets as soft whimpers escaped her. After hours of restlessness, she shot up in bed, covered in sweat as she cried out in fear. Fear of who or what, I don't know, but I can't help but feel inadvertently responsible.

She's lived a life filled with pain and secrets. She's closed herself off from the world, much like I have, because of her past—a past drenched in blood drawn by my father. And yet, the scars on her body tell me the loss of her mother isn't the only pain she knows. If I'm right about the information, or lack of, found in my father's ledger, then he's not only responsible for the wrongful death of Ariana's mother, but is also responsible for everything that happened to her after. Whatever she dreams of, whatever haunts her, it's because of my father. And that's why I can't stop thinking about her, why I've dug through every record my father has, why I've torn my office apart in search of the truth, Ariana's truth. But I've found nothing—nothing to take away the pain she doesn't deserve, nothing to give her the closure she desperately wants. Maybe it's for the best. I know as well as anyone that closure doesn't exist. And sometimes the truth only causes more pain. In Ariana's case, I fear that's exactly what waits for her.

"Alister, you with us?" Cassio asks.

"Yeah, um, continue," I say, redirecting my attention from my thoughts to the display of weapons before me.

Cassio Castellani is the head of the Castellani crime family out of Savannah, Georgia, and is a long-standing ally of my family. Though, you wouldn't know it given his laid-back take on the classic suit, the dangling earring, and his young age, which is only made more obvious with his clean shave. During their prime, the Castellanis supplied their unique weapons to all the crime families in North America and many outside the US. Lucky for them, the Department of Defense caught up to them before the FBI. In exchange for a pardon, Cassio's father struck a deal with the United States Armed Forces before his death. They've since legitimized their business and deal their arms only to the military. But, given our long family history *and* Cassio's undeniable feelings for Sophia, he was kind enough to make an exception for me when I called him a few months ago. Now, he's back with a brand-new shipment of guns, grenades, goggles, and God knows what else.

"I had this one made special for Sophia," he says, grabbing a thigh strap from the table. "It's equipped with a tracker, a knife, a USB for collecting intel, and mini Taser and mini flare."

"You packed all of that into a one-inch strap of leather?" Gio asks.

"You know me. It's all about efficiency and versatility." Cassio smiles, returning the device to its place. "How is Sophia?"

Gio and I share a knowing look as Cassio avoids eye contact. I glance at my watch. Thirty minutes before bringing her up—he's set a new record.

"She's good. Well, as good as she can be. I think she's more pissed than anything," I tell him.

"What do you mean?" His brows furrow.

"The men who tried to abduct her told her if she didn't go with them, they'd have me killed. But they were lying. I was meeting with one of my capos during the time of the abduction. She's just upset she got played." At that, thoughts of Ariana return to me. Sophia was lied to more than once that night. She just doesn't know it.

Cassio nods. "Any idea who ordered the attack?"

"Yes, actually," Gio says. He skips past the photo of Sophia and her ex, Caleb, since he ended up checking out and is no longer a suspect, and pulls up different angles of our two suspects from the party on his phone, which happen to capture an identifying mark on one of the men. "You see the tattoo on his neck? It's the mark of the Irish mob. We're thinking the men who came after Sophia are midlevel soldiers, like the mole they planted in your organization."

"Yeah, thanks for the heads-up on that. Even though we've legitimized, I guess certain bosses like to keep an eye on me to make sure they get first dibs if I ever get back in. Though, considering where I'm standing, I'm not sure you ever really get out."

"*By blood, I will meet my end,*" I mumble. Cassio nods. It's the same no matter which family or organization you belong to. The only way out is death. I suspect once I legitimize, if I survive to see the day, I'll face similar threats as Cassio. Perhaps more, seeing as I can't in good conscience allow another crime family to move into my city. That would put Sophia at risk just as much as she is now, if not more.

"We've tracked them to a pub on Bourbon Street," I say, doing my best to focus on the task at hand.

"Wait? In New Orleans?" Cassio asks. He shakes his head, knowing it's against the rules for members of other criminal organizations to come into my city without my permission. "They're either stupid or they're looking for a fight."

"And now that you're here, we're prepared to give them one," I say, taking one of the guns from the table. "The fact that they're still in New Orleans means they're planning another abduction attempt against Sophia. If they'd given up, they'd already be back in Boston or wherever their boss is based. Now that we've got our new toys, Gio and I and the rest of my capos are going hunting. We'll see which pig squeals first." At that, we all laugh and Gio flashes me a sinister grin.

"I pity the man who finds himself up against you," Cassio says. "But, before you go, I would like to make one request, if I may?"

"Of course."

I place my weapon back on the table as Cassio runs his fingers through his brown hair. Shaking off his nerves, he stands tall, meeting me eye to eye. His jaw clenches. And as a wave of seriousness clouds his amber eyes, I know. This is the moment he finally admits his feelings for Sophia. My fists instinctively ball until I remind myself it's Cassio, the man who's been in love with my sister since they were kids playing hide and seek through these very halls. I can trust him as much as I can trust anyone. And if he proves me wrong, I'll kill him, even if he is the Godfather of Guns.

"Alister, I know that you and Gio are more than capable of protecting Sophia. But, when I left those months ago, there was something in me that told me I should stay. For you. For her. Given everything that's happened, this time I can't walk away. So, I'm asking for your permission to stay and assist in your investigation in any way I can."

As Cassio speaks, I lower my head. His request is honorable, respectful, and not one I need to consider. It's just...the thought of my needing his help to protect my sister makes me feel weaker than I already do. But I'm not too proud to accept his offer. I've already fallen short when it comes to protecting Cara. And, if it weren't for Ariana—

"Of course you can stay. But not for me. I don't want you getting caught up in what's about to go down. Since you've already legitimized, and because I know you're in love with my sister..." I lift my eyes to meet Cassio's. He's taken aback by my bluntness, but he doesn't deny my observation. Good. I've got enough liars in my life to add him to the list. "I want you to stay for her. Protect her. Care for her. Be there for her in the ways I can't. And maybe, when this is all over, I'll feel comfortable with the inevitable."

"Inevitable?"

I smile and squeeze his shoulder. Cassio's is only seven years younger than me, two younger than Sophia, and yet, when I look at him, I see a child. Perhaps because that's what I see when I look at Sophia—a child who needs my protection, just like when we were younger, and I kept her from finding our mother's lifeless body sprawled out on the floor of our parents' bedroom.

I'm okay with Sophia being all I have. To be honest, my heart can't bear to love another, because as great as it is to love, it's also terrifying. It's terrifying to know that I may lose Sophia if these men have their way with her. But, even more so, it's terrifying to think that I'm all she has and that if something happens to me, she'll be left alone, defenseless, and heartbroken. As much as I don't want to let her go, I need her to find it in her heart to love someone else. If not Cassio, then hopefully someone just as decent and capable of providing for her. Because tonight is only the start of the war to come. With all wars, there are casualties. And there's a very good chance I will be one of them.

"She's upstairs," I tell him. "Go tell her the good news." Cassio nods and leaves Gio and me with a giddy smile spread across his face. I exhale and rest both my hands against the dining room table covered with instruments of death.

"How hard was that?" Gio asks, pouring me a glass of bourbon.

"Harder than you'll ever know." I down my drink and grab my weapon once more. "Call the capos. Tell them where to meet. We've got trespassers who need vacating."

It's close to midnight by the time we make it across the causeway to the pub, which means it's already packed with drunken civilians. *Great.* The crowd may help me and my men blend in, but it'll make it harder to find our targets. Even more so, it increases the likelihood that this ends bloody. With the entrance to the pub just up ahead, I stop my men for a weapons check. They reach inside their suit jackets, making sure they've got easy access to their guns.

"All good," they report.

"Good."

"Son, are you sure you want to do this? The boys and I can handle these lowlifes. No need for you to put yourself at risk," Vitale says.

"Vitale, don't pretend to give a damn about me. Besides, the only ones at risk tonight are them." At that, Vitale backs off, though he makes a good point. Since taking over from my father, I don't usually participate in small missions like this. It only increases my chances of being caught. And, if I go down, so does the entire organization. But, after what happened to Sophia, I can't sit this one out. I'm here to make sure Gio doesn't have any problems collecting our suspects for questioning. But Vitale and the rest of the crew can't know any of this. So, I offer them this explanation instead.

"Look, I told you gentlemen that war is coming. This may seem like a small mission, but it's not. The fact that those Irish scum think it's okay to invade our turf just goes to show that our enemies think we're weak. This is only the beginning. And, I don't know about you, but I'd rather cut the cancer out than let it spread until the point where there is no chance of survival for any of us."

They all nod, remembering that's exactly what happened to my dad. Cancer ate him alive, and though this is a metaphorical cancer, every word I say is true. If we don't get rid of them now, they'll come for Sophia. And once they have her, I'll have no choice but to turn myself over to them, essentially signing my own death warrant and relinquishing my crown to their king. And Sophia... Once I'm dead, so is she. At least, one can hope. Because if they don't kill her, they'll—

"Moving." I turn and do my best to flush the vile thoughts

from my mind as I approach the courtyard entrance to the pub. I unbutton my suit coat and move my hand to the gun holstered at my hip. As my fingers graze the rubber grip, my skin turns hot to the touch and the chatter and laughter of the pub's patrons lowers to nothing more than a hum. I take a deep breath as my body language shifts. My lips press into a flat line. My eyes narrow. Every muscle in my body is on high alert, stretching against the seams of my suit. I'm becoming him, the one they fear. And if they don't, they will.

"Parisi, you take the boss's left. I'll breach from the back," Gio says. As Gio leaves us, I offer him a nod of reassurance. He'll enter from the back and subdue our suspects before the rest of us make it inside. He'll let me know once he's got them unconscious and then I'll help him load them into the van we have Malik stationed in around back. With any luck, Vitale and the rest of the capos will be too distracted with rounding up the rest of the Irish soldiers to notice.

Parisi moves in front of me, crossing the threshold of the pub first. As we enter, I keep my eyes peeled for the mark of the Irish mob, as do my men. We take our time moving through the relatively small space, though we find no tattoos matching the ones of our suspects. Clearing the front, we make our way past the bar area and through a narrow walkway lined with bathroom and kitchen entrances to the back of the building. The closer we get to the back the less crowded it becomes, letting me know we've found them. I stop and give my men the nod so they can ready themselves. Though, truly, I'm hoping to give Gio a few more moments to execute his part of the plan. I glance at my watch. I should've heard from him by now. Maybe I should've gone with him. Maybe it was too big of a job for one person.

The vein in my forehead throbs as I imagine Gio lying at the feet of our enemies in a pool of his own blood. But, like so many times before, I push past my worst fears and continue moving toward the back. Parisi moves beside me while Gagliano and Vitale follow behind us. I tighten my grip on the handle of my pistol, readying myself for a quick draw. Though, as we exit the dark corridor that smells of stew and piss and enter the poorly lit back room, it's not Gio's dead body I find or even an armed gang waiting to slaughter us. Instead, I find a pool table, surrounded by half-naked women and a small group of men watching them as they bend over and drive long sticks into tiny balls. Gio's among them, sipping a scotch to blend in.

I exhale in relief at the sight of him. Though the moment of reprieve lasts only a second as Gio spots me and nods toward the door to my right. Of course. I guess they're not complete idiots. There's a camera above the door and no doubt an armed guard or two on the other side. If we approach, we'll be like fish in a barrel.

"Get comfortable," I tell my men. Immediately, they disperse, grabbing drinks and placing bets on the women's pool match. I do the same, joining Gio after grabbing a drink from the bar.

"How do you want to do this, Boss?" he asks.

I sip my drink, mentally running through my options. I have a device from Cassio that could do the trick, but there's no guarantee it'll work in our favor. There's only a handful of things that'll draw a man out of hiding—money, pride, and pussy.

My eyes shift from the pool table to the women surrounding it. What are the odds some of them belong to the very men I'm looking to draw out? That's when I see it. Among the ink sprawled over the blonde woman's shoulder is the mark I've been looking for. Gio follows my line of vision, spotting the woman.

"Go put your Southern charm to good use," I tell him.

Gio laughs. "I'm from Miami, which hardly counts as the South. And, besides, I don't think charm will do much for a woman like her." Gio downs the rest of his drink. He's right.

From the looks of her ink and pixie haircut, she'll be harder to wrangle than a bull. But, tonight, that'll work in our favor. I need him, or rather her, to cause a scene. It'll draw out her boyfriend and his backup. "You sure you don't want to give it a go? You and I both know you could use the practice," Gio jokes.

"Nice try," I mumble, taking his empty glass from him. Gio rolls his eyes and does as he's told. I should really give him a raise. As he approaches the woman, I back away toward the bar, setting our empty glasses down. Parisi and the rest of the gang take note and take up positions on either side of me with their hands ready for the draw.

The woman curses and takes a swing at Gio as he comes up behind her, making his presence known. She throws her drink at him but misses, sending the glass spiraling into the wall that separates us from the Irish soldiers. "This is it, boys. One, two—"

Like clockwork, the door concealing our suspects swings open. Out comes three men holding machine guns, the kind that will rip this place and everyone in it apart in a matter of seconds. Among them is one of the men who came after Sophia. I recognize him by his buzz cut and square-shaped head. Yet, there's no sign of the other one. Which means there's likely more men waiting in the room from which these came. There's no telling how many there are or how many guns they have. *Shit.* This is a suicide mission.

Vitale looks at me as his fingers twitch. I blink once, telling him to hold his position. When I return my eyes to the men approaching Gio, I find I'm the one who's garnered their attention. All three of them stop and stare as Gio holds firm.

"Good. You know who I am," I say, motioning for the bartender to pour me another bourbon. He does with shaky hands. I tip him a hundred and tell him to take the rest of the night off. As he leaves, so do the bar's patrons and women surrounding the pool table, leaving only my army and my enemies. I sip my drink. The longer the silence prevails, the more they are thrown off guard. I look them up and down, watching their hands turn red from their tight grips on their guns. Their faces shine with sweat. The muscles in their arms throb. All the while I remain calm, numb, so numb I appear to welcome death. Little do they know—I am death.

When I finish my drink, I set my empty glass on the bar and take a step forward. The rest of my men move with me, including Gio. We've got the Irish soldiers surrounded, but they've still got the upper hand and they know it.

"Now, now, gentlemen. If you were going to fire those weapons, you would've done so already. So, go on, put 'em down." They make no moves to lower their weapons. Yet, still, they do not fire. "Just as I thought," I say, taking another step forward. "Your boss doesn't know you're here, does he? Your very presence in my city is against the Rules of Civility, an act of war. And, if we were at war, you wouldn't hesitate to take me out. Yet, you don't pull the trigger. Which means you either just couldn't resist my city's charms or you've betrayed your boss and given your allegiance to someone new." That, or their boss isn't ready to wage a full-scale war against me, hence the abduction rather than assassination attempt. If they shoot me or my men, they'll create a conflict they're not sure they'll win without leverage. Sophia was meant to be their leverage.

"You screwed up, gentlemen. Now that you've been caught, this can only end one of two ways. Tell me who you work for and allow my men to escort you out of my territory or—"

Before I can finish my sentence, gunfire erupts. My ears ring as Gio lunges toward me, shoving me out of the line of fire. Bullets spray all around us, bursting bottles behind the bar and chipping away at the wood walls. Though, the chaos lasts for only a moment. When I look up, I find all three of the Irish soldiers dead on the ground as my ears fill with the sounds of civilians' screams coming from the front of the pub.

"No," I whisper. Gio stands, pulling me up with him. "No," I say again.

"What the Hell happened?" Gio asks, drawing my men's attention away from me.

"He aimed at me. I had no choice," Vitale says. He shrugs his shoulders as if he just dropped his hot dog on the sidewalk. I charge him, pinning him up against the wall.

"*What the Hell?*"

"Do you realize what you've done?" I ask him. He only looks at me with wide eyes. *"Do you realize what you've done!?"*

"*What?* Would you rather it was me dead on the floor?" Yes. Yes, old man, I would. But I can't say that. I can't give my own men a reason to turn against me, especially now that I'll have the full force of the Irish mob coming after me.

I shake my head and shove away from him. As sirens blare and screams echo from the front of the building, I pull my weapon and enter the room from which the men came. There's still a fourth man unaccounted for. And not only is he the key to finding out who ordered Sophia's abduction, he's now the only way I can stop this war before it starts. Assuming he is in fact a traitor whom his boss will be happy to have hand delivered.

Gio follows behind me as I enter the dark, smoke-filled room. There's a poker table in the middle with a spotlight hanging above it and a video monitor on the wall watching the room we just came from. The room is quiet, save for the sounds of police sirens and street traffic coming in from the outside.

"Still one room left," I say, motioning toward the slender door to Gio's right. He moves toward the door, and I follow behind him. "One, two." I kick down the door and Gio moves in, though we instantly regret it as the smell of shit and urine floods our nostrils. "He's not here," I say, lifting my suit jacket to cover my nose. I move rapidly around the small space as if it will somehow change our reality. "He's not here!" I yell. I lower my coat from my nose, holster my gun, and punch the tiny mirror hanging over the sink.

"Hey, hey, calm down," Gio says as shards of glass fall around us. "We can't let the others know why we're really here. We've got enough problems now that Vitale decided to be trigger-happy."

"I swear to God, I could fucking kill him. He just shot up our only lead. And now, we've got more heat on us than before." I shake my head and run my bloody hand through my hair. In the few shards remaining attached to the mirror's frame, I catch a glimpse of myself. I look tired, desperate, and deadly—everything I shouldn't be if I expect to maintain my men's respect. As if I even have it. Us looking weak has nothing to do with them and everything to do with me. Vitale may have pulled the trigger, but those men are dead because of me, because they wouldn't be in New Orleans if not to destroy me.

"Hey, I know you hate Vitale. We all do. But those men leaving New Orleans alive wouldn't have stopped the mob from coming for us. They came after Sophia, Alister. They're not going to stop. You know that. That's why we came here tonight. And even though tonight didn't go according to plan, at least you can rest knowing that there are three less men coming after your sister."

I know Gio's just trying to calm me down and talk me out of putting a bullet in Vitale's head, but I won't rest until I find the fourth man. He's the only one who can tell me which faction of the Irish mob is coming after me if it's even them he works for. The way the men looked at each other when I accused them of shifting alliances leads me to believe it's possible they are defectors. Though for my sake, I hope I'm wrong. The only lead I have is the Irish mob. But if the men who invaded my home have shifted their alliance, without the intel from the fourth man, intel I will strip from his bones if I have to, I'm back to square one.

"Come on, let's get out of here before the police complicate things," Gio says.

I brush the sweat from my forehead and wipe my bloody knuckles against my black dress pants. "Things are already complicated."

13

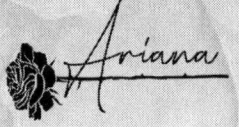

THE MOON HANGS LOW ABOVE THE MURKY WATERS OF THE swamp. Frogs moan and crickets chirp as I stand on the wooden boat dock just outside the abandoned shack the FBI uses as a last resort safe house. Though, tonight, this place is anything but safe. As if sensing what will happen next, a gust of wind rips past me, lifting my long, dark hair and the plaid blanket I have draped over my shoulders. I'm not sure if I should take it as a warning or a nod of encouragement. Regardless, the sound of Ray's footsteps as he approaches lets me know it's too late to back out now. This is happening. I just pray I can stomach it.

"He's waking up," Ray says, joining me at the end of the dock. "What now?"

I close my eyes and take solace in the sweet sounds of flowing water, knowing that what I say next will start a fight with the only friend I have. But I don't have a choice. Ray can't be a part of this, at least not more than he already is. With resolve, I turn to him and—

"Now, you leave."

Ray chuckles. "You're joking." Even in the dim light of the

moon, I can see the lightheartedness leave him when he realizes no, I'm, in fact, not joking. "No. *No.* There is no way in Hell I'm leaving you alone in the middle of the swamp with that psycho," Ray shouts, pointing back toward the shack. To his point, the place is a death trap even without the trained killer inside of it.

"I'm not asking you to *leave* leave. I just…I need to question him in private." I shrug.

"*Why?*" Ray crosses his arms in defiance. I exhale, rolling my eyes in frustration.

"Look, I've already involved you enough. I hated to even ask. I just needed your muscle and the van."

Ray nods, doing his best to keep his cool. "Involved me in what, Ariana? Who is he? What the Hell is going on?" Okay, cool lost.

"Ray." I drop my blanket to the ground and take both his hands in mine. I know I'm not playing fair. Ray cares for me…as more than a friend. Maybe I exploited that a little by asking him to help me with something I know could get him suspended, or worse. But that very reason is why he can't know that the man inside is Edgar Walsh, the Irish assassin who tried to abduct Sophia Amato six weeks ago. More than that, he's the man who's going to get me back in Alister's good graces, the man whose intel will be too good for Alister to turn me away—again. All of this—Edgar, the Irish mob, Alister—is against Bilieux's command. And, about fifty percent of the time, it's against my better judgment. But it's the only way I'll ever learn the truth of why my mother was killed.

"I need you to trust me," I tell him. "I'm going to be fine. He's restrained. And, if he somehow breaks loose, I have my gun. Not to mention some other toys."

"*Toys?*" Ray shakes his head. But his disapproval doesn't stop him from squeezing my hands and pulling me in for a hug. "Come here," he whispers as my chest crashes against his. His grip is suffocating, but I give in to him. I know he needs this, and I need him to walk away. "I don't know what's going on with you, Ari, but if Bilieux finds out, he'll fire you. You know that, right?" At that, I pull away from him despite his reluctance to let me go.

"If Bilieux figures out what's going on with me, then I will gladly let him fire me, because I don't even know, Ray." I cross my arms over my chest. "What's happening now, it's...complicated." I turn from Ray back to the water, praying he won't push the issue any further.

"Okay," he finally says. "I'll leave." He takes a step toward the house, then stops. I turn back to him. "But eventually, you're going to have to let someone in. Or else, whatever *is* going on, it'll consume you. It'll ruin you."

I nod as another gust of wind swirls between us. *Maybe it already has.*

Ray gives me one last pleading look before making his way around the cabin to the unmarked van he borrowed from headquarters. I don't move until I hear the engine crank and moan as he pulls away, leaving me alone in the swamp to do the very thing that haunts me. It's not that I'm afraid to interrogate Walsh. I'm afraid of what it may take to get the information out of him.

My heart races as I approach the shack. The wooden door creaks as I pull it open. I haven't even stepped inside, and his eyes are already on me—icy green and cold like death. I bite the inside of my cheek as if it will give me some strength I seem to be lacking. I take a step forward, leaving the door to the outside open so he can get a good look at what waits for him if he doesn't cooperate. The gators will enjoy a nice midnight snack. That is, unless the snakes poison his blood first.

Walsh watches me as I approach him, dragging his eyes up and down my body until I am only inches from the man who nearly beat me to death when first we met. The way he looks at me lets me know he recognizes me. His lips curl into a sinister smile as he grips the arms of the chair Ray has him strapped to. He's testing the strength of the ropes, not because he's afraid of what I'll do to him, but because he can't resist the urge to touch me, to hurt me, just like that night. Yeah. I've seen this look before. But unlike when I was younger, I now have the upper hand.

There. I've finally found the strength I need to rip the truth from his bones. It rests in my past. I nod and offer him a smile before turning and making my way to the kitchen table where a black duffel holds the various devices I've collected over the past few months. I take them out one by one, making sure Walsh can see them.

"If you think that's going to intimidate me, you're wrong," he says then. *Hmm.* Maybe it won't be as difficult to get him talking as I thought. I lower my knife to the table and turn to face him. "All this because I knocked you around a little. It seems a bit extreme." At that, I smile. He has no idea why he's here. I wonder if the truth will steal his smile.

"Well, I wouldn't call what you did *little* nor do I believe this is extreme punishment." I take a step toward him. "But this isn't about what you did to me. It's about what you tried to do to Sophia Amato."

At the mention of Sophia's name, his face goes pale, well, paler than it already was.

"You...you don't work for the Amatos. If you did, I'd know."

"And how would you know that?"

Walsh goes quiet, moving his eyes from me to the wall. I nod. I know that look too. Knowing he can't escape physically he looks for a mental escape. But he won't find one. I won't let him.

I return to the kitchen and grab my knife and a chair from

beneath the table. Returning to Walsh, I sit down directly across from him, meeting him eye to eye. Well, I would if he'd look at me. But I can fix that. Before Walsh's peripheral vision even registers my movements, I lean forward and slice a four-inch gash up his forearm. He screams, though not nearly as loud as I hoped, as he writhes against his restraints. Good job, Ray. The ropes haven't given an inch.

"*Hey, hey!*" I snap my fingers. "Look at me." His icy eyes shift into slits as sweat dampens his forehead.

"You're going to have to do better than that, sweetheart," he says.

I nod. "Yeah, I figured. But before you sign yourself up for a very uncomfortable night, just listen. Okay? Can you do that?" He doesn't say anything, but his eyes piercing into mine let me know I've got his attention. Alright, here goes nothing.

"You're right. I don't work for the Amatos. I work for the FBI."

"Is that supposed to scare me?"

"It should. You see, I'm a member of the Organized Crime Task Force, the same task force that studies criminals like you, like Alister Amato. Do you know what that means, Edgar?" His eyes narrow. "Yeah, I know your name. I also know that you died in a boating accident last year with three other men. Now, I'm going to go out on a limb here and say that you're not a ghost, though this is voodoo country." My eyes drift to his arm and the small pool of blood forming on the floor. "Ghosts don't bleed." I return my gaze to him, this time with a smile on my face. Two can play at this game.

"So." I slap my thighs and stand, pacing the room. "My guess is someone had you and your friends fake your own deaths so you could move around New Orleans undetected using false identities, all the while planning your attack against the Amatos. Why? I don't know." I shrug. "But you're going to tell me. And do you want to know why?" I stop as Walsh lifts a brow. He doesn't seem very impressed, but he's about to be.

"Do you want to know why you should be scared of me, Edgar?" I take a step forward and return to my seat just inches from him. "Because, during my time at the FBI, I've studied every criminal organization present in the United States, the way they operate, the way they torture, the way they get away with it. I mean, you're a part of this world, so you know what I'm talking about."

"Knowing and doing are two different things. You may know how to burn someone alive, but that doesn't mean you have it in you to do it," he says. "From the looks of you, I think you're nothing but a mouthpiece with a decent right hook. Untie me and we can put that mouth to better use than you spewing these words you can't even comprehend."

I lean back in my chair. "You know, maybe you're right. Maybe I don't have it in me to make you talk. But I know someone who does."

At that, I raise my brow, letting the weight of my words sink in. I hadn't planned on using the Alister card. If I was planning on just turning the man over to him, I would've done it already. But no. I need the intel. I need to prove to Alister that he needs me just as much as I need him. Let's just hope the threat of a visit from the Blood King is enough to scare some sense into Edgar, or else I may have to try my hand at torture, and he's right, I'm not sure I have it in me.

"So, here are your options, Edgar. Option one, you can tell me what I want to know. In exchange for your cooperation, I'll overlook your transgression against me and Ms. Amato, and have you put into Witness Protection. And before you say a dead man doesn't need protection, let me remind you that you were abducted by two federal agents. Now, my friend and I, we wore masks that will keep our identities safe, but we made sure our

FBI jackets were on full display of the pub's video cameras. When your friends realize you're missing and that you're in FBI custody, well, then you really will be dead. Because even if you tell me nothing, they won't be able to take that risk, will they? I mean, whatever mission that required you to fake your death and abandon your family for a year must be pretty important. Oh, and speaking of your family, I can arrange for them to join you in Witness Protection."

Edgar lowers his eyes as he considers my offer. "Sounds pretty sweet, huh? Well, option two is just as bitter, because that person who I *know* can and will make you talk, his name is Alister Amato—the Blood King of New Orleans. I may not work for him, but I will hand deliver you to him if that's what it takes. So, tell me, Edgar, is that what it's going to take?"

※

It was after two in the morning by the time I made it back home. Thankfully, the threat of a one-on-one with Alister was enough to get Edgar to tell me everything. And yet, as I sit on the back of my motorcycle waiting for the Amato guards to let me through the gate to see Alister, the information I gathered has me queasy instead of hopeful. I'd hoped in going after Edgar and gathering intel valuable to Alister, I'd prove my worthiness to him. Not to mention I'd have leverage that would require him to help me in exchange for the information, seeing as six weeks of begging and blackmail have gotten me nowhere. But, after what Edgar told me, I'm afraid my night in the swamp may have the opposite effect. Alister won't like what I'm about to tell him. In fact, it may just break him. And if he wasn't dangerous enough before, after he hears the truth, he will be. Let's just pray he directs that energy toward someone other than me.

"Alright, you're good to go," the guard says, handing me my

ID. I take it from him and try to offer him a friendly smile, but it doesn't work. He returns to his post as I kick up my kickstand. I'm surprised Alister agreed to see me. Maybe he's in a good mood. At least, one can hope.

The guard presses a button from his command booth and the large iron gate opens in response, revealing a gravel drive lined with moss-covered oak trees. I take a deep breath, doing my best to ignore the heart-racing anxiety coursing through me. Okay, no more stalling. It's now or never.

I rev my engine and set off down the path toward the grand mansion known to the world as Laroux House, named after the original owners before the Amatos purchased it in the late 1800s. The closer I get to the ancient home, the cooler the air feels as it pushes past the warmth of my leather jacket and through the holes in my black jeans. Just like last night, it's a warning. Because what happens next will change everything. Even if it is for my good, it won't be for Alister's. It'll break his heart—a heart, despite his constant denials, I really wish I didn't have to break.

As I pull through the circle drive, stopping just feet from the front entrance, the door swings open and out steps Alister. He's dressed in a white button-down and black dress pants, per usual. And yet, his facial hair is darker, thicker than I've seen on him before, and the wrinkles around his eyes are more prominent. As I cut the engine of my motorcycle and remove my helmet, Alister lowers his head and crosses his arms over his chest. Okay, not in a good mood. Noted.

14

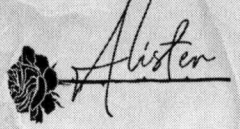

As someone who said she'd be a thorn in my side, and has been, I've got to give Ariana credit. She couldn't have more imperfect timing considering the epic failure last night was. Yet, it's last night's events that make her presence intriguing. She promised my guards her visit would be worth my time. Seeing as my men still haven't located the missing fourth man, I could do with some good news, or at least a healthy distraction from the utter disaster that is my life.

"Morning," I say, stepping down from the stoop to greet Ariana. Sophia is inside, which means she can't be. I've got enough to deal without adding a scorned sister to the list.

"Morning," she says. Her lips lift into a small smile, though there's something about her that's different from all the times before. Her arms hang rigid at her sides. Her shoulders are tense, as is her neck. And she looks at me with eyes I've never seen before. They are dark like an abyss just waiting to consume me. When I heard she was asking to see me, there was a part of me that thought it was another ploy, one the events of last night had me happy to play along with. But now it's clear she's telling the truth.

"I have a feeling I'm not going to like what you have to tell me," I say. She nods, lowering her eyes to the gravel. *Shit.* I take a deep breath and look toward the trees lining the drive. "Do I want to know?"

"I wouldn't be here if you didn't."

"I'm not sure I believe that," I say, turning back to her. "Just last week, you threatened to find a loophole in my agreement with the FBI to move up the impending investigation. Seems you'll do or say anything to try to convince me to help you."

"And yet, you agreed to see me." She looks at me with a raised brow as if she knows she's gotten under my skin. As she stands there in her leather jacket, her dark hair blowing in the crisp morning breeze, I have to admit, maybe she has.

"Perhaps I made a mistake," I say, quickly shoving the thought from my mind.

"Perhaps. But, speaking of mistakes, I've learned from mine. I know I've been a pest the past several weeks, and it's gotten me nowhere. Today, I'm changing things up and coming to you with information I think you'll find helpful."

Her brows crinkle as her plush lips part. In her eyes, I find the same hint of desperation I've seen time and time again. And yet, that isn't all. There's something about the way she looks at me, pleads with me. It's as if she doesn't want to hurt me, but she knows her next words will.

I look away from her then. Tension riddles my body as I anticipate what will happen next. "I'm listening," I finally say.

She nods, taking a moment to collect herself and— "After you dropped me off at my apartment, I remembered something about the men who attacked me, who attacked Sophia."

"If you're here to tell me they're Irish mob, you've wasted

your time and mine. I already know. Gio and I raided their hideout last night."

"Oh yeah?" She raises a brow. "I'm assuming it didn't go as planned."

"Why would you assume that?"

"Oh, you know. Just your cheery disposition is all." Despite the tension between us, she can't help but smile at her quip. To be honest, neither can I. I shake my head. She has a way about her that is unlike anything I've ever known before. Even in the midst of chaos, she finds a way to make me smile and relieve some of the hotheaded anger simmering in my blood. Yeah, I'd say she's gotten to me, in more ways than one.

"Fine. It was a complete shit show," I admit. "I'm surprised you didn't hear about it at work or even from your apartment since it's so close to Bourbon Street."

"Yeah, that's, um, a long story," she deflects. "Anyway, listening—remember?"

"Right, listening." I lift my hands in surrender.

"Well, now knowing that you found the rest of Edgar's crew, my intel may not be as valuable as I thought."

"Wait? Edgar? Who's Edgar?"

Ariana hesitates. "You didn't get a chance to interrogate them, did you? That's what you meant by *shit show?*"

At that, my lips fall into a flat line and tension returns to my muscles. She found him—the fourth man. More than found him, she interrogated him. That's the intel she's got for me. Though, given her nerves, I now fear the threat of the Irish mob is even greater than I thought.

"Ariana, tell me what you know. I can't deal with the suspense anymore."

She nods. "First, you have to agree to help me find out what happened to my mom."

"You know what happened," I say, my frustration evident.

"Then you have to help me find out why and who took part in the hit," she begs. I shake my head. *This woman.* "Look, Alister, I get that what's happening with you is more important. Your enemies are alive, and the threats made against you and your family are current. Even I can admit it. So, I'm not asking you to abandon your efforts to protect Sophia. I am simply asking that once the threat against your family has been neutralized, that you help me."

Ariana closes the distance between us and takes my hand in hers. She moves so quickly I don't even have time to react. Though, even if I did, I'm not sure what I would do. As Ariana intertwines her fingers with mine, her body only inches from me, I make no moves to pull away. Her touch is just as addictive as everything else about her I've come to know.

"Please, Alister," she begs. "You are all I have."

But you don't have me. I've got my hands full with Sophia and this business, this war. No. She can't. I can't. There's more than one reason why I don't let myself go there with any woman. And the absolute last person I will make an exception for is Ariana Valentine, an FBI agent no less. It's then that I pull my hand from hers and take a step back.

"I owe you nothing." Even as I say the words, I know they're not true. My father is the one who took her mother from her. He's the reason for her pain. And, even if that weren't the case, it still wouldn't change the fact that I want to help her. It's against my better judgment, but I do. I can't explain why, but the way my chest tightens as disappointment fills Ariana's eyes and steals the light from her cheeks tells me it's true.

"Fine. Then neither I you." At that, she backs away. But before she can get too far, I reach out and pull her back to me. Like the night we shared together, her body crashes into mine, so close I can feel her breath against my chest as she gasps. The simple sound does something to my insides I know can't be good. As much as I know I need to let her go, physically and otherwise, I can't. At least, not today.

"I didn't say you can leave," I whisper as my hand moves to her lower back to steady her.

"Well, unlike your soldiers, I don't need your permission," she says. "Now, either agree to my terms or let me go." She lifts her chin as if daring me to deny her again. She knows she's already won. Or else I wouldn't have stopped her.

I do as she says. I release her from my hold, but not because I want her to leave, though I should. I really should. "You drive a hard bargain, Ms. Valentine. One I will agree to."

Her smile is contagious as it spreads across her face. "Yay! And that's Agent Valentine to you."

"Yeah, I wouldn't throw that title around out here. The walls have ears. And while I may be fine with your occupation, there are some who could choose to use it against you *and* me."

Ariana nods. "Okay, well, in that case, maybe we should go somewhere more private. I don't think you're going to want an audience when you hear what Edgar had to say."

<hr />

THOUGH CASSIO and his men are rectifying the issue, there is still a portion of my property fronting the lake without any surveillance coverage. That's where I take Ariana for her to deliver Edgar's intel. We walk in silence until we reach the lake's edge. I cast my eyes upon the water, so peaceful and yet a painful reminder of what could've happened. What would've happened if— "Okay, I'm ready."

Ariana takes a deep breath. "Edgar Walsh is part of a four-man team sent to New Orleans by Joseph Cullen, the head of the Irish mob out of Boston."

I stand in silence as Ariana speaks, keeping my eyes on the

water. It's better this way. I don't want her to see me turn into *him.*

"They faked their own deaths over a year ago, so they could operate undetected while gathering intel on you and your family. Walsh said that Cullen was working with someone in New Orleans to take you down. He didn't know who."

"That's convenient," I grumble.

"I know. But there's more." I nod, still refusing to look at her. "According to Walsh, as far as they knew, this mission was undisclosed. Only Cullen, whoever their New Orleans contact was, and their handler, Avery Gallagher, knew of it. They were given a burner phone by Avery before they left Boston. It was how they communicated with Cullen. Or rather, how Cullen communicated with them." Ariana hesitates.

This is it—the thing she doesn't want to tell me but knows she must. My insides coil and burn knowing there is someone in my midst plotting against me. This entire time! How could I not — No. Of course I suspected it. I've suspected there was a traitor in my father's organization ever since the night my mother was killed. And now—now I have confirmation but no name, no face to punch, no body to destroy. My fingers shake as I fight the urge to hit something, anything. That rock over there, it'll do.

"Ah!" I grunt, crossing my arms to keep my hands from doing things they shouldn't. "Just tell me, Ariana." I turn to her, the sight of moving water nearly as suffocating as this news. It's then that I see the small wrinkle between her eyes. Her lips part the same way they did before. Now it is she who turns away from me. "No," I say, stepping into her eye line. "I want you to look at me when you tell me. If it's this goddamn hard for you, I...I need to see you so that I don't lose control."

She bites her lip as sweat dampens my chest. My heart feels

like it beats one thousand beats a minute as I wait for what she'll say next. Finally, she lifts her eyes to meet mine and—

"They only heard from Cullen twice. The night of the Halloween party when they were ordered to capture Sophia and..." She fights the urge to look away as her eyes glisten with tears.

No. No, don't say it. I half reach out to her, half stumble as I finally understand. I take Ariana's hand in mine and she brings her other to my neck to steady me. I shouldn't be this close to her. Not when she finally reveals the truth, making it real. I could hurt her if I'm—

"Say it," I whisper. My voice cracks with emotion as over Ariana's shoulder, next to the tree line, I spot her—Cara. Ariana brushes her thumb across the skin of my neck as if she senses the rage and heartbreak coursing through me. "Say it," I say once more, this time with more grit.

Ariana nods as I squeeze her hand, holding on to her for dear life. Finally, she says, "They were the ones who abducted Cara and brought her to the brotherhood. What happened to her was never the brotherhood's plan, though they went along with it. Cullen is the one who ordered the hit. It was part of his plan to dethrone you." Ariana's words rip through me forcing me to let her go for fear I'll break her if I don't. "Hey, hey," Ariana says, bringing both her hands to my cheeks. "Look at me. Look at me. You're in control." She nods as if it'll make it true. "You're in control."

As my blood boils inside me and my head aches with memories of the past year, memories now tainted with this revelation, I back away from her. "You need to leave."

"No. No, I'm not leaving." She takes a step toward me, but I put my hand out to stop her.

"Ariana, *go*." I give her the death glare, the one I hoped she'd never have to see, the one that's made grown men piss themselves at my feet. Still, she doesn't flinch.

"It's okay," she says. "It's okay to let go. It's okay to lose control. I won't judge you."

I shake my head and walk away from her. When I lose control, people die. So, if she won't leave, I will. I can't be near her, not when I'm this angry, this—

"Alister!" The bite in her voice stops me dead in my tracks. It shocks the rage right out of me. Though, as it leaves me, I wish it would've stayed. Because left in its place is a hollowness so all-consuming I feel as if I may succumb to it.

Light-headed, I drop to my knees and sit among the grass along the bank of the lake. I rest my head in my palms as emotion courses through me. This is why I still see her. This is why she haunts me. It's because her abductors, the men truly responsible for Cara's death, still breathe. I've killed countless men in the name of avenging my sister. I've bathed in their blood and yet it still isn't over. When will it end? Will it *ever* end? Will she ever truly have peace? Will I?

"Alister?" Ariana drops down beside me and brings her hand to my back. Like before, I welcome her touch, though it does confuse me. Ariana doesn't know me. She has no reason to comfort me at my lowest point, to stay even when I tell her to leave, especially after I've already promised to help her find her mother's killers.

"God," I moan, rubbing the ache from my forehead. "None of this makes sense," I say. Little does she know I'm talking about more than Edgar's claims against Cullen. And yet, even those aren't completely adding up. Word gets around in a world like ours, which is why I know that Joseph Cullen died over a year ago. Unlike his men whose deaths he helped fake, his body was found and positively identified by his daughter, the new head of the Irish faction in Boston.

"Ariana, Cullen died before Cara was abducted, which means whoever truly ordered the hit against my sister, whoever was contacting Walsh and his men via the burner phone, was not Cullen at all. It was the New Orleans traitor, the nameless man I will soon uncover or die trying."

As the words cross my lips, I turn to Ariana and find not an FBI agent sitting next to me nor even a woman only here because she needs my help. No. In Ariana I see a kindred soul, someone who understands my need to uncover the truth, someone who understands my need for justice. Which is why I know she'll grant my request to interrogate Walsh myself.

"I need to see Walsh."

Ariana pulls away from me, turning toward the lake. She's smart enough to know turning him over to me will make her an accessory to murder. Still, there's no way in Hell I'm allowing the man responsible for my sister's death to walk this earth when she can't.

"Ariana?"

"Alister, he's already in Witness Protection. It was the only way I could get him to talk."

As Ariana's words leave her, I'm sure I've heard her wrong. "Say that again."

"Alister..."

I turn away from her and push myself up off the ground. This time she doesn't follow. *Smart girl.* I pace the bank of the lake, doing my best to stay calm, but it's no use.

"The only way you could get him to talk!" I shout, finally turning back to her. "Why not bring him to me? I still would've agreed to your terms, saved you the time of interrogating him yourself *and* the FBI's resources you used to put him in WITSEC." I shake my head, biting my lip to keep from saying something more hurtful. "All you did...all you did, Ariana, was rob me of my chance to have justice for my sister."

"No," she says. "No, I saved you from yourself."

"What the Hell is that supposed to mean?"

"Alister, you and I both know that if I brought him here, you would've killed him. And then you would've had to live with that guilt."

"*Guilt?* Do you think I feel guilty for killing the men who raped and sold my sister or the man who raped and tortured her some more before killing her? The man who disintegrated her body in a barrel so that there was nothing left? Nothing left, Ariana. *Fuck no!* I don't feel guilty. And killing Edgar Walsh wouldn't have changed that and you know it."

"Fine." She stands. "Maybe you're right. Maybe you shouldn't feel guilty. But killing Walsh wouldn't have avenged your sister, Alister." She takes a step toward me. "There is *nothing* you can do that will avenge her. There is no justice for what they did to Cara. None."

"If that's true, then how is she supposed to let go, huh? How is she supposed to find peace?" It's then that my eyes find Cara once more, lingering. She's always lingering.

"Alister, Cara is gone. Her eternal rest, her salvation isn't in your control." Ariana closes the distance between us and takes my hands in hers. Deep down, I know she's right. It's not Cara who can't let go. It's me. I may not feel guilty for killing those men, but I do feel responsible for what happened to Cara. She was my sister. She was mine to protect and I failed. Maybe somewhere inside of me I think the more men I kill in her name, the more responsibility I place on them, the less guilt I'll have to feel. But that's just my foolish attempt at coping with her death.

"She's gone, Alister," Ariana says again. "Everything you've done since her death has been for you, not her. And that's okay. It's just not okay for you to think you have power over the dead. Of all the things you carry, this is one you need to let go."

I consider her words, unwilling to admit aloud that she's

right. If I do, Cara will hear and maybe she'll stop— I pinch my eyes closed to fight off tears threatening to fall. The truth is I'm not ready to say goodbye to her. I'm not sure I'll ever be. I suppose the silver lining of my looming war with the Irish mob is that I get to prolong my mourning period. I get to hold on to her a little while longer.

Clinging to my distraction, I open my eyes and say, "There's only one person left alive who may know the identity of the person in New Orleans working against me."

Ariana lets go of my hands and takes a step back. She's surprised at my sudden shift of subject, and, as realization dawns on her, she says, "We're going to Boston, aren't we?"

15

ALISTER AMATO IS THE MOST CONFUSING HUMAN BEING I'VE ever encountered. One minute he's this sophisticated gentleman who wears suits tailored to perfection and exudes self-control. The next, he's this brick wall of a man who looks as if he could burn the entire world down and rise from the ashes unharmed. His constantly shifting personality makes me realize how fragile his self-control truly is, and that scares me. Though, not enough to walk away from him and the assistance he's promised me, as is evident by my place on the leather sofa against the wood-paneled wall of his office.

Alister sits at his desk while he and Gio discuss the information I shared with him. I would try to contribute to their conversation, especially since I'm the one who will be accompanying Alister to Boston, but, instead, I'm consumed by memories of my most recent encounter with him.

I knew learning that Walsh and his men were the ones who abducted Cara would be difficult for Alister to hear, especially since he believed he'd rid the world of the men responsible months ago. And yet, I still could not anticipate his reaction. He was not only furious, deadly, but broken and on the verge of tears. The sight of him so emotional tugged on my heartstrings in a way I've never felt before. Seeing Alister grieve his sister, a person who was just as important to him as my mom was to me, makes me feel the pain of her loss all over again. It's a crippling, heartbreaking pain that is both tangible and intangible. What makes it worse, what makes my soul swell for Alister, is that there is no cure, at least not one I've found in the near twenty years since my mother's death. That is why I asked to join Alister in Boston, to be there by his side as he comes face-to-face with the man he believes will be his cure, the man he believes will lead to true justice for his sister. He'll need someone who understands his unending torment when Gallagher's answers fail to heal what's broken inside him.

However, just as Alister is confusing, so are my feelings for him. Why do I care about his pain? Why do I care about him? He's a criminal, one my vow to protect the innocent requires me to apprehend. And yet, he's so much more than that. From our very first meeting, I could tell there was more to him than I thought. And today only affirmed it. His pain is my pain. In his suffering and grief, I find myself, a kindred spirit plagued by the same demons. Though, I'm starting to fear there's something more between us than a common understanding of tragedy.

As we stood on the circle drive fronting the Amato mansion, there was something in the way he pulled me back to him, his movements so fierce and efficient, that took my breath away. In his eyes I saw something primal, something that made my insides quiver in both excitement and fear. It lasted only a moment and yet, it lasted long enough to awaken an urge, a desire in me that's long been dormant. As I take in the four walls of Alister's office and all that they encompass, I can't help but wonder what I've gotten myself into and if I'm prepared to face it.

"I need to know everything about him, Gio. I need to know where he eats, sleeps, fucks, and any unusual stops on his itinerary. Once we have all of that we can decide what the best course of attack will be for Ariana and me."

At the mention of my name my focus returns to Alister and Gio only to find Gio's face etched with surprise. Hmm. It looks strange on him. I thought he had only one expression—stern and obedient.

"Boss, are you saying you and Ariana plan to take down Gallagher on your own, in enemy territory?"

"There's a mole, Gio. It could be someone in this house, a maid, a cook, one of our men. We won't know who's plotting against us until we get to Gallagher, and if you leave with me, it'll draw too much attention. We can't risk tipping off the traitor before we're ready to take him out."

Alister looks at me then. Under normal circumstances, he wouldn't be able to speak so plainly about murder in my presence. But, since his deal with the FBI allows him free rein for a year, he's able to commit as many crimes as he wants until the bureau begins their investigation, which will be only on present-day criminal activity. I pose no risk to Alister, at least not yet.

"No one knows who Ariana is," Alister says then, returning his attention to Gio. "And if the night of the Halloween party tells us anything, it's that she can handle herself. It's the best of a bad situation."

"Handling herself and trusting her to have your back are two very different things," Gio says. He's not wrong. But Alister is right. He needs backup and yet he can't be seen bringing an army into Irish mob territory.

"That'll be all, Gio," Alister says then. Gio takes his dismissal humbly and leaves the office quietly as Alister focuses on his laptop.

I stand and make my way to the chair seated in front of his

desk. Still, Alister doesn't look at me. Perhaps he's still upset I refused to give him Edgar. Regardless, this partnership will never work if we can't learn how to communicate.

"Listen, Gio is right. In all the missions I've been a part of with the bureau, the ones that fail do so for one of two reasons." Alister looks at me then. "Poor intel or poor communication among the team. Like it or not, you and I are a team about to go after a very dangerous man in a dangerous city. We need to find a way to trust one another, at least enough to believe we won't let each other get killed."

Alister nods and leans back in his chair. "And how do you propose we do that? If you haven't noticed, I don't trust easily, and for good reason, apparently."

"Well, we have that in common. You've been surrounded by enemies your entire life and have very few confidants. That's a burden I understand, so much so I envy the bond you have with Gio and Sophia. I don't even have that."

"What about your task force at the FBI? You claim to trust them, and yet you aren't close with them."

"There are levels to trust or perhaps different kinds of trust. I trust my team to have my back in the field just like I have theirs. Our survival is linked to our collective efforts, and we're working toward a common goal. We all want to take down the bad guys." At that, Alister smiles. "That doesn't mean I trust them to know my secrets. Or maybe it's not a lack of trust I have in them. Maybe it's just my fear that they won't understand me, that they'll judge me. I don't know. I just…"

"Need to be able to trust me," Alister says.

"Yeah."

Alister nods. "Well, here's the thing. I can't promise you anything, Ariana. I'd like to. I'd like to be able to tell you that our plan will be foolproof. We'll go to Boston, find Gallagher, and everything will go without a hitch. But I can't promise you that. I've...I've made promises to people before, promises that I would protect them, and I haven't always been able to live up to those promises. If you need something to trust in, trust that I will always be honest with you, even if it isn't what you want to hear."

At Alister's words, I bite my lip. I'm not sure if he's trying to discourage me from coming or testing my desire to see this mission through, but his words certainly don't offer me the encouragement I was hoping to find. But he's right. Trusting him to tell me the truth is a good step in the right direction. It may even be a lifesaving one.

"Okay," I say.

"Alister, where is everyone? This place is deserted." I close my eyes as Sophia enters the office. Right. I imagine my inevitable conversation with her will go about as well as the one I'm currently having with her brother. "Oh, sorry. I didn't realize you had a meeting." Sophia does a double take as she recognizes me. "Ariana?" She looks between me and her brother. "Alister, what's going on?"

Alister stands and makes his way to Sophia. He grabs her arm gently so he can lead her out. Oh no. That'll only make her more pissed. "Let's discuss this elsewhere," he says as the two of them disappear behind the thick wooden door separating his office from the rest of the house. At least sixty seconds pass before my reality dawns—I'm alone in Alister Amato's office. Memories of the night of the Halloween party return to me. His office is always under guard. I stand zero chance of ever having an opportunity like this again.

At that, I stand and quickly move to the other side of his desk. I know he's agreed to help me find my mother's killers, but what if he changes his mind? What if our Boston trip is as big of a shit show as his recent attempt to collect Walsh and his men and he dies before he can help me? Well, I suppose that would mean I'm dead too and, at that point, the truth really wouldn't matter. Ugh. *Focus, Ariana.*

I shove my mental rambling to the furthest corner of my mind and scan over the documents atop his desk. Nothing worth looking at there. I then start tugging on desk drawers, all of which are locked aside from the one keeping the bourbon. *Figures.* I click the space bar on his laptop, praying it hasn't already shut down due to inactivity, only to find that it has. I sigh in frustration, that is, until I spot the USB drive jutting out from the side of the computer. *Jackpot.* I snatch the thumb drive and return to my seat just moments before Alister reenters the room.

"Trust, huh? I leave you alone for five minutes and you're already back to your old ways."

"What are you talking about?" I ask, playing dumb. But as Alister approaches me, his features tight with frustration, I know I've been caught. "Hey!" I cry out as Alister pulls me up out of the chair with one hand and reaches into my back pocket with his other. His fingers easily find the USB drive, and I roll my eyes. His office must be under video surveillance. Paranoid much?

"This was a test." Alister holds me in place as he lectures me on breaking the trust I'm sure I never had. Instead of pulling the USB from my pocket, he presses it into me. His unexpected, lingering touch draws a gasp from me as he presses firmly against my bottom, holding me by not only my arm but also my most tender flesh. As he does, I find the same look in his dark eyes as before. My body responds in kind, giving in to his touch rather than pulling away, even though I know I should. I really should. Thankfully, before my body overrules the sirens blaring through my mind, Alister lets go of me and takes the USB, tossing it back on his desk. "You failed." When he turns back to me, I no longer find the warm gaze that makes my insides melt. In its place is disappointment and a coldness that eats at me in the most unpleasant way.

"I'm sorry," I whisper. It's all I can say. Despite my reasons for going for the drive, none of them seem worth mentioning now. He told me he'd help me. He told me he would always be honest with me. What I just did proves I don't believe him. It proves I don't trust him, despite my desire to. I suppose because I've never been able to rely on anyone before and the memories of his constant denials are still fresh.

Alister brings his fingers to his temples and massages them as he considers what to do with me. Once I finally convinced him to let me accompany him to Boston, he said I should stick around until we came up with a plan. But who knows how long it will take Gio to gather the intel he needs, and he may not want to put up with me for that long.

"Just please don't send me back to the dungeon. That's all I ask," I blurt, assuming the worst. Alister looks at me with furrowed brows.

"Contrary to your belief, I don't make a habit of keeping people in my dungeon. It's only used under special circumstances. Given our common goal and our survival is depending on our collective efforts, I'm willing to let your transgression slide, just this once," Alister warns. "Though, clearly, you can't be left alone. So, come on. You've just earned yourself a date with the Devil."

"Dramatic much?" I ask as Alister moves past me toward the door. When he turns back, his lips are drawn into a wickedly sly grin.

"You wish."

After changing into exercise clothes, both of us in black leggings and tank tops, Alister leads me outside through the formal courtyard to the pool. What I find is a much different scene than the night of the Halloween party. Instead of blaring music and the ruckus of party guests, it's quiet, save for the soft trickle of water coming from a fountain. Instead of a chandelier-lit evening of ghouls and glamour, the day is cloudy and crisp. Atop the pool is a platform covering a portion of the water. Based on our attire and the kickboxing gloves Alister tosses at me, I can only assume it's meant to be our battleground. On any other day, I'd relish the chance to spar with the Blood King, but today's temperatures and the ice bath awaiting the loser of the duel make me hesitant.

"If this is your idea of a date, I can see why you're still single." At that, Alister laughs. Good. At least some of his tension from earlier has subsided.

"Would it help the illusion if I took off my shirt?" Alister asks, brow cocked. I roll my eyes and slip my hands into the gloves.

"Not exactly sure that's date appropriate either. More like the morning after." Besides, if he takes off his shirt, I imagine the ice-cold water will be the least of my worries.

"Well, if you hadn't gone snooping through my things, then maybe I could trust you to stay in the house while I work out. Unfortunately for you, that is not the case."

Alister hops up onto the platform before turning to offer me his hand. I give him a scowl filled with all the annoyance I can muster. Though, I have to admit, I'd much prefer this than sitting alone inside the mansion. Or worse, being left to deal with Sophia. I know I owe her an explanation, and I'll give her one, but right now, I've got my hands full trying to make sense of Alister and whatever urges he's awakened in me. I take his hand and he pulls me up to join him in one swift movement.

"Gio could use a day off anyway."

I nod, moving to the opposite side of the platform. "Fine. Though why you choose to duel over an ice bath is beyond me."

"It helps ease the sting of getting your ass kicked, and it also serves as great motivation to not let it happen twice."

"You know what, I'm looking forward to this. We'll finally get to see who would've won if my plan to interrogate you the night of the Halloween party had worked."

"So, we shall. Ladies first," Alister says, motioning for me to begin the duel. He's insane. If we both go full force at one another now, there'll be nothing left of us by the time we make it to Boston. But I can't let him best me. It'll offset the power dynamics between us, and he'll never see me as an equal. If that isn't enough of a reason to kick his ass, perhaps this is a test, just like the USB drive. It makes sense. He needs to see my skills for himself before settling for me as his one and only companion to take on Avery Gallagher.

Okay, Alister. You want a fight? I'll give you one. Just remember what you asked for.

I take on a fighting stance and slowly approach. What happens next is a dance in which both of us avoid each other's swipes, punches, and kicks. He's good. I've used moves on him that've taken down countless men. Yet, he evades them all.

"You're quicker than I would've thought," I say as thunder rumbles above us. "I thought your muscles would slow you down."

"You should know better than to underestimate your opponent."

"You're one to talk, seeing as you haven't gotten within twelve inches of me."

"I'm taking it easy on you, *bella*. I usually opt for a brutish use of force when facing off with an enemy."

"A-ha. Well, come on then. Show me what you've got, *tesoro*."

Alister's eyes flash with surprise at my use of Italian. He looks almost as surprised as I felt when he called me *bella*, the Italian word for *beautiful*. Though his surprise doesn't keep him from following up on my request. Alister charges me so quickly I can't avoid his long-reaching arms. He pulls me toward him, spinning me around so that my back presses into his chest. I'm thankful for the change in strategy. It would've hurt had he tackled me straight to the ground. Unfortunately for him, I won't respond to his gentle fighting style in kind.

As Alister tightens his hold on my chest, I grab his forearm and use it to stabilize myself as I propel my body forward. I swing my legs out and toward the ground, and Alister loses his balance, allowing me to slip between his legs as he tumbles forward. He catches himself against the wooden platform, which keeps him from falling, though not before I pop back up onto my feet and approach him from behind.

When I reach Alister, I kick him in the back of the knee to keep him down. He grunts, falling to his knees. Now I've got him right where I want him. I reach around his front, tightening my arm around his neck, much like he attempted to do to me before letting his manners get in the way. I lean forward, whispering in his ear, "When your opponent is bigger and stronger, you must be faster, smarter, and scrappier. I do believe you've been bested, Mr. Amato."

"Perhaps," he says as I release my hold on him. "But you did make one mistake."

"What's that?" I ask as Alister pushes himself up from the ground.

"Thinking a criminal would play by your rules." Alister turns to me, picks me up, and—

I scream as Alister throws, not pushes, *throws* me into the pool. It feels like a hundred pinpricks across my body. Within seconds, I begin to shiver.

"Asshole! You just couldn't stand to lose!" I yell as the salty water invades my mouth. Alister kneels, a boyish smile stretching his lips.

"It's not about winning or losing, Ariana. It's about preparing you for what's to come." At that, seriousness steals his smile. He's quiet for a moment. When his eyes return to me, there's a hardness in them, which is only amplified by the emptiness of his voice. "When you're in a fight to the death, you must be willing to kill. If you aren't willing to take a life to protect your own or the lives of the ones you care about, then you're as good as dead. It's a sad truth, but a truth nonetheless. One maybe you're not ready to hear."

"Hey! I grew up in a world sketched outside the lines. It's why, when I became an adult, I chose a path for myself where the lines are clearly drawn. Right and wrong. Good and evil. But that doesn't mean I don't know what it's like on the other side. The rules you and Avery Gallagher play by are different. I know that and I'm ready for it. So, don't take me out of the game before it even starts."

"Why?"

"What?"

"Why are you so insistent on coming? Not only is Gallagher a threat, but you barely know me. And what you do know of me is that I'm a dark, depraved monster who leaves a trail of bodies in his wake. You say you don't trust me, and yet, you've placed yourself at my side despite knowing what I'm capable of."

As Alister's words leave him, raindrops break free from the clouds above. As they hit my skin, the chill in my bones only intensifies, and yet, I don't move. His words have me paralyzed. There are many reasons why I want to go with him, most of which I can never say to him. I can never tell him I want to help him through his pain. I can never tell him I care for him and enjoy his company. Most of all, I can never tell him his very presence makes me feel alive in a way I've never felt before, so much so I am willing to overlook the utter stupidity of my choice to tether myself to him.

And yet, it isn't just his question that's left me speechless. He thinks himself a monster. And perhaps Agent Valentine would agree. As I said, I live in a world with starkly drawn lines, making decisions simple and the bad guys easy to discern. But I see more than a monster when I look at Alister. His very existence shatters my perception of good and evil and obliterates the box I've placed myself in for my own protection.

A loud rumble of thunder pulls me from my thoughts, drawing me back to Alister. Knowing I can't reveal to him my true feelings, not that I even understand them, I give him the only explanation I can. "I just…want to make sure you don't die before you have a chance to make good on your promise to me." It's the truth, just not the full truth. Alister nods and offers me his hand. I take it, though not to escape the water that's left my lower body numb.

"*Ah!*" Alister yells as I tug him forward. As he flies, crashing into the freezing cold water, I laugh.

"You forgot to double tap, Mr. Amato. Looks like this girl still has some life in her yet."

"Oh, you want a double tap? Okay. I can handle that," Alister says as he rips off his sopping wet tank top.

"No, no." I giggle as he stalks toward me with glistening chiseled abs and hair the color of midnight. "I submit. I submit," I squeal as Alister reaches me. But that doesn't stop him from wrapping his arms around my body and pulling me against his chest. As he holds me, I can feel the hardness of his chest, the strength of his muscles, the beat of his heart. His entire being cradles me, making me feel safe despite my vulnerable position. "I submit," I whisper once more as his dark eyes stare into mine.

"Smart girl." Though he's acknowledged my defeat, he does

not let me go. That is, until a rumble of thunder and snap of lightning pulls us both back to reality—the one where I'm the FBI agent who despises the monster within him and he's the Mafia king who hides his true nature behind expensive suits and legitimate business ventures.

"We should probably go inside, unless the final act of this date is me being barbecued by a lightning bolt."

16

Alister

"Son of a—" I cross the kitchen from the island to the stove, abandoning my turkey in favor of a pot of chicken stock now boiling over. I reach for the pot to remove it from the flames. Big mistake. *"Ah!"* As the searing-hot metal of the pot's handles connects with my skin, I drop the pot. Chicken stock, diced onions and celery, and whatever else the cook left in the fridge for our would-be Thanksgiving dinner splatters across the floor. I throw my hands up in defeat and dab away the sweat on my forehead. This is great, just great. Because I don't know who's coming after me and Sophia, I sent everyone home—the groundskeepers, the maids, the cooks. Like Sophia said, this place is deserted, all except for my security detail, Gio, Sophia, Cassio and his small legion of men meant to protect my sister, and our resident FBI agent, Ariana.

The storm that swept in almost a week ago now made it too dangerous for Ariana to return home on her motorcycle. I could've driven her in one of my vehicles, but I thought it best she stays, in case Gio's intel required us to leave for Boston without much notice. One night turned into five as the storm continued and Gio struggled to come up with enough intel on Avery Gallagher to form a plan. Now, the weather has cleared, and we have a plan to confront Avery tomorrow night at a showing of *The Nutcracker* at the Boston Opera House. But, before that, is Thanksgiving—the one holiday that there is no Historical Preservation Society party or gala or Mafia business to tend to. It's just for family. Since Ariana has no family and therefore has never had a proper Thanksgiving, I want to make this holiday perfect for her. Yet, without the help of my staff, I fear the only edible thing I'll be able to muster up is chopped celery and ranch dressing.

"And I thought I'd seen it all," Gio says. His lips draw into a smile stretching from one side of his face to the other as I turn back to the stove and switch off the gas burner.

"Now is not the time for jokes, Gio," I scold him, though I don't mean it. Every other day of our lives is a fight to the death. Today is one of the only days of the year we can take a breath and pray our enemies do the same.

"Fine." Gio makes the motion of zipping his mouth closed. "But there is one matter you should be aware of."

I give him a pointed look as I step over the slop now covering the terracotta tile. I make my way back to the island, grab a knife, and return my focus to the turkey. Gio knows not to bring business to my attention on Thanksgiving unless it's dire. Whatever he has to say, I'd rather take my frustration out on the bird than him.

"I'm listening."

Gio nods and takes a seat at the island across from me. "We received a call from the bureau. He wants to know why you're looking into Ariana." At that, I hesitate, my knife hovering over the slimy protein as I remember the deep dive I did on Ariana the moment I agreed to let her accompany me to Boston. To my surprise, many important records such as her birth certificate were missing. Though I'm not sure why I thought I'd have better luck than her. Ariana has the same FBI access I do thanks to my arrangement with her superior. She's been searching for the truth for years and all her findings have done is lead her to me. Yet, the lack of childhood records for Ariana isn't the only unusual thing I found. All records from her juvenile years were sealed. It must've caught Bilieux's attention when I put in the request to unseal them.

"Did you tell him to mind his business?" I ask as I begin slicing the turkey without method.

"He claims that's what he's doing. For you to look into Ariana, it must mean she's on your radar. How or why, he didn't know. But he's worried if she gets close enough to you, she may find out about his arrangement with you—his *real* arrangement."

"You mean he's worried she'll find out her boss, the man who suspended her for speaking out against the very deal that protects him just as much as it does us, is a crook on my payroll. He's worried she'll try to blackmail him into giving her her job back or worse." Gio nods. "Well, he shouldn't be. I've been keeping an eye on Ariana. And, besides, her interest in me is purely personal. And, even if she did learn of our arrangement with Bilieux, she needs me. She won't do anything to jeopardize our relationship." At least, I hope not.

"That may be, but I can't say the same thing for Bilieux. You know as well as I do that that snake will do anything to keep his secrets buried. If he thinks Ariana knows his secret…"

"The world learning of his affiliation with me will be the least of his worries if he so much as lays a finger on her."

Gio watches me with surprise as I slam the tip of my knife into the wooden cutting board. I stand up straight and run my fingers through my hair to try to cool off. This is getting too complicated. A week ago, I would've said Ariana has gotten beneath my skin. Today, I… I shake my head, shoving the thought from my mind. Nothing good will come of it and Gio is too perceptive not to notice. Yet, he's right. If Bilieux perceives Ariana as a threat, he'll stop at nothing to remove her, *permanently*. And I can't allow that. I won't. I look at Gio then.

"You should alert our associate that Ariana is under my protection. He's not to go near her—period. Once Ariana has learned why her mother was killed, I'll pay Bilieux a visit and have him reinstate her. He'll have no reason to worry about her blackmailing him when he can keep an eye on her himself and her work will keep her mind off whatever we discover about her mother. Not to mention being among her task force members will remind her of which side she's on. The bureau is already corrupt enough. I don't want Ariana growing so attached she starts crossing lines she shouldn't."

"You're worried about *Ariana* growing too attached?" Gio asks, though it doesn't sound like a question.

"Are you implying something?" My eyes narrow as the energy of the room shifts. Gio appears to be contemplating his next words carefully, but he wouldn't be my friend if he wasn't honest with me. Though his gentle delivery doesn't make the words any easier to hear.

"Alister, I see the way you look at her, the way you not only tolerate her but enjoy her."

"Your point?"

"My point is, maybe it's not Ariana who's at risk of growing too attached. Maybe it's you." At that, Gio stands and moves toward the exit that connects to the dining room. When he reaches the door, he stops. "It wouldn't be the worst thing in the world, you know, if you cared for her. Things are changing around here."

"Not fast enough, Gio. And not with any guarantees that let me know she would be safe by my side. You and I both know New Orleans will always need a king. It will always need rules, structure, an army that operates in the shadows to keep the monsters at bay. Even once we legitimize, to remain in New Orleans is to remain at war with whomever seeks this territory. There is no room for love in my life, Gio. And there never will be."

"Very well."

As Gio leave me, I take stock of my surroundings. Vegetables I don't know the names of cover the wooden island. A half-mutilated turkey I have no idea how to cook lies in front of me. And for what? What I said to Gio is the truth. I can't care about Ariana. I can't care about any woman without signing their death warrant. First my mom, then my sister—any woman who either is an Amato or is loved by one is cursed. And yet, so are the men who love them. So am I. Because the truth is, Ariana hasn't just gotten underneath my skin. She's found a way inside my heart. Perhaps she crawled in through one of the cracks left in the wake of my sister's death, or perhaps through the hole that's been a permanent part of me since my mother was taken from me. However, or whichever, there's a bit of warmth inside me that wasn't there before. It feels like a glowing ember somewhere deep inside the dark abyss that is my soul. It's small yet not easily extinguished.

I lean forward and rest my palms against the island as the window to my left allow the setting sun to cast a warm glow upon the room. My one day of peace is almost over and yet, it feels as if it hasn't even begun. Tomorrow will bring war, how deadly and how bloody only time will tell. Maybe that's why I wanted to make the best of today, not just for Ariana, but for me. I want to allow myself a day to feel the things I shouldn't, to feel the things I wish I didn't. Because I know that everything will change between us when Ariana finally sees me at my worst, when she finally meets the Blood King.

Ariana saw the remnants of my wrath when she investigated

the crime scene that led her to me. She saw glimmers of my darkness when she spent time in my dungeon. I'm a monster. She's seen enough to know that. And yet, somehow, she's overlooked every sin. Our very first night together she said she was still making up her mind about me. I pray Boston isn't the bloodbath I know it can be. But, if it is, her mind will be made for her, and she will never look at me the same way. She won't be able to lie to herself anymore about who I am, *what* I am. Maybe it's for the best. In my heart, I know it is. Yet my clarity doesn't give me peace. It only brings more pain—the pain of knowing I will never deserve a woman like her. I will never exist in her world, no matter how badly I want to. I will never break free of the shackles of this throne. I am forever the Blood King, and I am forever alone.

"Oh, sorry. Am I interrupting?" I straighten my back as Ariana's voice pulls me from my thoughts. She stands at the edge of the kitchen, appearing from the servant's stairwell. Her hair is pulled back low and loose. Soft curls fall forward, framing her face. She wears a short, shiny dress the color of gilded bronze. It looks exquisite on her. Yet, it's not the dress that chases away the demons inside me and stokes the flames of that flickering ember in my heart. It's the black combat boots strapped around her feet. Despite being dressed like a mini-Sophia this week, she hasn't given in to Sophia's heels. Her boots represent her and everything I admire about her—her strength, her humble nature, her willingness to fight for what she believes in and for those who need her help. As my eyes make their way back up her body, taking in every inch, they finally meet hers to find them filled with suspicion. "What's that look?" she asks.

"What look?" I do my best to turn away from her, to look anywhere but her, but I can't. As she moves closer to me, I'm transfixed by her.

"The one plastered all over your face." She comes to stand

across from me. She looks at me the same as before. Her chin tilts upward as she dares me to deny my feelings for her, my attraction to her. It's as if she's taunting me, yet I don't think she realizes what's she's doing. Good. If she felt for me the same as I feel for her, walking away from her would be next to impossible. And yet, walk away I must. Just…not tonight. I still have a few more hours before sunrise.

"You walked in on an epic failure," I say, ignoring the question I can't answer, at least not aloud. "I'm not much of a cook, but I wanted to make tonight nice—for you."

"*For me?*" Surprise widens her eyes as she takes a seat on the stool across from me and my butchered turkey.

"Yeah." I nod. "Thanksgiving is a special holiday, and I know you've never really had anyone to celebrate with. If you weren't here, given our lack of staff, I'd settle for a frozen pizza, a bottle of Bordeaux, and a night of card games with Gio, Sophia, and Cass. But you are here, so I'm, um, trying to make the best of what the chef left."

Now it is Ariana who is transfixed and speechless. Perhaps she is confused by my gesture. Perhaps the holidays make her miss her mom even more. Maybe celebrating is the last thing she wants to do. Unable to deal with the silence any longer, I ask her, "What's that look?" Hopefully she'll be more forthcoming than I was. She lowers her eyes then.

"I guess surprise, gratitude, appreciation," she whispers, refusing to look at me. "Though, I am wondering where you're going with this," she says as she shifts her attention from her fidgeting fingers to the bird between us. *Shit.* I was hoping she hadn't noticed. Guess I can't get much past her.

I lean forward as I massage the tension from my neck. "Well, I, um…was thinking I'd cut it up and cook it somehow."

"*Somehow?*" At that, I bring my eyes back to Ariana to find her brow cocked and a slightest rosiness to her cheeks. Now that's a look I'm familiar with, one filled with sarcasm. "You have no idea what you're doing, do you?"

"Not in the slightest."

Ariana nods and hops off her stool. She glides around the island through the beams of the setting sun, and as she comes to stand beside me, she appears to glow. The only thing that can make her more beautiful is the sun itself, bouncing off her dress and chestnut locks as she absorbs all its light and warmth. The very first night we met, I called her a fallen angel. Perhaps she was. But tonight…tonight she isn't fallen at all. She's just…an angel.

As the spilled chicken stock and wilted vegetables come into view, Ariana nods and crosses her arms over her chest. "I was wondering what that smell was. I'd say this is a cry for help if I ever saw one. First things first, that needs to be cleaned. Then, I need a casserole dish, butter and spices, and for the love of God, potholders," she says, noticing the bright red skin on my palms. She takes my hands in hers, assessing my wounds, and a waft of sweet cinnamon and caramel moves with her. I inhale it to keep my mind off her gentle touch and all the things it makes me feel.

"Well, now I feel bad," she says.

"Why?"

"I can't exactly boss you around if you're hurt. I was so looking forward to that." At that, we both laugh.

"My sweet Ariana, I've endured a lot worse than this. Boss me around all you like. For tonight, and tonight only, I'm all yours."

❦

SOMEHOW ARIANA FOUND a way to salvage dinner. She made baked turkey with mashed potatoes and roasted vegetables. She moved around the kitchen with ease once I found all the things she needed. In all my life I've never spent so much time in the kitchen. But it was nice to watch her, to see her in an environment she's comfortable with and yet not in combat. Now, she sits snuggled up in one of the chairs in the living room with a blanket draped over her legs as she sips a glass of wine. She fits so perfectly into the simplest parts of my life, my home. It's the other parts, the darker parts, I want to keep her away from.

Gio ignites the fireplace and pops on the record player, prompting Sophia to drag Cassio from his place on the couch to the center of the room. He pretends to protest but obliges my sister's request for a dance with a smile all the same. If only it could be like this all the time—simple, normal, happy. Then maybe Ariana could stay. Then maybe I could admit that I want her to. Gio joins me by the fireplace. He doesn't say a word but gives me a look I can read like a book. I glance at my watch. It's half till midnight. Only thirty minutes left to make the most of my one and only holiday with Ariana.

Do I test my self-control and ask her to dance? What if she sees straight through me and realizes the real reason why I asked her to stay all those days ago? It wasn't the storm or even our upcoming trip to Boston. I wanted her to stay because I want her. I want to be in her presence, to bask in her light. I know our time is limited. If we survive tomorrow, there will still a come day when the truth of her mother's past is revealed. She'll get what she came for and she'll leave my life forever. I want to make the most of our short time together, but she can't know that. For so many reasons, she can't know. And yet, as her eyes find mine, I can't stop my feet from moving toward her.

As I reach her, I extend my hand. "Would you like to dance?"

Ariana hesitates before standing. She downs the rest of her wine and places her hand in mine. I lead her to the center of the room, ignoring the weight of Gio's and Sophia's eyes on me. Using my free hand, I guide hers to my shoulder. As my fingers graze her soft skin, the ember inside me explodes, setting my entire body ablaze with tender excitement. Ariana grabs hold of my shoulder, and I move my hand to her lower back. It's a formal position with minimal touching, unlike my sister and Cass. And yet, where our bodies do connect, there is an electric warmth that makes me feel alive in a way I don't think I've ever felt.

My eyes lock with hers and I take a step back. Ariana stumbles forward, stepping on my toe and bumping into my chest. "Oh my God. I'm sorry. I've never really danced before."

"It's okay." I laugh. I bring my hand to her blushing cheek and tilt her face to where I can see her. "I'll teach you." And I do. Ariana is a fast learner. Soon enough we're dancing all around the living room, quick, slow, and then barely moving at all, yet we don't let go of one another. We've only grown closer.

"So, when were you going to tell me that you've been suspended from the bureau?"

Her eyes narrow, though she doesn't ask for an explanation of how I discovered her little secret. Good. She's smart enough to know she shouldn't want one. "When it was necessary. Turns out, it never was," she says.

I nod, tightening my grip around her waist as I know I've got only a few more minutes before the magic between us breaks. "*Why* didn't you tell me?"

Ariana huffs and looks from my shoulder to my face. She's reading me, asking herself if she can tell me the truth. She still doesn't trust me, at least not fully. I suppose I can't blame her. Finally, she says, "I didn't tell you because I thought you may not treat me with the same respect you would another agent who's still in the good graces of the bureau. I was afraid."

"Are you still afraid?"

Ariana's brows furrow as if it's the first time she's considered the question. "No." Her answer makes me smile and breathe a sigh of relief.

"Good, because you have no reason to fear me, Ariana. That I can promise you. And, for the record, I don't respect you because you're an FBI agent. I respect you because you're strong, smart, stubborn. And, because you've survived one of the most heartbreaking things a human can, and you didn't let it cripple you. You became someone who helps others avoid suffering the same fate. You risked your life to save Sophia, someone whose death the FBI wouldn't even blink at knowing our family's activities. You didn't save her because it was your job. You saved her because that's who you are. And that, Ariana, is respectable, admirable. Ultimately, it's why I agreed to let you come on this mission. Because, depending on how our time with Avery Gallagher goes, I may need you to save me from myself." Ariana nods as she processes my words, though confusion quickly overcomes her. "What is it?" I ask.

Her lips part as she brings her eyes to mine once more. "Is that all you think of me?"

17

Ariana

AS THE WORDS CROSS MY LIPS, I KNOW I SHOULDN'T ASK THEM. What do I expect him to say? What do I want him to say? Most importantly, what would I do if he revealed he feels for me even a glimmer of what I feel for him? Thankfully, it doesn't seem I'll have to make that decision, at least not tonight, as the clock, sitting atop the two-story fireplace, strikes midnight, and whatever spell cast upon us breaks, prompting Alister to let go of me and back away. He doesn't answer my question. And, rather than dissect how his silence makes me feel, I shift my attention from him to the four walls containing the remnants of the best Thanksgiving I've ever had. Sophia's heels lie haphazard on the gray rug anchoring the dark and cozy room. Empty wine bottles sit atop the grand piano. A fire still roars in the hearth to my right. And, as if the holiday itself were an album, brilliant throughout and yet, sure to end, the record player spins on a small table at the foot of the wooden stairwell. It produces only static, making the words left unspoken between Alister and me even more obvious.

"I wonder where everyone's off to," I say. To distract myself from the unreadable expression etched across Alister's face, I turn and begin picking up empty wineglasses and bottles and fluffing the throw pillows on the ornate, deep-set sofa. Perhaps I've revealed too much to him and he's getting scared. I must go about as I normally would to prove to him I'm not falling for him. Am I? Falling for him?

"I'd, um…I'd rather not think about where Sophia and Cassio have gone," Alister says, clearing his throat. I laugh, which somehow eases some of the gut-twisting nerves inside me. Still, I don't look at him. We need a moment for the status quo to reset. If I look at him now, I'm not sure what I'll find or what he may perceive in me. "Gio is probably asleep in his private quarters or preparing for tomorrow," he continues. I nod and grab the last of the wine bottles before heading through the dining room to the kitchen.

"Why didn't Gio spend today, well, yesterday, with his family? I'm assuming they're in New Orleans."

"No. He's from Miami, and his family is still there," Alister says, following behind me through the swinging door of the kitchen. I place the empty wineglasses and bottles on the island. When I turn, our eyes finally meet. And, unlike Cinderella, whose fantasy ended at the stroke of midnight, when I look into Alister's eyes my insides still tingle. He comes to stand beside me, and his arm brushes mine, reigniting the electric connection I felt between us on the dance floor. I do my best to ignore it and offer Alister a follow-up question.

"So, how did you and Gio meet?" I ask, taking a step away from him to sit on one of the barstools.

Alister smiles, letting out a small laugh. "Do you really want to have this conversation now? It's after midnight."

"Well, what else is there to do?" Because there is no way me being left alone on the third floor of the Amato mansion with nothing but my thoughts is better than this. Besides, after the night I've had, sleep won't come easy.

"Fine." As Alister gives in to me, he takes a seat on the stool next to me, once more closing the distance between us. *Careful, Ari.* Keep your eyes on his, not on his bulging biceps, not on the sprinkle of chest hair peeking out from his slightly unbuttoned shirt, and, most certainly, not his lips.

"When I was eighteen, I convinced my father to let me attend college somewhere other than New Orleans. I knew that it would be my only chance to escape this city, to have a somewhat normal existence. So, I ended up going to school in Florida, not far from Miami. But being the son of one of the most dangerous, wealthiest, and most sought-after men in America, I would always have a target on my head. Gio's family, one under my father's rule, was close by, and he was my same age. So, he became my roommate, bodyguard, and, ultimately, friend. When I had to return to New Orleans after graduation, he came with me. We've never been apart since."

"You said you wanted to escape this city, to be normal. It sounds like you didn't want the life laid out for you in New Orleans."

"I didn't. I...I don't." As Alister admits the truth, there's a sadness that takes over him. And yet, a clarity takes over me. Ever since I met Alister, there's been something about him that has lured me in, making me see the best in him despite the blood on his hands. At first, I thought it was the kindness he showed me after Walsh's men left me bloody and broken. Then, I thought it was our shared pain. The loss of his sister and the loss of my mother has forever scarred us in a way that makes it easy to relate to one another. Yet now I'm starting to see what draws me to Alister isn't his kindness or our shared knowledge of tragedy. It's his remorse, his desire to be good.

Alister and Sophia didn't ask to be a part of this world of

darkness. They were born into it. And from the day they were born, they've had a price on their heads and a target on their backs. What happened to Cara is evidence of that. And if the threat of death isn't enough, there are other ways this world has made them its prisoners. Sophia admitted as much when we finally cleared the air between us.

"Ariana, do you think you're the first ill-intentioned person to get close to me? My entire life I've had to worry about women and men befriending me or dating me for the wrong reasons. When I was a teenager, I met a girl while on a field trip from school. We started talking online and got close. It wasn't until I told my dad I wanted to go to the movies with her that he did a background check and realized she was a spy for another crime syndicate. When I was in my early twenties, I got played again. This time by a man who had absolutely nothing to do with the Mafia and yet knew I was rich. He just wanted me for my money. He wanted the money so bad, he deliberately poked holes in his condoms hoping he'd get me pregnant, so I'd forever be tied to him, even if I didn't marry him." At that, she turns away from me, shaking her head. *"It's because of people like that that I fell for Caleb. Well, I'm not sure I fell for him. I just…I felt safe with him. I mean, he had his own money and was from another country so that kept him from learning too much about my family. And even he turned out to be a lying, cheating asshole. But you?"*

I bite my lip and do my best to prepare to be obliterated. She has every right to hate me. I exploited her at her most vulnerable time. I—

"Ariana, Alister told me why you did what you did, what happened to your mom and how our father may have been involved." She turns back to me with glistening eyes and a sad smile. "He also told me that you were the one who saved me and that you almost died trying."

"He's being a bit dramatic," I mumble, and Sophia smiles.

"Yeah, well, he tends to do so. But I remember the man who led me away from the party. I remember how tight his grip was around my arm. I...I even remember the second one smothering me with the rag of chloroform while the other one held me against him." Her brows crinkle, and I wonder if this is the first time she's gone through something like this. It must have shaken her.

"If you hadn't been there, they would've done to me what they did to my sister." Her lip quivers. "And Alister...I don't think he would've survived losing us both." At that, her voice cracks and she turns away from me as emotion overcomes her.

"Hey." I reach out, resting my hand on her shoulder. "I...I wish I had the right words to say right now. I wish I could tell you that you're safe and nothing like this will ever happen again, but...I don't want to lie to you, not again, at least." Sophia nods. "But what I can tell you is that I'm here if you ever want to talk or just cry. I'm sure you feel like you have to be strong because if you're not, you're afraid Alister will—"

"Become even more oppressive," she says, a sad laugh escaping her. "Or worse." She said she was afraid Alister wouldn't survive losing her. Yet, something tells me she's worried about losing her brother in more than one way.

"I guess this is my way of saying I'm sorry for what happened to your mom," Sophia says, turning back to me. "I don't know how she got involved in this world, but I know that her death, like so many others, shouldn't have happened. It wouldn't have happened had our world not become so corrupt and void of the true essence of what the Mafia is about—family, loyalty, and honor. If I were in your shoes, I'd be doing the exact same thing you are—fighting for the truth at all costs. So, if it wasn't obvious, I forgive you, Ariana. Of everyone who's lied to me, at least you had an honorable reason for doing so."

Alister and Sophia are trapped, prisoners to their blood. That is their saving grace, the thing that lets me know I can trust Alister, that I'm safe with him, and that my feelings for him are valid, even if they are dangerous.

"Ariana, you've been fighting the Mafia and other criminal

organizations your entire adult life and for good reason. But it wasn't always like this, at least, not the Italians. The Mafia used to be about protecting each other when no one else would, when the laws of society were written against people like me. That's not to say that we didn't do horrible things in the name of protecting our own, but at least we had honor. Over the years, especially during the time of Prohibition, our outfit became anything but honorable. We got a taste of wealth, a taste of power, and we've clung to it ever since." Alister shakes his head. "This way of life is poisonous. It infects everyone who partakes in it, whether their choice or not. And once you're a part of it, you never truly escape it, no matter how badly you may want to."

"But what about now? You're the boss, Alister. You make the rules. You can choose to leave this way of life behind. I mean, you'll have to, unless you want to spend the rest of your life behind bars."

"Isn't that what you want?"

"*What?*" My brows crinkle as Alister's eyes narrow.

"I saw your suspension report. I know the outburst you had at work was about me. You wanted me to rot for what I did." *How did he...?*

"No. I wanted a chance to talk with you face-to-face, by whatever means necessary. There's a difference."

"Maybe. But no matter what happens to me, to this business, the only choice I have isn't between freedom or prison. It's between which cell I want to make my home. I may be king, Ariana, but I operate in a world filled with criminals, both those against me and those with allegiance to me. It's a world always on the brink of war, and talk of legitimizing the business will only rile my enemies and make my allegiances crumble."

"So, what are you saying? Are you just going to give up and give in to the role you've been forced to play? To sit atop a throne slowly but surely melting beneath you until the day you're arrested and become more vulnerable than you are now?"

"Why do you care?"

"*Excuse me?*"

"I said, why do you care? By the time the FBI comes knocking, you'll have the information you need, and our time together will be a thing of the past. So, why do you care what happens to me?"

"Because I do, Alister!" As the words finally escape me, I throw my hands up in defeat. "I know I shouldn't, but I do."

Alister's lips part. In his eyes, I find an expression I haven't seen before—a sense of hope that quickly fizzles. At least I'd like to think it was hope. It's probably just my wishful thinking.

"You're right. You shouldn't." The light leaves Alister's eyes and his jaw hardens, and I know my feelings aren't reciprocated. And, yet, what are my feelings? Just because I care about him and don't want him to go to jail for simply being born into a family of murderers doesn't mean I want to be in a relationship with him. I...I don't even know how to be in a relationship. Though, as I try to make light of my feelings for him, I know it's no use.

His soul speaks to mine. His body excites me. His touch intoxicates me, filling me with an unquenchable lust and longing that scares me and confuses me. Yet, I can't act on it. Because even if he did care for me as I do him, he's still a Mafia king. And from what he says, he always will be. It's hard to understand how someone as rich and connected as Alister can't walk away and start over somewhere new. And yet, he's right. The people of this criminal world operate by different rules and rule number one is—the only way out is with a bullet in your head. Or, in the case of my mom, a knife to the gut. Alister will never escape his demons. And I can't be me *and* be with him.

"Do me this one favor," I say then, lifting my eyes to meet

Alister's once more. "Let's play pretend. If you weren't the Blood King, ruler of men, Devil incarnate, what would you be? What would you do? Let me get to know the parts of you you're forced to keep hidden. Because when this comes to an end, I want to remember the real you. I want to remember the man, not the monster."

Alister takes a deep breath and spins on his barstool to face the wall. Yet, slowly, he extends his arm, opening his palm for me to take his hand. I intertwine my fingers with his and savor his touch almost as much as his words.

"If my life was my own, if I had no connection to the Mafia, I would've gone to college. I don't know where and I have no idea what I would've studied. I probably would've been an asshole because of my upbringing. Even without the drug money, my family owns half of New Orleans. That alone puts me in certain social circles, some more vicious than the criminal ones." At that, I smile. "I would've dated a lot, and partied. I would've wasted my parents' money on some useless degree and then traveled the world for at least a year, maybe five." Alister smiles as he gets lost in his mind, that is, until his lip quivers and his cheeks blush.

"Hey. Are you okay?" I ask, giving his hand a squeeze. He shakes his head.

"I just realized that in this fairy tale my mom would still be alive."

"Her death was connected to the Mafia?" Alister nods. "Oh my God. I'm so sorry."

"It's fine." Alister wipes his eyes before any tears can fall. "It's just...if she had never been killed, maybe it wouldn't be so hard for me to love. I mean, it's not that I don't want it. Of course I do. Who doesn't? But her death was the thing that made me realize I would never have it. I would never have love without the risk of losing it. And after she died, I just, I couldn't risk losing anyone else. So, I never allowed myself to get close enough to care, to fall in love, to risk heartbreak and the life of whoever was stupid enough to love me." Alister shakes his head. "In my perfect world, I'd return to New Orleans after traveling and I'd settle down. I'd fall in love, get married, have as many kids as the Lord would bless us with. And I would spend my days enjoying the simple things."

"Like cooking a meal or dancing in the living room?" I ask.

Alister turns to me. "Yeah," he whispers. "Things like that." Alister holds on to my hand a moment longer as his eyes drift to my lips. Maybe I've been reading him wrong. Maybe... Maybe he does care about me. The way he had Dr. Ramirez tend to my wounds after my confrontation with Walsh's men, the way he offered me his bed while spending the night of the Halloween party in discomfort, the way he bent over backward to make Thanksgiving the most amazing day of my life, the way he looks at me, holds me, dances with me, talks to me. The way his thumb caresses my hand right now.

I jump as he leans forward, stopping just inches from me. My heartbeat quickens as Alister brings his palm to my cheek, caressing my soft flesh. Is he going to kiss me? Do I want him to? Oh, who the Hell am I kidding? Of course I want him to! And yet, he does nothing more than brush a rebellious curl behind my ear and pull away as quickly as he approached.

"That's the fairy tale," he says then. "And this is not that." At that, Alister stands and leaves the room without another word.

"No. It's not," I whisper. As the door swings closed behind him, there is an ache in my chest that lets me know I'm in too deep. I've crossed the threshold of heartbreak. Now, there is no retreat without being broken in two. Thankfully, we've still got Boston and the truth surrounding my mother's murder to discover. We've still got time before I have to say goodbye.

18

Alister

With the way Ariana and I left things last night, I didn't get much sleep. All I could think of was her—the way she smells of cinnamon and caramel, the way her hand fits perfectly in mine, the way she looked at me when I nearly kissed her. Her warm eyes were so full of hope and innocence, a bit of fear, and yet, electric anticipation. It was that look that shocked me back into reality and cemented my then-shredded self-control. There's a part of her that cares for me, which means she can be hurt by me. And hurting her is the last thing I want to do.

"Interesting," Ariana says, pulling me from my thoughts.

"What's interesting?" I ask as I tip the bellmen for hauling up the mountain of luggage Sophia packed for Ariana. I knew I shouldn't have asked for her help. Seeing as all the two-bedroom suites were already booked, the bags take up most of the walking space in the small hotel room Ariana and I will share. I close the door and lock it as the bellmen leave and then proceed to dodge the Louis Vuitton trunks as I make my way to the bed.

"I pictured you more of a midcity penthouse kind of guy.

Instead, you bring me to a charming, Beacon Hill hotel with no more than four stories. That's interesting."

As Ariana gazes out the large windows overlooking the quiet brick street beneath us, I allow my eyes to linger on her for a moment. I was sure things would be awkward between us. In fact, I almost left her in New Orleans for fear of what staying in the same hotel room, same bed, would bring out of us. But, when I woke up this morning, everything was normal. Like every morning this week, she sat at the dining room table drinking her coffee. She met me with the same smile I've come to love, and immediately went into her normal good-natured ribbing. Relief washed over me as she acted like last night never happened. Though, I'd be remiss to say that relief was the only thing I felt.

"Yeah, well, it's not my typical vibe, but that's exactly why I picked it. We need to stay under the radar while we're here." Collecting myself, I drop my leather satchel beside the nightstand, remove my shoes and suit coat, push the sleeves of my dress shirt to my elbows, and lie down on the right side of the bed. "Beacon Hill is quiet, quaint, filled with tourists, and is close to a major interstate and public transport station should we need to make a quick getaway. Not to mention, it's only a ten-minute drive to the opera house." Ariana nods and turns to face me, her brows raised and her arms crossed. "*What?*" I ask.

"What if I wanted the right side? Now your germs are all over it."

"*My germs?*" I can barely keep a straight face as I try to figure out if she's serious or just giving me a hard time, as is her way. "If by germs you mean the stench of Italian leather from my private jet or the town car we took from the airstrip, then I think you'll be fine. Especially considering you're not getting the right side."

"Is that so?" She takes the few steps necessary from the window to the bed, plopping down beside me. "I guess you left your manners in the South, because Southern etiquette says the lady always goes first and that includes choosing her mattress real estate."

"Aha. Well, it's also proper etiquette, Southern or not, that the man sleeps closest to the door to fend off any unwanted company." At that, Ariana nods. "What? No rebuttal? No feminist commentary?"

Ariana shakes her head. "No. If you want to take a bullet for me, go ahead. But considering the blockade of Louis Vuitton between us and the door, I think we'll be okay."

"Right, well, one can never be too careful." At my words, Ariana looks from me to the bedspread, her smile fading, as well as the light in her eyes I've grown so used to. Oh no. I've got to do better at keeping things platonic between us. I don't want to toy with her feelings nor my own. And yet, perhaps her sudden change in mood has nothing to do with the things left unspoken between us and everything to do with the bed upon which we sit. I realize this arrangement isn't ideal for either of us.

"Hey, um, I'd offer to take the sofa, but there isn't one. And I triple-checked—there are no other rooms available to—"

"No, it's fine," she interjects, waving me off. "I mean, it's...it's not that I'm concerned about sharing a bed with you. I mean, I am, just not for reasons you're probably thinking."

"What do you mean?" I ask, moving to sit up straight as Ariana picks at the frayed fabric of her jeans for a moment, as if considering how she will answer my question. Though, I'm sure I already know. She's afraid of what she may do or say in her sleep. The night she stayed with me, I pretended to be asleep as the nightmares consumed and awoke her. But I heard everything. Which means I know her nightmares are about more than just her mom.

Finally, Ariana lifts her eyes to mine and says, "I'm a restless sleeper. I sometimes have night terrors. It's not something I can control." She bites her lip, as if there is more she'd like to say but doesn't.

I want to know what she dreams about. I want to know what happened to her and who hurt her. And I want to make them pay for ever daring to lay a finger on her. I imagine what she must've gone through, and my fingers ache and my shoulders tense, as if readying to throw a punch. No matter how badly I try to keep my emotions in check, I can't ignore the way my body reacts when I think of her in pain. I can't ignore the desire in me to protect her as if she is my own blood, as if she is mine.

"Alister?" she asks, drawing me back to the present.

"Sorry, um, don't worry about it, okay? When I sleep, I'm out like a log." At my quip, she smiles, her cheeks set aglow. She's so beautiful. And though I know her eyes have seen the worst of humanity, there's still a softness, an innocence to her that I admire. It's why I respect her, why I constantly want to be in her orbit.

"Well, there goes my bullet-proof vest," she says. As her sarcasm returns to her, she slings her legs over the side of the bed, stands, and makes her way to the leather Louis Vuitton trunk that's taller than she is. "I must admit, I was a little distracted while Sophia was packing. I caught a glimpse of the dress, but..." Ariana opens the person-sized trunk, and a bushel of pale gray tulle pours out, leaving her speechless.

"What is it? Did it get wrinkled?"

"Nope, but I wish it did." My brows crinkle. "Maybe then I could convince you to buy me something new with an actual bodice." Ariana pulls the mannequin from the trunk, revealing a dress I can't even remember Sophia wearing. Sure enough it has a deep-V neckline along with similar V-shaped openings beneath the arms. "The back is not much better," Ariana says, glancing at the back of the dress and then returning her frustrated gaze to me. Yeah, my dad probably vetoed this one. I mean, it's beautiful, it's just…

"To be fair, it offers more coverage than the dress you were wearing the night we met."

"That was Halloween, and I was on a mission to seduce you. I don't normally dress like—" Ariana waves in annoyance at the dress. "I don't even have the vocabulary to describe this." At that, I laugh. "It's not funny." Ariana puts her hand on her hip.

"It's kind of funny," I admit. "Besides, you need something a little *extra* given tonight's mission. It's not that I doubt your seduction skills, it's just, I need you to be undeniable tonight if we're going to get Gallagher alone." As the words cross my lips, I instantly regret them. Gio and I should've come up with a better plan, one that doesn't force the girl I like into the arms of my enemy.

"*Wait*," Ariana stops me. "Rewind. Your plan is to have me seduce Avery Gallagher?"

"It's a classic ploy, one you have experience with."

"Yeah, a botched experience and unoriginal is more like it."

"Who said it was botched?" Did I just say that out loud?

"Don't try to make me feel better." Ariana ignores my comment—*thank God*—in favor of shoving the mannequin back into its hiding place. "It's like Tinker Bell gone rogue."

"If Tinker Bell wore diamond-encrusted Vera Wang."

"Wait, those are real diamonds? That dress is by Vera Wang?"

"Let it sink in while you get ready. We leave in an hour."

As I watch Ariana move around the room in a fit, shuffling through shoes, jewels, makeup, and hair pins, I can't help but smile as my chest fills with warmth. However, as thoughts of what is to come burst through the towering walls I've built to house my feelings for her, the warmth is quickly chased away by an eerie chill. I hate that I care for her, because I know my feelings for her put her at risk. Hell, her being here with me now puts her at risk, but I couldn't stop myself from allowing her to come. I wanted this night with her, both because of my plan to confront Avery Gallagher and in spite of it. I want this time with her because she makes me feel normal. She allows me to pretend I could belong in her world rather than mine. And yet, it's because of my world and the fact that she knows darkness too that I know she's the one I need tonight, not Gio, not even Sophia. She's the one I need to talk me off the ledge, to keep me from starting a war with the Irish mob that may be the death of us all, but now that she's here, I worry I've made a mistake. I used to think Sophia was all I had to lose. I have never been more wrong.

WHEN ARIANA STEPPED out into the hallway of our hotel, I was speechless. Turns out Sophia knew what she was doing. She sent Ariana with all the tools and products to do her hair and makeup and tons of jewelry options to match the dress. The dress, albeit a bit revealing in the cleavage and side-boob area, is stunning on her. Diamonds cover her chest and stomach and drip down haphazardly through the pale gray pleated tulle like tears. Let it be a warning to any man who dares to touch her as they too will be left in tears.

As we move up the velvet-lined staircase of the Boston Opera House to our balcony seats, I wrap my arm around Ariana's waist and pull her tight to my side. She turns to me, surprised by the sudden move. But as the wandering eyes of the men around us return to their partners, I take it my point has been received. She's mine. And yet, she isn't. The whole point of her being here, of her wearing that completely captivating dress, is to draw the attention of Avery Gallagher, to make him want to touch her, do things with her, not me.

"Sorry," I mumble, releasing my hold as I'm reminded why we're here. And what a sour reminder it is.

Ariana doesn't say anything. Instead, she wraps her hand around my arm and allows me to escort her as a gentleman should. Her touch grounds me. And yet, the farther we make it into the opera house, the less gentlemanly I feel. Based on the light recon Gio and I did prior to our flight, I've already spotted three known members of the Irish mob among the crowd. Though no Gallagher yet. Just the thought of being in the same room as him, breathing the same air as him, makes my blood boil. So much so, I keep my eyes pointed away from Ariana as we make our way into our private seating area. It's more than me not wanting her to see the monster within. She's a distraction, a breathtakingly beautiful distraction. And right now, I have to stay focused if we're going to make it out of here alive. Avery Gallagher and his former boss may not have been the ones to order the hits against my sisters, but had Joseph Cullen lived, they would've. This man is my enemy, and we are in enemy territory. I can't forget that.

"Hey," Ariana says, moving her hand to mine. I allow my fingers to intertwine with hers, but do not turn to her. "We're going to survive this, Alister. And we're going to return to New Orleans and destroy whoever has been working against your family, whoever hurt Cara."

At the mention of my sister's name, I'm reminded of the night I thought I'd finally avenged my sister, the night I thought I had justice. Little did I know, there was so much more to the story. So much more and yet I almost died for a sliver of the truth. Not only me, but Emma. I promised her I'd keep her safe, that the brotherhood wouldn't touch her, but they quickly made me break my promise. I don't want to break a promise to another woman, which is precisely why I've offered Ariana no assurances. And yet, as I feel her skin against mine, the warmth of her body, the soft pulse of blood in her veins, I know I cannot let her walk into battle on my behalf without offering her these words. More importantly, I know I cannot say them without being willing to enforce them, even if that means going head-to-head with the Irish mob all by myself or walking away from the mission altogether. For her, I would do both.

With resolve, I turn to her. Her lips part in anticipation as I continue to hold on to her hand. "I want you to know that you're safe with me. I won't let anyone hurt you and I will kill anyone who tries."

Ariana appears to savor my words as I savor her stunning face and the delicate way her dark curls fall loosely around her cheeks, breaking free from the pins meant to hold them. Unable to restrain myself any longer, I bring my hand to her cheek, just like I did the night before. It's the same one one of Gallagher's men buried his fist into nearly two months ago. I brush my thumb over the place that was once red and swollen. I didn't know her then. I didn't trust her. Now that I do, I can't imagine allowing anything like that to happen to her again. And yet, it very well could if we go through with this plan.

"We can still call it off, you know," I tell her. "I can get to Gallagher another way. My quest for vengeance shouldn't jeopardize even more innocent lives. It shouldn't jeopardize you."

"No." She pulls away from me then. "No, you need to know who's coming after Sophia. If we return to New Orleans now, we'll be sitting ducks waiting for another attack."

"*We?*"

"Yes, *we*. If it wasn't obvious, I'm in this, Alister. Not just for tonight, but until the end. I'm not walking away. And I know the only reason you'd even consider abandoning the mission is to keep me safe. I'm telling you that isn't necessary."

She's right. It would test my self-control like nothing else to leave this city without stripping every piece of intel from Gallagher he has to give. But I would do it for her. I would do it to keep her from suffering the same fate as Cara. And yet, as the thought comes to me, I'm reminded that if I walk away without the answers I need, Sophia will remain at risk of suffering just that. Like I said, distraction. Because when I stare into Ariana's warm eyes, I forget everyone and everything else so much so it's dangerous. *We're* dangerous together, and not in the way that sends fear shivering down the spines of our enemies. But in the way that makes us vulnerable, and not just us, but my entire family, the people I've pledged my life to protect. So, she's right. I can't walk away. I guess I just wish she would. I don't know how I'll live with myself if something happens to her because of me.

I offer her a nod as the orchestra begins their piece, signaling the start of the production. Ariana reaches into her clutch and pulls out a pair of binoculars I remember seeing as part of Cassio's weapons display. "Here." She hands them to me. "They've already been programmed with Gallagher's information. When the lights go down, scan the room. Once we know where he is, we can keep an eye on him until he excuses himself for a drink or restroom break. It's then that we should attack. And, if a moment doesn't present itself during the production, we'll grab him on his way out." Ariana remains calm and calculated as she speaks. It's as if she's done this a thousand times before. For all I know, she has.

"Hmm, I guess you're right. I shouldn't worry about you."

"Oh, I don't know," Ariana says, relaxing into her chair. "It felt kind of nice."

As the lights dim around us, Ariana leaves me with a smile

before focusing her attention on the stage, though I let my eyes linger so I can live in this moment a little longer. Because what comes next won't be pretty or innocent or coy. It will be painful, dangerous, and bloody. And it may just change everything between us.

19

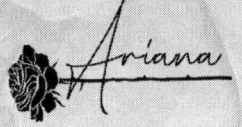

When the announcement for intermission is made, Avery Gallagher stands and excuses himself from his balcony seat and his three companions. From what Alister says, the man Gallagher is meeting with looks to be one of the mob's bosses. The other two men are his and Gallagher's security, which means we'll have to be quick and careful not just in interrogating Gallagher but also in escaping the opera house without drawing their attention.

"He left his detail behind, which means he's probably going to the bathroom," Alister says.

"It's time. He won't be without his security again."

Alister and I share a knowing look before exiting our private balcony and making our way through the throngs of people to Avery Gallagher, the man whose truth may change Alister's life forever. As we walk, it occurs to me, maybe Alister wanted to call off the mission for more than just my safety. Maybe he's afraid to know who in his inner circle has betrayed him. Because once he knows, he loses them. And he's already lost so much in his mother, father, and Cara.

I slow my pace as a wave of sympathy rushes through me. Alister isn't close with many people, at least, from what I can tell. If, by chance, the traitor is someone he trusts, it'll be even harder for him to hear and even harder for me to make sure Alister doesn't cross a line that may get us caught in enemy territory.

"Having second thoughts?" Alister asks, moving his hand to my lower back. His touch sends shock waves through my body, though they aren't strong enough to alleviate my nerves. I turn to him.

"No. I'm just...worried about you. We don't know what Gallagher will say. What if he says something you don't like?"

"You're worried I'll do something stupid," Alister says, seeing straight through me. As we round the corner and the men's restroom comes into view, Alister moves his hand from my back to my hip and pulls me with him to the side of the corridor. Hidden from view by a large marble column, Alister leans in and whispers, "Don't worry. No matter what Gallagher says, I won't do anything to put you at risk." His words do little to reassure me. And yet, as his breath tickles the delicate skin of my neck, it isn't my nerves that make the hairs on my arms rise. "I told you I'd protect you and I mean what I say, every word."

Alister pulls away from me, and there's something in the way his golden-brown eyes pour into mine that makes me believe him. Or maybe it's just wishful thinking because I have no other choice and I'm high on electric butterflies. Ever since last night, I've done my best to pretend that things haven't changed between us. But they have. I can feel it in every touch, every glance, and every word. Though none of that changes the fact that we are about to go about up against one of the most dangerous men in the country and our lives literally depend on my ability to be sexy. Yeah, easier said than done.

Alister peeks around the corner of the column while I use

the mirror from my clutch to check my reflection. The false eyelashes and pink lipstick Sophia sent me add a sultry yet innocent vibe to my pale gray, diamond-encrusted ensemble. I feel and look like a princess. Well, a princess with cleavage and sideboob. My ensemble will work well for the angle I play when I attempt to convince Gallagher to take me somewhere private. A man like him—rich, powerful, manipulative, and greedy—wants an innocent, naive damsel he can impress and dominate. So, that's what I'll give him, at least until Alister shows up and—

"Gallagher just came out of the bathroom. He's in line for a drink at the bar." Alister turns to me. "Are you ready?"

"Yeah." I nod.

"Are you sure?" Alister asks, sensing the hesitancy in my rigid stance.

"What if it doesn't work? What if I can't get him to leave with me?"

Alister gives me a once-over, taking in every inch of me. As his eyes meet mine, his lips draw up into a sexy smirk. "It'll work." Two words, short and to the point, and yet they make everything inside me turn to goo. *Focus, Ariana. This man is dangerous.* Though, as the thought comes to me, I wonder if I'm subconsciously referring to Gallagher or Alister.

As Alister peeks around the column again, he says, "Alright, he's next in line."

I nod and take a deep breath. "That's my cue."

❧

AVERY GALLAGHER IS tall with thick blond hair and a scruffy beard to match. Most notably, he's built like a brick house. Which means, even without his security, it won't be easy to subdue him. By the time I reach him, he's already gotten his drink and is preparing to head back to his seat. I know I'm meant to approach him, throw myself at him. But, as my eyes meet his, there are no words on my tongue. It's not that I'm afraid. I've taken down greater men than him. It's just... I don't trust the words that would escape me if I allowed them to. As my feelings for Alister continue to grow, I'm not sure I have it in me to outright seduce another man. So, I make my way past Gallagher, pretending to be lost. Seeing as I have no idea where I'm going, it's not a hard act to sell. And if Alister's compliments are worth their salt, Gallagher will follow behind me and aid his damsel.

"Are you lost, miss?"

Look who took the bait. At the sound of the unfamiliar voice with the slightest hint of a Boston accent, I turn. Gallagher takes a step toward me with his head slightly lowered as if to appear mysterious.

"It looks like I am." I begin to fan myself and look around in search of something, anything but Gallagher's green eyes. My disinterest in him will make him want me more. "It's so congested in here. I'm feeling a bit flush and was looking for a place to lie down." It's then that I return my gaze to Gallagher. He now stands only inches from me, so close I can smell his cologne and spot the edges of a tattoo along the top of his shirt collar. "Do you know of somewhere private I might catch my breath?" As the words cross my lips, I pull out every trick in the book—light, breathless tone, wide, doll-like eyes, and slightly parted lips he can't help but want to kiss.

Gallagher's lips lift into a smile, almost hidden by the beard taking up half his face. And yet, the small wrinkles stretched out from his eyes let me know he's fallen for my act. "I know just the place. Come. I'll escort you." Gallagher offers me his arm, which I graciously take. As I do, I catch a glimpse of a pistol hidden beneath his suit jacket. *Great.* He's armed and Alister has no idea.

As Gallagher leads me to a door just off the bathrooms, I fight the urge to turn around and search the crowd for Alister so I can warn him about the gun. No. There are too many people hovering around. If Gallagher sees him, he'll no doubt recognize him, and this will end badly for more than just us. Gallagher opens the door for me, and, with resolve, I take a step inside. The room is empty and dark, so dark I can't even tell what color the walls are painted. There's a couch to my right and some chairs to my left. At the far end of the room, there is an unmanned bar with high-end liquor and cigars ready for the taking. That explains the smell.

"Here, this should do well for you," Gallagher says, directing me to the sofa. "Can I get you anything to drink?"

Knowing I've got only a few more seconds until Alister shows up, I reach out my hand to Gallagher's. "What I want isn't a drink." Gallagher's smile widens as he takes a seat next to me. Without a word, he leans in, bringing one hand to my cheek and one to my thigh, using the slit in my dress to gain quick access to my flesh. As his lips crash into mine, I move my hands to his side, wrapping my fingers around the handle of his gun just as the door to the lounge swings open, filling the dark space with light.

I open my eyes, finding Alister watching me from the doorway as Gallagher moves his hand from my thigh up my waist to my—

"Avery Gallagher," Alister says, pulling the bearded man's attention from me just before his hand reached my chest. When Gallagher turns to face Alister, I slip the gun from his hip holster and move away from him. Thankfully, he doesn't notice. At the sight of Alister, his grin returns, only this time it is more wicked than lustful. He stands, every bit as tall as Alister. And yet, the lethal look in Alister's eyes and the way his jaw clenches and the vein in his neck throbs lets me know I've got nothing to worry about. Alister will destroy him. For our sake, I just hope he can do it quietly.

"Alister Amato," Gallagher says before turning to me. "Sweetheart, would you mind giving us a moment? Don't worry. I'll find you after." He winks at me, though I don't move. Alister uses Gallagher's brief distraction to close the distance between them. When Alister reaches him, he brings his hand to Gallagher's throat, shoving him against the wall so hard a picture falls to the floor.

"You do not speak to her. You do not look at her. *She's mine*," Alister growls.

"Then why did I have my tongue halfway down her throat?" Gallagher asks, a glint of pride in his eye even though Alister's grip strangles his words. I take a step toward them, moving my finger onto the trigger of the gun still hidden behind my back. It's then that a flash of silver draws my attention to the two men's waists where Gallagher is just moments away from gutting Alister.

"Drop it," I say, lifting the gun and aiming it at Gallagher's head. If this thing goes off, stab wound or not, Alister and I won't make it out of the opera house without being caught by Gallagher's men. But I won't stand by and do nothing. Gallagher turns to me, realizing how true Alister's words were. *I'm his.* Alister, once again, uses my distraction tactics to his advantage and maneuvers the knife from Gallagher, pressing it to his throat.

"One move and I end you," Alister says.

"That's if I don't kill you first," I add.

Gallagher looks between us without showing an ounce of fear. Yet, something in his demeanor does change. The tension in his shoulders relaxes. The intensity in his eyes dissipates. What's left is reason.

"If you kill me, you won't get what you came for," he says,

returning his gaze to Alister. "Seeing as you've broken the Rules of Civility to come here, I doubt you'll give up so easily."

Rules of Civility? What is he talking about?

"Lower the knife, and the gun." Gallagher turns to me, giving me a pointed look before returning his green gaze to Alister. "And we can have this conversation like gentlemen. Truth is, I've been expecting you."

"I bet you have," Alister bites out. Alister holds the knife to Gallagher's throat a moment longer, as if fighting the urge to end him here and now for even daring to move against him and his family. And yet, just as I feel myself about to talk him down, he pulls back, letting Gallagher go. The two men adjust their suits, as if they're buffing smudges from their armor. In a way, maybe they are. Gallagher's eyes drift down toward the knife still clasped tightly in Alister's palm, and Alister hands it to me for safekeeping. Gallagher nods.

"Will the lady be drinking as well?" Gallagher asks, moving to the bar.

"Does the lady have a pulse?" I ask, drawing a smirk from him.

With Gallagher focused on making the three of us drinks, I take a deep breath and return my gaze to Alister. As I do, I find his never left me. His eyes drift from mine down to my lips where they linger. *Oh no.* Is he upset I kissed Gallagher? I only did it to get the gun from him so he couldn't use it against us, against him.

"Are you okay?" Alister asks, breaking my mental spiral. His voice is strained and nearly inaudible.

"I'm fine," I say, though I am confused by his demeanor. Perhaps he isn't buying Gallagher's sudden offer for a cordial discussion. His guard is still up, which tells me mine should be too.

"Stay behind me, but close. Only use your weapons in an

instance of life and death. We're on their turf, which is already seen as an act of war. If we draw blood, we will have one."

I nod and follow Alister to the bar where Gallagher waits for us with three bourbons.

"I thought it would be fitting since you are the King of New Orleans," he says as we join him.

"How very original," Alister remarks. His body is still riddled with tension, though his words are a little less strained. Still, I keep my palm gripped tight around my knife and my trigger finger on high alert as Alister sits on the barstool closest to Gallagher and I on the stool behind Alister.

Gallagher sips his drink, though Alister doesn't touch his. Smart. He could've poisoned them when we weren't looking. After a moment of contemplation, Gallagher turns to us. His green eyes land heavy on Alister, as if he's ashamed of what he's about to say. I lean forward, waiting intently for Gallagher to reveal the truth.

"It's no secret the feud between the Italians and the Irish goes back generations. But that all changed, or so I thought, with the peace treaty your father brokered with the North American heads of organized crime. The Rules of Civility, a final gift to his son before he passed, one I'm sure he'd hoped would protect you and your rule."

At the mention of Alister's father, Alister sits up straight, as if it will help his body absorb his anger, or, perhaps, sadness.

"Unfortunately, my former boss, Joseph Cullen, had plans for your family's demise that predated the signing of the treaty." At that, Gallagher looks away from us and downs the rest of his drink. "When Cullen revealed he was sending four of our men to New Orleans, men I'm sure you've snuffed out or you wouldn't be here, I advised against it. It was only a few months after the treaty was signed—"

"You mean, a few months after my father's death," Alister

bites out. Gallagher nods.

"I told him he should give you a chance to become the great leader that your father was." Gallagher shakes his head. "That's when he revealed that he'd been plotting his takeover of the Amatos for nearly two decades. Nothing would stop him from getting what he wanted."

"And what did he want?" Alister asks, though the tone of his voice says he already knows.

"Power. More money. More influence," Gallagher admits. "From what I understood, it wasn't personal. It was just...business."

"Yeah? Well, your men made it personal when they abducted my little sister a year ago and even more so with their recent abduction attempt against my sister Sophia."

Gallagher's eyes widen in surprise, or perhaps fear. If he'd known how truly personal this is for Alister he may not have agreed to such a gentlemanly discussion.

"I thought the brotherhood abducted your sister."

"Yeah, so did I, until Edgar Walsh admitted it was him and his men who took her to the brotherhood. They abducted an eighteen-year-old girl from her dorm room in the middle of the night and turned her over to a group of sex trafficking predators who raped and sold her, only for her to be raped repeatedly until her owner had enough of her. Do you know it took me months to find the man who had her only to realize I was too late? I was too late, Avery. I spent weeks searching every abandoned warehouse and junkyard off the coast of Greece to find the barrel containing her body. Or should I say, the brown sludge that was once her body? *My sister, Avery!*"

Alister slams his fist against the bar as all the emotions of his past crash inside him like waves. I relinquish my knife to place my hand on his shoulder, emotion straining my own features. I want him to remember I'm here and I've got him.

Alister lowers his head, taking a moment to regain control of himself. Out of respect or perhaps shame for what his men have done, Gallagher looks away.

"I am truly sorry for what Walsh and his men have done to your family. I need you to know I had nothing to do with it nor did Josephine. I assume you know her father, the man who ordered the hit against your family, was killed shortly after he sent Walsh and his men to your city. Well, of course you know," Gallagher remarks.

"Because if I thought for a moment that you had something to do with my sister's death, I would've ripped your insides out and fed them to you the moment I walked through that door," Alister says, lifting his eyes to meet Gallagher's once more. The man across from him only nods. In his eyes I finally find the fear that only Alister can cast upon a man of his rank and stature.

Alister shakes his head and downs his bourbon in one hefty gulp. As he places the empty glass back on the bar top, his fingers shake, as if it's taking everything inside him not to crush the glass in his palm or worse, smash it against Gallagher's head. "Continue," Alister finally says. His words slip through his gritted teeth. Gallagher nods and does as he's told.

"As I said, Cullen died within days of sending Walsh and company to New Orleans. It was a car accident, no foul play suspected, at least by the police. I wasn't so convinced." Gallagher gives Alister a knowing look. "I thought you'd figured out what Cullen was up to and ordered the hit after taking out his men planted in your city. You were the only one at the time who had motive to kill him."

"If you thought I had your boss murdered, why wouldn't you come after me?"

"Because…Josephine had just taken over in the wake of her father's death. She knew nothing of the operation, nor did anyone else. I was the only one who suspected foul play and I didn't want to throw her into a war she wasn't ready for. Besides, I never agreed with Cullen's plans to take New Orleans. We don't need Italian territory to be strong and powerful. We're already your superior." At that, Gallagher smiles, teasing Alister as if it will lighten the mood. Yeah, I don't think that's possible. Alister doesn't even entertain his comment.

"With Cullen dead and presumably Walsh and his men, I tossed the burner phone I was meant to use to communicate with them and never thought twice about the mission. But you know that, don't you? You knew of Cullen's death before you got here. And, if what you say is true, that Walsh and his men are the ones who abducted Cara and attempted to abduct Sophia, then you know those orders didn't come from him." Realization dawns on Gallagher as Alister nods.

"I'm here for a name, Avery. You and I both know Cullen was working with someone in New Orleans to orchestrate these attacks. And after his untimely death, they are the one who ordered Walsh and his men to go after Cara, to go after Sophia. And, given what you've said about your former boss's twenty-year vendetta against my family, I'm starting to consider their attacks are just as old."

Gallagher's brows crinkle, as do mine. What is Alister getting at?

"My mother was killed in a hit meant to take out my entire family sixteen years ago. It was almost successful. Had I not heard the windows burst in their bedroom just down the hall from mine, they would've killed both of my parents and then snuffed me and my siblings out in our sleep. Still, I couldn't save her. They shot my mother. I can still remember the sound of her body hitting the wood floor, the vacant look in her eyes as blood gushed from her chest. So, tell me, Avery, who was your former boss working with? Who is to blame for destroying my family?"

As Alister reveals the truth of how his mother was killed, I close my eyes. He understands my pain even more than I thought. I knew his mother's death was connected to the Mafia. But I had no idea Alister witnessed it. Like me, he was a child when his mother was taken from him by evil men. The small part of me that feels vindicated, happy that his father suffered, is quickly snuffed out by my empathy for Alister. No child deserves to lose their parent so young and so horrifically.

At that, Gallagher stops. The light leaves him as his lips press into a flat line. It's as if he knows his next words won't sit well with the Blood King. I relinquish my final weapon, setting my gun on the stool behind me as I ready myself to restrain Alister, or at least attempt to if Gallagher delivers anything less than what Alister needs to hear. He turns back to Alister then as I scoot to the edge of my seat.

"It's true that Cullen was working with someone in your inner circle, someone eager for power though smart enough to know they'd have to sacrifice some of it just to survive the coup. Whoever worked with Cullen knew he couldn't take on your father, or you, by himself. Either that or he just wanted to use our soldiers instead of his own out of sheer self-preservation. But I never knew a name, Alister. I never even saw the guy. In the nearly twenty years that I worked for Cullen, I never even knew about his plots against your family until last year when I was told to help Walsh and the rest of them fake their own deaths."

"I don't believe you," Alister whispers. *Oh no.*

"What?"

"I said, I don't believe you."

At that, Alister grabs the empty bourbon glass from the bar and smashes it into Gallagher's face. Gallagher blinks, giving Alister enough time to charge him, tackling him to the ground. I stand and move out of the way as their struggle leaves barstools scattered and Alister's knuckles busted. Alister buries his fist into Gallagher time and time again until Gallagher finally blocks a punch and rams his knee into Alister's ribs. I flinch and look back to the gun and knife just a few feet away. What good would it do? Though Alister is more than capable of killing Gallagher with his bare hands, he won't. He still needs the name. And if he truly believes Gallagher is keeping it from him, he won't kill him until he reveals it.

"I'm telling you the truth, Alister." Gallagher pushes Alister off him using the full force of his legs. Alister flies backward into the opposite wall. Sweat covers his forehead, though he shows no signs of the struggle that just ensued, unlike Gallagher, who stands across from him with a busted lip, swollen cheek, and split temple. "You know I am. You just don't want to believe that this was all for nothing, that, just like you have been ever since your sister was taken, you're one step behind."

Alister pushes himself up off the ground, disappointment appears to quench his thirst for Gallagher's blood. It's then that his eyes move to the gun just within reach.

"No, no, Alister, don't," I say, as he grasps the gun and points it at Gallagher's head.

"If he's telling the truth, he's of no use to me," Alister says, his voice void of any emotion.

"Alister, you promised me you wouldn't do anything stupid." I look between the two men as Gallagher raises his hands in surrender. "Alister, if you do this, it will mean war."

Gallagher turns to me with a smile that sets every nerve in my body on fire. "Sweetheart, don't you know? We're already at war." As the words cross his lips, a sudden burst of light fills the room as the door behind me swings open. I turn just in time to see a small army of gun-wielding men, all tattooed with the mark of the Irish mob, enter the small space. I take a step back and—

20

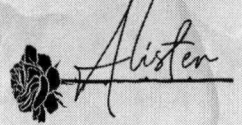

I WAKE WITH A CRICK IN MY NECK AND TENDER WRISTS AS I find myself restrained to a chair in the basement of one of Josephine Cullen's holdings. I should've known Avery's request for a cordial discussion was just him stalling until his backup could arrive. Who knows if what he said was even true? His men stormed the gentlemen's lounge so quickly, they had Ariana in their grasp within a matter of seconds. With a gun to her head and me outnumbered and out-armed, I had no choice but to let them take us. They walked us out of the opera house, and once they had us in a car, they drugged us so we wouldn't know where we were headed. Gio, of course, has been tracking us the entire time and is no doubt on his way given our unexpected change of course. But, as Ariana comes into view, I'm worried we won't be able to wait for him.

"They wouldn't," I whisper.

Ariana lies unconscious on the floor in front of me. Her hands are cuffed behind her back, and she's wearing nothing more than her underwear and corset. The way she is displayed before me makes Gallagher and his men's intentions clear. No. Gio will never make it here before they—

"Good, you're awake." Avery's voice pulls my attention from Ariana to him. At the sight of him and the two men accompanying him, my insides twist. She'll never be able to fight the three of them off. Even if she wasn't handcuffed, she'd be no match for them. No. I can't. I can't let what happened to Cara happen to her. I use all my force to try to break free from the cuffs clasped around my wrists with no success. "It's reinforced steel, Alister. A Cassio Castellani offering, before he legitimized, of course."

I bow my head in defeat, knowing the cuffs won't give an inch if Cassio made them. Although…

"Please," I beg. "Do what you must with me. Just let her go. She isn't a part of this."

"Isn't she? She was the one you sent to lure me away. The one who used her body, or should I say mouth, to steal my gun from its holster. The one who then pointed that gun at my head and threatened to kill me. All of it to protect you. So, yes, I'd say she's very much a part of this."

"She's innocent. Don't make her pay for my mistakes."

"Mistakes. Yes, let's discuss those." Avery begins to pace the room while I maneuver my watch, also a Cassio Castellani creation, using the built-in laser to melt the latch of the cuffs.

"Let's start with the obvious. You broke the Rules of Civility by coming here without permission. You engaged in hand-to-hand combat with me. You would've killed me had my men not shown up in time. And let's not forget your worst offense of all." At that, Avery stops. The light leaves him as his lips press into a flat line. I'm running out of time. "Walsh and his men, you killed them, didn't you?"

I don't answer him, nor do I tell him Walsh is alive. He doesn't care about those men. If he did, he would've avenged what he believed to be their murders a year ago. But he didn't. He wrote them off as a casualty of a war he claims he never even believed in and only brings them up now because he needs to justify what he's about to do to Ariana. But he can't. There is no justification for rape.

"Any one of those transgressions is an act of war, Alister. You know that. And yet, you sit here without remorse, without shame. That tells me you need to be taught a lesson." Avery moves toward me then, stepping over Ariana's body to rest his hand on my shoulder. I meet him eye to eye without flinching even as the laser burns my skin in its efforts to free me. "And so you shall."

As Avery shifts his attention to Ariana, I tug on the cuffs, but they still don't break. "There are other ways to teach someone a lesson," I say, hoping to stall him a few moments more. "Trust me, I know. I would never cross the line you're about to."

Avery turns back to me. "I don't like this any more than you do. But you broke the rules, Alister, the very rules your father wrote."

"Your men broke them first."

"Maybe. But we'll never know, will we? You see that transgression alone is worse than your presence in our city. The punishment for which is death." At that, Avery kneels and brings his hand to Ariana's cheek. He caresses her flesh before moving his fingers to her lips. "The thing is, I can't kill you without risking Josephine's life. Nor can I bring myself to put a bullet between this one's eyes, not when I still taste her on my tongue."

"You do this, and you'll have a war greater than anything you've ever seen," I warn him, silently praying it won't come to that. But make no mistake, if I can't break free and he does force himself on her, I will rain Hell down upon him.

"What happens next is on you, Alister," he says, his voice

void of any emotion. No. I've run out of time. "It's on you. Let her screams be a reminder to you. The next time you feel the urge to cross us—don't."

Avery motions to one of his men, who hands him a syringe filled with God only knows what. I grunt as I try to break the hold of the cuffs. They still won't give. *Just a little more, come on, a little more.* Avery shoots the syringe into Ariana's vein, causing her eyes to flash open and her body to lift off the ground as she comes to. Adrenaline. He wants her awake while he rapes her. I swear to God, I will—

"Well, hello, sweetheart. Nice of you to join us."

Ariana struggles against the grip of the handcuffs as she squirms, taking in her surroundings. Her chest rises and falls as the adrenaline speeds up her breaths. Finally, her eyes meet mine. I'm not sure what she sees in them, in me. Whatever it is, it slows her breathing and movements, as if she's gone numb. It's as if she knows what will happen next.

"There, there," Avery coos, rolling her from her side to her back. She cries out as her hands press into the wooden floor beneath her, taking the full weight of her body. Once he's on top of her, her wrists will be crushed. "I know you missed my little conversation with Alister, so here's the gist of it. You're going to suffer for your boyfriend's stupidity. Don't worry. I have no plans to kill you or him. Though, I suspect you may wish for death by the time you've taken all three of us." Avery glances toward his men, who now share in his wicked glee.

"I swear to God, Avery. You will pay for this in kind. And then you will die at my hand."

"Careful, Alister," Avery warns. "Things could get a lot worse for you *and* her."

"Do it," Ariana says. Her voice so quiet I can barely hear her yet her words draw both mine and Avery's attention. "Do it," she repeats. "You think you can hurt me?" Her lips lift into a sad smile as tears fill her eyes. "Whatever you think you're going to do to me, it's already been done."

As the words cross her lips, my heart breaks. I knew she'd faced demons before. The scars on her body tell me so. But her admission now reveals her past trauma is greater than I thought. I don't know who or how or why, but she's been hurt in this way before. And like Avery, I will make them pay for what they've done to her, and then I will put them down like the animals they are.

"Yeah? Well, we'll see about that."

As Avery moves his hand to the lace of her underwear, I break free. *God bless you, Cassio.* I lunge at Avery, tackling him to the floor much like I did before. Only this time, I don't hold back. Instead of using my fists to end him, I opt for the quicker method since I still have two others to fend off. I position the strap of my watch against Avery's neck and press a button. A single silver shank shoots from the strap of my watch into Avery's neck, severing his carotid artery. Blood sprays from his flesh like a sprinkler, wetting my face and shirt, though I don't have time to revel in it before I'm ripped off him by his two goons.

Ariana rolls out of the way as Avery's men nearly trample her in their assault against me. I quickly regain my balance and move toward them, making sure their attention stays on me. As I throw my punches, the reinforced steel of the handcuffs still attached to my wrist flies with my fist, adding to their suffering. Their faces split open under the metal's pressure, and I lean forward, snatching the holstered gun from one of them. They haven't fired, which means they're either new and don't know that my killing Avery justifies them killing me *or* Josephine has no idea what her men have been up to or the lengths they're willing to go to keep her reign intact. If they kill me, they'll be forced to explain what Avery almost did, what they were giddy to take part in. If they can subdue me and get me back to New Orleans without Josephine finding out, then there's nothing to explain, nothing to pay for. Oh, but I'll make them pay.

When the one to my left lunges toward me, I fire the gun. The bullet crashes into his head, burning the flesh surrounding the entry point due to our proximity. The second man stands still in surprise. I don't give him a moment to react. As the image of his sick face, smiling down at a restrained, half-naked Ariana, flashes through my mind, I pull the trigger, ending him like I have the others. His body falls to the now blood-soaked floor, and silence befalls the room as the weight of my actions settles on my shoulders.

As I take in the beaten and bloody bodies before me, I know I've royally fucked up. And yet, as my eyes find Ariana, crouched in a corner across the room, I know I'd do it again. My only regret is that their deaths were too quick.

I slip the gun into my waistband and grab my suit jacket from where it lies as I approach Ariana. Tears drench her face as she sits, motionless at the foot of the stairwell leading to, undoubtedly, more men I will have to slaughter if we hope to survive. When I reach her, I drop to my knees, drape my jacket over her shoulders, and work to remove her handcuffs. She doesn't say anything nor look at me. Instead, she slowly takes in her surroundings—the bodies, the blood, the bullets. This is exactly what I was afraid of. I never wanted her to see this side of me, the predator, the bloodthirsty monster within. And yet, I know I had no choice. Still, how will she ever see me as anything more now that she's officially met him—the Blood King?

Maybe it's for the best. She and I aren't even together and still Avery used her against me. Of course, he wouldn't have been able to if I didn't care for her. But I do. I really do. And yet, how can I be with her? How can I show her my true feelings when I know that doing so only puts her at a greater risk than she already is? No. She must see me as a monster if she is to remain safe. And yet, just like before, when I allowed her to accompany me, I can't bring myself to push her away, even though I know it's for the best.

Once she is free of the cuffs, I bring my hand to her cheek so I can get her to look at me. "Hey. Are you okay? Did they hurt you?" Ariana's glossy eyes meet mine as she pulls her tender wrists to her chest. She parts her lips, but no words come out. Instead, she slings her arms around me and buries her face in the crook of my neck. I pinch my eyes closed as I return her embrace. Our bodies press together so perfectly it's as if we're one person or, at a minimum, two halves of one whole.

"Thank you," she whispers. The quiet brokenness in her voice makes me hold her tighter. What just happened was traumatic, and yet something tells me her sadness is grounded in the past, the time, or times, when no one protected her from the man or men who sought to have their way with her. I pull back so that she may see the sincerity in my eyes as I make her this vow.

"Ariana, I can't promise you much, but what I can promise you is that no one will ever hurt you again. For as long as I live, I will protect you. I just...hope you can forgive the actions I must take to do so."

"Forgive?" Confusion washes over her. "Alister, there is nothing to forgive." Ariana takes a deep breath, tugging my jacket tighter around her. When she returns her gaze to me, I find her strength and determination has returned to her. "You saved me, in a way that, years ago, I could only dream of. You may think that isn't much, but believe me when I tell you it's everything."

Ariana's words uncoil the deepest parts of me, flooding my veins with relief. And yet, she's wrong. What I'm offering her isn't *everything*. It's only a fraction of what my heart wants to give her. But I don't argue with her. I allow her to feel what she needs to get through this moment. Though, as the sound of footsteps echoes down the stairwell, I find our moment of horror continues.

"That's a hefty promise, Mr. Amato. One I'm afraid will be short-lived." As Josephine Cullen, flanked by two guards, comes into view above us, I reach for my gun. "Uh-uh," she says, waving a warning finger at me. "After the mess you've made, I plan to take my time with you. If my men are forced to shoot you, it'll ruin my perfect canvas."

"Josephine," I say, standing with my arms raised in surrender. After what Avery and his men tried to do to Ariana, it goes against my better judgment to try talking rather than fighting. But, from what I hear, Josephine is a fair leader, one I pray believes my killings of her men are justified once she learns of their intentions. "I can explain."

"Explain?" She laughs, stopping just a few steps above us. "How can you explain coming into my city and killing my men? I thought you were smarter than this, Alister. You know, if the circumstances were different, I'd be inclined to pardon you given the tragic news of your sister's death. But..." She shakes her head, directing her gaze over the railing to take in my handiwork. "Your actions today have forced my hand."

"Please. They tried to rape my...Ariana." Unsure of what to call her, I simply use her name.

Ariana stands and turns to face Josephine.

"It's true," she says. "If nothing more, my appearance is proof of their intentions."

As Josephine examines Ariana, something about her demeanor changes. She takes a step closer, prompting me to move in front of Ariana.

"Relax, Alister," Josephine says. "I have no plans to make your girl pay for your sins. Though, there is something about her that is eerily familiar." At that, my brows crinkle, as do Josephine's as she reaches out to run her fingers through Ariana's curls. Ariana looks between me and Josephine, clearly just as confused as I am. "What did you say your name was?"

"Ariana—Ariana Valentine," she tells her. Josephine's eyes widen as if she's seen a ghost. She removes her hand from Ariana, letting it fall to her side.

"Valentine," she mumbles, more so to herself than us. "That's, um...very close to Valentina." She returns her gaze to Ariana. No. How could it be? "You look just like her."

"Wait. You...you knew my mom?"

Josephine nods. "And you. You were born here, Ariana, in this very house."

"How is this possible?" I ask, though Josephine's eyes don't leave Ariana.

"Come," she says. "We have much to discuss." At that, she turns her back on us both, though her henchmen make it clear they have no intention of letting me follow.

"I'm not going anywhere without Alister," Ariana shouts. "Either pardon him or you'll have to kill us both." Ariana's waited her entire life for the answers Josephine is willing to give. Would she really walk away from the truth for me?

"Very well."

21

"Stay close. I don't trust her," Alister says, pulling me back to his side. Too dazed to trust my own judgment, I happily sink back beside him as we, changed out of our formal wear and into Josephine's casual offerings, follow behind her through her luxurious Irish-inspired townhouse. My heart beats quicker than it should as sweat dampens my palms. As Josephine Cullen, the head of the Irish mob, prepares to tell me of her relationship with my late mother, I feel I understand what Alister must've felt coming face-to-face with Gallagher and the brotherhood. The anticipation is killing me, and yet, the confusion pulsing through my head is just as painful.

I've known all along that the deeper I dig into my mother's past, the more complicated my view of her may become. She wouldn't have been murdered by the head of a criminal organization without cause. If my mother knew Josephine Cullen, then she was likely working for the Irish mob against the Amatos, which is more than enough reason for Alister's father to order the hit against her. I can't say I blame her for wanting to destroy the Amatos' drug trafficking business, but, aligning herself with the Cullens isn't exactly innocent. It makes me wonder how deep her roots in organized crime went, and how much of what she endured, what I witnessed as a child, was her choice.

Josephine leads us into a formal tearoom, and I look up at Alister. His eyes focus sharply on Josephine's back. Yet, feeling the weight of my gaze, he slides his fingers through mine, giving my hand a squeeze. He lets me know he's here with me and not in the deepest, darkness parts of his mind that seemed to consume him while facing Gallagher. My blood still races at the thought of what could've happened if Alister hadn't fought them off, but that isn't the only memory that has me so wired I feel as if I may faint.

Whatever you think you're going to do to me, it's already been done.

At that, I lower my eyes to the floor, gripping on to Alister's arm with my free hand to help steady me. It's not that my encounter with Gallagher and his men dug up the memories of my tragic past, as if they are so easily buried. The trauma I suffered as a seventeen-year-old girl at the hands of my foster father is always with me. It's a piece of my story, just like my mother's murder, that haunts me and yet has also made me who I am. What's overwhelming isn't the truth I've spent the past eleven years learning to live with. What scares me is that now Alister knows. He knows another one of my secrets, something no one else does. It makes me feel connected to him in a way I'm sure will only cause me pain. And yet, as he holds my hand, as he protects me against men who seek to harm me, as he stands by me in the face of news that may change everything for me, severing the connection I feel with him is the last thing I want to do.

"Please, have a seat," Josephine says. Alister and I move toward the small wooden table centered in the room with black walls and large stained-glass windows overlooking some part of Boston, assuming we're still in Boston. Alister lets go of my hand

and pulls out my chair for me. I take my seat first. Alister second. Josephine sits last so that she is directly across from me. She then proceeds to fix herself a cup of tea using the delicate tea set separating us and her. "For you," she says, reaching out to hand me the cup. It's filled with black tea made creamy with milk and sugar. "I made it the way your mother used to like."

At her words, my mouth falls open. All these years, I've only ever had a few memories of my mother to cling to. Most of them aren't ones I like to remember. Perhaps that's one of the reasons why I've worked so hard to learn the truth of not only why my mother was killed, but who she was. I want to know her. I want to know what music she liked, what her favorite flower was, where she grew up, did she ever fall in love? I want to know everything. And yet, as Josephine sits across from me, more aware of my own mother than I am, the sight of the teacup stings. It's easy to fight for a ghost, especially one of a person you never really knew. You get to pretend they were perfect. You get to imagine the life the two of you could've had had things been different. The truth will shatter those illusions.

What if what Josephine has to say isn't what I want to hear? What if my mother wasn't a good person? What if she was no better than Alister's father or Alister himself? And yet, hasn't he shown me there is more to him than his blood and birthright? There is light in him just as much as there is darkness. If I can accept him, then I can accept my mom, even if she isn't the mother I've wanted to believe her to be.

I reach out and take the teacup from Josephine, quickly setting it down in front of me before my shaky hands get the best of me. Josephine lowers her eyes, as if wondering how to begin. "Leave us," she says to no one in particular. Though, quickly and quietly, her guards do as she says, closing the door to the tearoom behind them. She is as formidable as she is beautiful. Long fiery red locks surround her face, the perfect complement to her icy blue eyes. There are few wrinkles on her face, though there is an air of wisdom about her that suggests she's older than me and Alister. If she knew my mother, perhaps they were about the same age. The thought makes me look at her closer as I imagine how eighteen years would've changed my mother, at least, the memory of her I have.

"I'm not sure where to begin," Josephine says, redirecting her attention to making her own cup of tea. "I suppose I should start with an apology. I'm not sure what led to your encounter with Avery," she says, giving Alister a quick glance before turning back to me. "But nothing warrants the treatment you nearly received at his hand. My men are loyal to a fault. As a woman leading an organization such as this, I face more than my fair share of threats. Avery had the best of intentions in sending a message, but, admittedly, he went about it the wrong way. I would never condone such an assault. For his actions, I apologize, and I thank you, Alister, for protecting Ariana."

"You speak as if you know me," I say, surprised by my interruption yet unrelenting.

"I did, a very long time ago," Josephine says. She sips her tea as if it will give her strength. I do the same, bracing myself for what may come next. "When your mother, Valentina, was sixteen, she was sent by her family to stay here. She was pregnant." Josephine nods, her eyes glazing over as if she's remembering back. Oh, what I would give to share her memories, to see them for myself. "Teenage pregnancy is a taboo enough issue, especially when you come from a Catholic family. But, your mother's family, who they were and the plans they had for Valentina, only made things more complicated."

"What do you mean?" My brows crinkle as Alister wraps his arm around the back of my chair. I look between him and Josephine as she turns to me, confusion contorting her features.

"She doesn't know? If she's with you, then she must know," Josephine says.

"*Know what?*"

Alister gives the slightest shake of his head, prompting Josephine to take a deep breath. She turns back to me. "Ariana, your mother was part of a powerful family in New Orleans, a family like mine, like Alister's. I never knew her last name, but... she was Mafia, born and bred."

"*What?* No." I shake my head.

"It's why she was sent here, so that she could have her baby, have you, in secret before returning to New Orleans to live out her responsibility to her family."

"Responsibility?"

Josephine shakes her head. "I don't think she knew what her family had in store for her. All she was told was that '*her father had other plans for her.*' We were both only kids at the time. We didn't know much about the business or even the customs of our organizations. Knowing now of the less than pleasant history between the Irish and the Italians, I know that Valentina's family must've had some sort of secret alliance with mine. Or else my father never would've taken your mother in."

"Not to mention, this would be the last place anyone from New Orleans would look for her," Alister says. "The peace treaty between our families was only recently signed. All those years ago, the Amatos and the Cullens would've been the greatest of enemies even if not at war."

"*Wait. Wait.* Just...slow down," I say as frustration coils inside me. I look between Alister and Josephine once more as they both sit in silence, allowing me a moment to put the pieces together.

The idea of my mother being part of the Mafia baffles me, and yet it makes perfect sense. I always wondered how an innocent woman could get so caught up in the world of organized crime it would warrant a hit by the head of one of the most powerful bosses in the country. But if her family had some sort of secret plan for her and an alliance with a known enemy of the Amatos, then it would explain everything. My mother's father, *my* grandfather, was working to overthrow the Amatos from the inside. Perhaps he planned to use my mother to form some sort of an alliance with another crime family or even a criminal organization outside the Mafia. I know it's archaic, even twenty years ago it would've been, but in the world of the Mafia, arranged marriages in exchange for alliances are common so long as the girl is a virgin. That's why my mother's family wanted to keep her pregnancy, keep me, a secret.

"Gallagher said that Joseph Cullen had it out for the Amatos for nearly twenty years," I say, turning to Alister as realization finally dawns on me. "It's possible that my mother's family, then and now, are the ones who've been coming after yours this entire time."

Alister looks at with me with sad eyes and a tight jaw as the irony settles between us. I came to him because I believed his father killed my mother, or at least ordered the hit. I believed him to be the only person who could help me learn the truth. And yet, the truth is, my mother's family, *my family*, may be responsible for the deaths of Alister's mother and sister *and* responsible for the recent attacks against Sophia. I can only imagine Alister's father fought to the learn the truth behind his wife's murder just as fiercely as Alister has fought to bring Cara's killers to their knees. And yet, despite their efforts, it is I who has brought Alister face-to-face with the truth, just as he has me to mine.

I reach out to him, placing my hand on his cheek as if I may relieve some of the tension in his features. "I'm sorry," I whisper. He shakes his head and, interwining his fingers with mine, moves my hand to his knee.

"You didn't blame me for the sins of my family. I won't blame you for the sins of yours."

I offer him a sad smile, thankful for his mercy. And yet, it does nothing to quench the guilt inside me. To think that my blood could cause such pain, could be so greedy and power hungry, disgusts me. I've wanted for so long to know my mother, to know where I come from, where she came from. But now? I'm starting to think Alister was right to turn me away. This truth isn't one I want to believe. And yet, without it, I'd still have so many questions. Even still, I do.

"Tell me more," I say, returning my attention to Josephine.

She nods and sips her tea. I suppose now she understands why we came to Boston, why Alister needed to meet with Avery Gallagher face-to-face. I'm sure she and Alister will need to discuss the extent of the attacks made against Sophia in private. But, for now, I need to know more about my mom, like who my dad was and how my mom ended up back in New Orleans with me if she was sent here to have me in secret.

"Valentina was furious with her family when she arrived. She and your father were in love. He wanted to marry her, even though he was only a few years older. Still a kid, just like us. But your mother's family didn't want her to marry Sandro."

"Sandro? Is that my father's name?" The name feels both foreign and familiar, like a stranger who has suddenly become so embedded in my soul, it feels like he's always been there, just waiting for me to find him.

"It was what Valentina called him. Could be his name or a nickname. What was obvious was how much she loved him. She wanted to have you. She wanted to marry him. She wanted the three of you to be a family. And she, desperately, held out hope that you would be. She believed Sandro would stop at nothing to find her. She said he was from a family like hers. He had the money and resources to bring her home to him. And yet, months went by. Her belly grew. Each day Sandro didn't come, her hope waned. By the time you were born, she'd given up on him. Her hope was quickly replaced with fear and determination. She knew that her father would come to take her back to New Orleans after you were born, forcing her to give you up for adoption. Despite her heartbreak and feelings of betrayal by Sandro, she loved you, more than anything. She didn't want to give her father a chance to take you away from her, so she tried to run."

"From here?"

Josephine nods. "You were only days old. She was in no condition to leave the warmth of this home or the care of the nurses my father provided her. And yet, she packed a bag in the middle of the night with the intention to flee. She didn't even tell me of her plans. That is, until the next day, when I woke and found her still here. She was crying. It was the first time in her near nine-month stay with us that she realized she was our prisoner and not our guest. She lived with that knowledge for a year, repeatedly trying to escape but always failing. Finally, just after your first birthday, someone from Valentina's family came for her."

"You don't know who?" I ask.

"No. I was at school when they came for your mother. When I got back, all that was left was a note. She thanked me for being her friend during the hardest time of her life. She said she was returning to New Orleans with her uncle. She said she knew this day would come. She was sad to leave but her uncle agreed to let her keep you. She said it would be better than living as a prisoner."

Tears fill my eyes as I imagine my mother, at only sixteen, being turned away by her own family, forced to live and give birth in a stranger's home, and, even more so, trying desperately to flee into the cold New England night—all for me and because of me.

"But she was a prisoner," I say then, biting my lip to keep it from quivering.

"What?"

My eyes flash to Josephine. I want so badly to break, but I can't. Not when there's still so much I don't know. So much she can tell me.

"I know I don't have all the answers. Hell, I wouldn't be here if I did. But my memories tell me my mother wasn't welcomed back into the fold with open arms. I grew up in a dump, Josephine, a dump I was hardly ever allowed to leave. I didn't go to school. I didn't have friends. And my mother wasn't any better off than I. She didn't even shop for our own groceries, not that she had the money to. A man would bring them and place them on the counter. He would then seek payment by taking my mother into the bedroom we shared and doing godawful things to her. I didn't know back then what went on behind that closed door, but I'm old enough now to understand—the sounds, the bruises on her body, the bulges between his and the other men's legs. She was more a prisoner there than she ever was here. For ten years, she lived as such. Well, I guess nine, since my first year of life was spent here."

"What are you saying?" Josephine asks. Her eyes widen and she leans forward, gripping the edge of the table.

"My mother was murdered when I was ten years old. No doubt it had something to do with her father's secret plan for her, perhaps even his secret alliance with your family. She died for him!" I yell, slamming my palms against the table as I stand. So much for not breaking. "But he was nowhere to be found when she needed him the most because he is the one who banished her to Hell along with the uncle who retrieved her from here, luring her home under, no doubt, false pretenses. Her family wasn't there for her because they didn't care about her, about me. They used her as a whore for their personal gain. If she hadn't hid me when they came to kill her, they probably would've done the same to me. And all for what? More money? More power? More influence? It's all useless, just like you!"

"Ariana," Alister says softly, reaching out to console me.

"You could've helped her. All those times she tried to run, you could've helped her," I say, my anger giving way to more sadness and more tears. As I sit, I rest my head against the table and cry into the wood, and Alister rubs his hand up and down my back.

"I did. I did try, Ariana," Josephine says softly. "Even when I hadn't heard from your mother in nine years, I didn't hesitate when she reached out to me, asking me to help her leave New Orleans for good."

"What? What are you talking about?" I lift my head to face her, though I can barely see her through the tears. I wipe them from my eyes as Josephine stands and walks to the buffet server pressed against the wall. Atop it she finds a wooden box engraved with a depiction of red roses and returns to us, holding it. She gives the box to me, and I'm surprised by its weight. "What is this?"

"It's everything I have left of your mother. She was a dear, dear friend, Ariana. I loved her. And I did do everything I could to help her. Am I useless? No. Did I fail Valentina? It seems so." At that, my brows crinkle. Josephine nods toward the box, prompting me to open it. Inside I find a gun, the source of the unexpected weight. Yet, my attention quickly shifts from it to the passports, money, letters, pictures, even the little stuffed elephant toy my mother must've left behind in her rush to return to the city that did nothing but abuse her.

"Most of what you'll find is from your mother's time here. There are pictures of her when she was pregnant with you and of you after you were born. It was the early ages of modern technology, and I'm pretty sure my father tracked all my online activity, so all that was safe to use was an old Polaroid camera I found in our basement. Valentina wanted to have the photos to share with Sandro when he came for her."

"Why would she leave these?" I ask.

"She was afraid my father or our guards would find them if she kept them herself. She assumed my father was aware of her family's plan to make her give you up for adoption. She didn't want to take any chances that they may be destroyed, so she had me keep them safe for her. After she left, I found the elephant toy underneath her bed. I kept it to remind me of you." Her icy eyes fill with tears as she smiles. She really did care about my mom, didn't she?

"What I think you'll find most interesting are the passports and the letter just beneath them," she says, redirecting her attention from me to the box. My cheeks tighten with emotion as I move past the passports to get to the letter. I want so badly to look at them and the picture of my mother I know they must hold. But it's something I think I need to do in private, that way I don't have to hold back my emotions. Though as I open the letter and run my finger over my mother's handwriting for the very first time, my emotions overtake me just the same.

"She wrote to me nine years after she left Boston. I hadn't heard from her since. Every day I think of how lucky we were that I found her letter before my father. Though, as it turns out, he still managed to thwart your mother's plans." I press the letter to my chest, using it to channel my mother's spirit while Josephine continues. "Her letter was short and vague. All that was clear was that she needed my help. Knowing the world I belonged to, she tasked me with having passports made for the two of you. She also asked for money, an unregistered weapon, and, if possible, means to flee the country. She didn't say why she needed to leave or what the past nine years had been like for her. I had hoped to learn more when I made my way to New Orleans with the items. She'd set a date, time, and location in her letter. It was a spot in Audubon Park overlooking the water."

"I know it. On the rare occasion she took me out, we would go to the park and have a picnic by the water. Those moments are my favorite memories of her," I whisper, wiping the tears from my cheeks. Josephine does the same. "The day she was supposed to meet you, she didn't show, did she?" I ask. Josephine shakes her head, lowering her eyes to the table.

"Instead of Valentina, it was my father who met me. Seeing as I still have our only correspondence, I can only assume the people I tasked with getting me the passports and the weapon betrayed me. My father must've warned Valentina's father or uncle or both. He followed me to New Orleans just to let me know she wouldn't be coming, and I was never to speak to her again. From what you've said here today, I guess it would've been more appropriate for him to say I *will* never speak to her again, because he and her father had already killed her."

As the words fill the air between us, I can barely hear them. I'm too consumed by thoughts of my mother trying to flee, trying to protect me. If what Josephine says is true, my mother wasn't killed because she was a spy. She was killed trying to escape a life of abuse. She was killed trying to keep me from suffering the same fate. And yet, as I make sense of all that Josephine has said, her last words finally register, and I immediately turn to Alister. His furrowed brows and tiny wrinkles on his forehead tell me he shares in my confusion. He looks from me to Josephine.

"Wait. Are you saying you believe your and Valentina's fathers had Ariana's mother killed? According to Ariana, her mother was killed in the way of the Amatos. It was a hit, one ordered by my father. At least, we assume so," Alister says.

"No. I don't think that's right," Josephine admits. I turn to her. "Domenico wouldn't have ordered a hit against an informant without knowing who they worked for. Since we don't know who Valentina's family was, it's possible your father knew of their betrayal and dealt with them as well. But he didn't know of my father's involvement. And, if he knew of Valentina's, I doubt he would've had to dig deep to learn of my father's."

"And he wouldn't have just let Cullen go if he knew he'd been working to destroy him," Alister adds.

"So, are you saying Alister's father never knew of my mother's betrayal? You're saying she was killed by her own blood, the same people who forced her to spy on the Amatos?"

"We may never know the truth, Ariana," Josephine says. "But, if your mother's family was trying to use her against the Amatos, they wouldn't have been able to allow her to escape their control out of fear she could turn against them and reveal everything to Domenico. He would've forgiven your mother for her honesty and because, it seems, she had no control over the role she was forced to play. But he would've slaughtered them for their actions against him, including my father. Yet, he didn't. That makes me think he had no idea who was working against him. Even still, if what you remember about your mother's murder is true, that she was killed in the way of the Amatos, my guess is her family wanted to use your mother's death to frame the Amatos. They were determined to use her, in life and in death, to dismantle the New Orleans criminal underworld and rebuild it under their rule."

22

Alister

To say Ariana and I left Josephine's frazzled and with more questions than when we first arrived would be an understatement. Before leaving, Ariana walked slowly through the home her mother once lived in, taking in every nook and cranny as I held on to her, keeping her upright. I can only imagine she was looking for a connection to her mother. She was trying to find her essence among the antique furniture and family photos of people she'll never know. All she found was more pain and an even greater desire to punish the men responsible for the torment her mother suffered. Just as I feared, this quest for the truth is consuming her, pulling her deeper into the darkness that her mother fought in vain to escape. Part of me is thankful for Josephine. She's the only person alive who knows that part of Ariana's mother's story. And yet, as Ariana sat silent and numb on the way back to the hotel, holding on to the box of her mother's things with so much force her fingers appeared to cramp, I can't help but regret bringing her here.

    She had to have known learning the truth of her mother's past would change everything for her. Given the little I know about Ariana's life since her mother's death, I'm guessing she expected to welcome the change. But learning that her mother was not only a spy for the Mafia but was actually born into it and was betrayed by her own family is not the truth I imagine she'd hoped to discover. No. This...this truth will haunt Ariana perhaps more than the unknown. It will make her dig deeper as she tries to find the remnants of her family so she can bring them to justice for what they did to her mother. But that, like her presence in my life, will only put her in danger. And yet, knowing that her family is likely the enemy I've been searching for, I can't not look into them. I can't turn my back on this lead just to protect her. And there is no way she'll walk away now that we're so close to learning the truth.

I shake my head and sip my coffee as I wait for Ariana's and my order at the Thai place across the street from our hotel. After everything that's happened in the last twenty-four hours, I need a moment to process and so does Ariana. God. I can't even imagine what must be going through her head. From what nearly happened with Gallagher and his men to receiving answers to questions she's had for the better part of her life, it's too much. I glance at my watch and pray the food is ready quickly so I can get back to her. She shouldn't be alone right now, no matter how much she wants to be. But what will I say to her when I get back? What can I say?

Josephine said Ariana's mother belonged to a powerful Mafia family in New Orleans, which means they were, *are*, one of the three families under Amato rule. I know enough of my family history to know that the families of Gagliano, Vitale, and Parisi have made up the New Orleans branch of the Amato organization for generations. Even when the leaders of those families die and are replaced by a younger generation, the family itself remains. I remember looking at my father's records for the year Ariana said her mother was killed. There were very few hits that year and nothing that would suggest the slaughter of an entire family, which would be the punishment for Valentina's family's crimes if my father had known. That, accompanied with the reality that my capos are still from those long-time associated families, lets me know my father never caught the man or men plotting against us, the man or men responsible for my mother's death. There's still so much unknown, especially when it comes to Ariana's past, but what I am certain of is that the Gaglianos, Vitales, or Parisis have betrayed me. And I will die before I let them spill any more Amato blood.

Still, the assurance I feel knowing my suspects have dwindled to three individuals does nothing to calm the bit of nausea in my gut. Among my men is not only the one responsible for destroying my family and Ariana's, but also is Ariana's father, assuming he's still alive. Josephine said Sandro was a member of another crime family in New Orleans. It makes sense. Young Mafia women are heavily supervised by their parents and guarded at all times, making it difficult to form relationships with those outside the organization. But Sandro? No one with that name comes to mind. He'd be quite a bit older than me, but not as old as my dad was. As the boss, I know most of the prominent men in our organization by name, which makes me fear Ariana may yet have another deceased parent. Perhaps her mother's family had him killed when he impregnated their teenage daughter. Can't say I blame them. At least for that.

"Boss?" At the sound of Gio's voice, I pinch my eyes closed and let out a sigh of relief. He takes a seat across from me. Since Ariana and I used the private jet, it took him longer than usual to get here. Thankfully, things took a turn for the better with Josephine, albeit an unexpected turn.

"Coffee?" I ask, pushing the pot to his side of the table.

"That bad, huh?" Gio pours himself a cup, looking a bit

worse for wear. It's been a while since he's had to make an emergency exfiltration trip.

"You have no idea." I down the rest of my coffee and fill him in on Ariana's and my findings—Josephine's innocence, her late father's twenty-year plan in the making to destroy my family, what Avery almost did to Ariana, and how Josephine offered us both more information than we know what to do with.

"I'm assuming Avery is dead. The fact that you aren't leads me to believe Josephine is telling the truth about Ariana's mom. You killing Avery was like someone killing me. She wouldn't have let you get away with killing her right-hand man if she didn't care about Ariana nor if she was in on her late father's plans to destroy you."

I nod. "I thought the same thing. Though, I'm not so sure it's a good thing she's telling the truth. I mean, for us, yes. After my chat with Avery, I felt like we were back to square one. I couldn't trust him. But with what Josephine said, I'm certain that he was telling the truth. One of our capos is plotting against us of their own accord. They are the ones responsible for every horrific thing that's ever happened to my family," I say through gritted teeth. "Given what they had planned for Cara and Sophia, perhaps my dad's cancer was a silver lining. It took him out before they could. But Ariana?" I shake my head. "She's spent her life bringing men like me to justice only to now learn she's of the same world, the same darkness. How is she supposed to accept that? How am I?"

"What do you mean?" Gio asks.

"I don't want this life for her, Gio. An FBI agent digging around in Mafia business without backup and the support of the bureau is a dangerous thing. Not to mention, if by some chance, her father, Sandro, is still alive, she'll never be able to pull herself away from the Mafia. She's spent her entire life alone. She won't easily go back to that." Though as the words cross my lips, I realize they apply to more than just Ariana. I share in her loneliness, forever cursed to keep love at arm's length because of who I am and the enemies I've inherited. Ariana's and my time together is limited. I know that as well as she does. Yet, I still can't help but wish things could be different. The day she leaves my life will be a dark one as the loneliness I've become all too accustomed to returns."

"Well, if you're really that concerned, we find her father first. If he's alive, we change that. Then she'll have nothing left to cling to in the dark."

"No," I say, a bit too quickly. Ariana's too smart to be fooled. If I was responsible for her father's death, if I stole her opportunity to know him, even if he is a monster, she'd never forgive me. And as much as I know she needs to, for her own good, I don't want her to hate me. Her hatred would break me in ways I've never been broken before, an explanation I don't offer Gio. "But there is someone you can find for me," I say as flashes of Ariana crying and shaking in the basement of Josephine's come back to me. Gio leans forward. "I want you to look into Ariana's past. Someone hurt her. Perhaps more than one someone. I want to know who they are and where they are. I plan on paying them a visit."

"How chivalrous of you." At the sound of Josephine's voice, I turn and Gio stands, positioning himself between me and her. She looks him up and down. "And here I thought we were past shows of strength," she says, turning her attention back to me. "I've come alone, Alister. You and I need to speak in private."

Even with the coffee I just downed, I don't have enough energy left for another of Josephine's chats. Still, I don't plan on being in Boston for more than one night, and I need all the intel I can get before returning to New Orleans. Though, as I send Gio away and Josephine takes her seat across from me, something tells me she isn't here to discuss her father's former accomplice.

"What are you doing here, Josephine?" I ask, knowing the only reason she showed me any mercy before was because Ariana was with me.

"I remembered something else after you and Ariana left. Since I hope to never see your face again after this wretched night, I figured I shouldn't wait to tell you." Hmm. Guess I was wrong.

"I'm listening."

"After my father confronted me in New Orleans and told me to stay away from Valentina, he brought me back to the hotel and told me to wait for him until he returned. Me being me, I did the opposite. I followed him, thinking he'd lead me to Valentina. If I could find out where she was, then I could try again to help her. This time I'd do a better job at keeping my father in the dark. But he didn't go to her. Instead, he went to a strip club called the Temptress."

"You're kidding," I say.

"No. Why?" Josephine furrows her brows, unaware that the Temptress is one of my family's holdings, a legitimate one. Though, despite this, the debauchery that takes place between its walls makes it the perfect location for certain drug sales to go down. It's one of many of my family's legitimate holdings that have secret operations overseen by one of my capos.

"Just, continue."

Josephine, displeased with my abrasiveness, purses her lips. Still, she does as I ask. "I couldn't hear what was being said or even see the face of the man with whom my father met, but he did meet with someone. Given our discussion earlier, I'd bet millions he was meeting with someone about Valentina, perhaps the one who has betrayed you. I know it may not seem like much, but, in my experience, an old dog doesn't learn new tricks.

My guess is, if your traitor used the Temptress as a meeting ground before, he's still using it now."

I nod and bite the inside of my cheek to keep from cursing. I know her assumption isn't proof, but two coincidences aren't exactly coincidence at all. Walsh and his men told Sophia that they had eyes on me and would kill me if she didn't go with them. I thought they were bluffing, seeing as I was meeting with Gabriel Parisi at the time of the attack. And yet, Josephine's mention of the Temptress suggests I may be wrong about him, the capo I trusted the most, aside from Gio. Because it is his responsibility to oversee the drug operations out of the Temptress. His and his alone.

"Alister? Alister, are you okay?"

"No." My voice is so low the word is barely audible. "I think I know who's plotting against me. I think I know who is responsible for Valentina's death." And my mother's and Cara's.

Josephine nods, a sense of uncharacteristic nervousness contorting her features. "I suppose no matter how hard we try to avoid them, the wars of our fathers will always become ours. With that in mind, I will leave you with this advice."

As Josephine contemplates her next words, all her natural charisma leaves her along with her arrogance. I lean forward, not wanting to miss a word. Josephine may be my enemy on most days, but today, she is a fearless leader willing to offer me the guidance I desperately need.

Finally, she says, "When our world begins to crumble around us, we often think we need to burn it down and start over just to survive. But, like a wildfire, once we light the match, there is no controlling where the fire will burn or who it will claim. I know you feel betrayed."

"*Betrayed?*" I scoff. "No, my father was betrayed. I am...I am vengeful, filled with a lethal lust for the blood of my enemies I've never felt before."

"That's why I urge you, Alister, to maintain your control and handle this like a leader, like a king, not an angry little boy who takes his fist to his Legos."

"Is this meant to be your advice? Because it doesn't sound like anything more than a good scolding."

"What I'm saying is, what we do is a delicate balance, knowing when to protect with force and when to protect with sacrifice. Knowing when to negotiate and when to stand firm. The ones we love are the safest when we maintain the balance. If we tilt in either direction, we either become too soft and easily taken advantage of or too unpredictable, so much so our own people fear us. And then they turn on us. If you are to protect the people you love, Alister, if you want to end this vicious cycle of violence, then you need to replace the traitor with someone formerly aligned to them. Often, it's a family member of the same name, same blood. It gives the family their dignity back and helps soothe the pain of losing their loved one. Because no matter how treacherous the crimes of your enemies are, there will always be loved ones who mourn them, loved ones who can easily become enemies if you don't find a way to bring them to your side."

"I hear you. But how do I know I can trust them? How do I know they won't come after me the same as they did my father?"

"You don't," Josephine admits. "But you must be merciful as much as you are feared if you are to maintain the support of your people. It's the only way you'll be able to keep her safe."

I nod, savoring Josephine's advice, though the mention of *her* draws my attention and instantly makes my insides tighten. "You mean Sophia?" I ask.

"The fact that you have to ask for clarification is all the answer you need, Alister." At that, Josephine shakes her head more to herself than at me. "You care about Ariana," she says then, returning her gaze to me. As the words settle between us, I find myself sitting up straighter, as if ready to defend my feelings for the woman I know I shouldn't love but do. *Wait. Love?* My silent confession steals the words right off my tongue. The sad look on Josephine's face lets me know it's better this way.

"I don't know how the two of you found each other, but your feelings for her are obvious. Too obvious. Why else do you think Avery sought to use her against you?"

"This is the lecture I was expecting," I mumble.

"It's not a lecture, Alister. It's a warning. You need to stay away from her. Our world destroyed her mother, her family. It's already got its claws into Ariana, and yet, she can still escape it if you just let her go. You know it's the right thing." She nods. "And I know I have no claim over her or right to even say these things to you. But I also know that this life, a life with you, is the last thing her mother would want for her. I've already failed Valentina once. To remain silent on this matter would be to fail her again."

"This is one of those times I'm meant to protect by sacrifice," I say. Her words aren't new to me. I've been telling myself all the same things. "It isn't so easy, Josephine. Not when walking away from her means sacrificing the part of me that is the most human, the most normal, the only part of me I actually like."

"I know your burden. But if it was easy, it wouldn't be a sacrifice. If it was easy, it wouldn't be real. Take pleasure in the fact that it is. Hold on to that pleasure even as you let her go."

23

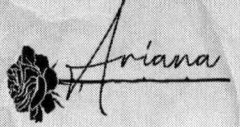

As my fingers graze the wooden box containing mementoes from my mother's past, my chest aches. I never got to bury my mother. The closest thing I have to a grave site is the place in Audubon Park where we'd have our picnics. This box changes that. It holds pieces of her and her story, *my story*, that allow me to feel close to her even though she's never been further from me. And yet, I hesitate to open it, to look at the pictures of her when she was happy, when she was young and innocent, before her family stole her light, because I know what's inside is all I'll ever have of her. Opening this box is like saying hello and goodbye all at once. It is her urn and this, this is finally the closure I've longed for ever since that fateful day that never made sense.

Repositioning myself on the bed, I set the box in front of me and brush my damp locks behind my ears. Slowly, I open it and remove the pistol, placing it on the bedside table. The night I met Alister, I asked him in a rhetorical fit why my mother didn't run. Why she didn't, at a minimum, have a means to protect herself. Turns out she sought just that—a better life for her and her daughter and a means of attaining it. I shake my head as fresh tears fall. Josephine should be glad her father is dead, because if he wasn't, he wouldn't live another night.

As I rummage through the box, I pull each item out slowly, saving the pictures for last. There isn't much—the elephant toy, an old sweatshirt, and a small journal. After all those years, the sweatshirt smells like wood, but I inhale its scent anyway, knowing that once it smelled liked her. The elephant toy rattles as I lay it next to me atop the fluffy white comforter. I can't help but smile at the sound. I pull the journal into my lap, and I lean back against the wooden bed frame and make sure my face is dry of tears before opening it. I wouldn't want any to fall and smudge my mother's handwriting. Though, as I read the first entry, I realize not crying isn't an option.

August 2, 1992—*I'm scared. I did something, something bad, and now I'm being punished. All my life, my parents have done everything to protect me, so much so, I've hated them for it. But now I see why. I'm... I'm pregnant. And I don't know what will happen next. Will my parents disown me? Will Sandro still love me? And what about my baby? What kind of life will he or she have? Will I even be allowed to be a part of it? God—please, help me. I know I messed up, but please. I need you.*

August 22, 1992—*I told Sandro. I couldn't keep it inside any longer. He said he loves me, and he wants to do right by me. I've never been more relieved. I love him so much and I always thought we would get married, just not so soon. But, if Sandro is willing to marry me and provide for me and the baby, then my parents should have no reason to force me to give it up. But I can't be sure until I tell them. And so, my relief is quickly replaced with nauseating fear. Sandro said we should tell them together. He doesn't want me to go through any of this alone. But I know my father. This will infuriate him and break my mother's heart. Our family will be ruined. No. I can't let Sandro anywhere near my parents. My father may hate me once he learns the truth, but he won't kill me. I can't say the same for Sandro.*

November 22, 1992—It's been too painful to write. Even now, tears drench my cheeks and my hand shakes. I thought I was protecting Sandro by telling my parents of my pregnancy alone. And maybe I did. But I'll never know because my parents sent me away. It's been months now and no one has come for me, not even Sandro. I'm worried he's dead. But, perhaps, more so, I'm worried he doesn't love me anymore. Does he think I chose to leave him? Does he know the truth—that my parents sent me away? Does he even care? My belly has started to swell, though not much. I'm going to have Josephine, the daughter of the man who's keeping me hidden, take pictures. I want to show them to Sandro when we're finally reunited. At least, that's what I tell myself. Believing he's still out there and he still loves me is the only way I'll make it through this. And I have to make it through this, not just for me, but for my daughter. My daughter. MY daughter. It doesn't feel real to say or think, but I'm going to be a mom. How do I even do that?

My mother's fear, insecurities, and, ultimately, sadness echoes through every entry the further into her pregnancy she gets. I can remember being a teenager. It wasn't easy. But it was nothing compared to what she went through—getting pregnant, fearing being abandoned by her family and her boyfriend, feeling insecure about how to be a mom when she herself was nothing but a child, and then everything that happened after I was born. As I flip through the journal, the entries become shorter and less frequent until they just stop. My mom doesn't reveal anything about the man who came to take her back to New Orleans. And since the journal was left behind, she must have left Boston in a hurry. Perhaps she didn't want to leave at all. Perhaps her uncle forced her to write Josephine that note so that she wouldn't come looking for her. As questions rumble through my head like the hunger tearing at my insides, I move the box to the side and close my eyes.

I thought this would be my closure. In a way, it is. I now know parts of my mother's story I never could've imagined, including how she ended up at the mercy of the Mafia and that she was betrayed by her own blood rather than slaughtered by Alister's father. And yet, with all this information comes new questions. What would make my mom's family so desperate to overthrow the Amatos they'd sacrifice their own daughter? Why didn't my mother's father come to get her instead of her uncle? Why did it take a year for him to show up and why did he allow my mother to keep me if the entire reason she was sent away was to have me in secret? Perhaps he just wanted leverage over her. Maybe he threatened to take me away from her if she didn't do what he said. The sick bastard. And yet, my nameless uncle isn't the only man I'm infuriated by.

I've never thought much about my father. Before my mother died, I don't remember it occurring to me that I didn't have one because I never saw other kids with their dads. Being with my mom was the only normal I knew. But as I got older, I began to realize any man who would abandon his child in the way I was abandoned, along with my mother, wasn't worth knowing. For all I knew, my father was one of the men who visited my mother. If you can even call it *visiting*. But now I know the truth. My father was rich, powerful, dangerous, and connected enough to find my mother if he wanted to, but he didn't. I suppose Alister did say no one would look for my mother in Boston. It was enemy territory. Somehow, I don't think it would've stopped Alister. He would never stop searching until he found his lost loved one, as is evident in his relentless search for Cara.

I allow my anger to ease the sickening sadness creeping through my veins, or at least I try to. I tell myself I'm angry at my father because it's easier to believe than the alternative. After everything my mother's family did to take the Amato throne, it's possible they killed my father before I was even born. At that, my lip quivers and fresh tears fall just as the door to the hotel room swings open. I quickly wipe my cheeks as Alister arrives, worry etched across his face as he holds a brown paper bag filled with warm deliciousness. But my efforts do nothing to fool him or ease the heart-wrenching sorrow twisting my insides.

Alister enters the room slowly and quietly. His golden-brown eyes melt into mine, but there are no words spoken between us. I look away from him then as memories of what nearly happened with Gallagher work their way to the front of my mind. It feels so long ago, though it wasn't. In more ways than one, this day has stripped me bare. And Alister has witnessed every moment. All day, I've fought through the awkwardness that last night left between us and now I've more to battle. Though, as Alister sets my food on the bedside table and pulls up a chair next to me, I'm not sure how much fight I have left.

"You don't have to do that, you know?" Alister says as I reach for a plastic fork.

"Do what?"

"Hide from me." His words draw a sharp breath from my lungs, prompting me to abandon my fork and food and close my eyes as if it's possible to disappear. As I do, Alister remains silent, as if he knows that's exactly what I need rather than comforting words or even a consoling touch. He's right. Silence is best, because if I were to tell him what this day has done to me, I wouldn't know where to begin. Though, as I escape into my mind, it's not to hide from him. It's because I *can't* hide from him. When Alister looks at me, he sees straight through me. I've allowed him to break down all my walls and now I feel naked in his presence. And I'm not sure how I feel about it.

"Do you remember when I asked you how your life would be

different if you weren't beholden to the Mafia?" I ask, opening my eyes.

"Yeah," Alister whispers.

"Well, it got me thinking how my life would be different if my mom was still here." Alister leans forward, listening intently as I stare blankly at the wall ahead.

"At Josephine's, I said that my mom received frequent male visitors with less than honorable intentions. Somewhere along the way, I think their interest started to shift from her to me. The night my mother was killed, the man who dealt the final blow asked her where I was. She told him that I was already gone, and because of his own efforts to keep me hidden, he would never find me. She said, *'Good luck finding a ghost.'* I've lived like a ghost all my life, but it wasn't until that night that I truly felt like one—invisible and detached."

I turn to Alister and, in his eyes, find a warmth that wraps around me so tightly it feels as if his gaze alone can glue the broken parts of me back together. It's then that I say, "With you, it's different. I'm so used to hiding from everyone, keeping people at arm's length. But I can't hide from you, Alister. In a way, I don't want to. But that doesn't mean that I'm not scared for you to know me, to know what happened to me, to know my truth."

"You can tell me anything," he says as he reaches for my hand, giving it a gentle squeeze.

"I know," I whisper. As Alister's palm covers mine, I savor his touch, though only for a moment before I pull my hand from his. "It's just...I've never told anyone before."

"What you dream about," Alister mumbles as he sits up straight, drawing his hands back into his lap, and my chest tightens. "The night of the Halloween party, I only pretended to be asleep."

My mouth goes dry when Alister admits the truth. Memories

of that night return to me. I shot up in bed covered in sweat, my cheeks damp with tears. The only solace I found was in Alister's sleep, but he heard everything. *Everything.* "You've known this entire time."

"I suspected and I prayed I was wrong."

I lean forward and rest my face against my knees, shielding myself from Alister's view. Like I said, I'm naked in front of him. There are no secrets between us, and it is the most comforting and terrifying thing I've ever experienced, well, almost.

"You weren't wrong," I finally admit.

I sit up straight and move to sit in front of him with my legs crossed. Once more, Alister reaches out and takes my hand in his. This time I don't pull away from him. What I'm about to say might be my darkest secret of all, even darker than my memories of the night my mother was killed. I need his strength to say the words, to admit the truth forever etched into the essence of my soul. And I need him to be my foothold so that I'm not consumed by the memories of the vile acts of evil men.

"Before I joined the bureau, I made sure my records were sealed. The last thing I've ever wanted was anyone's pity. I guess after so many years of not getting it, I became numb to it. Numb to everyone's ignorance and indifference. Numb to my own horrific past. At least, in my waking hours. I don't have as much control over what haunts me behind closed eyes." As my heartbeat quickens, pounding against my flesh as if my most vital organ wishes to rip itself from me, I take a deep breath and ignore the way my body begins to shake.

"After my mom died, I was placed in foster care. During my time in the system, there were a few different homes all with their own challenges. There were bullies at school and at home. I was behind intellectually, and with so much turmoil and uncertainty in my past, it made it hard to connect with the other kids.

I was an easy target. And their attacks left me with scars, emotionally *and* physically."

Alister's hand tightens around mine. I lift my eyes to meet his and find, unlike the warmth they once offered me, they are now cold and dark as death. I bite my lip and continue.

"After a while, I was finally placed in a decent home. There were no other kids, so no bullies. I was there for a couple of years in high school before I aged out of the system. Weirdly, that was the closest I ever felt to being normal, to having a real family. My *parents* were older and a little more well-to-do than my others. I was able to attend a great school with a guidance counselor who helped me apply for scholarships to colleges. I was able to work and save up before turning eighteen. And my *parents* had never had children of their own, so they had a lot of love to give. At least, they did. But, um…everything changed when my foster mom died."

Alister closes his eyes then. The muscles in his face tighten as if he knows what I will say next. As the words rest on my tongue, they taste bitter. Though the shaking has stopped, my body feels heavy, so heavy I feel as if I may faint. I take several deep breaths to combat my light-headedness.

"Hey," Alister whispers. "I've got you. I know that no one else ever has, but I do."

Alister lowers his eyes as if he's just made a promise he knows he can't keep. I look away from him then as I'm reminded of last night and the way his demeanor changed the moment he realized we were getting too close. He let me in, and I saw the real him—the him that wants a simple life filled with love, the him that wants me. This is that moment for me, the moment where I choose to let him in completely or turn him away for good. I know I should do as he did. The painful expression in his eyes and the tightness of his cheeks makes it clearer than ever—whatever we feel for one another will never be enough to defeat our differences, our pasts. What I feel for Alister is the closest thing I've ever felt to love or being in love, and yet I still hesitate to tell him the truth—the complete truth.

I lower my eyes then and find our hands still clasped tightly together. I move my thumb against his hand, caressing him as he did me. I lift my eyes to meet his once more, and the darkness has left him. What remains is a softness, a gentleness that welcomes me in and makes me feel safe. In his eyes, I find my resolve to finally open the door to my past and to my heart.

"My foster mother passed only a few weeks before my eighteenth birthday. Her death filled my foster father with an unrelenting bitterness and darkness. In his loneliness and despair...he raped me." I press my lips firmly together to keep them from quivering as I finally say the words I've only ever said once before—the day I reported him to the police and had him arrested. After that day, I swore to never speak the words again. Who would I tell anyway? I've never had anyone close enough to care. Well, there is Ray. But, for some reason, I just never felt like opening up to him like I do Alister. Alister, whom I refuse to look at.

"After it happened, I stayed in abandoned buildings until my eighteenth birthday. I needed to be sure I wouldn't be placed in another home. After all, they'd never offered me any real safety. Once I turned eighteen, I reported him, and he's been in jail ever since. And I've been..." I hesitate and pinch my eyes closed as the weight of my admission finally hits me. "Haunted ever since."

As the words cross my lips, I open my eyes to seek solace in Alister's presence. Though, as I look at him, the events of that tragic night play within my mind on a loop. In my memories, his frame is more vivid than his face. He wears a dark button-down shirt with khaki pants. He enters my room and closes the door behind him. As he walks closer, I wrap my covers tightly around me, sensing something is wrong. That's when he brings his hand to his belt buckle and—

"All of this is to say, deep down, I know, whether my mother lived or died, I've always been destined to suffer at the hands of a monster. Her death saved me from one and fated me to another." I shake my head, my throat raw with emotion. "So, as I sit here and look at what's left of my mother, my *real* mother, and I think about everything I learned today, I can't help but feel disappointed and disgusted. Because there was never any hope for either of us."

24

Alister

Ariana pulls her hand from mine and wipes her falling tears as I do my best to restrain myself. All I want to do is pull her into my arms and never let her go. That, and rip her rapist to shreds with my bare hands. But, in this moment, I can't do either of those things. Not only am I over one thousand miles away from the man who is as good as dead, but I don't trust what my body would do if I were that close to Ariana. And, right now, the last thing she needs is more unwanted advances and shallow words. I mean everything I say. I meant it when I told her she doesn't have to hide from me and that I'm here for her. But for how long?

Josephine's words, or should I say *warning*, are seared onto my heart, inescapable and inevitable. Even Ariana said her mother's death freed her from one monster and fated her to another. Her presence in my life lets me know it fated her to more than one. I would never hurt Ariana in the way she's been hurt before. But those who seek the Amato throne will stop at nothing to claim it, as is evident by the life of secrecy and servitude Ariana's mother was forced to live as she spied against my family for hers.

Josephine is right. I can't allow Ariana to become a victim of the same world, the same darkness her mother strove to protect her from. Which means I can't hold her. I can't touch her. I can't swear to her that those who hurt her will suffer a greater pain, even though they will. Most of all, I can't tell her I love her, and I will protect her until my last breath, even though it's the truth. Because our love wasn't meant for the light of day, only the shadows. And, eventually, the sun will rise, chasing away the darkness that has haunted Ariana since birth, and with that rising sun will be the end of us. What a joyful and wretched day it will be. At that, I lower my head and console Ariana in the only way I can.

"Maybe there is hope." I lift my head to look at Ariana, and I find her staring back at me with parted lips and wide eyes. She holds her breath, as though unsure of what I will say next. "Josephine tracked me down while I was out getting food. She remembered something more she thought would be helpful to us."

"What did she say?" The words scrape through Ariana as the weight of my revelation settles onto my shoulders. I have three capos based in New Orleans, aside from Gio. One of them will lead us to Ariana's father, if he's still alive. Another is responsible for every horrible thing that's ever happened in both of our lives. Once we return to New Orleans, it won't be long until a truth twenty years in the making is revealed. And with that truth will be our goodbye.

"She said...she said she followed her father to a strip club in New Orleans after he thwarted her plan to help your mother. He met with someone, someone she believes was his partner in the city."

"The man responsible for my mother's death," Ariana whispers.

I nod. *And my mother's and sister's.*

"Did she know who?"

I shake my head as my emotions swirl inside me. All this time. All the lives lost. Could Gabriel Parisi really be responsible? He's older than me, but not by much, which means any vendetta he has against my family would've been inherited from his father. I'm not aware of any blood feuds between my family and his, but the same can be said for my other capos as well. Sometimes wars like this are bred of nothing but greed and a lust for power. But, even in the mind of a monster, is a throne really worth the abuse Valentina suffered? No. There has to be more to this story. And whether or not I believe Gabriel Parisi and his father before him are capable of such evil, he's the only lead we have and it's one I can't ignore. The more time that passes, the more likely it is that whoever is working against us will strike again. And this time, Sophia may not be their only target.

"She didn't know," I say then. "But I might. The club he visited is called the Temptress. To this day, it's still owned by my family and is a hub for both legal and illegal transactions. I have a man who oversees the latter, off the books, of course. We're going to pay him a visit."

"The Temptress," Ariana whispers. She lowers her eyes then as if she isn't surprised by the very news I found disturbingly shocking.

"Do you know it?"

"Months ago, when I realized your presumed connection to my mother's murder, I began investigating you, searching for evidence linking your family to mine. It was at the Temptress that I found a photo of my mother taped to the wall along with hundreds more, presumably of women who worked at the club. But...there weren't any records of anyone named Valentina having worked there."

"Why are you just now telling me this?"

"Because there was a part of me, no matter how badly I tried to ignore it, that thought I could be wrong. There was a part of me that wondered if the woman in the photo really was my mom or if I was just so desperate for something, anything, that I was clinging to a lead that was nothing more than a coincidence. And, on top of it all, I didn't want to offend you."

"Offend me? How could you offend me?" My brows crinkle as confusion washes over me.

"Because, if I was right, if my mother did work off the books at a strip club owned by your family, especially given what occurred at our home, it could only mean one thing."

It takes me a moment to follow Ariana's train of thought, but once I understand, I wish I didn't. "That she was being sold for sex by my father, which would make the man who raised me no better than the men who sold, bought, abused, and murdered my sister."

"Yeah, I, um…didn't think that would go over well," she says.

"You're right. It probably wouldn't have."

I sit up straight and clear my throat as I absorb this latest blow. This is too much to process. First Gabriel isn't who I thought he was and now my father? When will the secrets and betrayal end? My father knew I never wanted to be king because of how corrupt our outfit had become. Still, he assured me there was no other way. That if I didn't take the throne, it would be thrust upon Sophia, which would all but sentence her to death seeing as the men of our world would never accept her as their boss. So, I fell in line. I became the son he wanted me to be. And, after his death, I did everything I could to lead our people as he did. I defended his name against every slander. I swore up and down that my father couldn't have known what the brotherhood truly was, because he never would've sold to their organization if he knew the truth. I speak of my father as a businessman who was respectable and honorable. Have I been lying to myself? Have I been blind to his ways while hating myself for my own?

At that, I lean forward, resting my elbows on my knees and burying my face in my hands. I don't want to believe my father was a monster. And I know that Ariana's evidence, if you can even call it that, of illegal sex work happening in one of my family-owned businesses doesn't mean my father sanctioned the activity. Just like the man who killed Ariana's mother tried to frame my father, this could be another one of his ploys. Still, the split second I considered the alternative, that I truly didn't know my father as well as I thought I did, is enough to make me question everything. I do horrible things to maintain my power and, ultimately, the safety of my family. No doubt my father did equally horrible things, especially after he lost my mother. And yet, none of this compares to what Ariana discovered about her own family today.

I've always known of the darkness tainting my blood and everyone who shares it. But nothing could've prepared Ariana for what she learned today. Even still, I'm not sure she's realized the extent of our discovery. By birth and blood, she is a Mafia princess and likely the rightful heiress to one, if not two, fortunes. Whatever we discover in New Orleans will change everything for us both. And yet, it still won't change the thing that matters most.

"It's almost over, isn't it?" Ariana asks then. Once more, I sit up straight, taking in the beautiful raven-haired woman before me. As if reading my mind, she looks at me with lifeless eyes and drooping lips. We both know she isn't only referring to the investigation.

"Yeah, I think it is," I say. At that, I stand, leaving Ariana to her thoughts and pad Thai. That is, until she stops me.

"Alister," she says, her voice so soft and broken. I stop at the foot of the bed, but do not turn to face her because I'm afraid of what I may see if I do. Perhaps, more so, I'm afraid of what she'll see as my cheeks tighten and my eyes blur with budding tears.

"No one has ever known me the way you do. I've never let them. After living like a ghost for twenty-eight years, you make me feel seen for the first time."

She hesitates, allowing her words to invade my core and give life to the parts of me that burn for her. Only, as her words stoke the flames of love inside me, it isn't a warmth they provide. Rather, a scalding pain so intense, there is no mistaking that my heart is breaking, both for her and because I can't have her.

"I don't know how to give that up when this is all over."

As Ariana admits what I've feared ever since the night we met, a single tear drips down my cheek. That night I pushed her away because I was afraid of what this world would do to her and of where her search for the truth would lead her. Now, more than ever, my fears are cemented. She can't be an FBI agent *and* a Mafia princess. She can't remain safe *and* know her father, assuming he's still alive. And yet, as it stands, I'm her strongest foothold in this world of darkness. I'm the one she doesn't want to lose. I'm the one she's risked her life for her. I'm the one who's put her in harm's way. And, so, it is I who must break the bond between us, even if in doing so I break my own heart.

With resolve, I stand tall. "I don't know either, but you have to. *We* have to."

25

Alister

The flight back to New Orleans was quiet and not much has changed in the way of Ariana's and my communication since we arrived back in the Crescent City yesterday evening. She stayed at her place last night, which is good and somehow excruciating all at once. The halls of Laroux House are empty without her sarcasm and dark without the light only her soul can provide. Yet, I know it's for the best. If Gabriel Parisi proves to be the man we've both been searching for, this week may be my last with Ariana. And whatever is happening between us will finally end, for better and for worse.

Cassio loaned Gio and me a few of his men to accompany us to the Temptress, though I had him stay behind to protect Sophia in case things go sideways. Until I know the extent of Parisi's plots against me, assuming he is guilty, I can't trust my own soldiers. Who knows where their allegiance lies? Cassio's men are in an unmarked SUV in the alley behind the club, waiting for my order to infiltrate. Ariana will meet us back at Laroux House after Gio and I have collected Parisi.

The night sky, tainted with the spoils of sin, is a suffocating dark haze hovering over us and the ancient buildings that make up the French Quarter. As Gio and I make our way down Bourbon Street, the neon signs of surrounding businesses reflect in the fresh rainwater covering the street, turning the beaten-up concrete into a colorful rainbow one might find in a children's game. This street may be filled with players, but the games afoot are not for children nor the weak of heart. Drunken tourists and locals alike move past us, completely unaware of the thin line between their world and ours. A hypnotic blend of jazz and zydeco music pours out of the restaurants and bars, a perfect representation of the two worlds that exist here—the loud, obnoxious, and oblivious world of the innocent and the dark, melancholic, and tortured world of those who operate in the shadows.

Among the string of illuminated doorways, there is one that is lit by nothing more than the soft yellow glow of a French lantern. There is no sign advertising the debauchery that occurs just beyond the threshold. And yet, those who know, know. The Temptress finds its home in a three-story building that dates to the 1700s. On the top floor, New Orleans' sleaziest elite gather to enjoy their sinful pleasures while overlooking the throngs of partiers thrust upon our streets from a place of silent superiority. Shrouded by a weathered facade not many would dare to enter, the Temptress provides an illusion of anonymity wealthy men and women crave. But, among them, is not where we'll find Gabriel Parisi.

As Gio and I enter the club through the barely lit doorway, we are met with an even darker lobby. Instead of venturing up the wooden stairs to where our wealthiest patrons reside, we continue straight toward the door that leads to the main level club. The small, red neon sign hanging above the door is the only light within the small space. It casts a red glow upon Ariana's skin as she waits for us, dressed in her classic all-black ensemble of jeans, tank top, and leather jacket. My muscles tense with anxiety and my heartbeat quickens in my chest. She isn't supposed to be here.

"Took you long enough," she says, crossing her arms over her chest.

"What the Hell are you doing here?" I ask, my voice low.

"Waiting for you. Isn't it obvious?" Ariana cocks her brow as I shake my head at her quip.

"You can't be here." I take Ariana by the arm and drag her toward the exit.

"What the Hell is wrong with you? Let go of me!" Ariana struggles against my grasp, but my grip is unbreakable. "Alister, stop! You're hurting me!"

As Ariana cries out, my jaw tightens in frustration. Still, I do as she asks. Once free of my grip, she adjusts her jacket as I stare blankly ahead at the door separating us from the street. That's when I say, "If you think I'm hurting you, what do you think the men in there will do to you, if given the chance?" I turn to Ariana. Her features are mostly hidden by the darkness surrounding us. Yet, I still manage to register her defiance in the way she stands before me.

"I'm with you. I'm safe." If only it were that simple.

"You being with me is what puts you in danger, Ariana." I can't keep the frustration from my voice. "After everything I've told you about my mom, my sister, after what almost happened at Josephine's, how do you not get that? Why do you think I told you to meet us at the house? You can't be seen with me by those who wish to harm me! I care about you too much!" When I finally admit what I swore I'd never say, I turn away from her and punch the nearest wall. "*Fuck!*" I shake my hand, the skin on my knuckles split open. My rage is met with the sting of reality, in more ways than one.

"You see how easy it is for you to lose your temper? That's

why I'm here, Alister. Because if Gabriel admits to being the man responsible for your sister's death, I don't trust you not to kill him before I get the answers I need." Ariana quickly moves toward me and jabs her finger into my chest for emphasis. She has a point, but it still doesn't negate the consequences of her being here.

"Alright, you two, maybe we should lower our voices or else we'll blow the entire mission before we even make it through the door," Gio says. At that, I take a deep breath and do as he says.

"I lose my temper when I have a reason to. Boston was one thing, Ariana. This is another entirely. As an Amato holding and hub for drug sales, this place is crawling with mafiosi. Under normal circumstances, the Temptress would be one of the safest places in the French Quarter for me and those I care for. But, tonight, it's different. No one comes after a king without an army. Whoever is working against my family was smart enough to employ the help of the Irish mob, but that doesn't mean they don't have an army of their own—men who've pledged their loyalty to me now turned as spies. I can't trust any of them, especially not with you."

Now that I've finally shared my true feelings for Ariana, the ember inside me that's simmered ever since we first met explodes, and when it does, I'm relieved of the weight of my emotions and yet filled with a desperation all at once. I'm desperate both to protect her and to love her. Most of all, I'm desperate to be loved by her. Through the darkness between us, I try to discern her reaction. I know she cares for me. Maybe not in the same way I do her. But, in some way, she does. And yet, her self-control proves stronger than mine as she refuses to bend to my affection.

"I hear you. But you're the one who told me I'd have to learn how to give you up. Now it's time for you to take your own advice. If your care for me is what puts me at risk, then stop caring. If that's too difficult for you, I'll go in alone. No one has to know I'm with you."

"Like Hell!" As Ariana tries to move away from me, I block her path to the club entrance. She sighs in frustration and lifts her eyes to mine. Now, closer to the door, I can see her better. In her eyes, I see the fierce, stubborn, independent woman I love. Yet, I also see fatigue and impatience. She's tired. Tired of searching for the truth, of coming so close only to leave empty-handed. Maybe she's even tired of me. It takes everything out of me to be in her presence and not be with her. Perhaps she's plagued with the same emotions, at least a fraction of them.

I take a step back and stand tall, moving my eyes from her to anything but. I'll never not care for her, but she's right. I need to shove her from my mind long enough to collect Parisi so that we can both finally get the answers we need and end this, for better and for worse.

"Fine," I mumble. Gio takes a step toward us, ready to hear my commands. "I'll take the lead. Gio, you follow behind Ariana." He nods. "I want you within arm's reach at all times," I say, pinning Ariana with a look of stern warning. She nods. I do the same, still not at ease with my decision to let her accompany us. Though, it's not like I have much of a choice. "Are you ready?"

"I've been ready for eighteen years, Alister. The better question is, are you?" Ariana cocks her brow as she poses the question I know the answer to and yet can't admit. Of course I'm not ready. Gabriel Parisi is my friend, at least, I thought he was. If he has betrayed me, I won't just have to kill him, I'll have to erase his entire family—Ariana's family. Unlike when I went up against the brotherhood, this isn't an execution I'm looking forward to doling out. Though, as thoughts of Cara return to me, my hesitation subsides. I may not like what happens next. I may not be ready to face the man who took everything from me. But face him, I will. I've lost a mother to betrayal, a sister to greed. If I don't end this now, it will be my cowardliness and nothing more that destroys what's left of my heart.

"Let's go."

※

AS WE ENTER THE CLUB, it takes a moment for my eyes to adjust to the pink overhead lights that illuminate the otherwise red space. Red velvet chairs surround white tables adorned with poles, while floor-to-ceiling curtains of the same fabric hang along the back wall of the club, separating the VIP booths from the main floor. It's there that we will find Parisi. But, before we reach him, we've got other bullets to dodge. For our sake, let's just hope they remain figurative.

I glance over my shoulder to make sure Ariana and Gio are behind me and then proceed through the club, turning away the women who approach and avoiding eye contact with the scantily clad performers dancing atop the tables to the melodic notes of a haunting song. Though, theirs aren't the only eyes I feel on me. All around the perimeter of the room, men stand from their tables and watch as the three of us walk in silence. Likely Parisi's underlings, they know who I am and that I wouldn't be here if something wasn't about to go down.

As the overhead lights shift from pink to red and the black booths of the VIP lounge come into view, I move my hand from my side to my hip, readying myself to pull my gun from its holster, my eyes locking with Gabriel's. At the sight of him, my lips press into a flat line and rage bubbles in my blood. The bounds of sanity threaten to burst inside me with each step I take. As much as I want this to be over, I don't want it to be Gabriel. Though, as he sends the women in his booth away, his friendly expression leaving him, I fear my original suspicion was right. The music blaring through the surround-sound speakers intensifies, as if sensing what will happen next. It works with the adrenaline racing through my veins to drown out any hesitation, any fear, any anxiety left inside me. Ariana was right. She shouldn't trust me not to kill him.

"You're hereby relieved of your duties for the night," Gio says, stepping forward to address the two armed guards standing outside Gabriel's private booth. As my underboss, Gio oversees all of my capos, so he sees the soldiers more than I do. They recognize him and obey him. Though, not without first glancing at Gabriel and leaving us with a wary gaze. I maintain eye contact with the one on my right as he passes by me and Ariana, and I fight the urge to reach out to her and pull her closer to me. But as much as I want her by my side, claimed as my queen, I must remain indifferent for her own safety. Even if Gabriel turns out to be innocent, others who wish me ill may still be present tonight.

With Gabriel's armed guards dismissed, he stands and brings his palms together in front of him. He means to disarm me. By keeping his hands visible, he wants me to believe he isn't a threat. Despite our friendship, I am not so easily convinced. Gio takes a step inside the booth. He glances from side to side, checking for additional men or weapons that could be used against us. Finding none, he motions for me and Ariana to join him. I take a step back and allow Ariana to enter first, our eyes meeting long enough for me to register her fear. Her chest rises and falls more rapidly than normal. Her hands shake with nerves as her forehead glistens with sweat. Ariana and I may not have known each other that long, but in our time together, we've come face-to-face with many challenges. Not the least of which were three men who restrained and tried to assault her. And yet, through it all, I've never seen her this afraid. I'm not sure I've seen her afraid at all. As she turns away from me and sets her sights on Gabriel, I realize she isn't scared of facing him. She's scared of what she may do to him if he is proven to be whom we suspect.

I once asked Ariana to save me from myself. I never thought I may have to return the favor. But that look in her eyes lets me know I might. With Ariana safely away from prying eyes inside the booth, I do one last perimeter check for anyone or anything suspicious. I count at least ten men standing at the ready. The question is, do they await my command or Gabriel's or someone else's? Not wanting to wait around to find out, I step into the booth and tug the red velvet curtains closed behind me. As I turn to Gabriel, confusion contorts his features, and an uneasiness settles upon his shoulders. He moves his eyes from Gio to Ariana to me.

"Boss, is there something I can help you with?" At his words, Ariana's fists ball and she parts her lips as if readying to obliterate him. Seeing her close to unraveling forces me to suppress my own anger long enough for us to make it out of the club without drawing any more attention than we already have.

"Perhaps, Gabriel," I say, taking a step forward and reaching for Ariana's hand. She turns to me, surprise distracting her from her rage, at least, for a moment. "But you'll have to come with us. Is that a problem?"

"No, of course not." Gabriel takes a step forward, which I counter by stepping in front of Ariana.

"Not that way," I growl. Gio motions toward the door to the alley behind Gabriel. He looks between the three of us once more. If I'm reading him correctly, he knows he's in trouble, but I'm not sure he knows what for. Then again, if he is guilty, he's a master of manipulation, covering his tracks, and framing others to protect his own hide. He won't be easy to crack. But something tells me, if he is guilty, it won't be long until his traitorous forces come for us. And when that happens, I'd much rather be at Laroux House than here. Gabriel exits the club through the door and is immediately guided by Cassio's men to the unmarked SUV. Gio follows behind them and Ariana and I behind him.

"We're not riding with them, are we? I don't think I can stomach the hour drive without tearing him into him," Ariana says, her eyes focused on Gabriel's back.

"No," I say. At that, I let go of her hand to brush a strand of hair behind her ear, caressing her cheek ever so slightly. The simple movement draws her attention just as I hoped it would. "No, you're riding with me."

She nods. "How are you so calm? I was fine. I'm always fine, but when I saw him, I just…"

"Wanted to jump out of your skin and on top of him," I finish her sentence. "Yeah, I feel the same way. The thing is, we can't both give in to our emotions. If we do, we'll burn this place to the ground. And then where would we be?"

Ariana nods as she absorbs my words. She and I both know they apply to more than this moment as does her answer.

"Dead. We'd be dead."

I admitted that I care for her. I didn't use the word *love*. I didn't prove my affection for her in the ways I want to. But it's out there. Like a rose lying between us just waiting for her to pick it up, I'm waiting for her to admit her feelings same as I did. But, if she does that, our goodbye only becomes more painful, even though I would give anything to hear her say it, just once, that she cares for me. Until then, whatever she may feel for me is only a figment of my imagination—a dream I wish could be reality. But, as in this moment, so then. Our love would be the death of us just as much as it would give us life.

I nod and take a step back. "Exactly."

26

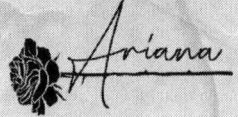

Being back at Laroux House makes my heart ache in a way I didn't expect. Though perhaps it isn't the place, so much as the purpose. Parisi left the Temptress with us willingly. That was two nights ago. Ever since then, Sophia, Cassio, and I have been doing a deep dive into him and his family's past while Alister and Gio interrogate him in the dungeon. Just the thought of what they must be doing to him makes me nauseous, even though on his first night with us, I begged Alister to let me have ten minutes alone with him. The slightest possibility that he may be the man responsible for my mother's death made me want to hurt him in a way I've never wanted to hurt anyone, well, with one exception. Thankfully, Alister refused my request. I say *thankfully* because the more I learn about Gabriel Parisi, the more I believe he's innocent.

In addition to developing state-of-the-art combat weaponry, Cassio also creates cyberintelligence weapons in the form of various codes and viruses. To be honest, I don't understand how he does it. But somehow, he's developed a back door that grants us access to most, if not all, pertinent sources of information.

That, plus Alister's access to the FBI database through none other than Supervisory Special Agent Bilieux—*what the actual Hell*—has given us everything we need to conduct the most thorough of thorough background checks on the presumed criminal mastermind.

We've checked Parisi's phone records, property records, and bank accounts. We even tapped into the security cameras at his home and throughout the city, tracking him to and from the Temptress. He hasn't spoken with anyone with connections to the Irish mob or even any of the other capos. He doesn't own or rent any properties that Alister doesn't already know about. We even searched for properties under possible aliases. Nothing. And his bank accounts don't reveal any suspicious expenses, like money used to keep Walsh's crew hidden in New Orleans for an entire year, or deposits, well, aside from the disguised drug money Alister vouches for.

I even took it a step further and searched his travel records. After Joseph Cullen died last year, it's possible the New Orleans traitor may have found another partner to help him take down Alister. But, on all fronts, Gabriel Parisi checks out. He's either that good at covering his tracks or he's innocent. And seeing as Alister wasn't entirely convinced of his guilt to start with, I'm leaning toward the latter.

My eyes scream for a break, so I close the laptop in front of me, and take in my surroundings. I'm not sure when Cassio and Sophia left or where they disappeared to, but I'm thankful for the private moment to register the gravity of my investigation. From my mother to Alister to Walsh to Gallagher to Parisi, every decision I've made has led me here, sitting three stories beneath the earth in the Amato Blood Cellar—*yes, Blood Cellar*.

There's a wooden cabinet behind me, full of books, photographs, and records I'm sure no one outside of the Amato bloodline has ever seen. Behind me, to my left, is the stone staircase leading up to the main house, or, if you know where you're going, it will also take you to the dungeon. The room is anchored by the most gorgeous wooden table Alister says his ancestors brought with them from Italy. It is flanked by a red and gold tapestry of the Amato family crest and a wall of portraits. There is one for each of the Amato bosses, the first of which is nothing more than a pencil sketch. And finally, the focal point of the room and its namesake, the wall of blood that stares back at me.

Pressed into the ancient stone wall of the Amatos' underground Blood Cellar, *and* makeshift war room, is a mahogany bookcase of sorts. Except, instead of books, it is full of tiny bottles containing the bodily fluid of the prominent victims of past Blood Kings and the current one, Alister himself. Each king, dating back to the late 1800s, has a section of shelves dedicated to their kills. According to Alister, the bottles don't necessarily represent every fatality, but they do represent every hit, which sometimes has more than one victim. Each vial is labeled with the initials of the deceased and the date of death, which corresponds to the record of hits kept by the boss.

The first thing I did once Alister explained what exactly I was looking at was check for any labels beginning with a *V.* Alister has said there is no evidence suggesting his father had anything to do with the murder of my mother. Plus, after learning of Josephine's father's involvement in the plots against the Amatos and the fact that Alister's father never sought revenge against him for the death of his wife, I'm inclined to believe it's true. My mother's death was just another of the traitor's schemes to frame the Amatos, just like, as we've recently learned, the placement of my mother's Polaroid in the Temptress. Still, I had to double-check and, of course, I found nothing. *Nothing.* That's exactly what I feel when I look at the wall that should scare me straight and send me running in the opposite direction of all things Alister Amato.

Exhausted, I rest my arms on the wooden farmhouse table in front of me and bury my face in them. My body needs rest, but my mind refuses to grant it. If Parisi is innocent, then there are only two suspects remaining. Now that Alister has finally given me the keys to the kingdom and revealed the names of his capos, I have everything I need to put my hard-earned investigative skills to use and end this. And yet, perhaps that's the cause of my nausea just as much as what occurs on the other side of the stone walls surrounding me.

As thoughts of Alister and the past few months dance through my overworked brain, tears of frustration sting as they fill my closed eyes and force themselves out. I'm tired—tired of pretending I don't care for him, tired of being warned to stay away from him, tired of getting so close only for him to pull away again and again.

I sit up straight, pressing my back firm against the intricate woodwork of the chair I sit in, and I realize my decisions over the past few months have not only led me to an unlikely physical destination but also an emotional one.

I'm surrounded by one thousand reasons why Alister and I shouldn't be together. Forget all things Mafia and Alister still has anger management issues, unresolved childhood trauma, and a serious issue with his self-worth. That's just off the top of my head, and all these things are reasons for me to walk away. Yet, I can't because I'm just as screwed up.

I shake my head and wipe the remnants of tears from beneath my eyes. He thinks we're so different, that we come from two different worlds, that being with him puts me in danger. But I've never known another soul so like mine. And, whether he'll ever admit it or not, the fact is, the day I was born I inherited the same enemies and the same world of darkness he did. I just didn't know it. We aren't so different, are we? Yet, as I take in my surroundings once more, I wonder if I should be relieved or royally disturbed. It doesn't matter though. Whatever I feel for Alister, no matter how badly I want to find a way to be with him, to convince him to let us try, I can't focus on any of that so long as the past threatens our present.

I reach for my phone and text Sophia to bring me some coffee when she returns—*if* she returns. The clock on my phone says it's after nine p.m., and the likelihood of us solving this case tonight is slim to none. It took days to investigate Parisi. Now, we have to repeat the process times two. At that, I roll my eyes and stand, stretching out my arms and legs, which are sore from prolonged sitting and slouching.

"None of this makes sense," I mumble. Twenty years. *Twenty years!* I know Alister said that greed and a lust for power are often all the motivation someone needs to start a war. But, if what we believe is true, if the same person is responsible for Alister's mother's death, and mine and Cara's, and they have truly been coming after the Amatos for nearly two decades, then they have to have a damn good reason for it. This is personal. It has to be.

This all started during Domenico Amato's reign. Plenty of people want power, money, influence. But who wants revenge? Clinging to the small burst of energy coursing through my veins, I sit at the table once more and grab a pen and paper. Across the top of the page I write Domenico's name and then list out everything I know about him that may be pertinent to the case. A lot of this information I gathered during my initial three-month investigation into the Amatos before Alister and I ever met, but since then, Alister has revealed even more to me. Along with the Amato records I now have, maybe the real catalyst for this war will present itself. Our enemy is a master at covering his tracks and maintaining his secrets, but there is one thing he can't hide, manipulate, or rewrite—his motive.

According to the Amato records, Domenico led the Italian Mafia presence in New Orleans and Texas for thirty years, expanding across the gulf all the way down to Miami during his reign. He was young when he took the throne, only twenty-eight compared to Alister's thirty-one. Neither of them was old enough to have had enemies of their own upon becoming king. We know that Alister inherited his father's enemies, but how did Domenico acquire them?

I grab the black book containing the record of hits and instead of looking for details regarding my mother's murder or even Alister's, I flip to the beginning of Domenico's section and begin strumming through his past. Or, at least, I would if an entire page for the year 1992 weren't missing. "What the?" I run my finger over the tiny jagged edges of the missing page. If I hadn't been looking so closely, I may not have noticed them at all. And yet, it's clear, with 1991 preceding the missing page and 1993 following it, 1992 is the year we need to investigate. Coincidentally, or perhaps not at all, it's the same year my mom got pregnant with me and was sent away to stay with the Cullens in Boston.

I run my finger over the jagged edges again. It's possible that Alister or even his father removed the page. Perhaps Domenico didn't want his son knowing about a hit gone wrong. Or maybe Alister knows more than he's been letting on. Maybe this entire thing has been a ruse. He turned over all his family records knowing I'd never be able to discover the one truth I'm interested in. But there's only one way to find out. I stand and make my way to the wall of blood before me. If either Domenico or Alister tried to hide the truth, they wouldn't have stopped with ripping out a page in a book that only they have access to. They would've gotten rid of all evidence linking them to the crime, especially the biological evidence. Thumbing through the vials of blood makes the hairs on my arms rise and bile tickle my throat. I'm not sheepish by any means. I'm an FBI agent for Christ's sake. But the idea of hoarding the blood of your victims is too similar to a serial killer hoarding his victim's body parts, teeth, and hair for me to be comfortable. Finally, I find a single vial covered in dust labeled with the year 1992 and the initials *C.V.* I remove it from its place and return to the table with a sigh of relief.

As I take my seat, I place the bottle on the table and wipe the dust from my fingers on my black leggings and tug the sleeves of my cream-colored sweater down from where they are bunched at my elbows. The sight of the vial lets me know Alister didn't lie to me, which eases some of the tension in my muscles. Yet, touching the vial has left me with a chill. The blood inside represents a person now dead, killed at the hands of Domenico Amato or, at least, his men. It represents death, pain, betrayal, secrets. Whoever this person was could be the reason why all of this began. Why else would someone try to erase the record of his or her death from the Amato history books? Speaking of history books, where in them do I begin my search for the identity of *C.V.?*

"Come on, Sophia. I could really use that coffee."

I scan my eyes over the books, photos, and various documents lying on the table in front of me. *C.V.* could be anyone. There's not even a guarantee that he or she would be in any of Alister's records since it's possible they were from a competing criminal organization. *Okay, think, Ariana.* It's not much, but I've begun investigations with less. Eyes wide with anticipation, I reach for my laptop and type in Agent Bilieux's username and password to gain access to the FBI database. While suspended, my login is deactivated.

At the thought of Bilieux, anger roils inside me. I'm not

saying I didn't deserve to be suspended. My behavior was entirely unprofessional. But now knowing that the only reason Bilieux granted Alister unprecedented prosecutorial immunity for a year was to keep his own secrets hidden pisses me off. On top of that, he practically stalked me to ensure I wouldn't go near Alister at the press conference in the park all because he was afraid if I got too close to the Amatos, I'd learn his secret. I shake my head. I knew there was something up with that deal from the start, but I had no idea Agent Bilieux was corrupt. Now that I know the truth, I'm not sure what I will do with it. Alister assured me he'd handle Bilieux, and I'd have my job back as soon as we finished this investigation. But I don't know how I'm supposed to work for a man I can't trust. Still, I'd be lying if I said I didn't see the silver lining.

If Alister was behind bars, I'd never be this close to learning who killed my mother and, potentially, a lot more. I also never would've had the chance to get to know Alister. My heart never would've been opened in the way that it has, in the way that only he could. And, perhaps most of all, Alister never would've had the chance he so desperately deserves to leave the Mafia behind and start anew. Perhaps that's what keeps hope alive inside me. We spoke about it once, briefly, but enough for me to realize Alister doesn't share my hope for a time without war. He said, *"No matter what happens to me, to this business, the only choice I have isn't between freedom or prison. It's between which cell I want to make my home."* He doesn't believe there is a way out of the darkness, even though he knows he will drown in it if he doesn't break free. But I know him. Alister Amato places the safety of his family above all else. He will find a way to save Sophia from jail, from death. He will find a way to save himself. And, one day, his world won't be so dark and dangerous. Maybe then he won't be so afraid to love me. At least, that is the hope I cling to, especially now, as I feel our investigation coming to a screeching end.

Within the appropriate search engine, I add in my suspect's initials, year of death, and plug in search parameters for New Orleans and the surrounding area. If this doesn't turn up anything, I can always expand my search later. But as the results begin filling the screen of my laptop, it's not a lack of information that's the problem—there are over one hundred results of deceased men and women that meet my search criteria.

"Okay, narrow by cause of death," I mumble. I remove all suspects who died from natural causes and those under the age of eighteen. I didn't know Domenico Amato, but he did raise Alister and Sophia and they would never hurt a child let alone order a hit on one. "Alright, now that's more manageable." Thirty-five results remain. Let's hope that one of them fits the profile for our mystery victim—Italian, most likely male, mysterious, sudden, or violent cause of death, and, most importantly, someone who knew or at least ran in the same circles as Domenico. This is profile A, the one I'm betting is the winning concoction of attributes that will unearth *C.V.'s* real identity. In truth, our mystery man may not have even been from New Orleans nor be Italian nor have known Domenico on a personal level. He could've been an outsider. But I still stand by my theory. What's happened over the last twenty years, from my mother's death to Alister's mother's and sister's, it's all too personal to be anything but revenge. Domenico had been king for only a couple of years when the hit against *C.V.* was ordered. He was young and possibly reckless. Maybe he made a mistake. Maybe he killed an innocent. Maybe that is the sin his children have been forced to pay for.

"I come bearing gifts." I jump as Sophia and Cassio enter the room. She holds a silver tray topped with a fresh pot of coffee and an assortment of donuts, bagels, and croissants. "Oh, sorry. I thought you would've heard us coming down the stairs," Sophia says.

"I'm too in my head," I say as I rub the sleep from my eyes before returning my focus to my too-bright computer screen.

"Maybe you should call it a night. We heard Gio and Alister talking on our way down. Even they have ruled out Parisi."

"Yeah, I know," I bite out. "That's exactly why I can't sleep. We've wasted days going after the wrong man, which has only given the real killer more time to plan his next attack."

"She's right," Cassio says. "We are running out of time. Though, I'm not sure how much progress any of us will make if we don't get some sleep."

"Quiet, just silence, *please*!" I yell.

"What's going on in here?" Alister asks as he and Gio join us. Both look as tired as I feel. Though, based on the bloodstains on Alister's white button-down, my guess is his fatigue is just as emotional as it is physical. I take a deep breath and turn my laptop so that they can see what I've found, my eyes thanking me for the reprieve. They ache almost as much as my head.

Alister takes a step forward and squints as he reads the death certificate for a middle-aged man killed in a house fire in 1992. "The name, Alister. Look at his name." As realization dawns on him, he lifts his eyes from the computer to meet mine, and I know that sleep is the last thing any of us are getting tonight.

27

Alister

The black walls of my bedroom are made darker by the seemingly starless night filtering through the windows on either side of my bed. Even the most natural beacons of light have chosen to hide on this night of great revelation, a night of such darkness it can lead only to a day of death. I sit with my back against the wooden bed frame as I ponder our discovery. As I do, I am met with silence, stillness. It's as if not even a cricket dare chirp nor fleck of dust dare float for fear I will pounce and obliterate it just as I plan to the man who betrayed my father and sought to extinguish every last glimmer of light in my life before executing me just as he did my mother. But, to my surprise, it is not anger or bloodlust or even relief I feel as I anticipate what the morning will bring. Nor is it peace or hope that tomorrow will put an end to the threats I face.

Ever since the night my mother was killed, just down the hall from the room I'm in now, I've been filled with an unrelenting anger and fear. It has crippled me, causing me to live a life without love or hope. In many ways, Ariana changed that. She broke down every wall inside me and found the parts that desired love and to love and she nurtured them. She gave rise to emotions I thought myself incapable of. She made me fall in love with her without even trying. And yet, even she could not give me back my hope.

For over a year now, I've been hunting the man or men responsible for my sister's abduction and her eventual death only to learn that they are likely the cause of more than just the death of my sister, but also the inhumane murder of my mother. We don't have hard evidence to back up this theory—yet. But I can feel it in my bones. He took her away from me, from Sophia, from Cara, who was only a baby. He destroyed our family with one bullet. And yet, he is only one man, one enemy, one of many. Tomorrow, I will have my answers and his suffering for his crimes against my family and Ariana's will begin. But his death still will not give me back my hope. In this world, upon this throne, there is none to be had.

As I stare blankly into the darkness, it is that truth, above all others, that weighs heavily on me. For months now, I've allowed myself to be distracted by this investigation, by Ariana, by what I feel for her. Now that I finally know the name of the man who plots against me, there is nothing left to distract me from my reality. I am numb, empty, just as I was the day my father died and I was forced to take on his burden, the burden of being king. Tomorrow will not free me of this crown nor the enemies surely biding their time, waiting for the perfect moment to attack now that Cara's death is public. Nor will it eliminate the potential for rebellion once my followers learn of the FBI's looming investigation. My enemies will never stop coming for me, for one reason or another. It is because of this that tomorrow is not a day to rejoice or celebrate or even anticipate with the joyful glee commonly associated with revenge. No. Tomorrow is nothing more than a goodbye. Goodbye to one enemy and hello to the next. Goodbye to the distraction that has kept me from slipping into the abyss of depression. Most of all, goodbye to the woman who made me realize I'm capable of love. I will love her for the rest of my days, though I will not subject her to the burden of being my queen. I will protect her in a way no one ever protected me.

As emotion tightens my cheeks and leaves my throat raw, I turn my gaze upon Ariana, who sleeps next to me. She rests in perfect peace, her dark locks sprawled across the silky, charcoal sheets, her lips parted as she dreams, hopefully of happy things rather than the horrors from her past that haunt her, while mere inches away, I sit in silent agony. It is the most excruciating torture to know her and be unable to have her. Yet, I know if I were to make her mine, any chance she has of happiness, true happiness, would slowly but surely evade her and be replaced by the same hopelessness I've endured for the better part of my life. I will sooner die than see her be consumed by the world her birth would have her inherit. Only, now, keeping her from the darkness won't be as easy as me simply walking away from her, as if leaving her could ever be simple or easy.

Ariana was right. The only thing powerful enough to spark a war of this nature is revenge. Former capo to my father, Carlo Vitale, his wife, and, presumably, their teenage daughter, Valentina Vitale, were killed in a house fire in October 1992. After all of Ariana's efforts to discover her mother's identity, the truth resided not in the year 2003 nor even in New Orleans, but eleven years prior and nearly two hours away on a rural estate. Only, per the diary Josephine gave Ariana in Boston, we know the real Valentina was already in New England at the time of the fire.

Arson was never officially suspected, but that doesn't mean anything, not when you've got detectives, officers, and the FBI higher-ups on your payroll. This was a hit, one my father botched. No matter if he discovered Carlo's plots against him, which I can only assume he did, he would never order the death of a child, at least I don't think he would. Regardless, among the burnt remains of an old Victorian home meant to be Carlo's private palace for plotting his attacks against my father, the bones of an adolescent girl were found. Knowing Carlo and his wife had a teenage daughter, my father may have influenced the medical examiner to say the deceased was Valentina without completing the appropriate DNA testing to determine otherwise. I can imagine the guilt he must have felt and his desire to move on from the incident as quickly as possible. So, he fast-tracked the investigation, no doubt paying off whomever necessary to make sure no one had any reason to ask questions or dig deeper into the tragic events. For all intents and purposes, Valentina Vitale was dead. Only, she wasn't. Someone took her place. And her death, I can only assume, was the true catalyst for the war that has plagued my family ever since.

According to my father's records, after the death of Carlo Vitale, his brother, Christio, was brought into my father's inner circle, now residing in mine. It's common practice, according to Josephine. To avoid a war, you transfer the wealth and position to the nearest kin, hoping and praying it's enough to buy their silence and their loyalty. Well, it wasn't. Because on that day in October 1992, unbeknownst to my father, Christio Vitale didn't just lose his brother and sister-in-law. I believe he lost his soul. Because shortly after Christio stepped into his brother's shoes, his wife and daughter, Veronica, left him, never to be seen again. Convenient or coincidence?

A teenage girl died in that fire. If it wasn't Valentina, perhaps it was Veronica. Perhaps that is why Christio Vitale took up his brother's efforts to destroy my family. Perhaps that is why he attempted to eliminate all evidence that would speak to his motive, unaware of the Blood Cellar. Perhaps that is why he used and abused Valentina, ultimately killing her and trying to frame my father for it. He blamed her and my father for what happened to his daughter. If he had access to my father's hit book, enough to rip out an entire page, then he also would've had the opportunity to add an entry, explaining the previously unexplainable ink blot for the year Ariana's mother was killed.

While the theory that Vitale's daughter, Veronica, was killed in the hit that took out Carlo and his wife along with the idea that Vitale, Ariana's great-uncle, is the same man who orchestrated the attack that killed my mother is just that, a theory, we were able to find hard evidence linking Vitale to the Irish mob, specifically the hit squad he sent after Cara and Sophia. We conducted the same background check on him as we did Parisi. Even in the short amount of time, we found property records and bank records connecting him to the apartment Ariana and her mother used to live in and a second location security camera footage shows Walsh and his men frequenting, at least before they were exterminated from my city. Christio Vitale is our man. He's Ariana's blood. And yet, it's not her mother's side of the family I fear will keep Ariana tethered to the darkness. No. It's her father's.

At that, I sink down under the covers, bringing myself face-to-face with a sleeping Ariana. I move my fingers to her hair and savor the silky feel as the strands slip through my fingers. She smells of warm amber and sweet vanilla. I wish I could bottle her scent, wash my sheets in it, and bathe in it. Alas, it would only be a painful reminder of the woman I can't have.

After discovering Vitale's guilt, Gio took off to plan a course of attack while Cassio and Sophia retreated for some much-needed rest. But Ariana refused to sleep, knowing that a look into her mother's past might reveal the identity of her father. She passed out before she could identify him. So, I brought her here, unwilling to part from her, and I continued the search. For nearly thirty years, Ariana's father has believed Valentina was dead, and so too was his unborn child. The moment the two of them learn of each other, they won't tolerate being separated again. So, where does that leave me? How am I supposed to protect her from the Mafia when her own father is Mafia? There's a part of me that wants to use this revelation as an excuse to remain in her life. But the moment I think it's possible, I am transported back to the night when I came face-to-face with my mother's lifeless body. She lay next to me on the ground, her hair sprawled out much like Ariana's is now. As the images flash through my mind, I pull my hand from Ariana's hair and roll onto my back as tears drip down my cheeks. Though, I am quickly drawn back to her as Ariana begins to shake.

"Hey, baby." I gently try to wake Ariana, but she is too consumed by her nightmare.

"*No. No. No!*" she screams as she slings her arm into my chest. Writhing against the sheets, she fights an imaginary demon. Only, he isn't so much imaginary as he is a thing of her past. I swear to God, I'll kill him.

"Hey, Ariana, Ariana." She turns away, and I wrap my arms around her and pull her to me. Her back rests against my chest as I restrain her arms and whisper in her ear, coaxing her out of his grasp and into mine. "You're safe. You just need to wake up. Wake up, baby." Slowly, her frantic movements stop, and her breathing slows. Small beads of sweat dot her forehead as she finally opens her eyes. "It's okay," I whisper. "I've got you. I'm right here."

Once I'm sure she is alright, I loosen my grip and remove my arm from her waist. Only, she stops me before I do. Ariana spins to face me, directing me to keep my arm wrapped tightly around her. As her eyes meet mine, our faces only inches apart, I don't believe my heart has ever beat so fast. "Don't let me go," she says then, and once more my throat aches with emotion. I can't. I can't do this. As much as I want to comfort her, I won't make promises I can't keep. I won't lead her to believe there's a future between us when I know there isn't. There can't be.

"But I have to." With my truth, cold tears escape my eyes onto my warm cheeks, leaving an icy trail in their path. It's a painful reminder of what my life before Ariana felt like and the cold loneliness I'm destined to return to. We've been playing this game of push and pull for months now. But it's time for it to end.

As my words settle on her, they land differently than all the times before. I've told her from the start that she wouldn't find happiness with me. I've told her she shouldn't care about me, that this isn't a fairy tale. We both knew this would never work, that every touch, every look, every time we tried to ignore the fact that we are from two completely different worlds we were playing with fire. And yet, knowing this would end doesn't make it hurt any less now that it has. Her lips quiver, though only for a moment before she presses them into a flat line, doing her best to conceal her emotions. It's an act we should both be better at by now.

"I'm sorry," I say, and all the words I've been keeping inside rip from me. Maybe I'm wrong to say them. Maybe hearing them will only make this harder for her. But I can't spend the rest of my days apart from her without her knowing how I truly feel, what she truly means to me. I can't give her much, but I can at least give her that, assuming she even wants it. "Ariana, I..." I bring my hand to her cheek as she moves hers to mine, wiping away the remnants of my tears. "I love you. I'm in love with you." As the words cross my lips, Ariana gasps in surprise, and her eyes fill with tears of her own. I wipe them away as they fall, pulling her tighter against me with my other arm still wrapped around her. "Maybe I shouldn't say it. Maybe I should keep it inside. But I..."

"No," Ariana says, shaking her head. Her gaze follows her movements as she moves her fingers from my cheekbone lower and lower, raking them across my stubble until she reaches my lips where she rests her thumb. Her touch makes my insides tighten yet my heartbeat slow. "No. I want to hear it. I want to know that this wasn't all in my head." As Ariana's eyes meet mine once more, in them, I find the same pain of heartbreak I've grown too accustomed to.

"It wasn't. I promise you, it wasn't." As tears drip down her cheeks, I wipe them away with my thumb while Ariana moves her hand from my face to my hip. "The night we met, I wanted to shield you from this world, from the pain it brings. In a way, maybe I even wanted to shield you from me, because my track record with women is nothing short of tragic. I was harsh and cold and unsympathetic."

"You were trying to protect me before you even knew me," Ariana whispers.

"Yeah, I guess I was. But you weren't having it. You were stubborn, willful, independent, and capable, as proven in your pursuit of me all those weeks before Edgar Walsh brought us even closer. You promised me you'd be a thorn in my side, that you'd pester me until I complied, and you were and did. But you were also the best part of my day, a bright light shining through the darkness." As I speak, I move my hand from her cheek to her neck. The warmth of her skin tickles my insides, which only makes this moment that much more painful. "By the time you came to me with the information from Edgar Walsh, I was already falling for you, but the days since then have only intensified my feelings. Since my mother's passing, this place has never really felt like home. But you changed that. You brought life back into these walls just like you did my heart. From wrestling to cooking to dancing to just talking—one simple moment with you is better than a million without you."

"Then why are you doing this? Why won't you give us a chance, Alister?"

"Ariana—"

"I know your concerns. I know all the reasons why we shouldn't be together. *Trust me.* I've thought about it and wrestled with it as much as you have. But I am willing to take the risk. I'm willing to have my heart broken by you. I'm willing to put myself in the line of fire if it means that I can finally feel loved. And not just by anyone, Alister, but by you. I want to be loved by *you*. I want to spend my days and nights with you. I want to be the one you talk to, the one you dance with, the one you argue with, the one you trust to help you carry the burdens that no one else sees. And not just for one night or one week or even one month. I want you, Alister. I know I shouldn't, but I do. And if you feel the same way, then why can't we at least try? Because I am not some fragile wallflower that needs protecting every minute of every day. I have lived through Hell, Alister. I have gone up against the Devil more than once and I've survived. I know there are certain unique perils that come with being by your side, but I can handle them. *I can.* And if I can't, then at least I lived and I loved. Because before you, my life was filled with the same darkness you speak of. So, please, please just give us a chance to have the happiness we both deserve. *Please.*"

Ariana pleads with me with her words, with the way her eyes widen in anticipation, with the way her fingers dig into my skin. She holds her breath as she waits for my response, and I savor every second, just as surprised by her admission as she was by mine. I've felt the connection between us for weeks and I'm sure she did to. But to finally have it validated with such powerful words, it's... It means everything to me. It's as if she has reached inside me and wrapped her hand around my heart. She alone holds the power to protect it and destroy it. But there is one power she does not hold over me. Even Ariana cannot make me forget the way my mother was taken from me, then my sister. She cannot make me forget the role I'm forced to play and the dangers that come with it. My love for and loyalty to Ariana is unquestionable and unsurpassable. But it is because I love her that I cannot be with her.

I loosen my grip around her waist as I surrender to my fear and the weight of the crown I'm forced to wear. "I'm not willing to take the risk, Ariana. Not with you." I push myself up and rest my back against the bed frame. I take a deep breath. With a small amount of distance between us my self-control has a minute to replenish itself. Though Ariana soon adjusts, sitting up opposite me. There's a rigidness to her that lets me know she's hurt, and she's done. I nod to myself. As disappointment drains her, I feel her hold on my heart disappear. Left in her place is an empty pit that will certainly never be filled.

"I have lost so many people, Ariana. And I know I'm supposed to be strong and not let it get to me." At that, I smile a sad smile. "In my world, weakness gets you killed. So, I...I pretend like I'm okay, like what happened to my sister and to my mother before her has only made me more dangerous, more lethal. And maybe it has. But it's also left me terrified, anxious, and empty. And I wish I could break free from it. I wish I could flip a switch and be willing to take the risks you are. Because I'm not afraid of loving you, Ariana. I'm not afraid to tell you how I feel, to hold you in my arms, to open my heart and soul to you. I'm afraid of the world bearing witness to such love, because I know it will stop at nothing to rip it from me, to rip *you* from me. And that I won't survive."

I shake my head as Ariana moves her hand to my shin. She offers me a comforting touch this time, rather than one filled with longing. "If protecting you means I must give you up before someone can take you from me, then that is what I'll do. As hopeless and weak as it sounds, I..."

"You are hopeless, Alister. But...you are not weak." As Ariana moves her hand up and down my shin, softly, slowly, gently, she says nothing more. I suppose because there is nothing left to say, but there is still so much between us that has yet to be explored. Perhaps it's better this way, and yet knowing my memories of Ariana are all I'll have to cling to once the sun rises only adds to my heartbreak. For they are far too few.

"*Mi tesoro.*" Ariana's voice lifts the hairs on my arms and pulls me back to her with bated breath. Slowly, she moves toward me, caressing my leg. Her lips part as her eyes graze my body, at least what she can assess through my gray sweatpants and white tank top. There's something about the way she looks at me and the way her fingers dig into my thigh as she moves them higher and higher that makes a certain appendage swell, despite her touch ceasing just inches from where it fills the crotch of my pants.

"Yes, *mi amore?*" I ask, my throat raw. Though, for once, not with emotion, rather, anticipation. It's then that Ariana brings her hand to my abs and continues her alluring caress up my body to my neck and, eventually, to my cheek. As she runs her fingers across the stubble on my face again, I close my eyes and take a deep breath, one I hope will settle the carnal craving building inside me. I want this. *God, I want this.* But she has to make the first move. To claim her body after breaking her heart would rival my most chilling crimes. But if she wants me to, this is a request I can wholeheartedly meet. I open my eyes and find a softness in hers, an acceptance of our tragic end, and yet, a longing still for something more.

"I once told you there was never any hope for me. I was always fated to be hurt by a monster. Perhaps there was never any hope for us either. But that doesn't mean we weren't destined to love one another, destined to touch one another, to devour and claim one another." As she speaks, she leans forward, bringing her lips so close to mine I can practically taste her. Though they do not touch. In this position, her chest presses against mine and her brunette locks drip softly over my shoulder as her sweet scent fills my every pore. Still, I do not touch her, because I know once I do, I won't be able to stop.

Finally, she says, "Give me tonight, Alister. If the world cannot bear witness to our love, then love me in the dark without inhibition. Touch me. Do everything with me. So that when the sun rises and we are forced to bottle our feelings once more, I, *we*, may have this moment to cling to—a moment to last a lifetime."

At that, Ariana brings her lips to mine, and they are just as soft as I always imagined them to be. She tastes like sweet vanilla and sugared caramel, which only makes me want to kiss her more, bite her, *devour* her as she said. But is this really wise? Can we so easily wake to a new day and pretend this night never happened? Then again, I don't think the purpose of tonight is to forget. It's to remember—remember every caress, every embrace, every moan, every whimper, every laugh, every swear. I want those memories as much as the air I breathe, if not more. And so, without a moment's more delay, I give in to her kiss.

28

ALISTER TASTES LIKE STOUT BOURBON AND SMELLS OF WINTER pines. His kiss is warm, yet his touch is icy, electrifying. Though, perhaps it's just my nerves, because the moment Alister brings his hands to my hips, pulling me onto his lap, my entire body floods with warmth. This isn't the first time I've been with a man since my assault, but it is the first time it's meant anything. And, since tonight is not only our first time together but our last, I want to savor it.

As Alister moves his hands under the hemline of my cream-colored sweater, I pull my lips from his. Alister stops his movements as concern contorts his features. "Are you okay?" he asks, his brows furrowed, producing a small wrinkle in the center of his forehead. His lips part as he waits for my response. They are red from our embrace yet glisten with the faintest hint of my lip balm. This gorgeous man loves me. I can see it in the way he looks at me, his eyes searching my body for any signs of harm. I can feel it in the way he holds me, firm yet gentle. It's as if he's afraid I'll disappear. And yet, his touch and his gaze only echo his words.

I can't begin to express what I feel as I replay Alister's declaration of love over and over again in my head. What he said was everything I wanted to hear and everything I didn't. But I do understand. I do. As much as it hurts me to accept, I know what it's like to be crippled by inescapable demons and unrelenting pain. I pray it isn't always like this. I pray he does find the peace he so desperately deserves. But I know that's something only he can do for himself. And maybe he has to do it alone, just like I did, just like I do.

As I look at him, taking in the strong bridge of his nose, the sharp line of his jaw, I know tomorrow will be one of the hardest days of my life. I will not only come face-to-face with the man who took my mother's life, but I will say goodbye to the only man who has ever loved me, the only man who has ever made me feel whole. Just like Alister cannot fathom a better life for himself, I cannot fathom a life without him. Yet, tomorrow aside, tonight I am more than okay. Tonight, I am with the man I love. I am with my best friend. I am with my protector. I am with my partner in crime and against it. And I am happy. For as long as the moon hides the sun, I am happy.

At that, I adjust myself over top of him, and he moans as I rest atop his swollen appendage. I can't help but smile at the sound. I like him like this—disarmed, unbuttoned, and at my mercy. Though, considering the way his eyes shift, filling with a certain primal lust I've seen only a few times before, perhaps it is me who is at his mercy. "I am perfect," I whisper as I bring my hands to his black hair. As I do, I close my eyes and memorize the way it feels, soft yet coarse. A lot like him, I suppose.

"Yes, you are," he says then, bringing his lips to my neck. I smile and let out a soft laugh as he kisses my delicate skin, working his way from behind my ear down to my collarbone. It's then that I open my eyes and wrap my arms around his neck.

"I pulled away because I wanted to see you. I want to see

the way your eyes gaze upon me as you undress me." As the words escape me, I lift my chin as if daring him to do just that.

"I'm going to have my hands full with you, aren't I?" He smirks.

"Did you expect anything less? Though a certain prodding lets me know I too will have my hands full *and* other areas as well." At that, we both laugh, me even more so when I feel his dick jerk in response to my words. Hmm. He likes the way I talk to him, and I like the way his body feels so close to mine, so close I can almost make out the shape of him through my thin leggings.

"I love you," he says then. Bringing his fingers to my hair, he brushes it over my shoulder. "Whatever happens next, I want you to remember that."

"What do you mean whatever happens next?"

"I mean..." He blushes and lowers his eyes to where our bodies connect. Once more, he brings his hands to my hips, slowly lifting the hem of my sweater. Only, this time, I don't pull away from him and he doesn't stop. Gently, Alister pulls the sweater from my body, revealing the lacy bra concealing my breasts. It offers me a final bit of coverage, allowing me time to get comfortable being this exposed in his presence. Although, this isn't the first time I've felt naked before him; figurative nudity is different than physical.

As Alister tosses my sweater to the side, he moves his eyes to mine. They do not venture lower. "I want to take this slow. I want to savor every minute with you," he says. "But my body may not allow that. At least, not at first." At that, my brows crinkle. Alister moves his hand to my neck and guides my mouth to his. He kisses me, his movements starting slow and soft, yet quickly speeding up to rapid, hard, and desperate. Simultaneously, his hands wrap around my hips. His grip tightens as he deepens our kiss, so much so it hurts. When I whimper, he pulls away.

"Do you see what I mean? Do you see what you do to me? I want you. I crave you so desperately I'm afraid I may hurt you. If I do, tell me and I'll stop, or have me make it up to you after in any way you choose. But, whatever you do, don't forget I love you."

"You could never hurt me, not when I know your intentions, your heart." I rest my palm on his chest and allow the delicate thud of his beating heart to calm my last remaining nerves. "Trust me, I've been hurt before and what hurts isn't so much the physical pain as it is the emotional. Knowing someone took something from you, took a piece of you..." I shake my head as Alister instinctively moves his fingers to the places on my body where I wear my scars. "You aren't taking anything from me, Alister. You are giving me everything, every piece of you in exchange for every piece of me. And, for the record, I love you too. I know I've said a lot of things tonight, but I'm not sure I've said those three words. I love you, Alister. Now, make love to me, fuck me, do whatever you want with me. Just be with me. Claim me as yours, even if only for tonight."

As I speak, Alister's expression shifts from tangible lust to something deeper, gentler, though equally as desperate. Alister pushes himself up and me along with him. I tighten my grip around him as he lifts me and lays me down among the silky charcoal sheets and pillows. I rest my head on them as Alister removes his shirt and positions himself overtop me. As he does, I take him in in all his glory. His arms and abs are chiseled to perfection. Looking at him, I realize I'm discovering muscles I didn't even know existed, and as my eyes move to meet his, I find he is admiring me as well. His dark gaze drifts from my waist up to my breasts. As his eyes move so does his hand. His touch is gentle despite his hands having a natural roughness to them. As he touches me, caresses me, I can't help but think of all the men he's bested, the weapons he's wielded, the death he's delivered with these same instruments. Knowing him capable of such terror and torment makes his loving touch even more arousing. His palm reaches my breast, and I gasp in pleasure, prompting him to lower his lips to my cleavage. As his lips embrace my skin, I surrender myself to him, every part of him, the beautiful and the ugly, the chivalrous and the monstrous, and everything in between.

When his lips leave me, his eyes return to mine. "You asked for everything. You deserve everything. So I will make love to you. I will fuck you. I will tease and devour you. And I will hold you. Because you deserve nothing less." His words leave me speechless and my body aching with anticipation.

Alister pushes himself up once more. He stands to remove his pants, but I stop him.

"Allow me," I say. I hop off the side of the bed, standing to join him. Slowly, I rake my fingers over his abs until I reach the waistband of his pants. All the while, Alister watches me with hungry eyes and parted lips. I lower myself to my knees, tugging his pants down with me. His sweatpants reach his ankles, and my own hunger is amplified by his well-groomed region and throbbing erection. It sticks straight out, forcing us to remain at least six inches apart. That is, until I envelop his length in my mouth. I know he told me of all the things he wishes to do to me. And, God, I wish it too. But what of the things I wish to do to him?

Alister moans as I take him inside me. I move painfully slow, so painfully he is forced to bring his hand to the back of my neck so that he can control the pace. I let him fill me over and over again, savoring every stroke. As he moves in and out, I feel like one of those cliché fictional girls who talk of his extreme length and how pleasurable it is to give a blow job. But what can I say? I love every minute of it. It's my gift to him, before I let him take me. And *take* he does.

Alister pulls himself from my mouth without finishing. He brings his finger to my chin, lifting my gaze and body toward him. I stand, allowing Alister his turn to undress me. He spins me around so quickly I throw my arms out to catch myself against the mattress. I gasp as Alister approaches me from behind. He brings his hands to my hips, making quick work of removing my leggings. As they fall to my ankles, Alister bends down and removes them from my person. I am left in nothing but my nude, lacy lingerie. As Alister returns to a standing position, he drags his hands up the backs of my legs. His touch ignites every nerve inside me, even more so as he slips his fingers beneath the fabric of my underwear, squeezing my bare, tender skin. I lean forward, resting my hands against the mattress as I push my bottom out further so he can have full access. He leaves a kiss on my tailbone before continuing to trace the curves of my body. Though, before he reaches my breasts, he stops.

"You said you wanted to watch me as I undress you. But that's only half the fun, *mi amore*." At that, he tugs on my hair, prompting me to look straight ahead where I find a mirror staring back at us. Alister crouches over me, leaving wet kisses along my shoulder blade all the way down to where my bra clasps together. All the while, he maintains his grip on my long, brown locks. I watch him, *us*, as he undoes my bra. It falls from my body, leaving my breasts dangling and vulnerable. Gently, Alister tugs on my hair as he stands upright. His movements pull me with him. My back rests against his rock-hard chest as I stand in front of him. As he releases my hair, I lower my eyes to the floor, knowing what will happen next. I take in a sharp breath, my nipples standing firm in anticipation of his touch. Though, instead, Alister brings his hand to my chin. He caresses my jawline before directing me to look at the mirror once more. I do as he commands, finding solace in my surrender.

Through the mirror, I watch him as his dark eyes examine my flesh. The muscles in his arms clench as he forces himself to take things slow with me, though I imagine his self-control will only last for so long. As his hands cup my breasts, I gasp and close my eyes in pleasure. It feels so good to be touched by him, to give myself to him. As he kneads my skin and has his way with my most sensitive peaks, thoughts of tomorrow threaten my ecstasy. This is a moment I wish I could live in forever. I knew being with him would be amazing. I even knew it would only make our goodbye that much more painful. But I never could've imagined it would be this exhilarating, this magnetic, this *perfect*. And now, my heart breaks even more than it did before, because as amazing as this moment is, I know it will be short-lived. Even still, I cannot pull away from him. I cannot steal my own happiness when I know the rising sun will do it for me.

When Alister's hands abandon my breasts in favor of my lower region, I open my eyes and watch as he removes my panties. Now there is nothing left separating us. There are no clothes to hide behind, no secrets to keep us up at night, no words left unspoken. I am his and he is mine, even if only for tonight.

Alister spins me to face me. Perhaps he senses the sadness inside me threatening to escape. "Are you okay?" he asks. He brings his palm to my cheek, and I lean into his touch. I nod and offer him a smile. I'm not sure he believes me, but his next movements certainly give rise to feelings, both physical and emotional, that take the place of my other thoughts.

Alister picks me up and returns me to the bed where I lie on my back. "Spread your legs," he says, nudging them open. I do as he says. As he crawls between them, I take note of my body's slippery response to his other embraces. Though, as he wraps his arms around my thighs, locking me in place, I realize nothing prior could've prepared me for the sensation of Alister Amato's mouth on my clit. I gasp, my mouth opening as he takes me into his.

"*Ah!*" I moan. As his tongue teases me, I arch my back and push my pelvis upward, shoving myself into his face. He laughs in response and tightens his grip on my thighs. He takes advantage of my position and buries his face into me once more. As he continues demonstrating his knowledge of the female body, his unrelenting assault on my most sensitive area creates a burning sensation between my legs. I give in to it. Nothing consumes me except him, his tongue, and his touch. I grab on to the sheets, clenching them for support as I find my release. As I do, my body twitches and thrusts as it aches for more, as it aches for him—all of him. When I finally settle, relaxing into the bed, Alister brings his mouth back to me, this time lower than before. I cry out as he licks the cum from my body. He didn't lie when he said he'd *devour* me. As his tongue slips inside where his dick should be, I reach down and yank his head up by his hair.

"Put it in," I say, my voice hoarse from all my moans.

"*Yes, ma'am*," he replies. His words draw a smile from me as he repositions himself, his face just inches from mine, and I bring my hands to his flushed cheeks. As much as I've enjoyed our encounter so far, I miss him.

"I love you so much," I whisper. As I bring my lips to his, I taste myself in his kiss. Though, only for a moment. When Alister—*finally*—thrusts inside of me, I gasp. My lips lift from his. As I take him in, I see that's exactly what he wanted. He wanted to feel my reaction to his body, from the tips of my curling toes to my plump, ripe lips. He smiles as my body opens for him, taking in every inch.

"All of my love is yours, Ariana. I will never touch another woman as I've touched you. I will never love another woman as I love you."

"Never is a very long time," I whisper.

"As long as forever, which is how long my heart will belong to you." Alister's words settle between us, and my lips quiver as, once again, my emotions threaten to escape. I meant what I said when I told Alister he wasn't weak. If he loves me as much as he claims to, as much as I truly believe him to, then pretending otherwise must be next to impossible. And yet, he's prepared to live a life doing just that. That takes a level of strength and resilience I fear I lack. "Now, lie back and let me love you." I nod and do as he says.

Alister wraps his arm around me, pressing his palm into my back. He holds me in place as he thrusts into me. He gives me everything—every inch, every ounce. His length rips through me, tearing at my too-tight insides. The pain is a consequence of years of loneliness and abstinence. But soon enough, my body adjusts and wraps around him as if I'm made for him and him alone. His movements alternate from quick and hard to slow and gentle. In his own way, he makes love to me and fucks me all at once. And I savor every moment, even initiating a few positions of my own. I meet his loving touch *and* his aggression, his stamina, his pace. We move as one in a way I never knew humans possible. That is, until exhaustion overcomes us both.

29

I DARE NOT LOOK AT THE TIME NOR LET MY EYES DRIFT TO THE muted light pouring in through the windows on either side of the bed for fear the moment will shatter. Just let me lie here. If not forever, then at least for a little while longer. I rest my head on Alister's well-groomed chest. It is damp with sweat as is mine, but I don't care. Our skin melts together as if we are one. Even our breaths, which have yet to steady, release in sync with one another. Alister wraps his arm around my body, cradling me. I snuggle into him, draping my arm over his torso. We lie naked against one another with our bottoms covered by silk sheets. He caresses my hair and my back while I find solace in the steady beat of his heart and the warmth of his body. Yet, his touch is no longer enough to chase away the sadness the rising sun brings.

Unable to keep them inside any longer, fresh tears fall from my eyes, dripping down my warm cheeks onto Alister's chest. As they do, Alister steadies his hand, resting it on the blankets surrounding us. Yet, he does not say a word. He need not ask why I cry, because he knows. Perhaps he feels as I do—heartbroken and at a loss. As I lift my heavy head to meet his gaze, I find I am right. His eyes are red with emotion, his cheeks tight and damp with tears of his own. At the sight of him, I break. The sounds of my heartbreak no doubt echo through Laroux House as I wrap myself around Alister's body, refusing to let him go. He gives in to my touch, pulling me against him so tightly it hurts. And yet, the pain of his arms crushing my ribs is nothing compared to the pain in my chest. It feels as if someone has cut my heart from me. It burns. It stings. My insides are left raw and empty. I've felt this pain before. When my mother was killed before my eyes. When I was raped by the man meant to protect and provide for me. And yet, it has never felt quite like this.

"Please," I whisper. "Please, don't..." I can't bring myself to say the words. Just the thought of him leaving brings on a new wave of tears and all the hoarse blubbering, snot pouring, and head aching that comes with them. As I shed my weight in tears, Alister still does not say anything. Yet, his grip doesn't loosen nor do his tears cease to fall. I know he loves me. I know he does. I know this hurts him just as much as it hurts me. That's why it's so tragic. We love each other, but we're both too hopeless for it to matter.

"You should...you should take a shower," he says then. His voice is so hoarse he can barely get the words out.

"*What?*" I look to him, confused. "No. *No!* This isn't happening. I'm not ready. I'm not ready for this to be over." Alister nods. He presses his lips together in a flat line. Perhaps to keep from letting his own cries of agony out or maybe because he too isn't ready.

"I'll...I'll join you."

"*What?*"

"I'll meet you in there. I just...need a minute."

I can hear the pain in his voice as he speaks. He shifts in the bed beneath me, pushing himself up to rest his back against the headboard. His movements force me to prop myself up as well.

I'm confused by him. What does a shower matter and why does he *need a minute*? Nevertheless, I am too emotional and too desperate for another moment with him to care. Knowing that he has never lied to me before, I toss my legs over the side of the bed, stand, and make my way to the bathroom, passing by the mirror that holds a hundred memories. I'm not sure I'll ever look at another mirror again without thinking of him, without thinking of us. In that, I find respite.

I open the wooden door to the bathroom and am met with a similar aesthetic as Alister's bedroom—moody, masculine, and sophisticated. Dark navy blue walls and mahogany-stained wood cabinets anchor the space and are complemented by white marble countertops, brass fixtures, and slate gray tile floors that lead into a massive shower, the walls of which are adorned with even larger slate gray tiles. As I take in the space, my eyes flick to the ornate brass mirror hanging above the sink. In its reflection, I find Alister. He watches me from the bed. I've never seen him more broken. My lips quiver, yet I keep a third round of tears from spewing.

I remember speaking with Sophia. It was after she learned the truth of who I am, after I apologized for lying to her. She thanked me for saving her the night of the Halloween party, but not just because she was afraid of what those men would've done to her. She was afraid of what her death would do to Alister. She feared he wouldn't survive the loss. I know Alister places his family above all else. His love for me is no comparison to his love for his sister. And yet, as I look at him, I wonder—will he survive this? Will I?

Determined not to make things any harder on him, I take a deep breath and suck down the rest of my cries as I maneuver around the bathroom. I turn on the water in the shower and pull out two towels from the vanity. Just as the water reaches the perfect warmth, Alister enters the room. He's put on sweatpants, which strikes me as weird considering he's coming to take a shower. Perhaps he was cold. At the sight of him, I cross my arms over my chest, taking note of my own nudity.

"Are you ready?" I ask.

He tries to offer me a smile but fails. Instead, his lips droop once more as he shoves his hands into his pockets. "As I'll ever be," he says then. I nod and take a step toward him. I'm thankful for this moment, however awkward it is. I wrap my arms around him and pull him in for a hug. It isn't sexual or even romantic. Yet, it is filled with love—the kind of love that is so selfless it hurts. I want the best for him. I want him to be happy. I want him to find peace in his life, even if he can't do that with me by his side. That's how much I love him. That's how much he loves me—enough to walk away, even when all either of us wants is to stay.

"I love you, Ariana Valentine. I always will. Never forget that."

I smile, just when I started to believe I'd never smile again.

"I'll never forget," I whisper against his chest. Alister brings his hand to my hair for what will likely be the last time. He runs his fingers through the long, brown strands as he brings his lips to my forehead. I close my eyes, relishing these last few moments with him. Then—

"*Ah!*" I gasp. An unexpected pinch draws my attention to my shoulder, where Alister pulls a syringe from my flesh, the effects of which are nearly instant. I grab on to his arms as my legs go weak and my vision begins to blur.

"I'm sorry," Alister whispers. As the weakness overcomes me, he lowers me to the ground where I rest my head on his lap. "I'm sorry," he says once more. A cold tear drips from his eye onto my cheek as his face blurs to something unrecognizable. Its sharp prick against my numbing skin is the last thing I feel before the darkness consumes me.

My head is heavy as my sleep breaks. Slowly, I open my eyes, wiping away the residue of my slumber only to be met with a certain brightness that is familiar and yet unexpected. The white walls of my bedroom greet me rather than the black of Alister's as does the pale comforter and the cream-colored sleeves of the sweater Alister discarded from my body just the night before. "No," I whisper. I toss my blankets to the side and force myself out of bed as realization finally comes to me. My bedroom stands in stark contrast to Alister's, which only makes my presence here sting that much more. Everything is the opposite of his. Everything is as it was before I ever knew Alister Amato. This room is a time machine, transporting me back to my old life, a life without Alister, a life without love. As if our goodbye wasn't painful enough, *this*, this physical representation of our breakup, if you can even call it that, is the final blow I wasn't prepared to take.

He drugged me. He... My stomach twists with the truth, and I move toward the French doors on the opposite side of the bed. I reach for the olive-green velvet curtains and pull them back with as much force as I can muster. As the bright light of day fills my room, warming my skin, I realize *what* Alister did isn't as important as *why* he did it. By now, Alister, Gio, and Cassio's men will have made it to Vitale's. For all I know, he's already dead. *No.* Alister wouldn't do that to me. He wouldn't. I deserve my time with Vitale just as much as he does. He knows that and yet he drugged me so that he could go alone. Perhaps he doesn't want me to see what he plans to do to Vitale. Perhaps he thought he was protecting me. I shake my head as I sink to the floor, resting my back against the body of the French doors.

"I can't. I can't do this anymore." As more tears threaten to fall, I find myself so exhausted I think I'd be content to just stay here, to give up any chance I may still have to confront the man who murdered my mother. I know he won't live through the night. Alister will make it so. And, the truth is, I just...I don't think I can stomach another goodbye. I don't think I can bear to see Alister, to be in his presence, to be forced to walk away from him again. Maybe he did me a favor. Maybe I should thank him for forcing me out of his life, because I...I never would've left.

"*I never would've left*," I whisper. As a roar of agony escapes me, I bring my hand to my chest as if it will help ease the pain. I lower myself to the floor and rest my head upon it, despite the fact that I can't remember the last time I swept. I cry until there are no more tears inside me, though I still do not move. That is, until my eyes focus on the armoire in the corner. Taped to the back of it is the Polaroid of my mother, the one that told me Alister Amato would lead me to the man who stole everything from me. And he did. Only now, Christio Vitale has taken more from me than my mother. He has taken my heart, my love, my Alister. And Alister has taken my one chance at vengeance.

As my sorrow gives way to anger, I push myself from the floor, grab my purse from the nightstand, and make my way through my apartment to the exit. It will break me to see Alister again, just as much as it breaks me to be apart from him. But I will never forgive myself if I let my heartbreak get in the way of avenging my mother. I'm the one who started this. I'm the one who's going to end it. Though when I yank my door open, my momentum is stalled by the man who loves me. Only, just not the right one.

"Good, you're alive."

"*Ray?*"

"It's been so long you've forgotten my face. *Perfect.*" Ray forces his way into my apartment as I stand stunned. What is he doing here? Better yet, how do I get rid of him? I haven't seen him since the night he helped me capture Edgar Walsh. That's not to say he hasn't tried calling and texting, but I haven't known what to say to him. I never did give him the explanation he wanted when it came to Walsh and our night in the swamp. And I can't tell him about Alister—not that I've been working with him for weeks now, not that I've fallen in love with him, not that I slept with him, not that he broke my heart, and especially not that he is about to commit a murder, one I will likely help him with.

"Ray, I...I was just on my way out." I feel bad. Ray has been a good friend and he deserves some sort of an explanation. He truly does. But not now, not today, especially when the sight of him only makes me think of Alister.

"Ariana." *Uh-oh.* Ray's use of my first name rather than Ari, accompanied by his exasperated tone, lets me know I'm in trouble and he isn't going to leave without a fight—a big one. "Look, there is a lot I want to talk to you about. Like how you've been MIA for months now. How you had me help you kidnap a man who turned out to be connected to the Irish mob only to then offer him asylum in WITSEC. And how you've been avoiding my calls and texts ever since. Oh, and let's not forget, where you've been sleeping for weeks on end now."

"What are you talking about?" I cross my arms in defense.

"Do you honestly think this is the first time I've come to your apartment looking for you? This is just the first time you've been home." I nod and close the door he left open. Does he know? About Alister? About all of it? If he's truly been so worried about me that he's been staking out my apartment, then it's possible he's done other things, like follow me to Laroux House. Though I imagine if he knew what I've been up to, he would've found a way to confront me long before now, especially since my relationship with Alister is an utter violation of Bilieux's orders. If Bilieux found out, it would be grounds for termination. Not that I give a damn about that corrupt bastard.

He can try to fire me all he likes. Alister will— I stop myself as thoughts of Alister threaten to overcome me once more. "And yet, none of that is why I'm here," Ray says then, shoving his hands into his jeans pockets.

"Why are you here?" I ask. Ray takes a deep breath. The somber expression he wears is strikingly different from the Ray I remember—the blond-haired, blue-eyed, happy-go-lucky guy always ready with a smile and a joke. "Ray, what is it? Just tell me." I slap my hand against my thigh. It's then that his brows crinkle and he takes a step toward me.

"Wait, have you been crying?" At that, my lips part and I lower my eyes to the floor. "*Ari?*" Ray closes the distance between us. Bringing his hand to my chin, he lifts my head, forcing me to look at him once more. The simple movement makes me think of Alister. Everything makes me think of Alister! I bite my lip and pull away from him, fighting tooth and nail to hold my emotions inside. Not only can I not tell Ray the truth, at least not today, I also don't have time to have another breakdown. I have to get to Vitale before Alister kills him.

"I really have to go," I say then. I turn and reach for the handle on my front door, but Ray stops me from opening it by pressing his palm against the wood. "Ray. What are you doing?" I do not turn to him as he speaks, though I can hear the hesitancy in his voice. Whatever it is, he doesn't want to say it, he doesn't want to believe it's true. *Oh no.* He knows.

"There are whispers around the bureau that you've been investigating Alister Amato for months now, despite Bilieux's orders. I don't think I need to explain how bad this could get if you don't find a way to refute the rumors and fast. Bilieux doesn't need another reason to fire you. Giving him one may make your suspension permanent."

At that, I turn to him. In his eyes, I find worry. "Knowing this, when I didn't answer—"

"I thought there was a chance you were dead, Ariana." He brings his hand to my cheek. No. *No*, not like he does it. *Please*. I can't. "Please tell me it's not true."

"I...I can't do that, Ray. And I also can't let you touch me like that, ever, ever again." Shock and sadness contort Ray's features as he lowers his hand. I step around him, putting an entire room's width between us. "Look, I...I will tell you everything. I will. But right now—"

"Right now, what? Where do you have to run off to? To see him?" As Ray loses himself in his hurt and anger, I welcome the guilt I feel for lying to him and denying him. It eases some of the sadness I fear is permanent. He shouldn't have found out this way. He shouldn't have found out at all. But how? How could those rumors have been started? No one in the bureau cares enough to keep tabs on me except for Ray, and even he didn't know of my investigation into Alister until he heard a rumor. *Bilieux*.

Alister told me that Bilieux suspected I'd approached him. He didn't know why or how, and he certainly didn't know the extent of our relationship. But he knew our paths had crossed or else Alister never would've used his FBI login to look me up. That put me on Bilieux's radar in the wrong way, as if I wasn't already. Alister assured me he'd handle Bilieux, but what if Bilieux plans on *handling* me first out of fear I've gotten too close to Alister and have learned of his corruption. By spreading a rumor around the bureau that links me to a known criminal, he's creating an easy motive for my murder. Ray is worried Bilieux will fire me, but I think he's capable of getting rid of me in other, more permanent ways.

"Ray," I say, stopping his tangent. "Ray, you have to leave."

"*What?*"

"You can't be seen with me, not while these rumors are circulating." I begin pushing him toward the door. Alister said that my being seen with him while there was a target on his back put me at risk. Now I fear the same for Ray. If Bilieux thinks I know his secret and that I've told Ray, he won't just come after me. He'll come after us both.

"What? *Why?*"

"*Because!* I've already dragged you into this mess once. I won't do it again. You helped me capture Walsh and put him in WITSEC. That was for my investigation into Alister Amato. If Bilieux finds out, he'll have just as much reason to fire you as he does me. So, you need to leave." At that, I pull the front door open and step aside for Ray to leave.

"No. No, Ariana, I'm not going anywhere until we talk." I throw my hands up in exasperation. Though, my peripheral vision picks up on movement that draws my attention from Ray.

As Christio Vitale along with three armed men appear in my open doorway, my eyes go wide with horror and my entire body goes numb. I guess I don't have to worry about Alister killing him before I get my face-to-face. Though, as his green eyes bore into mine, an evil smirk tugging at his lips, I wish he had.

"You should've listened to her, son."

30

Alister

My lungs fill with steam while the taste of eucalyptus lingers on my tongue. As I stand, half-naked in the bathroom that holds far too many memories, it invades my nostrils and fills my being as if it has the power to make me breathe easier, but no such power exists. There is no cure for the raw agony coursing through my veins. There is no treatment that can erase the memory of her touch, her voice, her body, her spirit. There is no soap able to wash the scent of her from my skin and my sheets. These are the memories we both wanted. These are the moments we both sought to cling to. Yet, I never imagined them to be so torturous, so debilitating. They haunt me. *She* haunts me.

As I stare into the ornate mirror, it is not my damp, towel-draped figure that stares back. It's her. She stands before me just as she did only a few hours before. And like before, her eyes are bloodshot. Her cheeks are red and stained with tears that never cease. She is the picture of utter heartbreak. As she takes me in, her gaze shifts from one of pity to one of horror as I prick her skin with the strongest possible dose of my cook's most recent creation. Memories of her falling into me come to me. I lower my gaze from my mirror to my arms as if I might find her in them. Alas, they are empty, as is my heart, as were her eyes as she drifted out of consciousness.

Desperate for a distraction, I slather shaving cream onto my face and reach for my straight razor. I imagine Ariana caressing my cheek, running her fingers through my stubble just as she did the night before. As my chest aches with the thought of her, I bring the blade to my skin and begin removing the source of the memory. I fight the urge to lean into its sharp edge. If I bleed, then at least I have a reason to feel as I do. As it stands, I have no right to break, to cry, to yell, to mourn the loss of her, because it is I who pushed her away. I ruined us. *I*...I broke her. And maybe she could've forgiven me for that. But after this morning, she'll never trust me again. She...she'll hate me.

If only she had hated me from the start, saying goodbye to her wouldn't hurt so much. But she saw me for me and for the man I want to be, and she loved me. *She loved me.* And that is exactly why I did what I did. It's why I can't have her anywhere near Vitale, at least not until I have him in my custody, restrained, where he can't hurt her. Because as much as she loves me, I love her. I love her with everything that I am. Every crevice of my heart belongs to her. It is a love so powerful that I've never felt anything like it. It's different from the love of my family. It's...it's all-consuming. It's as if she is mine and mine alone to protect.

Maybe I was wrong to do what I did. Maybe I could've talked her out of accompanying me to face off with Vitale. But if her presence at the Temptress told me anything, it's that she won't sit quietly behind. And I...I couldn't bear to be in her presence any longer, not when I know I can't have her. I can't touch her. I can't claim her. I can't love her. It is an impossible task, one that only makes the end of this investigation and thus, our relationship, that much more tragic. We knew this day would come. We knew that being together wasn't possible. Perhaps it even goes without saying that we knew we couldn't be friends. Even that innocent of a relationship could draw my enemies to her. But now I fear an even more permanent separation may be necessary because I don't know how to exist in the same world as her. I don't know how to walk down the streets of the French Quarter and not search every shadow for her. I don't know how to let her go, even though, after this morning, she may be ready to do just that.

I pull the razor from my face and bring it to my wrist, gritting my teeth as I hold it over my throbbing veins. My hand shakes as the voices in my head argue over what I should do next. I need her to hate me. I should be happy I finally gave her a reason since my business and blood weren't enough to turn her away. I should be relieved. And yet, relief is the last thing I feel in her absence. The sounds of her cries and the look on her face as I held her before the drug took effect make me desperate for an escape. I *want* to feel the pain of the blade slicing into my skin, because at least then I can escape this unrelenting mental torment, this disease of conflicting emotions. At that, I give in to my urge, unable to restrain myself any longer. Yet, as my blood escapes through the tiniest sliver of open skin, my thoughts of Ariana only intensify.

I think back to the first night I met her, the night I saw her scars. That was the moment my soul succumbed to her. That was the moment her safety became my responsibility, whether I liked it or not, because the marks on her body let me know no one had ever protected her before. I remember wondering if she'd hurt herself, if the pain of her life's tragedies had gotten the best of her, but it didn't. No. She...she remained strong.

I pull the razor from my flesh and throw it with all my force. It crashes against the slate wall of my shower, and the handle separates from the blade, both pieces falling among the bloodstained clothes piled in the corner. I throw my hands out and rest my weight on the vanity before me. I lower my head and do my best to calm my breathing, inhaling what's left of the eucalyptus steam. She was strong. She *is* strong. She will survive this, just like she did the loss of her mother, the bullies of her childhood, and the man who used his own grief as an excuse to rape her, the man I've made certain will never hurt another soul again.

Ken Clarke, handcuffed and still wearing his orange prison jumpsuit, fights against the grip of the officers on my payroll. "What is this place? Where have you taken me?" I stand with my back pressed against the hard cinderblock wall of the abandoned building that serves as ground zero for my drug business. He can't see me. The room is large and empty, a decoy in case anyone comes looking for things they shouldn't. All the windows have been boarded up, casting the entire space in darkness. The only light comes from a single fixture hanging above the bottomless metal chair, which my men strap Ariana's rapist to. The light illuminates his graying blond hair, the sunspots on his pale, weathered face, and the ice in his crystal blue eyes. Prison has not been kind to him. Though, I imagine he will long for the comfort of his cell and the company of his cellmate once he becomes acquainted with me. Little does he know, mine is the last face he will see.

He's spent over a decade of his twenty-year sentence in prison for his assault against Ariana, who was then just seventeen. Her age at the time of the crime is the only reason he received the maximum penalty. And yet, he is still eligible for parole as early as next year. That simply won't do. In no universe will I allow him to live alongside her.

"Please. This has to be a mistake. You've got the wrong man."

"No," I say, emerging from the darkness. "You do." He doesn't know who I am, but he knows he should be afraid. As his lips part and his eyes widen in fear, a wicked smile tugs at my lips. It's rare for me to take

joy in inflicting pain, but today I will make an exception. As I reach into my suit jacket, he flinches. *Pussy.* From my coat, I pull a white envelope filled with cash and instructions on what to do with his body after I'm finished. I hand it to my inside man. "For your trouble." He gives me a nod, takes the money without saying a word, and the two of them leave the way they came.

"Wait! Wait, you're just going to leave me here? What is this? Corrupt bastards!" Clarke yells. *Man, you'd think over a decade in prison would've taught him a thing or two about keeping his mouth shut. I suppose it's never too late to learn.* At that, I sling my fist into his cheek as my men disappear through the exit. Blood spurts from his mouth, spraying across the concrete floor. The blow silences him, giving me a moment to remove my suit jacket and adjust the sleeves of my button-down.

"Who...who are you?" he asks, gargling his own blood.

"Wrong question," I say, throwing my fist into him again. *To be honest, I've got more creative ways of punishing him than with my fists. But, after this morning, it feels good to punch something.* "Would you like to try again?" I cock my brow, wiping the blood on my knuckles onto my shirt. He shakes his head. I nod. *He's a fast learner. Unfortunately for him, I'm not done reorganizing his face.*

As I pound my fist into his flesh, I black out. I lose myself in the blood, in his screams, even in the silence once he is no longer able to speak. I'm not sure how much time passes before I come to. When I do, Ken Clarke is unrecognizable. He is nothing but bruises and blood and even that is not good enough. *It will never be good enough to make up for what he did.* As I take a step back, once more wiping the blood from my fists, I step on something—a tooth. The sight of it prompts me to inspect the floor surrounding Clarke, which is where I find more teeth, pools of blood, and suddenly become aware of the smell of urine. The scene is enough to steady my hand and allow myself a moment to catch my breath. I turn away from him and return to the wall from which I came to grab the broom propped against it.

I didn't get to take my time with Avery Gallagher. Had he raped Ariana, I promised him he would suffer in kind, and I meant it. I think it only right Ken Clarke suffer the same fate I had planned for Gallagher, since he did, in fact, rape the woman I love, my defenseless, sweet, Ariana. He was supposed to protect her. He was supposed to care for her, provide for her. No, he wasn't her real father, but he was a father figure. She was under his care, and he not only failed her, but abused her. Perhaps that, just as much as her mother's murder, is why Ariana struggles to open up to people. She is afraid of being abandoned, afraid of being betrayed by those she trusts. Her scars are more than just physical. She is haunted by what he did to her both in her dreams and in her daily life. This man will never know the pain he's caused. Just as the men who committed the same offenses against Cara will never know the true consequence of their crimes. Perhaps there is a bit of peace to be found in her death. She wasn't forced to live with the pain of what happened to her, at least not for very long.

I lower my eyes to the ground and return to Clarke, broom in hand. He doesn't move as I approach him. His chin sags against his chest. I kick his leg to draw his attention. I want to know that he hears me, that he understands why this is happening to him. And I want him to look upon the broom with fear just as Ariana was forced to watch him stalk toward her, just as she was forced to lie on the ground, restrained, waiting in silent agony for Gallagher and his men to rip her clothes off.

"My name is Alister Amato," I say through gritted teeth. "And you raped the woman I love."

"I...I never..." I kick his leg once more as he struggles to speak.

"Ariana Valentine!" I yell. If he can't speak, at least he can listen. "She was seventeen and she was in your care and you...you hurt her in the most unspeakable of ways." I lean forward, jabbing my finger into his chest as I speak. Finally, I have his attention.

"It was only one time," he says. He's so quiet, I can barely hear him. Yet, his sentiment is impossible to miss.

"It was only one time," I repeat. His words dumbfound and enrage *me, so much so I have to force myself away from him for fear I'll kill him before he has a chance to truly suffer.* "One time." *I pace the floor in front of him, though my anger quickly consumes me and draws me back to him. I step forward and take his face in my hands.* "We aren't playing baseball with women's bodies, you sick fuck," *I yell, mere inches from him.* "You don't get three strikes. You get one. And, unfortunately for you, you used it on the wrong girl."

"Ariana," *he whispers.*

"You don't get to say her name. Say it again and I sew your mouth shut."

I tighten my grip on his shredded cheeks. That is, until he notices the broom still clutched tightly in my hand.

"What is that?" *he asks, his eyes shifting from me to it.*

"This? This is going to hurt." *At that, I release him and—*

Ariana may hate me. I may hate myself for breaking her heart. But at least I know she'll be safe—safe from Ken Clarke, safe from Vitale, safe from me. In that, I find respite from the raging war inside. That is, if I can get my shit together and finish this. I take a deep breath and allow my thoughts of Ariana to settle. When I return my gaze to the mirror, I'm pleased to find it empty of her reflection. Vitale has had twenty years to plot his revenge against my family. No doubt he's stockpiled weapons and recruited extra soldiers off the books. There is no room for distractions today nor weakness.

I wipe the remaining shaving cream from my freshly shaven face and make my way to my closet where I opt for tactical attire instead of my typical suit. I slip into the black cargo pants, tucking my black T-shirt into them, and, doing my best to keep my face void of emotion, make my way downstairs to find Gio, Sophia, and Cassio waiting for me.

As I reach the bottom of the stairs, Sophia's sadness is undeniable. She looks at me with pity rather than the worry I half expected. She must've heard Ariana and I last night *and* this morning. Cassio stands next to her sharing her expression while Gio stands across the room, dressed similarly to me, none the wiser. I move my eyes to the floor and clear my throat.

"Are we ready?" I ask.

"Yes, Boss," Gio says. "Cassio's men are waiting for us in the vans along with more weapons than Christio Vitale could ever imagine. We're ready."

I nod. "We have one stop to make first," I say, lifting my eyes to Gio. His brows furrow in confusion. I always entrust Gio with planning our missions. Everything from entry to exit, to transportation, to our formation, to the kinds of weapons we use. But, even with the element of surprise and Cassio's surplus of high-tech gear, Vitale has us at a disadvantage. I can't be sure he hasn't turned some of my private soldiers to his cause, which is why I've kept them at arm's length for weeks now and haven't entrusted them with Gio's and my plans of attack. We will be outnumbered. But there is one person I can trust outside of Gio and Cassio, one person with an army of his own who has just as much motive as me to see Vitale brought to his knees—Alessandro Gagliano, Ariana's father.

I cross the room to Cassio and offer him my hand. I don't plan on losing today, but I'd be an idiot to operate with blind confidence. Cassio stands up straight as he shakes my hand. "If anything happens—"

"It won't," Cassio says, cutting me off. "But if it does, Sophia will be safe with me for as long as she chooses."

I nod and offer him a smile. "Thank you." At that, I move to my sister. Neither of us utter a word, because we wouldn't know where to begin. Instead, she throws her arms around me and nuzzles her head against my chest. I return her embrace, my throat raw with emotion.

Sophia is aware of our plan. Gio, I, and our men will infiltrate

Vitale's compound here in New Orleans. It'll be a bloodbath, one, without Gagliano's men, we may not all survive. If we do, Sophia will have her moment with Vitale once we've extracted him and brought him here to Laroux House. If she doesn't hear from us, she and Cassio will take the jet to his home in Savannah. She'll be safe there. And, whether he chooses to fight with us or not, Gagliano will be reunited with his daughter. However much I'd like to shield Ariana from the Mafia, if something happens to me and Gio, her father will be the only one left with the means and desire to keep her safe. Despite my inability to be in her life, I will never stop protecting her, even if it is from the shadows.

"I love you, brother," Sophia says then.

"I love you too." At that, I pull away from her and stalk toward the door as if walking fast will allow me to escape my emotions and not just the emotions of potentially seeing my sister for the last time or even the utter agony of saying goodbye to Ariana. As I reach for the handle and open the door of my childhood home to the chilly winter breeze carrying the scent of moss and evergreens, I am not only walking away from the two women who mean the most to me, I am going to avenge the two women who were taken from me.

As I step from the stoop to the gravel drive, making my way toward the black van waiting for me, my eyes drift to the oak trees just off to the side. It is among them that I find Cara. It's been a while since I've seen her. But as I take her in, I see it's been worth it. The gray-blue skin of her ghost has warmed to her natural tone. Her face is free from tears, mascara smudges, and any signs of dishevelment. Similarly, her nightgown is no longer torn and stained, and she finally looks like the sister I remember. Her improved appearance lets me know that the truth truly has been revealed and the man responsible for her death, and my mother's, will finally meet his end. I know she isn't real. I know her ghost is nothing but a figment of my imagination, a visual representation of my own journey to make peace with her death. Still, seeing her reinvigorates me and reminds me of the purpose of this mission and of everything I've endured over the last year. The memories of her and my mother focus my mind and ease the ache of heartbreak. That is, until Gio finally takes note of Ariana's absence.

"I thought Ariana stayed the night," Gio says.

"She did," I mumble. As I reach for the handle on the passenger side of the van, I hesitate. I don't care to have this conversation in front of the men waiting for us inside. I turn to Gio to find his brows furrowed and his eyes narrowed. "I decided it best she doesn't accompany us today."

"And she accepted that?"

I purse my lips as memories of the morning threaten to take hold of me. "Not exactly." Gio nods and lets out a sigh. Perhaps he pities me, same as my sister. Only, I imagine his pity isn't so much out of concern for my heart rather what Ariana will do to me once she wakes. As the thought threatens to unravel my focus, I push it from my mind and open the door to the van. Whether I live long enough for Ariana to hate me or die before she gets the chance to, one way or another, this ends today—all of it. If we don't get on with it, the anticipation may kill me first.

31

Alister

As we arrive at Gagliano's townhouse in the French Quarter, the skies above fill with stormy clouds as thunder rumbles. It's a three-story brick building with black doors and shutters and a wrought iron terrace adorned with greenery that wraps around the second story. As the wind kicks up, the ferns hanging from the second-story awning begin to blow and the gas flames of the street-level lanterns are snuffed out. That's not a good sign. Given my hesitancy to bring Gagliano into the fold, it's enough to give me pause.

"You okay, Boss?" Gio asks, stopping a few feet away. I shake my head and shift my gaze to the quiet street. It's not that I don't trust Gagliano. I mean, sure, I don't know him that well. Just a few months ago, I was questioning who between him and Vitale I trusted the least. But there is no doubt in my mind that when he learns his daughter is alive and that Vitale is the one who killed his love, Valentina, he will join our cause. I suppose it's that certainty that makes me hesitate.

Once Ariana and her father are reunited, her life will change forever. She'll be a Mafia princess. She will forever be connected to murderers, drug dealers—criminals. And between her father meeting with associates at his home and her attendance at Mafia-only parties and events, it won't just be Gagliano she'll be exposed to. The mere thought makes me clench my fists. I know what this world will do to her. Perhaps, even more so, I know what the men of this world will do to her, or, at least, try. And if they learn she works for the FBI, they'll kill her and her father, suspecting them spies. Deep down, I know the last thing I should do is walk through that gate. But I also don't have a choice if I hope to survive today's events nor do I have it in my heart to keep Ariana from her father, even if the thought of them being in each other's lives makes my skin crawl.

"Boss?"

"I'm ready," I say. It's a lie. Nevertheless, I tap my hand on my back and side pockets, feeling for my weapons, and then continue through the wrought iron gate leading to Gagliano's courtyard.

An armed guard stands at the end of the pass-through. Once he recognizes us, he immediately steps aside and communicates over his comms that we've arrived. I give him a good once-over, assessing his abilities to maintain the safety of the home. If Ariana will be spending even a minute here, I need to know she's protected by the best. Perhaps I should just find a personal guard for her myself, though I doubt she'd accept the gesture. I make a mental note to find someone with stealth, someone who can watch her from afar without tipping her off. A woman, to be certain, or a eunuch.

"Mr. Amato," Gagliano says. He appears, dressed in a tan suit, on the second-story wrap-around porch overlooking the stone courtyard. "What a lovely surprise." *Yeah, lovely.* "Please, have a seat. I'll have my cook send out some refreshments and be right down."

"That won't be necessary. Please, join us now." Gagliano's

smile leaves him as he registers my stern tone. He nods, tugs on the lapels of his suit, and follows my command. It occurs to me I should treat him with a bit more respect considering my feelings for his daughter and the fact that I'm here to ask for his help. However, I'm not sure I have the capacity to tidy up my manners on this day of all days.

Gagliano makes his way down the white-painted steps, and the three of us sit at the table situated between the fountain that anchors the space and the raised bed of white roses against the brick wall of the compound. As their sweet scent drifts in the chilly breeze, I wonder if Ariana will like them. She did say how much she loved the gardens at Laroux House, specifically the roses.

"Boss. Boss? *Alister?*"

"Hmm?" I turn to find Gio and Gagliano staring at me. "Right, um." I clear my throat and sit up straight. "Might we have a bit of privacy?"

"Certainly." Gagliano motions for his men to disperse. As they do, I take note of their placements, as does Gio. It's why he's always one step ahead of his opponent, though my interest in them is for a different reason entirely. There are four men who guard the main entrance and courtyard. Normally, I'd say it's a bit overkill considering the modest size of the place. But, given the circumstances, I'm pleased with the number as I am with the additional three who guard the second-story bedrooms and offices.

With all his men out of earshot, Gagliano shifts in his chair. "What is this about, sir?" he asks. As he speaks, I detect a bit of unease. Perhaps he's heard of my confrontation with Parisi. While no one saw me lay a finger on him, there were plenty of witnesses that know I was the last person to see him before his lengthy unexplained absence. Gio returned him to his wife last night. Still, perhaps Gagliano fears he will be next. Though I realize that those same witnesses could've reported back to Vitale. Perhaps our so-called element of surprise isn't as surprising as we thought. *Shit.*

"Right, um, I wish I could handle this more delicately, but, unfortunately, we don't have much time." Gagliano looks between us. His lips droop with worry. The simple movement draws attention to the wrinkles surrounding his mouth, which remind me of his age. He isn't old by any means. He's in his forties. And yet, the silver streaks through his black hair and the loose skin around his brown eyes say otherwise. He lost the love of his life before he was even twenty. Not to mention his child. Even though Valentina and Ariana survived past what Gagliano believed was their end, Ariana has still lived an entire life, twenty-eight years, without a family, and he without his daughter. Even given my intimate acquaintance with loss, that kind of pain is unimaginable.

I lower my eyes from his gaze and do my best to offer him the respect and patience he deserves as I reveal all that we've uncovered about Valentina's family, her death, Vitale's vendetta, and the fact that his daughter is alive.

As Gagliano absorbs all that I have to say, his demeanor shifts from uptight and cautious to restless and surprised. He stands from his chair and paces the length of the courtyard more times than I can count. He's quiet yet deep in thought until finally, he stops and drops to his knees in tears. He buries his face in his hands. Gio and I avert our eyes, giving him a moment. As his cries echo through the open-air space, my body stiffens. My thoughts of Ariana are unrelenting despite my best efforts to keep them at bay. His wails of both heartbreak and happiness serve as too stark a reminder of Ariana's cries. It's a sound I'm not sure I'll ever get out of my head.

"My daughter's alive," Gagliano whispers, wiping his face with his handkerchief. "My daughter." He stands and, slowly, makes his way back to us. "I...I didn't even know it was a girl. Valentina, she—" His lip quivers, forcing him to take a moment to collect himself. "All this time, I thought Valentina died in that fire and I have lived with that guilt for almost thirty years."

"Guilt? Why would you feel guilty? It was my father who ordered the hit against Carlo. If it had been Valentina in that house, her death would've been my father's fault, not yours. Even still, Veronica's is."

"No," Gagliano says, shaking his head. "There was never any hit."

"What?" Gio and I look at each other, confused. We have evidence to believe otherwise—the missing page from my father's hit book, likely torn out by Vitale to cover up his motive for coming after my family, and the blood vial labeled with Carlo Vitale's initials. My father recorded Carlo Vitale's death as if it was a hit and then Christio came along and did his best to remove the evidence. I understand Vitale's motives but not my father's. If it wasn't a hit, then why would he document it as such?

"Valentina's father moved the family out of New Orleans shortly after she became pregnant. I can only assume it's because she told her parents the truth and he didn't want anyone witnessing their family's shame. But even the privacy of the country wasn't enough for him. When I would go to visit her, he refused to let me inside to see her. This went on for weeks before I told my father. When I finally did, he went to your father, Domenico, for help. I hoped that they could reason with Carlo and arrange a marriage between me and Valentina. But... when they arrived at Carlo's country estate, everything went sideways."

"How so?" I ask. Gagliano takes a deep breath as his shoulders slump. It's obvious these memories are painful for him.

"Carlo attacked them. It never made sense to my father or

yours. Your father never had any reason to believe Carlo had anything personal against him, which is why it was so easy for Domenico to move Christio into Carlo's place. Now hearing of what Carlo was up to all those years ago, I understand. He didn't attack them on a whim, angry because of Valentina's pregnancy. He...he took advantage of their presence and he tried to dethrone a king. He failed. My father and yours were forced to kill Carlo and his wife that day. And because there was no evidence to suggest that Carlo had ill intentions toward your father, he feared that if his people learned the truth, that he was involved in the murder, especially after the third body was found, they would rebel." I nod. It's a valid thought.

If you kill one of your capos without good reason, none of them will feel safe under your rule. And a king is only as powerful as his army. Thankfully, in my case, there is plenty of evidence proving Vitale's guilt. And with Gagliano as a witness, I'll have no problem ridding him from my ranks. Though, perhaps that explains why my father documented Carlo's death as a hit. If anyone ever found out that he was present the day he died, he could at least say it was a hit even if it truly wasn't. It's not a fool-proof solution, but it was something.

"They were there because of me. Valentina got pregnant because of me." Gagliano shoves his finger into his chest, shaking his head. "Even with what you've told me today, I am still not without blame when it comes to what happened to Valentina. She was sent away because of me. Her family turned against her because of me."

"You weren't the one who forced her to live like a slave, Alessandro. And you aren't the reason she was sent away," I tell him. "That was her father's doing. And after his death, her uncle picked up where he left off by using her to destroy my family. Though, perhaps his motives are a little more understandable than Carlo's simple desire for power."

At that, Gagliano nods. "The fire was meant to cover up Carlo and his wife's true cause of death and, most importantly, any evidence linking back to my father and Domenico. I suppose that explains why Vitale hasn't added my family to his list of enemies over the years. Perhaps Carlo had told him of his plans against Domenico, at least enough for Vitale to suspect foul play in his brother's death. But he wouldn't have had a reason to suspect my father, especially if he didn't know that I was the father of Valentina's baby."

I nod. "You're right. He couldn't have known or else he would've made you suffer the same as he did Valentina."

Gagliano clears his throat. Perhaps I shouldn't have told him everything about the treatment Valentina suffered at Christio's hand. But if I didn't, Ariana would feel like she had to and I don't want her to have to relive those memories, as if she can ever escape them.

"My father swore to me they checked the house and found no one else there," Gagliano says. "But it's not uncommon for people in our line of work to have secret hiding places, especially for our children. But if what you say is true, Valentina was already in Boston, and it was Veronica Vitale who died that day."

"We believe so. Which would explain why Vitale could be so ruthlessly cruel to his niece and why he's kept coming after my family all these years. Unlike his brother, he doesn't care about power. He was happy enough to promise Joseph Cullen of the Irish mob most of what he would gain so long as he helped him destroy me. That kind of motivation is only sparked by one thing—revenge."

"So, what do we do now? When do I get to see my daughter?" Gagliano asks.

"In good time. But first, we need your help taking down Vitale once and for all."

"Whatever you need, consider it yours. In a way, it kind of

already is." At that, Gagliano smiles. It's an odd expression given our task. But I know that look. It's one only Ariana can bring about. He's excited to meet her, and while I was worried about just that, there's something about him that puts me at ease. I suppose because I see the way he speaks of her mother, the way he mourns her, the way he still loves her even after all these years, even after marrying and building a family with another. Valentina has always had a claim over his heart. That is something I recognize because I know what it is to love someone that deeply. Yet, like him, I fear I also know what it is to lose that someone.

I stand to stretch my legs as Gio meets with Gagliano's head of security and informs him of our plan. My phone buzzes in my pocket, and I have half a mind to ignore it completely. If there was an emergency at the house, Cassio would handle it rather than call me, given our mission. And if it's work, as in the actual businesses I run that don't involve drugs, it can wait. Yet, an uneasy feeling in my chest prompts me to pull it from my pocket. Ariana's name appears on a text notification, and my mouth instantly goes dry. I didn't expect her to wake this soon nor am I prepared for what she has to say now that she has.

With a heavy heart, I open the text. As the image of Ariana tied to a chair, beaten and bloody, sears into my eyes, I fight the urge to throw the device against the nearest brick wall. My blood boils inside me. My heart beats so quickly it feels as if it may rip out of my chest. I spin on my heel to face Gio as my words evade me. I bring my hand to my heart as my phone slips from my grasp.

"Boss?" Gio runs toward me as I drop onto one knee. He instantly spots the phone and reaches for it before Gagliano can see. *Thank God.* He shouldn't see her like that. I...I shouldn't have to see her like that. But this is exactly what I've been afraid of. This entire time. *That monster!*

"I can't...I can't lose her. I can't lose her, Gio. Not like this," I say, my voice cracking. Gio's eyes narrow as he takes in the image.

"What's going on?" Gagliano asks. "Is it Sophia? Does he have Sophia?"

Gio shakes his head and meets my eyes once more. There it is. He now shares the same look of pity Sophia wore just a short while ago. "It's not Sophia," Gio says, shoving the phone into his pocket. "But there is an address." I nod, pushing myself up from the ground.

"It says *come alone*."

"Yeah, that's not happening," Gio says, crossing his arms over his chest.

"What choice do I have, Gio? I won't let him hurt her. I won't let him kill her because of me." At that, I sling my fist into the brick siding of the pass-through. "*Ah!*" If my knuckles aren't raw enough after this morning's visit with Ken Clarke, the bricks certainly make them so. I suck down a slew of curses as I shake out my fingers, now bloodied.

"We will figure it out," Gio says, taking a step toward me. "We've got a two-hour drive to do so."

"Two hours? What?" At the mention of *two hours*, the same amount of time it took him all those years ago to visit Carlo Vitale's country estate, Gagliano finally understands. "He has my daughter, doesn't he?"

32

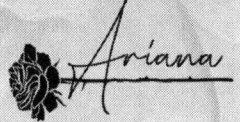

MY FACE STINGS AND MY HEAD IS HEAVY AS I COME TO. FUZZY images of a fight dance behind my closed eyes as soft drops of water land on my skin, casting a chill upon me that combats the warmth of my wounds. As I open my eyes, my senses return, and the pain of my injuries becomes more prominent. My chest aches as if I've been kicked. My sweater is ripped, revealing cuts along my arms. I lower my gaze to take in the haphazard pattern of blood staining my shirt, and it feels as if a scab on my lip cracks. I wince as the coppery taste of blood skates across my tongue. Where am I? What...what happened? *Ray!* I shift in my seat to search the burnt remains of the unfamiliar place, which only adds to my discomfort as the ropes restraining me to my seat dig into my wind-whipped skin. Among the charred rubble, I do not find Ray. Though what I do find is unsettling.

From where I sit in what appears to be the basement of a home long since destroyed, I can see straight through to the sky. Pine trees sway along the backside of the skeleton-like building. Their shade only adds to the chill of the wind and the random drops of rain escaping the storm clouds overhead. The remaining exterior walls of the two-story home, which I can only assume is Carlo Vitale's country estate, are charred black. All the windows have burst from their casings. The shards of glass lie on the ashy ground, mixing with broken sticks of wood and remnants of furniture and clothing long since forgotten. Yet, despite the disheveled nature of the home, there are structures that remain —a brick fireplace two stories tall, flooring I wouldn't trust, and a stone stairwell through the center. It remains intact like the cinderblock walls that maintain the shape and privacy of the basement in which I sit. It is around the perimeter of the room and upon the stairwell, stretching far above me, that armed men stand. Though, their mere presence is not what I find unsettling. It is their vantage point. If I am where I think I am, then I am surrounded by an open field, save for the pine trees on the backside of the property. While the men patrolling the decrepit space may be easy targets for a sniper, the likelihood of one setting up for a shot without being spotted is slim. This isn't going to end well.

Movement draws my attention to my left where, through a doorless frame, Christio Vitale enters wearing a spotless light gray suit. His sinister green eyes meet mine immediately. He walks slowly, befitting a man of his age. As he reaches out to me, I pull away. My resistance only makes him smile. He takes a step closer, and unable to move any farther from him, I flinch as he brings his hand to my split cheek.

"Such a shame," he says then. "If only you would've come willingly, none of this nastiness would've been necessary." At that, he removes his hand and takes a seat across from me.

"Willingly? Why would I go anywhere with you willingly?"

"Well, I am your great-uncle, after all. But you know that, don't you?"

"What I know is that you are nothing to me." He laughs and crosses his legs, clasping his hands atop his knee. "Where's Ray?"

"You needn't concern yourself with him."

"Well, I am concerned. Where is he?"

Vitale exhales in frustration. "We left him where we found him." His careless tone strikes me, setting my mind in a tizzy.

"Alive?" Vitale lifts his hands as if he's weighing oranges. "You son of a bitch. He had nothing to do with this."

"*This.*" Vitale nods, moving his eyes from me to take in our surroundings. "And what do you think you know of *this*, this place, this war—me? Where do you think we are, Ariana?"

As fury radiates inside me, I sit silent. Please, please don't let Ray be dead. He doesn't deserve to die. He doesn't even understand—

"You know, I never wanted any of this. It was my brother, your grandfather, who was involved with Domenico Amato and his business. He was the one who started all of this by allowing himself to believe he could dethrone a dynasty over a century in the making." At that, Vitale nods and shifts his gaze back to me. "The day this house was engulfed in flames, the day my brother died, was the day he told me of his plans. They weren't exactly actionable. At the time, Valentina was too young to play her part, at least, the part Carlo wanted her to play."

"And what part was that? Marry her off to the heir of some competing criminal syndicate? Use their men and arms to take down the Amatos, like you tried to do with Joseph Cullen and the Irish mob?"

"My, my. You've got it all figured out, don't you?"

"Well, it's a bit of an unoriginal scheme."

"You're right. It was. Mine was so much better, at least before Valentina put it in jeopardy." He smiles, and the simple gesture pulls my rage from what he may have done to Ray to what he most certainly did to my mother. As memories of the night my mother was killed flash through my mind, a rush of warmth courses through my veins. I am sitting mere feet from the man who took everything from me. It doesn't seem real. It doesn't feel real. But it is. As more rain falls from the clouds above, stinging my open wounds, I know I've experienced few things more real than this. If only I weren't restrained, I'd—

"Valentina was beautiful, spirited, and strong—like you, at least before—"

"Before you forced her to be your slave?" My throat is raw as the words scrape through me. Finally, after all this time, I will get the answers I've been searching for. Despite everything I've learned with Alister's help and Josephine's, I want to hear it from the horse's mouth. I want to know every tragic detail so that when I find my way out of these restraints, and I will, I won't feel guilty for the things I plan to do to him.

"Your mother understood that the Amatos had to be stopped. When she learned of what Domenico had done, killing her entire family—"

"You mean the lie you told her about an unprovoked attack that not only claimed the lives of your brother and his wife, but your daughter? Right? That's why you've done all of this. That's why you never stopped." As I speak, all civility leaves the man with the slicked-back gray hair. Vitale jumps out of his chair and reaches me within seconds. He pulls his arm back and smacks my already bruised and bloody cheek with all his might. "*Ah!*" I cry out as my head snaps to the right under the weight of the blow.

"You should have a little more respect for the man who provided for you all those years," Vitale whispers. His breath smells of old cigars laced with whiskey. He's so close, the mere smell burns my nostrils. I want to tell him to fuck off, that he didn't provide for me, my mother did. But I don't. One, because, in a sick way, he sort of did provide. And two, because I'm not ready to take another hit. Vitale backs away from me then, wiping the sweat from his brow with his handkerchief and adjusting the lapels of his suit. How can he be sweating at this temperature? Once collected, Vitale returns to his seat and his story.

"You're right. I did tell a lie to get her back to New Orleans, because I needed her cooperation, albeit, in a different way than her father planned for her. Carlo sent Valentina away because he didn't want anyone to know she'd been defiled, let alone been impregnated. But, once I had her back under my thumb, a dead girl no less, I used her in quite the opposite way." As a wicked grin spreads across Vitale's face, I press my chapped lips together to keep more antagonizing words inside. I knew it. There's no way my mother would've agreed to the life that befell her in New Orleans, even if she blamed the Amatos for her parents' deaths. And considering Vitale's blatant use of force against me, I can imagine he kept my mother in line in a similar way once she realized how he truly planned to use her to take down the Amatos.

"Valentina became a go-between for my spies," Vitale continues. "They'd visit her without drawing anyone's suspicion. We all have our whores, after all. When my men would gather new intel on the Amatos, they'd share it with her. The sex she provided was their reward for a job well done. She'd then share the information with me in exchange for a roof over her head, food on the table, and, of course, being able to keep you. It was a system that worked. The more I learned about the Amatos, the more elaborate my scheme to destroy them became and thus, the more drawn out." At that, Vitale pauses. He lowers his gaze from me to the ground as if lost in thought. Finally, he says, "It's an indescribable thing to lose the person you love the most. But you know that, don't you? Your mother was that person for you, just as my daughter...my daughter was that person for me. She was taken from me," Vitale admits. "Domenico Amato was the one who killed her, but she died because of your mother," he says, pointing his finger at me.

"How can you blame her? She was just a child."

"She was a child," Vitale agrees. "Which is why her pregnancy was such a disgrace. It was that shame that sent Carlo and his family out of the French Quarter to here, two hours away from me and my sweet Veronica. That's why my daughter was with me the day that I came to see my brother. I hadn't seen Carlo since the unexpected move, and I wanted to check on him. Veronica missed her cousin, so she asked to tag along. If your mother hadn't gotten pregnant, they never would've moved here. And even if my brother continued with his idiotic scheme, my daughter would not have died that day."

Vitale turns away from me and blinks away what might be tears. It's hard to tell in the poor light as the storm clouds above continue to darken and rumble, threatening a downpour rather than the light trickle currently irritating my skin. I could feel bad for him, if he hadn't retaliated against my mother, who was nothing more than a teenager at the time. There is no excuse for what he did—none. His daughter's death was tragic, but so was my mother's and all the pain she suffered before he finally ended her. Not to mention his ruthless assault against Alister and his family. His vendetta against Domenico, I understand, but going after his wife and children...

"When Carlo told me of his plans, I left. I went for a drive to process all he'd said and calm down. I knew that if he went through with it, he'd end up dead, but he wouldn't listen. He was greedy, stubborn, and stupid. I took my time searching for the right words to convince him to abandon his plans. By the time I made it back to the house, it was already engulfed in flames. There was nothing I could do to save them." He shakes his head and clears his throat as the memories haunt him. "In the days that followed, everything went seamlessly, *too seamlessly*. It was immediately ruled an accident even though my brother had just had an inspection done before moving in. And then, when Domenico Amato came to me about taking my brother's place in the business, I could feel it in my bones—he did this. Somehow, he found out what my brother was up to, and he killed him. I didn't have proof. In fact, it would be years before I knew with certainty. But the day I accepted Domenico's offer and took my oath was the day my plan was hatched." At that, Vitale nods as if thinking back over his greatest hits. It's sick.

"When my attack against the Amatos failed, I was forced to lay low. And, in doing so, I took pleasure in Domenico's suffering. Losing his wife broke him. He became paranoid and withdrawn from everyone except his children. He put all his energy into preparing them for the world they'd inherited, mostly Alister. But even the girls were taught things no ordinary Mafia princesses are. He trained Alister to fight and kill. He taught him the ways of the Mafia and of the world. Alister had to be perfect in his mother's absence, because anything less and his father's worry for his children would consume him. He wanted to ensure they could take care of themselves so that they wouldn't suffer the same loss he did. And that's when it occurred to me. I would not grant Domenico a quick reprieve from heartbreak. I would force him to live without his wife until the day came that I would take what's left of his family. I would take his children from him, one by one."

Vitale looks to me then as I absorb his words. This explains why Alister is so afraid of love, no, afraid of loss. It's not just because of the pain of his mother's untimely death, but because of the pain his father suffered as he was forced to live without her. Alister had to be strong because the death of his mother broke his father. And ever since, he's been afraid of suffering the same pain. Perhaps even afraid of neglecting those in his care because of his all-consuming grief. And most obviously, he's afraid of not being perfect. He's afraid anything less will put his sisters in jeopardy, a feeling I'm sure was only intensified after Cara's death.

"It's a pity cancer took Domenico before he had a chance to witness what I had planned for his children. Nevertheless, his death did not ease the pain of losing my daughter. Perhaps nothing ever will. But I am owed Amato blood for Domenico's hand in Veronica's death. And Amato blood, I will take."

"But you've already taken so much—Alister's mother, his sister. Let's say for one second I buy into your creepy, senseless Mafia logic, the Amatos have paid their debt to you in full two times over."

"No." Vitale shakes his head. "I lost my *only* child. While one dead Amato child is tragic, it is not the same."

"You're crazy. Alister has done nothing to you! Nor Sophia, nor Cara! And no matter what you believe about my mother, she was just a girl who fell in love. Your daughter's death was a tragedy, and you did not deserve to lose her the way you did, but my mother was innocent. She never deserved your wrath. She didn't deserve any of it."

"And what of you?"

"*Excuse me?*"

"What do you deserve? The way you speak of the Amato siblings and even my connection to the Irish mob, it's very *familiar*. I suppose you're the reason Alister has gotten so close to the truth. After nearly twenty years of manipulating him and his father, I knew something or someone must've tipped him off for him to suddenly question Gabriel Parisi the way he did."

So, he knows about Parisi. Perhaps that's what led him to me. He must've seen me at the club that night with Alister. *Damn it.* Alister was right. I shouldn't have gone in with him.

"Actually, that was your screwup. We only learned Joseph Cullen, before his untimely death, was working with someone in

New Orleans after your men's botched abduction attempt against Sophia. You led us straight to your secret squad of hitmen."

"Hmm," Vitale mumbles to himself as he tilts his head to the side. "Tragic what happened to Joseph." As Vitale speaks there is an unsettling gleam in his eyes.

"You killed him, didn't you? You…you got what you needed from him, Walsh, and his crew, and you got rid of him so you could control his men with them none the wiser. Gallagher thought Alister was responsible for Cullen's death. You'd hoped the Irish would go to war with the Amatos of their own accord and do your dirty work for you after Domenico's death, but you settled for their help in secret when they didn't take the bait—using them to abduct Cara and trying to repeat the process with Sophia."

Vitale nods once more, his eyes narrowing. "And who was it that thwarted that attempt? I was told it was a woman with dark hair, someone my men had never seen before in all their time surveilling the Amatos. It was you, wasn't it?" At that, Vitale laughs. "We could've been quite a pair had I had my way with you."

"And what way was that?" I ask as my mother's final words echo between my ears. *Good luck finding a ghost.*

"Oh, come on, Ariana. You're the smart, well-educated FBI agent with an act for profiling. You tell me."

My blood runs cold, and not because of the wind or even the rain. For him to know I'm FBI, Vitale must have been aware of me longer than just the few days since my appearance at the Temptress. That, or he has an inside man at the bureau, like Alister, or possibly both. Regardless of how he found out, he knows. And if his track record has proven anything, it's that he gets rid of people who know his secrets, especially those in positions of power. My status as an FBI agent only makes me more dangerous to him.

As my grim reality sinks in, so does understanding of why Vitale wanted to know where I was the night he took my mother from me.

"You said you wanted to take Domenico's children from him, because he took Veronica from you. You wanted to do the same thing to my mother—the woman you blamed the most for your daughter's death." I lift my eyes to meet Vitale's and find his lips drawn into a sly grin. "You let her keep me because I was your leverage to keep her in line. But even that plan had an expiration date, didn't it?"

Vitale nods, pleased with my deduction. "I planned to use Valentina for all she was worth until you reached your sixteenth birthday, the same age Veronica was when she died. And then I planned to take you from her, so that she could know the feeling of what it is to lose a child before I killed her."

Tears of pity well in my eyes. I once told Alister that there was never hope for me or my mom. Vitale's admission only makes it even truer. He was always going to destroy her, one way or another. At that, lightning cracks overhead. It illuminates the sky, though only for a moment. It makes me think of Alister and the day we wrestled in the rain. What I would give to be in his arms right now, shielded from this man and all the pain he represents.

Vitale stands and crosses the small space to where I sit. He reaches for me again and this time, I don't have the will to pull away from him. He brings his hand to my chin and tilts my head so that my eyes meet his. "You were meant to be my replacement, Ariana, my second chance at having a family. As it stands, I see you've chosen my enemy over me." *What?*

As the clouds above break and more lightning ensues, they shed rain down upon me with such ferocity I feel as if I could drown in it. Vitale retreats toward the stairwell where there is some overhead cover from the remaining floorboards while I sit stuck in ashy mud.

"You know, I've known Alister almost all his life," Vitale calls out. "He was just a boy when I first met him. None of his other siblings had even been born yet. And in the time since, I've never seen him keep the company of a woman or even look at a woman the way he looks at you."

Vitale's lips lift into a wicked smirk, and my stomach twists inside me. Christio Vitale has his own reasons for coming after me. I am his great-niece. That makes him interested. I know the truth about him. That makes him lethal. But if my encounter with Avery Gallagher and Alister's warnings of what someone would do to me to get to him are worth anything, then I'd be a fool to think my presence here has nothing to do with my relationship with Alister. As the rain drenches my clothes and hair, I struggle to keep my eyes trained straight ahead. But I have to. I can't let Vitale out of my sight, especially now that I know why I'm truly here.

"And what do you know of how he looks at me?" I ask.

"Enough to know you're the key to ending the Amato reign once and for all."

33

Alister

It's a long drive from New Orleans to the country estate where Ariana is being held hostage, and it's only made longer by the pouring rain and snapping lightning overhead. I suppose the one bright side to the storm is it kept my mind focused on the road and not what Vitale has done and is doing to Ariana, at least, for the most part. But as I turn from the time-worn road onto the private gravel drive leading to the structure housing Ariana, Vitale, and his men, I can no longer keep my mind at bay. Images of Ariana bruised and bloody flash through my mind. He went after her because of me. She's in pain because of me. And who is to say she isn't already dead? The mere thought makes my heartbeat quicken in my chest. I'm not prepared for this. I'm not prepared to see her lifeless body, to touch her ice-cold skin. I never will be. But I have no choice. If there's a chance she's still alive, I have to do everything I can to get her to safety, even if that means giving Christio Vitale what he wants—my crown and my life.

When the gravel road dead-ends into soggy pasture, I stop the SUV and take a deep breath. As the dark storm clouds above give way to early nightfall, my headlights are the only light shining in the field. They shine for many yards yet reach only the edge of the decrepit structure, no doubt full of armed men and yet completely shrouded in darkness. Though, in their path, I do find two figures, tall and jacked. As menacing rain dances across my windshield, I watch as the two men walk toward me. They are dressed in tactical gear, like mine, and wield rifles.

"I'm about to go dark. Position check?" I say, speaking into my comms.

"Team 1 and Team 2 are almost in position. They'll move closer once Vitale's men have their attention on you. But Team 3 is still five, ten minutes out to target," Gio says, his breath ragged.

"Which is it, five or ten?"

Gio hesitates, filling the frequency between us with sounds of rainfall, breaking limbs, and rustling leaves. "Give me ten," he finally says. At that, I lower my head and close my eyes. He and I both know we may not have ten minutes. As much as we thought we were prepared, Vitale turned the tables on us when he took Ariana. We're playing by his rules now, and who knows what he has in store for me and for her. And if his men spot ours before Gio is in sniping position, I'm as good as dead and so is Ariana.

As the men reach me, I whisper "Copy" just in time for them to open the door and pull me from the vehicle into the chilly night.

"Mr. Amato, we've been expecting you." Despite their respectful words, their movements are anything but. They leave nothing to chance as they search my person, removing all the weapons they find. In truth, I expected nothing less and would've done it myself had I had time. As they toss the gadgets aside and lead me toward the disheveled structure, rain soaks my clothes and casts a chill upon my body. The sensation makes me think of Ariana. She's been out here for hours now. "You know I expected more of a fight. That picture must've done a real number on you," the man to my left says.

His words gnaw at me, and I press my lips into a flat line and clench my fists. It takes everything in me not to kill him right here and now. But I can't. Without a sniper, I'm going in blind. I have to be patient. Gio has never let me down before. He won't start now. At least, that's what I tell myself as the two men lead me through mud and ash until we reach the ground-level entrance to the home. When we do, both men fall back and shove me through the threshold.

As I stumble into the small, square-shaped room lit by battery-operated lanterns, my eyes immediately scan the perimeter. I count six men plus the two who corral me from behind. Yet, none of them make any moves to approach me. The man behind me shoves me forward, forcing me farther into the space. It's then that Ariana comes into view. She sits in the center of the dilapidated structure, soaked to the bone, still restrained to the same chair from hours before. Her chin rests against her torn, stained sweater. Her wet hair sticks to her skin, shielding her face from view. She's so still, so—

I run to her and reach her in seconds. To my surprise, no one stops me. As I drop to my knees before her, I fear it's because they want me to see her, to assess the pain they've inflicted. I brush her hair behind her ears and her face comes into view, but she does not respond to my touch. She doesn't even shiver, despite her body being ice cold. At the sight of her, I break, unable to hold in my emotions any longer. Tears steam down my face, mixing with the pouring rain. I want nothing more than to shield her from it and from all the predators lurking in the shadows. Yet, I can't bring myself to do anything until I know she's still with me.

"Ariana," I say, my voice strained. "Ariana." I bring both

hands to her cheeks and gently lift her to look at me. "Ariana," I say again. My lips quiver as the bright yellow light of the lanterns shines on her wounds. Her lip is split as are her cheeks in various places, no doubt a result of her taking a fist to the face. The rest of her body is in a similar condition. It looks as if someone came at her with a knife. I lower my eyes to take in her hands. Her knuckles are just as bloody and torn as mine. She gave them Hell. Unfortunately for her, they gave it right back. As I bring my eyes to her face once more, my heart tightens in my chest. She still hasn't moved. *"Mi amore?" Please, please, wake up. I can't lose you like this. I—*

Finally, her face twitches and I feel her take on a little of her own weight. "Ariana, it's me, Alister. I'm here. I'm here, baby." I coax her out of her sleep, breaking all my rules in the process. Vitale and his men wouldn't have taken her if they didn't know what she means to me. There's no use in hiding it now, as if I even could. Slowly, Ariana opens her eyes, and I immediately wrap my arms around her. "Thank God. Thank you, God," I say as I rub my hand on her back to help warm her up.

"Can we go home now?" she asks. Her voice is weak, and her question lets me know she's still out of it. Maybe it's for the best. She doesn't need to see what happens next. She just needs to survive. That's all I need from her.

"Alright, that's enough." I release Ariana from my grasp and lower my head as Vitale's crackling voice rings in my ears. Almost immediately, two men pull me from Ariana, forcing me down on my knees in the mud as Vitale makes his way between us. Ariana rouses at the noise, finally aware that this isn't over. It's only beginning.

"You see?" Vitale turns to her then. "I told you he'd come." A wicked smile spreads across his face as he returns his attention to me, blocking Ariana from my sight.

That's right, you bastard. Keep your eyes on me.

"To think if I would've held your mother hostage rather than killing her, I could've had my revenge on your family a long time ago." At the mention of my mother, I grit my teeth and fight to free myself from the men holding me down. Surely, Gio has had enough time to get in position by now. "Uh-uh!" Vitale wags his finger at me before planting a single punch on my cheek. It only makes me smile.

"Well, that tickled," I say. No wonder he's spent twenty years building an army and operating in the shadows. If he had to face me one-on-one, he wouldn't stand a chance. Vitale smiles, though it does not touch his eyes nor lift his cheeks. He nods and walks toward Ariana. "Wait, no."

"How about this? Does this tickle?" Vitale pulls back and barrels his fist into Ariana's cheek. She cries out as her body collapses under the force.

"Hey, you want to hurt someone, hurt me! You hear me, Vitale. Hurt me!" I yell, once more fighting against the men who hold me. *Come on, Gio. Where are you?*

Vitale turns to me then. "I think I am." At that, he returns his attention to Ariana. *Fuck this.* As Vitale lays into Ariana, I break free from my captors' grasp. Using the knife they somehow missed during their search, I slit both their throats and turn my attention to Vitale. The sounds of the scuffle draw his gaze from Ariana to me. Though, as I grip the rubber handle of my blade, readying myself to take out the wannabe king, the blaring sound of gunfire rings through the small space. It is only made louder as it bounces off the cinderblock walls surrounding us. The sound stuns me. I don't even feel the first bullet enter my shoulder. But the second one, the second one is hard to mistake. When another round of gunfire echoes around us, a second bullet rips through my chest, bringing me to my knees.

"*No!*" Ariana screams, tugging at the ropes that bind her.

As I bring my hand to my chest, my knife falls among the

rubble, out of reach. I draw my fingers back to find them covered in blood, which is quickly washed away by the falling rain. Vitale walks toward me, taking in the bodies of his men left in my wake. *There you go, old man. Come closer.* The first two bullets missed everything vital. While a third might kill me, if I end Vitale before he ends me, his men may very well jump sides. Without a leader, a paycheck, and a promise of power, what do they have to fight for? Even without my knife, I can kill him within seconds. Although, a quick death would ruin my elaborate plans for him.

"I heard the gunshots. If you're still with me, Boss, hang on. I've almost got visual. This damn rain is fucking everything up," Gio says through my flesh-colored earpiece. I'm running out of patience, but I manage to muster a little more knowing that Ariana's and my best shot at making it out of here alive is with Gio's help. As it stands, Vitale stops just out of reach.

"I came alone," I say. "I did what you asked. Now, please, let Ariana go. Take me instead."

Vitale's eyes narrow as he looks down on me like I'm nothing more than a dog he aims to break, but I don't care. As he hesitates to speak, I look past him to Ariana. She sits, drenched and alert. Her hands grip around the arms of her chair to the point her knuckles are white while her face is a combination of reds and purples. The sight of her is even more of a reason to give Gio the extra time he needs. I will make Vitale suffer for what he's done to her. One day of torture for the murder of my mother. One day of torture for the murder of Valentina Vitale. One day of torture for the abduction that resulted in the death of my sister. And one day for daring to lay a finger on the woman I love. When I'm done with him, I will gut him like the pig he is and then I'll toss his rotting corpse into the wild so that the true beasts may devour what's left of him. I wonder if he will feel it— the birds pecking, the insects nibbling, and the alligators taking what's left. I suppose he'd be lucky if that's all he felt. Where he's going, the Devil has much more sinister ways of inflicting pain. At that, I move my eyes back to Vitale and hold his gaze as I fight through the white-hot pain spreading through my shoulder.

"You did what I asked," Vitale agrees. "But there are still two things I want from you."

"And what are those?"

Vitale takes a step toward me then. As he does, I ball my fists. *Come on, Gio. I'm running low on patience and time.* As if sensing the end is near, the rain finally stops along with the thunder and lightning. The silence left in its wake gives way to other sounds—my ragged breath, Ariana's shivers, and Vitale's demands.

"First, I want your crown. Or, should I say, ring." Vitale looks to my hand where he finds the ring of my family crest. Though it features the Amato family crest, it represents an organization much larger than my blood kin. It represents power and the control I wield over ten Mafia families stretching across the Southern United States in addition to my own. By giving him my ring, I give up my power and the loyalty of the ten families. The protection they provide their king will transfer from me to him and then he will be unstoppable. That is, if he survives to exact such power.

Upon request, I remove the ring from my finger without a second thought or dropping his gaze. His lips spread into a wicked grin as he takes it from me. He believes he's won. Good. The moment he places the ring on his finger, he will feel invincible. And that's when his guard will be the lowest.

"You know, I never desired power the way my brother did. I've taken it from you as part of my plan to destroy you and what's left of the Amato legacy." He places the ring on his finger then. "But now, I'm starting to understand the appeal."

"It's a curse, Vitale. One I am happy to pass on to you and your line. Although, I suppose your line ends with you. Unless you let Ariana live, claim her as your long-lost niece, and pass on the crown to her. I know men have a longer reproductive shelf life than women, but somehow, I doubt you've got any other options."

Vitale laughs and begins pacing the space between me and Ariana, ashy mud kicking up with each step. It splatters against my pant legs where I remain on my knees before him. "Do you think I am so easily manipulated? More importantly, do you think it's wise to so blatantly reveal your greatest weakness? My men have already been to Laroux House. I know Sophia is gone. Wherever she is, you were smart to send her away. You bought her another day, week, maybe a month tops before I find her. But losing her won't break you, will it? Not anymore, at least. You see, now you have someone else occupying your heart, mind, and soul. Someone else who you'd do anything for, even give up your throne despite knowing that your weakness will result in your sister's death." At that, Vitale turns toward Ariana.

"Ariana Valentine is not my heir. She is nothing to me. Isn't that right, sweetheart? Nothing but a ghost from a painful past I'd rather forget. And yet, she is everything to you." As Vitale turns to me, my chest tightens and my stomach flips. I know I've run out of time. *We've* run out of time. "Ariana Valentine has brought the Blood King to his knees and cast the last of a great dynasty into the mud like the worthless trash that he is and represents. She has served her purpose, a purpose her mother could not fulfill. And now, she dies."

Vitale takes a deep breath, turns to his men, and says, "Grab the knife. Slit her throat with the same blade he used to kill my men, and then do the same to him. The Amato reign ends tonight."

"*No!*" I yell. As I push myself up from the muddy ground, I am quickly brought back down by an electric charge that sends my body into shock. The water soaked into my clothes only prolongs the effects of the volts. My body twitches, writhing in the mud as one of Vitale's henchmen grabs the knife from the ground and stalks toward Ariana. I try to fight through the pain and push myself to my feet, but it's no use. I even try to call out to Gio, even though it will blow his cover and the cover of my men. But the charge is too strong. All I can do is grit my teeth and take it as Vitale's man pulls at Ariana's hair, forcing her to look to the sky. The simple movement exposes her throat. *No, God, please, don't take her from me.* I won't survive it. I can't lose her too. I can't—

As the man standing behind Ariana brings the bloodstained blade to her flesh, the sound of rushing wind swoops through the space. Fewer sounds have brought such a smile to my face as it is followed by the collapse of the knife-wielding henchman.

"Team 3 is in position, if it wasn't obvious." As Gio gives me the go-ahead, the sweet sound continues. Bullets zip through the air, eliminating the men surrounding us while Cassio's men storm the building and work their way through the men stationed throughout the other levels of the decrepit home. One by one, my enemies fall as the electric pain pulsing in my bones slowly subsides. Some land among us in the basement-like place. Others crash through what's left of the wooden floorboards, landing haphazardly throughout the property.

As Gio takes care of the men stationed closest to me, Ariana, and Vitale, our captor, the wannabe king, turns pale. He takes in the room, now cluttered with the bullet-ridden bodies of his followers, in horror, quickly realizing the hard truth I've been forced to live with ever since he invaded my home and took my mother from me. Alliances are as fickle as the wind. A crown does not make you powerful. An army does. And the men you want fighting for you can't be bought, bargained with, or manipulated. Only respect breeds true loyalty, and only true loyalty breeds true power.

Vitale spins around, searching for a soldier to defend him as I ball my fists and force myself up from the mud. Finding no one, he looks at me with wide eyes filled with bone-chilling fear. His face flushes bright red with the sting of loss, though this night is far from over and he knows it. At that, Vitale takes off. He runs out of the building the same way I entered, but my legs do not move to follow him. Instead, I go straight to Ariana.

"Alister—"

"Shh," I whisper as I drop to my knees in front of her. I grab the knife from the ground beside us and use it to cut the ropes from her wrists and ankles. "I'm going to get you out of here, okay? Everything is going to be alright. You're going to be alright." My words are just as much reassurance for me as they are for her. Ariana is weak, whether she realizes it or not. She hasn't eaten or had any water in hours, during which she was soaked by rain and chilled to the bone by winter winds. Even without her injuries, she's endured enough to warrant a hospital visit. With them, she could lose consciousness at any second. Knowing this, I work quickly.

Though Gio will maintain visual on us until I can get Ariana to Gagliano's men, we have no idea how many forces Vitale has. He admitted to sending some to Laroux House in search of Sophia, which means they aren't all present here tonight. Still, I'd rather Ariana be long gone from this wretched place in case Vitale has any more men set to deploy.

"But you're bleeding. You were shot and electrocuted. And, and...Vitale's going to get away with it, with everything. He's... You're..."

Ariana lifts her trembling hand to my cheek. As I cut the last of the rope from her feet, I lift my eyes to meet hers. Her eyes shine bright in the soft yellow light of the lanterns surrounding us. They well with tears, even though she is too dehydrated to have water to spare. I lean into her touch and let out of a sigh of relief. Yes, my shoulder hurts. Yes, my legs still tingle with residual volts of electricity. But Ariana is alive. And perhaps it's nothing more than her fear of my mortality or that she doesn't have enough energy left inside her to hate me, but she looks at me with so much warmth, so much love, her gaze alone chases away the chill of the night, of my rain-soaked clothes, and of seeing her at the mercy of my greatest enemy. She doesn't hate me.

"I'm fine," I say. "And Vitale isn't getting away with shit. He just thinks he is. Now, put your arm around my neck so that I can—"

"You came for me," she says then, her voice cracking with emotion. My brows crinkle in confusion. *Did she think I wouldn't?*

"Ariana, of course I did. Of course I did." At that, I lean forward and kiss her forehead. There's so much more I want to say, but I don't because nothing has changed between us. The sight of her now lets me know that it never can. Everything I've ever told her has been the truth, even if she hasn't always wanted to hear it, even if I haven't always wanted to say it. I will always love her. I will always protect her. But I can't be with her. And after what happened tonight, she should finally understand why. I almost lost her tonight. The very knife I brought to battle could've been the death of her, my love could've been the death of her. That is a tragedy I can't endure. I won't.

"Team 2—standing by." As I pull away from Ariana, the leader of Gagliano's men lets me know he and his team are in position. I take in Ariana one last time as— I jump at the sudden noise and spin to find the body of one of Vitale's men sliding down the stairs just a few feet away.

"Boss, you need to move. More of Vitale's men are breaching the building from the back."

"Copy," I say. "Team 2—move to target." Out of time, I lift Ariana from her seat and cradle her against my chest. She winces as my grip digs into her cuts and bruises. "I'm sorry, baby, but we've got to go. Gio, cover us."

"You got it, Boss."

With Ariana in my arms, I make my way to the threshold and wait for Gio's word to move outside the building. The sounds of gunfire and men talking fill my ears as I stare out into the night in search of the SUV meant to take Ariana from here back to New Orleans where she'll be under the care and protection of her father. As the SUV comes into view, bullets zip through the air, quiet and quick. With Gio having handled the last of Vitale's men on the frontside of the building, he gives me the go-ahead to move toward the SUV. "Hold on tight, baby," I say. Ariana does as I say, and I take off running toward the black SUV. As I reach it, the doors to the back seat open on both sides. Out come two of Gagliano's soldiers tasked with protecting Ariana. They move to flank the SUV, positioning themselves between Ariana and me and the house in case any of Vitale's men notice us and try to attack before I can get her settled.

I place Ariana directly into the van, not giving her a chance to stall or argue with me about her staying. "Alright, you're going to go with these people. Enzo here is in charge," I say, pointing to the driver. He gives Ariana a friendly nod. Then I direct my attention to the woman in the passenger seat. "This is Hannah. She's a nurse. She's going to make sure you get the treatment you need for your wounds. These other guys are part of Enzo's team. They will all work to keep you safe and get you back to New Orleans in one piece." Ariana shakes her head, visibly overwhelmed by everything that's happening. "Ariana, don't fight me on this, okay? You're in no condition to fight, and I can't take down Vitale if I'm worried about you. I need you safe." At that, I bring my hand to her cheek one last time, caressing her softly. She nods in agreement. *Oh, thank God.*

Just as I reach for the car door, Ariana leans forward and, wrapping her arms around my neck, she kisses me. After everything that happened between us this morning and almost losing her to Vitale, I thought I'd never feel her lips on mine again. Though, as our lips move together, I can't ignore the uncharacteristic roughness due to her dehydration nor the taste of her blood on my tongue. They are stark reminders of our tragic reality.

As she pulls away from me, she says, "I love you, Alister Amato. Stay safe. I'll be waiting for you to come home." Her words hit me like a bag of bricks, the pain of which is etched all over my face. "What is it?" she asks, noticing my change in demeanor.

I close my eyes as the sounds of her cries from this morning echo through my mind. It occurs to me then, just as I've meant everything I've said to her, her words have been laced with the same honesty. She told me she didn't know how to give me up. She begged me not to let her go. All this time, I've seen her strength. I've told myself she can handle it. She'll survive because she is a survivor. But even survivors reach a breaking point. I should know. And after everything she's been through, after so much loneliness and heartache and never having anyone show up for her, now more than ever, she isn't capable of letting go. She isn't capable of accepting that this is over, because doing so will break her. Truly and tragically, it will break her. And that devastates me, even more than knowing I must live a life without her.

I hate to do this here. In fact, I hate having to do this at all. We agreed that after last night, we'd bottle our feelings and go about our normal lives, however not normal they are. But I suppose neither one of us have been very good at living up to our bargain. Now, I have to set her straight. I have to say goodbye for the very last time.

"Ariana, these men aren't mine and they aren't taking you to Laroux House."

"What? What are you talking about?" Confusion washes over her. I take a deep breath and—

"Enzo and his team answer to Alessandro Gagliano. He is one of my capos, but most importantly, he's...he's your father, Ariana." I know this is a shitty way of telling her. As with everything with our relationship, the timing is anything but perfect. But I suppose it's better she knows now than to have her arrive at his home in the French Quarter and have no idea who he is. "By the end of the week, everyone associated with Christio Vitale will be dead, as will he. With their deaths, your identity will be safe, and your father and I will work out a way to make sure it stays so."

"Alister—"

"*No, Ariana.* You almost died tonight because of your association with me. I made the mistake of allowing myself to be seen with you by members of my world once. I won't do it again. This...this is goodbye, Ariana. For the last time, goodbye."

"No, no, Alister. Don't do this. We can figure this out —together."

I shake my head and step away from the vehicle, motioning for Ariana's new guards to join her. They do and are quickly forced to restrain her as she tries to claw her way to the now closed door. "*Alister!*" she screams. It's yet another sound I'll never be able to get out of my head.

34

Alister

As Enzo pulls away, taking with him the only part of my heart that still beats, the SUV disappears into the black night and the sounds of its tires against the gravel drift away. The lonely road ahead of me is like a magnet that refuses to release me. My legs feel heavy as my eyes refuse to leave the space I last saw Ariana. It's as if her very being calls to me and I want nothing more than to chase after her. And yet, I stand rigid and empty as the silence of the night gives way to the sounds of bullets and dying men.

"Boss, Vitale is trying to escape through the forest. I'm going to assist Team 3." Gio's voice pulls me back to the task at hand before the pain of heartbreak has time to take root just as it did this morning. I have an entire lifetime to feel it, and feel it, I will. But right now, I have to stay focused. Until Christio Vitale is dead, Ariana remains at risk and my mother and sister remain unavenged.

Finally, pulling my eyes from the road, I say, "Copy. I'm on my way."

Before joining Gio, I stock my cargo pants with weapons I find on the ground. Some of them I recognize as my own, the ones discarded by Vitale's men upon my arrival. Others I grab from the bodies of dead soldiers as I make my way around the house toward the woods. By now, all of Vitale's additional forces are inside and have their hands full with Cassio's reinforcements. There's a clear path to the tree line, which I'm thankful for given my still-bleeding shoulder.

As I move through the woods, I see why it took Gio so long to reach his position. The dark night may serve as excellent cover, but it also makes it impossible to see clearly more than a few feet in front of you. Not to mention thorny brush, long hanging limbs, and uneven terrain make moving quickly troublesome. One wrong step and you've got a broken ankle. All of this slows me down in catching up with the group, but it also means Vitale couldn't have gotten that far given his age and weight.

I crouch down to make my body a smaller target in case Vitale somehow called his men to come find him. Keeping my pistol pointed to the ground yet my finger ready near the trigger, I slowly move through wet grass and fallen pine straw, thankful the snakes have already entered their time of hibernation. As the wind kicks up, the trees begin to dance. I stop and press myself against the rough bark of a nearby tree as the swaying limbs cast shadows that look like men upon the poorly lit ground. I move my finger to my gun's trigger in an abundance of caution. *One. Two.* I step from the cover of the tree out into the sliver of moonlight with my pistol raised to find no one nearby. Though, the moment of silence and stillness does give way to another sense. I turn, lowering my gun to my side, as the sounds of voices, no, grunts, make their way through the towering, slender trees to me.

"Gio, do you have visual on Vitale?" The sounds grow louder

and more precise, and I move toward them. It isn't just grunts of exertion I hear, but a sort of scraping, as if someone is dragging something or someone across the forest floor. "Gio?" I ask again.

"Negative. Sophia thought she saw something and took off after it before I reached her and Cassio. We're trying to find her now, but she…she isn't responding to comms."

As Gio's words hit me, bone-chilling fear courses through my veins accompanied by a wave of nausea. I move toward the sounds that seem to grow louder by the second as déjà vu riddles my mind.

> *My legs go numb as Sophia's dark hair and sparkling dress come into view. I nearly trip at the sight of her. She lies on the gravel path just up ahead. She isn't moving. She—*
>
> *"Sophia!" I yell and sprint the last few steps to her. I drop to my knees and immediately pull her into my arms. Her body is limp. "Sophia! Sophia, wake up. Wake up!" I shake her, managing to fight through my fear long enough to realize she's still warm. "Gio, check for a pulse," I say as he drops down beside me. He brings his fingers to her neck as I hold her, unable to let her go.*

As memories of the night I almost lost Sophia, to Vitale no less, crash through me like waves on a beach, I break out into a sprint, heading toward the sounds that make me fear the worst. Like the night I sprinted from Laroux House through the gardens, I nearly trip in pursuit of my sister, catching myself against the rough bark of the trees as I search the shadows for her. By taking Ariana hostage and holding her over two hours outside of the city, Vitale forced me to make a choice. Either come alone, leaving my defenses with my sister, and die. Or come with an army and leave my sister unprotected. No matter which choice I made, he knew he would capture at least one of us, the last remaining Amato heirs. But I made a choice he didn't expect, one far too long in the making, and yet, one I pray I don't live to regret.

As movement in my peripheral vision draws my attention, I turn to watch Christio Vitale, pale, blubbering, and struggling to walk with an arrow through his leg, fall face-first to the ground as another arrow soars through his shin. He lands among the pine straw and the moonlight reflects off his pale suit as if seeking to wave the white flag of surrender on his behalf. With Vitale on his belly, finally put in his place after twenty years of scheming, treachery, and heinous, despicable murder, this war is finally over. But who is responsible for its end?

My eyes drift from Vitale up through the arrow's path to find Sophia. The one I've always sought to save is the one who ended up saving us all. She stands several yards away with her bow still trained on Vitale. Her body shakes as she appears to fight against her emotions in search of the restraint needed not to pepper him with more arrows. I'm not even sure if she sees me, but I see her—*finally*. She's no longer the little girl who rushed out of her room at the sounds of gunshots in desperate need of protecting. She's no longer the teenager who trusted too easily or the young adult who loved too hard. I see her now not just for her intelligence, beauty, and desire for independence, but for her strength, resilience, and capability to survive without me. I see her as the woman who saved me when the brotherhood had me bested and the woman who, with a single shot, ended a war twenty years in the making.

"Alister, do I really have to do this? It's summer. I want to spend time with my friends," Sophia says as I lug her bow and arrows down the gravel path of the tree-filled gardens at our family estate.

It's a hot summer day here at Laroux House and our proximity to the lake only makes the mosquitoes worse. Still, allowing Sophia to skip her training isn't an option, not only because Father declared it so, but because I'm set to leave for college in a few days. The thought of leaving her and Cara, who's only five, behind, especially after— Anyway, it, um...it turns my stomach. Sophia is only thirteen, so Dad hasn't yet begun her firearms training, but if I know she's proficient with the bow, I'll be able to sleep at night. At least, I hope so.

"Look, I get it. But Dad has a meeting, so he's entrusted your practice to me. Besides, I'm leaving in a few days, and I want an excuse to hang out with you before I do."

Sophia rolls her eyes but does as she's told. She takes the bow from me and directs her aim at the nearest target set up about twenty yards away, half hidden by a tree. She nails it on the first try, turning to me with her brow cocked and an unimpressed smirk. That is, until movement catches her eye.

"What the Hell is that?" she asks.

"Language," I scold her, despite knowing I would've said a lot worse. "I took the liberty of updating the course. You've proven yourself with stationary targets, but, in real life, your targets aren't going to wait for you to shoot them. Some will run from you, others will run toward you, lunge at you, come at you from behind. The one thing they won't do is stand still. So, now, neither will these targets. Now, you better shoot it before its timer expires. If you miss it, the entire course speeds up, increasing the difficulty just like if you miss a real target, allowing more to surround you."

Sophia groans as she takes aim once more. Though, as she moves through the course, there is a sparkle in her eye that says she won't be satisfied until she runs it perfectly. She's competitive that way.

After over an hour of trying and failing, Sophia collapses in exhaustion and from the steamy Southern heat. I sit next to her on the concrete bench situated beneath a large oak tree in the formal rose garden. She's red-faced and panting for oxygen as she inhales the water.

"Look, Dad and I are hard on you. We know that. But you understand why, right?"

Sophia only nods. It's been two years since our mother was killed, yet it feels like just yesterday. All our emotions are still so raw, so much so that we don't talk about them for fear of breaking. Instead, we train. We run, shoot, and study different fighting styles. The older we get, the more weapons we're exposed to. My training as the heir to the family business has been the most extensive, but my father has insisted on Sophia taking part in certain activities as well. Cara is too young to do any of it, which makes him feel helpless, whether he ever admits it or not. I suppose his sense of helplessness in the wake of my mother's death has somehow bled its way into me. I see how hard Sophia trains, and yet the thought of her truly having to put her skills to the test makes me queasy. I protected her the night the men came for us, the night our mother was killed. I will always do my best to protect her, but what if I can't? What if I'm not there?

"I want you to run this course every single day, alternating between morning and night. It doesn't matter if it's one hundred degrees or flooding. It doesn't matter if you have a headache or if you're sick or if your best friend's hamster dies. Your enemies will pick the most inconvenient times to attack, and you have to be ready to protect yourself, Sophia, at all costs."

As I come to, Sophia lowers her bow, her eyes meeting mine. They are filled with sadness and yet not an ounce of fear. All the training paid off. "She was my sister too. She was my mother too." Sophia stalks toward Vitale, who still tries in vain to escape us.

I move to assist her in restraining him, but am halted by the sharp, searing pain in my shoulder made more prominent by my reprieve. "Ah!" I wince. Though as my eyes move to assess my wound, my attention is drawn elsewhere.

Cara stands next to me, dressed in her typical light-wash

jeans and white tank top. Her long, raven-colored hair blends with the night while her bright red lips make me remember all the times I scolded her for appearing too grown for her age. As she stands beside me, she looks like herself, free from the torn, stained, and ghoulish reminders of her tragic end that have haunted me for months now. She watches Sophia with a smile on her face as she barrels into Vitale. Her warm amber eyes seem to smile too. Is this real? Is she really here? I reach out to her, but stop myself, deciding I'd rather not know. She looks at me then. Her gaze is almost enough to bring me to my knees.

"Just because I was unprepared doesn't mean Sophia is. You don't have to worry about her anymore, Alister, or me." At that, Cara steps away from me.

"Wait," I call out to her. I glance toward Sophia, who's got her hands too full with Vitale to notice. *Thank God.* Maybe the blood loss has caused me to hallucinate. It wouldn't be the first time. Regardless, I know this will be the last time I see my sister.

Cara turns back to me then. "Don't worry, Alister. Where I'm going, there is no fear. No pain. And I won't be alone. It's time you remember that you aren't either." She looks at Sophia one last time before returning her gaze to me. "I love you, brother. I always have. You were never to blame for any of this."

At that, Cara turns and walks through the forest. Her small frame darts in and out of patches of moonlight until I blink. When I open my eyes, she's gone. Our encounter was so brief, I question if it even happened. Yet, as I stare into the forest, my eyes trained on the path she took, the tension in my muscles releases and the ache in my head subsides. I wonder if this is what peace feels like—a sudden relinquishing of responsibility and guilt. I know I will never stop mourning my sister. Even after all these years, I still cry for my mother. I long for my father. The pain of loss comes and goes, always destined to return. But perhaps now, when I think of Cara, when I cry for her, when I long for her, I can take comfort in the pain rather than feel ashamed by it. I can let it serve as a reminder of her, rather than of my greatest failure. Perhaps that is a burden I'm meant to give up to make room for the place inside me Ariana has laid claim to and yet will never inhabit.

As I turn back to Sophia, I find Cassio pulling her off Vitale and Gio handcuffing him. As Gio breaks the stems of the arrows, Vitale squeals. The first of many. I walk toward them, and Vitale closes his eyes as if he thinks I will gift him a quick death. I move past him and go straight to Sophia where she cries into Cassio's shoulder. I'm thankful for him, for his support of my family, for his men who fought alongside us. But, most of all, I'm thankful that he loves my sister in a way that allows her to be both vulnerable and strong. Though, I could punch him for allowing her to run off after Vitale all on her own, I suppose I can't blame him for not being able to keep up with her. I trained her myself, after all. I extend my hand to him, and he takes it. Though no words are spoken between us except this simple request: "May I have a moment alone with my sister?"

"Of course," Cassio says. At that, Sophia pulls herself from him and turns to me, confusion etched into her brow.

"Our men have taken the house. It's all over. We'll get him loaded up and sent back to Laroux House," Gio says as he and Cassio pull Vitale to his feet and force him to march.

"Wait," Sophia says, moving toward them. "On your knees," she commands Vitale. He hesitates. I'm not sure if it's because she's a woman or if he simply can't kneel due to the arrow stems still lodged into his legs to keep him from bleeding out too quickly. As he's done for me a million times before, Gio enforces the Amato command. He kicks Vitale in his shins, leaving him no choice but to fall before Sophia. With him at her feet, she smiles, and then shifts her attention to his right hand where the ring of the Amato crest resides. She takes it from him, and then holds it before him, allowing him to take one last look at the thing he spent his entire life trying to achieve, and yet ultimately failed because he couldn't grasp the concept of what it truly means to be powerful, what it truly means to be royalty.

"An Amato king bows to no one," Sophia says then. *Except his queen*. At that, Sophia motions for Gio and Cassio to take him and they do. We watch Vitale struggle as he moves through the forest slowly. Gio results to threatening the use of an electric wand, like what Vitale used against me, to speed him up. *Ouch*. As the three of them disappear into the darkness, I wrap my arm around Sophia and pull her into my chest. She nuzzles against me, instinctively bringing her hand to my shirt, now drenched in blood. She pulls her hand back at the unexpected feel to take a closer look. "You're bleeding," she says, her eyes filled with concern.

"So are you," I say then, tilting her hand to show off her bloody knuckles.

"Well, it was well earned," she says.

"As was mine."

As I hold her, my lips lift into a small smile. I can't remember the last time we shared a hug like this. For nearly a year, I kept our sister's death a secret, which caused me to be unfairly distant toward her. And when I was finally forced to tell her, things became even more complicated between us. She resented me for keeping the secret, which created only more distance, leaving me to obsess over finding the men responsible for what happened to our sister. Losing Cara retriggered the same hopelessness I felt when my mother died and amplified it tenfold. No matter Sophia's capabilities, I saw her as nothing more than that little girl in her nightgown needing to be sent back to her room for her own good. I treated her like a ward, not like a sister. Maybe now that can change.

Sophia turns to me. "I believe this belongs to you." She

offers me my ring. I hesitate to take it, knowing what it represents. "Alister, I know you've felt like a failure, like what happened to Cara was your fault, like I'm your responsibility, especially since Dad died. But I am my *own* responsibility. And what happened to Cara was twenty years in the making. It wasn't your fault. And whether you choose to believe me or not, you *are* a worthy king. You are strong, honest, fair, caring, and selfless, a bit too selfless, if you ask me." At that, Sophia wipes the remnants of tears from her cheeks and places the ring on my palm. "So, take it. Take it because it's yours by birth and blood. Take it because it's yours to discard, not someone else's to steal."

Sophia's words strike me. *Mine to discard.* She makes it sound as if I can choose to walk away. But I've never— No one has ever given me that choice.

"I know you ended things with Ariana, and I know why you did it. I'd be lying if I said I don't agree with you. You worry for her safety, and you have every reason to, especially given our past and events of late. Vitale is just one enemy. When others hear of the brotherhood's involvement in Cara's death, of how close Vitale came to ending the Amato line, and of the FBI investigation that awaits us in the new year, more will come. New Orleans will be flocked with those who want us dead and won't hesitate to use the ones we love against us."

I nod. I'm not sure Sophia and I have ever agreed more. Though, I still don't understand where she's going with this. She takes a deep breath and—

"Which is why I want to give you this choice, the choice you should've had from the beginning, but no one ever offered. You can choose to remain king. There are plenty of reasons to do so —family legacy, power, the ability to wield an army, to maintain the status quo in this wretched criminal underworld. Or you can choose to walk away, to abandon it all for love."

What? I pull away from her then as the sting of heartbreak returns to me. "You know I can't do that."

"What I know is you've always had a reason to stay and never a reason to leave. But everything's different now. I have Cassio and you have Ariana. You don't need to protect me anymore, Alister. If you choose to remain king, I will support you. But I will no longer be the reason for your misery."

"Sophia, you're not—"

"Cassio asked me to accompany him back to Savannah after things settle down here. I've said yes." I take a step back from her and shove my hands into my pockets. A swarm of conflicting emotions dance inside me. There's a part of me that's angry Cassio didn't ask my permission, as is the gentlemanly thing to do, not to mention a requirement in our world. Then again, Cassio is no longer a part of our world, at least on most days. And it is for that reason that I allow my anger to subside and remind myself of why this is exactly what I've always wanted for my sister—a love and a life far from not only New Orleans but the Mafia itself.

"I'm happy for you, Sophia, truly." I reach out and give her hand a squeeze.

"I wish I could say the same for you," she replies.

"Sophia..." I shake my head. Though as I prepare a speech on why what she's proposing is impossible, my mind can't help but imagine it—a life without the Mafia, a life *with* Ariana.

"I once asked you to let me make myself useful and now I'm telling you. If you decide to relinquish the throne, I will help you figure out how to do it. Cassio and I both will. I can't promise we will succeed, but if there is anything in this world worth fighting for, worth sacrificing for, it's love, the kind of love that is uncontrollable and unrelenting, the kind of love that brings air to your lungs, that speaks to your soul, that makes you feel alive.

It's the kind of love I see between you and Ariana, a love that burns so brightly it tethers between tragic and magic."

"The way you speak it's as if there isn't really a choice at all."

"Don't pretend that your heart hasn't already decided. You've just been waiting for permission to finally go after what you want and I'm giving you that, Alister. Now, all you have to do is take it. So, what will it be?"

35

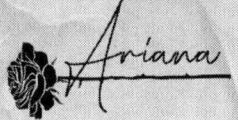

ONE MONTH LATER

The French Quarter at Christmas is no different than any other day in New Orleans. Sure, every column and antique streetlamp throughout the historic district is covered in Christmas lights or wrapped with green garland and topped with a red velvet bow. Every window and door is adorned with a wreath. Every wrought iron balcony is decked out in perfect harmony. And let's not forget the oak trees in the parks and at residences alike now covered in fairy lights in addition to the Mardi Gras beads never collected and the Spanish moss that allows the city's mystery and magic to prevail even during the jolliest time of year.

What the South lacks in snow it most certainly makes up for in decorations and festivities. And though perhaps its most known for its booze and music, it's not just the residents of New Orleans who embrace Christmas to the nth degree but also the businesses. While the carriage-riding crowd carols at Jackson Square, the midnight Santa runners pregame on Bourbon Street. The street musicians change their tunes, playing jazz versions of traditional Christmas carols. Famous restaurants and bars update their menus and compete to see who can make the best Milk Punch and other Christmas inspired cocktails. My personal favorite is the Mrs. Claus' Cookie martini at Sazerac, but I digress. Because like every other day in the Crescent City, the streets are filled with men and monsters alike, homes and hearts are tainted with secrets, and even the festive fuss cannot cleanse the darkness threatening to consume us all.

As I turn off the loud and lively Bourbon Street and continue toward my apartment, flanked by one of the two bodyguards assigned to me by my father, the night air fills with a violinist's sharp and sorrowful rendition of "*Jingle Bells.*" As the song concludes, the man hits a note that sounds like a cross between a Mariah Carey whistle and a woman's cry of terror. The eerie sound forces me to tug my leather jacket tighter around me as it amplifies the chill even the bustling Christmas crowds can't help me shake. After hours in the wintery winds and rain and the all-consuming rage and fear I felt coming face-to-face with the man who murdered my mother, perhaps the icy sensation has permanently attached itself to me just like the memories of that eventful night.

It's been one month since I was held by Vitale, since Alister said his last goodbye and shoved me into a car full of people I didn't know, sending me away to none other than my father, Alessandro Gagliano. The sheer shock of it all has almost been enough to quell the ache of my breaking heart—almost. Alister and I had a deal, one I myself initiated. But when I was at Vitale's mercy, when I feared I would die, Alister was the only person alive I wished to see. I suppose I got my wish, which has only made it even harder for me to bottle the feelings I know I must. He came for me, he risked everything to rescue me, including his life and Sophia's. His actions only made me fall in love with him even more. Yet, his final goodbye made it painstakingly clear—while the rest of my world has changed, our ability to be together never will.

I haven't spoken to Alister since that night. I've tried calling, texting only to get no response. I even went to Laroux House a few times, not to beg him to be with me, but just to make sure he was alright. Taking down Vitale was just as emotional for him as it was for me. Not to mention the last time I saw him he'd been shot, and Sophia was in the wind. But his guards wouldn't even let me through the gate. Yet, while the distance between Alister and me has only grown, so too has my relationship with my father—*my father*! I still can't even think the word while keeping a straight face.

I've gone so many years not only without a father but thinking the worst of the man I never knew. Add to that my unfortunate experience with my last father figure—I suppose that's the nice way of putting it—and my past has left me hesitant to welcome another man into my life. When I think of my dad, when I get coffee with him, when I have dinner with him and his wife and children, even today, when I spent Christmas with them, I can't help but be transported back to when I was ten years old and twelve and sixteen. Each time I entered a new foster home, I always wondered how long it would last and how it would end. What would I do to make them give me up? Or what would happen to me to make me want to leave? It was a cycle of fear and hopelessness that seemed to never end. I can't help but feel those same emotions now. The more I get to know my father and his family, *my family*, the more I grow to like them and the more I worry something, or someone, will separate us just like our differing worlds separated me from Alister.

Perhaps those same emotions are what have kept me from opening up to people over the years, especially Ray. Maybe I've always kept people at arm's length because the moment I allow myself to care, the moment I open up to them, I fear I'll lose them. Thankfully, I haven't lost Ray yet. After a few days in my father's care, he received word that Vitale and his associates had officially served their sentences and had been neutralized. There's a part of me that wishes I could've seen him suffer or at least been the one to put the bullet in his head or carve the X into his chest. But the other part of me knows that if I did, I'd be haunted by my own actions just as much as I am haunted by his. With Vitale's death and my body's recovery well under way, I was free to leave my father's and the first thing I did was search for Ray.

I found him at his apartment with injuries similar to mine. Once he learned I was alive, I thought for sure he'd be angry at me, for not only putting him in the position I did but for lying to him about Alister, about everything. Instead, he gave me the hug I truly needed, and I told him everything. I told him about my mom, my childhood, and my assault. I told him not only about my investigation into Alister, but my feelings for him. I even told him about Vitale. Well, I suppose that's the one thing I sort of had to tell him seeing as Vitale and his men put him in the hospital for two days. Finally, keeping his identity secret for his own protection, I told him I met my father, a mafiosi just like the man I love. He didn't say anything at first. In fact, I'm sure we sat in silence for over an hour as *Seinfeld* played in the background. Finally, he reached over to me, offered me his hand, and said, *"I'm sorry I pushed you to open up. I had no idea what you were holding in."*

"It's okay," I told him. As worry etched into his brow, I asked, *"What now?"*

He took a deep breath and said, *"This world you've been navigating, I've only ever seen it through one lens, that of an FBI agent. I don't want to see you get caught up in something not only dangerous, but illegal. But I know you well enough to know that nothing is going to stop you from getting to know your father, just like nothing stopped you from going after Alister Amato. And I'd rather you not have to go through it alone. I guess what I'm saying is, if you're in the market for a friend, I'd like to fill that role, and not as the flirty coworker friend who secretly, or not so secretly, wants to date you, but as a true, stuff-our-faces, gross-each-other-out friend."*

I still smile when I think about it. Though, it's impossible to think about that moment without remembering what happened next. Bilieux called me. I was hesitant to take the call in front of Ray, seeing as the one thing I hadn't told him was of Bilieux's side deal with Alister. Not to mention my suspicions that he may be behind the rumors about me circulating the bureau. Not that starting rumors is anywhere near the level of despicable I'm accustomed to. Though, I suspected his intention for spreading them may be. Still, I answered it. He acted like he knew nothing of my relationship with Alister or the rumors Ray warned me about let alone that I'm aware of his secret corruption. And, you know what, maybe he doesn't or, should I say, *didn't*. But there was one thing he should've been aware of that he pretended he knew nothing about. And that's what gave him away.

The day Vitale attacked us, Ray woke to find me missing and my apartment trashed. He immediately called Bilieux and told him everything, hoping that Bilieux would try to find me. God knows he had the resources to. He did nothing. It wasn't obvious at first since Ray was the only person who knew of my abduction. He couldn't get to the bureau to see Bilieux's efforts to find me, or not find me, due to his stint in the hospital, which Bilieux followed up, conveniently, with paid leave so that Ray could more properly recover. As Bilieux went on and on about me rejoining the task force in January, not once did he mention Ray's call or ask if I was okay. Nothing. When the call ended, a sense of unease washed over me. Did Bilieux not search for me because he'd hoped someone else would take care of silencing me? Or because he knew I'd be taken?

Bilieux had already made one deal with one Mafia king to line his own pockets. With Alister's time on the throne presumably limited due to the FBI's impending investigation, it's possible Bilieux sought a new king to bargain with. Or, perhaps, Vitale sought him out. Perhaps his relationship with Bilieux is how he learned I'm FBI. Regardless, my former boss was definitely hiding something, which is exactly what I texted Sophia to tell Alister.

Days later, SSA Bilieux was found dead. I guess it's a good thing I didn't tell Ray of my suspicions. Thinking me or rather, Alister, responsible for an agent's death may have been too much for him to accept. But I know Alister wouldn't have killed him without proof that he posed a threat to either his family or me. If my suspicions about Bilieux are correct, Alister protected me from him. Though, he isn't the only evil he's vanquished in my name.

In the weeks since Vitale's capture and death, the news has been filled with stories I can only assume Sophia is behind, unless the Amatos have some PR professional on retainer with an iron-clad NDA who knows how to clean up certain messes, specifically bloody ones. It's actually interesting to see how they operate, to see how they've kept their secrets for over a century. While an eyewitness claims she saw Christio Vitale fall into the swamp, his body subsequently dragged away by an alligator, similar reports of freak accidents have covered up the deaths of his associates. Even Bilieux's death was ruled a suicide. But among the cover stories was one I didn't expect.

According to Police Chief Hayward Jenkins, Ken Clarke, a prisoner serving a twenty-year sentence for sexually assaulting a minor, was killed while being transported to New Orleans East Hospital one year before he was eligible for parole. At that thought, I step off the busy sidewalk into an alley to catch my breath. I bring my hand to my chest as brief memories of my assault flash through my mind. It's been over ten years since I last saw Ken Clarke, since he came into my room and forced himself on me. I've come a long way since that night, the night I learned what it truly means to be helpless, the night I vowed to never feel that way again.

I suppose that's why I fell so hard for Alister so quickly. The night Ken Clarke raped me was the night I realized I was truly alone, and it was on me to ensure my safety from there on out. But, from the very first night I met Alister, there was something about him that made me feel like I wasn't alone. Even as he turned me away, he made sure my injuries were tended to and I had a bed to sleep in. He...he took care of me, even though he owed me nothing, even though I was the enemy for all intents and purposes. I'm not certain that Alister is behind Clarke's death, but the timing seems too coincidental for him not to be. The transport occurred the morning after Alister and I made love, the morning we were meant to say goodbye. I suppose getting rid of Ken Clarke just like Bilieux is his way of doing just that, cementing his words with actions that tell me it's over. He's ridding the world of the monsters who seek to hurt me or have hurt me in the hopes that I can move on and live a life without fear, a life without him.

I return to the sidewalk and give my bodyguard, Marcel, a quick nod to let him know I'm okay. As I continue toward my apartment, the crowds continue to thin the farther I get from Bourbon Street, letting me know I'm almost home. Thoughts of home make me remember the moment I saw Alister while still at Vitale's mercy. I was so out of it at that point a lot of that night is a blur. Well, until it wasn't. I vaguely remember asking Alister, *"Can we go home now?"* Maybe it's just what I was thinking. Maybe I didn't actually say it. Regardless, that's what I wanted. I wanted him to pull me into his arms, take me back to Laroux House, and never let me leave. Well, maybe that's a bit much. I just…I didn't want him to leave me again, to push me away, to tell me all the reasons why we can't be together instead of the one reason we should. But over the past few weeks that hope has waned.

I *am* going home—home to my one-bedroom, first-floor apartment with three locks on the door, a love seat instead of a full couch because *space*, and far too many books for my own good. The only thing that's missing is a cat to fully embody my singledom. And, in one week, I'll officially return to my old life. Well, with a new confidant in Ray, a Mafia capo father who doesn't know I'm an FBI agent, oh, and two bodyguards who take turns following me around. I suppose I should tell my father the truth before Marcel and Timothee figure it out for him. Perhaps that revelation will be the thing that forces him to exile me from his life. Alister always said I can't be a Mafia princess and an FBI agent at the same time. Then again, maybe my admission will be the thing that brings us closer to one another, the thing that finally eliminates my fear of him abandoning me. I suppose only time will tell.

When I reach the pedestrian-only alley lined with old buildings turned into apartments and businesses alike, I turn and walk toward my apartment halfway down. Like the rest of the historic district, the streetlamps are wrapped in green garland and topped with red velvet bows. It's nice, especially considering decorating for Christmas has been the last thing on my mind. Come tomorrow, it won't matter anyway. But for tonight, I enjoy the shades of red and green and the way the lights hanging from the second-story balconies illuminate the concrete walkway. Though, as I reach my front door, I find they illuminate more than the ground.

At the sight of the bright red package, Marcel picks up the pace so he can inspect it for me. But as the cool winter breeze catches on the gift tag tied with a gold ribbon, I see who it's from and grab it before Marcel reaches me. I motion for him to fall back as I quickly unlock my door and enter my apartment before he can protest. I close the door behind me and immediately lock it before placing the box on the coffee table in my living room. As the package sits, small and unassuming, I take a step back and imagine what could be inside.

A million thoughts race through my mind as I pace the small space. Maybe it's a gun. No, he would know I already have one. Well, more than one. Besides, it's not heavy enough. Maybe it's a watch, like the one he wore in Boston. That did come in handy. A burner phone so we can have private conversations? Maybe a plane ticket to somewhere where I can meet him off-the-grid and we can prolong our not-together-but-totally-in-love-with-each-other relationship? I roll my eyes as my desperation breaks through the tough-girl facade years of loneliness have allowed me to master.

"Okay, this is stupid. Nothing has changed between us. It's Christmas," I say as I move to my kitchen in search of some wine. "It's just a gift. It means nothing because we are *nothing* to each other." The untrue sentiment makes my heart squeeze and my mouth go dry with all the emotions I've spent the past month trying to suppress. At that, I ditch the wine for whiskey. I grab a glass from the cabinet and retreat to my couch, bottle in hand. Whatever is inside, it changes nothing. I know this. Hence the eighty-proof alcohol. And yet, my heart won't listen. There is a part of me that hopes this gift changes everything between us. The thought seems impossible after our last meeting and the past month. But there it is—a glimmer of hope resurrected by none other than a perfectly wrapped gift adorned with an ivory gift tag with nothing more than the letter *A*.

As I plop down on the sofa, I take several deep breaths and a shot of whiskey to prepare for what happens next. Okay, three shots. My tongue numb with liquid courage, I discard the ribbon and slowly remove the wrapping paper. Inside the gift box is another box, although this one is much smaller, made of red leather, and is accompanied by a small note. I take another shot. I'm going to be pissed if this ends up being from some other A-named person. All this anticipation for nothing. But who do I even know—? *Focus, Ariana. No more shots.*

With all the liquid courage I can muster, *literally*, I open the box to find a necklace. "Whoa." On a gold chain hangs an oval-shaped ruby the width of my thumb. It's surrounded by mini pear-shaped diamonds. It's stunning. But, up close, I see that it is much more than that. As I lift the box to inspect the stone closer, I see that it is embossed with the Amato family crest, the same crest Alister has hanging on the walls of his office and the Blood Cellar, the same crest embossed onto the family heirloom ring that represents his power as the Blood King. At the sight of it, my lips draw up into a smile and my chest warms. Though, perhaps that's just the whiskey doing its job.

I'm hesitant to read the note, hesitant to risk this feeling of warmth abandoning me. To stall, I pull the necklace from the box and fasten it around my neck. It's heavy, which means it's not easily forgotten, and its beauty makes it impossible to ignore. Perhaps that's the point. Perhaps this is Alister's way of reminding me of him and of signaling to his allies, those who would know the Amato crest, that I fall under his protection. Or perhaps it's nothing more than a farewell gift, something he found discarded in the Blood Cellar that he has no emotional connection to whatsoever. As my thoughts run rampant, I finally bring myself to read the note.

I need you to trust me. Until we meet again. —Alister
PS Merry Christmas

Confusion washes over me as I flip the note over in search of something more. That's it? That's— *Until we meet again.* I stare at the note, specifically those words, until my eyes cross and my vision blurs. Alister has always been so careful with his words, careful not to make false promises. And this...this makes it seem like—

No. I put the note back on the table, stand, and return to my pacing. No, no, he said we could never be together. He said his enemies, of which there are plenty, would use me against him. After what happened with Gallagher and Vitale, I know he's telling the truth. But...but if he no longer had enemies, if he were no longer the Blood King, then...? Is it even possible? He's said a million times before it isn't, that even if he left New Orleans, abandoning his throne entirely, his enemies would still hunt him. Because until he's dead he is the rightful leader of the Amato criminal organization. At that, I stop as my worry consumes me. *Trust me.*

"I do trust you," I whisper. I have no idea what he's planning, but he's up to something. And that *something* gives me hope. And, for better or worse, I'll cling to it until the pain of loving him is greater than the pain of losing him. And I'll pray that that day never comes.

36

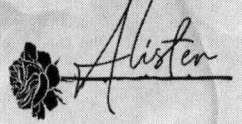

My parents' bedroom is just as I remember it. The walls are painted white. The floors are made of deep mahogany wood. Beautiful brass chandeliers and sconces hang from the ceilings and walls while the fading light of day filters in through the floor-to-ceiling windows once shattered by Vitale and his men. As I examine the room I haven't entered in years, I find everything as it should be. The windows, once broken, have been replaced. The floors, once covered in my mother's blood, have been scrubbed. The bed still has the same white down comforter. My mother's jewelry sits out atop her vanity while my father's slippers wait for him in the same exact place they always have.

This room is like a museum preserving the last remnants of my parents' lives. Perhaps that's why I've avoided it all this time. Between these walls, it feels as if they are still here, as if I should see my father walking out of the bathroom or my mother searching for something in her closet any minute now. But they are gone. And outside this room, I feel their absence so immensely that pretending, even for a second, that they aren't, that they can hear me, feels like a lie. Alas, today I welcome the lie.

As I move farther into the room, I blink away the memories of the night my family was changed forever and ease down onto the edge of the bed. Despite its absurdity, I'm almost afraid to ruin the perfect preservation of the room, afraid to breathe new life into it. As the old bed frame creaks under my weight, kicking up the most dreadful scent of mothballs and potpourri, it lets me know it feels the same way. In truth, I don't know why I'm here. Perhaps to tell my parents that I got him, the depraved bastard who took everything from us. *I got him, Mom.* As the thought comes to me, my throat aches. Or maybe I want to tell them that I met a girl. She's beautiful, smart, relentless, and strong—a fighter. *I think you'd like her, Dad. I think Cara would too.* At that, I move my eyes from the room before me to the leg of my black jeans. This is already hard enough and this room holds too many painful memories to allow my eyes to travel. *This.* There it is. The real reason why I'm here. I've come to say goodbye.

When Sophia told me she'd help me leave the Mafia for good a month ago now, I believed her. But I also believed it would be impossible without damning us both to a life on the run, which isn't a life at all. Still, I knew I'd underestimated my sister for long enough and she was right. After so many years with only one reason to remain atop the throne I never wanted—my family—I now have a reason to abandon it altogether. I now have a love worth fighting for, a shot at happiness worth pursuing. So, we put our heads together along with Gio and Cassio. We ran through every possibility and every outcome only to come up with one actionable plan.

I know you won't agree, Dad. After you and Grandpa worked so hard to maintain our family legacy, I'm sure you're rolling in your graves right now. But the truth is, I'm giving up the crown. The crown, the business, the power, the army. I'm giving it all away because it makes me a target. No. It makes her a target. And I couldn't live with myself if I lost Ariana in the same way you lost Mom, in the same way I lost Mom. I hope you can forgive me.

The new year will bring a new war. My enemies will flock to New Orleans once they hear of how close Vitale came to taking the throne, not to mention word of Cara's death is still spreading. They'll see my weakness as an invitation to try their luck. On top of that, there is the FBI's investigation, which could end with not only me in jail but everyone who works for me, including Ariana's father, which I cannot allow. I won't. Just as I desire a chance to love Ariana, to have her in my life day and night, she deserves a chance to know her father. And with my plan in motion, my initial hesitations regarding their relationship will ease. Alessandro Gagliano cannot be beholden to the Mafia nor prosecuted for his involvement in the Amato crime family if the Amato crime family no longer exists. So, there it is—the one way for me to avoid a war, protect my people, give them the choice I never had, allow Ariana a relationship with her father, and us a chance at happiness once and for all. I must abolish the Italian Mafia in New Orleans, and then I have to run.

It sounds simple. It's anything but. You see, I can't just walk away from the throne, book a flight, and never return. I must make it so that no other Cosa Nostra family may control this territory, *my* territory. Because if they do, they'll always see me and Sophia as threats. There will always be those who believe us to be the rightful leaders, and so they will hunt us. But if I relinquish my crown to a competing regime, one with a leader powerful enough to fend off all incoming threats, no Italian will stand a chance at taking it from them. But, while I am abolishing Italian rule, I am not leaving my people without a choice. I've found a leader with a vested interest in Ariana's safety who will welcome my capos, their soldiers, and their associates into their ranks, if they so choose. My capos' lives will change very little along with their bank accounts, and this will maintain the peace needed for an easy transition of power as will my absence.

For my men and other criminal outfits to accept the regime change, I must disappear. I must make it known that I have sanctioned this, and I am not a threat to the new power. And I must remain off-the-grid until the FBI concludes their investigation into me and the business that will soon enough no longer exist. If they find me innocent, I will be free. If they find me guilty, then today is my last day in the Crescent City. If they find me guilty, then the last time I saw Ariana truly was the last time. And our goodbye truly was goodbye.

At that, I run my fingers through my hair and take a deep breath. I didn't think it would come to this. Or maybe I did, it's just... Sophia gave me hope. Over the weeks, Ariana has consumed my every thought. Everything I'm doing is so that we can be together, free from the shackles of this world and its enemies. But there are still so many things that can go wrong. There is still a chance it will all be for nothing, that I'll be found guilty and forced to live out the rest of my days as a fugitive, not only without the drug money but without the income from my legitimate businesses. It will be a hard and lonely life, and the fear I've grown accustomed to over the years will only be amplified. Because I won't just be hunted. I'll be defenseless. That is why I haven't told Ariana of my plans. That is why no matter how badly I want her to, she can't come with me.

"Boss?" Gio knocks on the door as he enters the room. "She's here." I nod. As I turn to him, the reality of what I'm doing sets in. Gio wears his typical deep navy suit with a white button-down and a 45-caliber strapped to his waist. Whereas, I am, uncharacteristically, dressed in jeans, a long sleeve T-shirt, and leather jacket. That is because when I leave this place in mere hours, Gio will stay behind. He will inform the capos of the regime change and make sure things go smoothly while eliminating all evidence of our illegal doings from Laroux House and other business locations throughout the city. He fought me on the decision at first. In over ten years, we've never been apart for more than seventy-two hours. But there is no one I trust more than him to handle this most delicate matter. Not to mention the capos already respect him, and Sophia will have her hands full with running the legitimate Amato businesses from the safety of Cassio's compound in Savannah. "Are you ready?" he asks.

At that, I stand. "As I'll ever be."

Gio gives me a nod and returns downstairs, leaving me a final few moments alone in the place with the most painful of memories. I close my eyes and listen. I can still hear the bullet as it echoes through these very walls, ripping through my mother's body. I hear her collapse against the hard floors. I hear the men taunt my father. *It hurts, doesn't it? Losing the woman you love.* My lips press into a flat line as I open my eyes. For years now, I've replayed those words over and over again in my head. As I grew older, I felt a shift inside me as if they weren't just taunting my father. They were taunting me. They were threatening me and any woman I dared to love.

"Not anymore," I whisper then. "You don't get to control me anymore."

I cross the room to my father's dresser and my mother's vanity. I have far too many painful memories of them both. I search for something that may trigger a happier one I can cling to while away. I find it in my father's cross pendant. He always wore it tucked beneath his shirt collar as if it was a reminder of his own mortality. And now, I shall wear it too as a reminder that my days are limited and that everything I'm sacrificing now is so that I can spend the rest of them with Ariana, happy and safe. But what of her? Has our time together truly been enough to spark a love that will last a lifetime? For me, it has. But for her...

The way I left things with her was harsh and I haven't spoken to her since. There are still months before the FBI begins their investigation into my family unless the new task force leader moves up the timeline now that Bilieux is gone. That would allow me to return to Ariana sooner, but it would also increase the likelihood of a guilty verdict since Gio will have less time to get rid of evidence. All of this is to say that it could be a year or more before I'm able to return to Ariana. What if our time together isn't enough? What if she finds comfort in another? I suppose I can't blame her. I wouldn't. A normal, safe, and happy life is all I've ever wanted for her. But I'd be lying if I said the thought doesn't give me pause, that it doesn't make my blood boil, that it doesn't make me want to go get her right now and drag her with me regardless of her wishes. I want her to remember us, remember me, not for the monster this world forced me to become but for the man I am when I'm with her and the man I still wish to be. But is it fair of me to ask her to remember, to ask her to wait for me? No.

I bite my lip then as my eyes spot a red leather box on my mother's vanity. I don't have to open it to know what's inside. Though I am king, I am not the only Amato to wear the mark of our family. While my father had his ring, now passed to me, my mother and sisters had necklaces and brooches made of rubies and diamonds that bear the family crest. Every piece was hand-made in Italy before my ancestors immigrated to America, but unbeknownst to them was what the jewelry would come to represent. There are more of them stowed away somewhere, but the ones my family wear are special in that they've been outfitted with trackers. Completely undetectable, of course. The pieces are as functional as they are beautiful. I often wonder how things would've been different if Cara had been taken during the day rather than at night. If she was wearing her brooch, I could've tracked her. I could've found her. At that, I pick up the box and open it, taking in the beauty of the deep red stone.

Perhaps it isn't fair to ask Ariana to wait for me. And, considering her reinstatement to the FBI, it's most certainly best she doesn't know the extent of my plans to install a new leader of the criminal world here in New Orleans. But is it too much to ask her to trust me? Trust that everything I have done and will do is because I love her, even if she grows to no longer love me? I don't know. Maybe a reminder of our time together would only cause her more pain. Yet, the pit in my stomach lets me know I can't leave this city without giving her the necklace, without in this small way claiming her as mine.

I cross the room to my father's nightstand in search of a pen and paper. Finding just what I need, I hesitate. There isn't much room to say all the things I want to. Perhaps it's for the best. So, instead, I scribble my one basic plea—*Trust me*. There's a lump in my throat as I imagine how she will receive it. Perhaps she'll shove the necklace in the most cluttered drawer of her armoire never to look at it again. But maybe, just maybe, she will wear it. She will keep me close to her heart and allow me a glimpse into her life for however long this transition of power and investigation separates us. With resolve, I take the note and box in my hand and make my way downstairs to the dining room to finish what I've started.

When I enter the room filled with a massive oak wood table, I find Josephine Cullen sitting at the farthest end of it. She is flanked by her head of security, Avery Gallagher's replacement, just as Gio waits for me, standing behind my usual seat closest to the door.

"Mr. Amato, how nice of you to join us. I was beginning to think you'd changed your mind," Josephine says.

"Not at all. Just taking stock of a few things before I take my leave." I turn to Gio. "See to it Ariana receives this—tonight."

"But, Boss, the meeting," Gio protests.

"Go now," I tell him. Gio nods and does as he's told. As he closes the French doors behind him, I realize that that may be the last command I ever give him. How fitting?

"I have to say, Alister, I was surprised to receive your call," Josephine says as I take my seat. "It's not every day a territory of this size is delivered on a silver platter. If our fathers could see us now..."

"Yes, I've done my fair share of imagining their reactions. Mine would probably kill me before he let me remove this ring from my finger," I say, holding up my hand to examine it one last time.

"Well, I'm not as much interested in your ring as I am your signature. We Irish have our own customs and crowns."

"Right," I say then. "Shall we get on with it then?" I ask, moving my eyes to the papers.

"Yes," Josephine says. "Though, first, I must ask. Why me? I mean, there must be twenty people you thought of before me, what with your connections in Mexico and the Caribbean."

I lower my pen and meet her gaze. "You're the only one I can trust to look out for her. You're the only one I can trust not to bow to an enemy, who is free from weaknesses."

"You mean a husband, children," Josephine says, a glimmer of sadness in her cool blue eyes. "It's okay," she says then. "This world isn't a burden to all who inhabit it. I quite enjoy ordering around grown men and, of course, the smell of money."

At that, I smile and reach for my pen once more. As I sign away my territory, my birthright and greatest burden, a weight upon my shoulders is instantly lifted. I suppose I've been carrying it for so long I've forgotten it was there. Slowly, a smile spreads across my lips. I am doing this for Ariana. But, equally so, I am doing this for me. I am finally shedding the shackles of the Amato name and blood and, with the stroke of a pen, ending a reign over a century in the making.

"Blood is my beginning. My blood I will defend. Or, so help me, I will burn. By blood, I will meet my end."

As I recite the Blood Oath for the final time, I stand, knowing that what I've just done will either be the best decision of my life or the worst.

37

ONE YEAR LATER

As Ray and Sabine close in behind me, I dig my toes into the gravel and propel myself faster beneath the oak trees of Audubon Park. After a year of training together, I've finally got some competition. Well, that and Ray is trying to impress our task force's most recent recruit. I would say he's predictable, always going for his female coworkers, but my six-month suspension made me forget how much we work. There's really no time to meet someone outside the bureau between cases. Not that I've been looking. Besides, when I'm not working, in therapy, or with Ray, I'm with my dad. He and I have breakfast once a week and a weekly family dinner with his wife and my three half siblings. I have two brothers and a sister all under the age of twenty. You'd think they'd be skeptical of me, especially Gia, but after thirteen years of being the only girl, she welcomed me in with open arms. To my surprise, so did Stephanie, my dad's wife.

I can remember shortly after they came into my life, or rather, I came into theirs, my dad sat me down and told me he'd never stopped loving my mom. He didn't want me to think that Stephanie was a replacement for her and that my siblings were meant to replace me, the child he lost so many years before. He said it may not make sense to say it's possible to be in love with two people at once, but that when my mom was taken from him, the place in his heart that she inhabited, that *we* inhabited, was forever reserved for her and the life he never got to live.

Hearing him speak of her broke me and made me happy all at once. My mom's journal reveals her concern that Sandro had stopped loving her, that that's why he never found her, found us. It would make her happy to know that wasn't the case at all. He never stopped loving her, even once he accepted that she was gone and with her so was any chance of them being together. And yet it breaks me, then and now, to think of the pain my father went through when he lost my mom. It is a pain I know all too well and a tragic reality I fear I'll soon enough be forced to accept.

Alister was last seen entering Prague a year ago. That is where he flew to when he left New Orleans, and yet, his jet has remained parked and his whereabouts unknown ever since. I still don't know why he left. I can only assume it has something to do with the FBI's investigation into him and his business, but that ended months ago. He was cleared of all charges, or rather, suspicion, since Bilieux's deal prohibited the use of any previously gathered evidence, and by the time the investigation began, there was nothing left to find. And with Bilieux gone, Ray is the only other person in the bureau who knows of my relationship or past relationship with Alister. Thankfully, he never pushed me to divulge anything I learned during my time with Alister to our new boss, not that I would've. I'd sooner quit before I betray Alister. With the money I inherited from Christio Vitale's estate as the sole heir it's not like I have to work. Though I'm certain I'd go crazy if I didn't, especially without Alister to keep me company, or rather, keep me busy.

But, a year later, I'm wondering if he still has the same loyalty to me.

I keep replaying the words *trust me* over and over again in my head. And I have trusted him. But the more time that passes, I can't help but wonder what am I trusting him to do? Am I trusting that he made the right decision not just in leaving me, but breaking up with me? Or am I trusting him to return to me? That's what I originally thought seeing as his note also says, *until we meet again*. But if he's going to return to New Orleans, if he's going to return to me, then what is keeping him?

As various scenarios dance through my head, I push myself harder and faster, fighting against the wind chill while inhaling the earthy scent of the swaying oaks as the finish line nears. Perhaps he's taking time for himself, learning to make peace with his past like I am. We both have our fair share of demons that haunt us. While I have made progress in the year since he left—I am no longer plagued by nightmares—there are certain wounds that may never heal, wounds that lie dormant until pricked by a certain event, memory, or conversation. While I have long accepted this, which is perhaps why I put off going to therapy for so long, I'm not sure Alister can accept a lack of perfection. Is he waiting to become whole before he returns to me? With the trauma that he's been through, that may never happen. But it doesn't make him any less worthy of love or capable of loving me. Although, as saddening as that thought is, it is not the worst of those that worry me.

Perhaps his world caught up to him. He always spoke of his enemies viewing what happened to his sister as an invitation to challenge him, and then after what happened with Vitale... Is that why he left? To draw his enemies away from New Orleans, away from me? Or did he leave in defeat, essentially giving up his throne to whomever can claim it first? No. That doesn't make sense. If he did that, he'd never be able to return. Not to mention my job would've been a lot more complicated over the past year with turf wars leaving dead bodies all over the French Quarter. As it stands, it's been relatively calm, so calm a lot of our time has gone to tracking international criminal syndicates rather than domestic ones.

I shake my head as confusion consumes me and do my best to lose myself in my run. But it's no use. My mind like my heart is still completely occupied by the man with the raven-colored hair and golden-brown eyes. As I reach my finish line, the place along the pond where I share my happiest memories with my mom, I'm forced to confront a less than happy thought, one that's been consuming me for months now. Maybe I need to accept that Alister Amato is gone, and he isn't coming back. Though the mere thought leaves me with an ache greater than any run ever could. I'm not ready. Even after all this time, I'm not ready to give up on us. While our time together was fleeting, our love is not. It was, *is* a love to last a lifetime, even if we are destined to spend our lives apart.

"Girl, how did you get so fast?" Sabine asks, stumbling through her finish as Ray trails behind her.

"She secretly has wings. It took me six years to figure it out, but she has wings. I'm calling it," Ray says. When he reaches us, he falls to the ground, red-faced. Though, I imagine on a day like today he'll cool down fast enough.

"He's right," I say with a soft laugh. "Anyway, thanks for joining me. I know it's Christmas and you've got to get back to your families."

"Well, what about you?" Sabine asks. "Don't you have plans?"

I cross my arms over my chest as the wind seeps through the fabric of my black running shirt. "My family actually decided to do things on Christmas Eve this year. So, no, not really." Sabine looks at Ray, who looks at me. "No, no, I'm not trying to impose. I have like ten hours of Christmas movies waiting for me. Plus, I'm picking up takeout from the Court of Two Sisters."

"No," Ray says, pushing himself up from the ground. "No, you're coming with me. My mom always makes enough food to feed a small army, and besides, no one should spend Christmas alone. That's something the *old* Ariana would do, and *you* are not backsliding, you hear me?" He immediately crosses his arms and raises his brow as if daring me to protest.

I laugh. "*Fine.* I just need to go home, shower, and change."

"I'll come with," Ray says. "That way we can pick out our white elephant gifts together."

"White elephant gift?" Now it's my turn to raise my brow.

"My dear, Ari, you have so much to learn."

THE COOL CHRISTMAS breeze hurries me along as I fumble for my keys and unlock my door. Ray scurries in behind me. "Oh, look at you. You finally put up a Christmas tree," he says as I close the door behind us.

"Yeah, well, I had a little more time on my hands this year than last," I say, kicking off my tennis shoes. "So, how fancy should I dress? I've heard the stories of your mom's parties. I can only assume jeans are a no go."

"Whatever you wear will be fine," Ray says. "Though, I wouldn't go as fancy as this."

"Fancy as wh—" I turn to find Ray standing beside an open person-sized Louis Vuitton luggage trunk, the kind I've only seen once before. And yet, what it contains is unlike anything I've ever seen. Inside the trunk is a mannequin dressed in the most gorgeous strapless ball gown in existence. The skirt is made of ivory tulle with enough petticoats to take up half my living room. Draped over half of the ivory skirt is red velvet fabric that gathers at the hip to form a rose. "Oh my God," I whisper as my eyes drift from the hem up to the neckline. The corseted bodice cinches in at the waist, creating the most beautiful, classic shape. The bodice itself is a combination of white and red lace made to look like flowers. And yet, it is not the stunning nature of the dress that steals my breath. It is the red ruby and diamond necklace draped around the mannequin's neck, which tells me exactly who this luxe gift is from.

"There's a note," Ray says. I take a step toward him, speechless, as my throat aches with emotion. I reach out to him so he can hand me the note. "Ari, are you okay?"

"More than okay," I say, my voice raspy. Finally, I move my eyes from the dress to him.

"You won't be needing that white elephant gift, will you?" he says, my reaction giving it away. I laugh and pull the note from its deep red envelope.

You are cordially invited to a
Christmas Ball
An evening of cocktails, music, and dancing.
hosted by
THE AMATO FAMILY
with the Historical Preservation Society of New Orleans
Saturday, December 25
From 7:00 p.m. until 11:00 p.m.
Laroux House
443 King's Lane, Mandeville

38

Alister

To mark my return to New Orleans, Sophia has outdone herself with organizing our most glamorous Christmas Ball yet. While the grand marble staircase leading to the second floor is adorned with candles on each step and the banister is draped with green garland, the white walls and floor of the ballroom overlooking the gardens of Laroux House are illuminated by the glow of Christmas trees along the perimeter of the room. Each tree is decorated with ornaments in shades of red and pink, while strands of pearls, diamonds, and lace add a delicate touch that complements the oversize crystal chandelier hanging from above.

An Amato tradition, the party has slipped to the wayside the past few years, which makes this year's ball feel even more special. It represents a new beginning for us all. While Sophia and Cassio are living happily married in Savannah, Gio has maintained our family home and started up a new business under the fully legitimized Amato Family Holdings umbrella. It's a private security firm made up largely of my former soldiers and associates who chose not to join Josephine's regime. Speaking of which, I hear the transition has gone smoothly. She, of course, is based in Boston, but has chosen a worthy proxy to manage the southern territories. I say *worthy* not because I've met him, but because he somehow managed to keep a war from occurring in the same streets Ariana calls home. I've stayed aware enough of the underworld's dealings to make sure she's remained safe, but that's all the interest I have in it. And now that I'm back and Gio has our own personal army installed and outfitted with custom Cassio Castellani creations, everything is ready for our next chapter. After all this time, I can only hope Ariana is still willing to have me as part of her story.

I pull the black velvet ring box from my pocket to take in the eight-carat emerald-cut stunner. It's a bit big for Ariana's more demure taste, but if she chooses to accept my proposal, I want her wearing a ring that is impossible to miss. That way I'll feel justified in my reaction to whatever man is dumb enough to approach her.

"Alright, brother, the guests are starting to arrive," Sophia says as she makes her way to me with Cassio in tow. Marriage looks good on them, though I'm not sure I can say the same thing about Sophia's dress. The strapless neckline of the bloodred gown is far too low, the waist far too tight, and the hip-high slit reveals more of my sister than I'm comfortable seeing.

"*Really, Sophia?*" I ask before pinning Cassio with a stern look. "You let her out looking like that?"

"Hey, you know how futile it is to argue with your sister, especially over her wardrobe," Cassio says, raising his hands in surrender. "Not to mention, if anyone makes a move on her, I am more than capable of handling them." At that, Sophia kisses him on the cheek. I see she's trained him well. I wonder if Ariana will try the same with me. I wonder if I'll let her get away with it.

"Well, I might as well wear it while I can. Before long, I won't be able to fit into anything I own." Sophia and Cassio exchange a knowing look before she turns her gaze to me. It's then that her words finally hit me.

"Wait. Wait, are you?"

Sophia nods. "I'm pregnant."

"Oh my God! Congratulations," I say as I offer them both hugs. "A new Amato heir. Wow."

"Makes it all worth it, doesn't it?" Sophia asks, moving her hand to her stomach. "Because of you, our baby never has to know the same pain we did. He or she will never have to carry the same burdens or live with the same fear."

"Because of *us*. And yeah, yeah, it does make it all worth it. Though, hopefully, your pregnancy won't be the only reason."

Sophia nods. "Have you heard from Ariana?"

"Not yet," I say, refusing to give in to the worry lurking in the darkest corners of my mind.

"You will," Sophia says then. "And don't worry, her dress is far more modest than mine. It's a combination of white and Amato red to represent not only our family but our hope, *your hope*. May *both* our futures be bright, brother."

At that, Sophia motions for the staff to open the French doors to the cool December night just as our first guests make their way up the back stairwell from the horse-drawn carriages. The sight reminds me of the night Ariana and I met. She crashed into my life like a bull. To say I wasn't ready for her would be an understatement. But tonight, I am ready, ready to claim her, to love her, to pledge my life to her. I only hope she gives me the chance.

⊱❦⊰

AFTER BREAKING free from another incessant conversation about my sudden year-long absence, I glance at my watch. We're an hour and a half into the party and there's still no sign of

Ariana. Whatever hope and excitement I had coming into this evening has officially vanished. As I make my way toward the exit, I grab a bourbon from a passing server. By the time I've made it to the concrete stairwell leading down to the quiet gardens, I've finished my drink and long for another. Alas, that would require returning to the party with far too little food and far too many guests. All of New Orleans high society must be in attendance, all except for the one woman I hoped to see. Resolved in my retreat, I abandon my empty glass and continue down the steps until I reach the last one, where I take a seat to wallow in my sorrow.

I should've come back sooner. I just...I wanted everything to be perfect for her, for us. I wanted Laroux House fortified, our army in place, and all my business dealings handled so that the moment I saw her, it could just be the two of us. I could lose myself in her warm eyes, in her gentle touch without a worry for tomorrow or even next month or next year. I want that time with her. But what if all I did was rob us of that time? What if I truly did lose her?

I shake my head. Even now, I lie to myself. I tell myself I stayed away for so long because I wanted to make a perfect life for us, but the truth is, *I* wanted to be perfect.

While I've made progress with my grief, I wanted to find a way to let go of my insecurities and my feelings of inadequacy. Just because I've relinquished my throne and walked away from my life of crime doesn't mean I carry any fewer sins. I am a murderer, a monster. My soul is still stained with the blood of others. My mind is still riddled with the screams and cries of the men I've tortured. It's because of this that I've never felt worthy of Ariana's love. I thought I could find a way to heal that wound, to forgive myself, to believe myself a man worthy of her heart. But that is a wound only she can heal. Only she can make me feel worthy, and yet, her absence tonight only reaffirms that I'm not. She was never mine to love, only mine to—

The soft click of a horse's hooves against the gravel draws my attention to my right. The path through the shady gardens upon which the guests arrive is dark, lit only at the end by two antique streetlamps. I stand and move toward them as the clicking, no, galloping grows louder. As I move, my eyes widen in anticipation and my heartbeat quickens in my chest. Could it really be her? Please, please let it be her. Through the darkness, a horse and its open-air carriage emerge. I can't see who the passenger is. Still, the sight of it makes my legs go numb with nerves. *Come on. Come on.* As the horse reaches the end of the path, the driver hops from his post, revealing the most beautiful raven-haired woman who has ever existed, my love, Ariana.

Unable to be apart from her a moment more, I push through the prickly sensation in my legs and run to her. "Allow me," I say, sending the driver on his way. As Ariana's warm eyes meet mine, her pink-painted lips draw up into a smile that tugs on every part of my soul letting me know I am finally home. Unable to speak, I offer her my hand. As she takes it, her simple touch is too irresistible. I need more. I need her. *Now.* I move both my hands to her waist and pull her from the carriage in one fell swoop. She squeals at my touch. It's the cutest sound. As I lower her to the ground, she grabs hold of my arms to help with her balance. But she needn't worry. I never plan to let her go again.

"I was beginning to think you weren't coming," I say, moving my hands from her hips to her lower back, pulling her tighter against me. She parts her lips in response, giving in to my touch. Yet as she lifts her eyes to meet mine, it isn't submission I find in them, rather fire.

"You made me wait for you an entire year. The least you can do is wait an hour or two for me." At that, I laugh. In her presence, it comes so easily to me, everything does because Ariana doesn't just represent love or even hope to me. She represents freedom. She *is* my freedom, my lifeline. Yet, she will also be my keeper just as I will be hers. She will remind me of the best parts of me while loving my ugly. And I will protect her from all who would do her harm and love her enough to chase away any fear of abandonment, any taste of loneliness. She will never know such pain again.

"I'm going to have my hands full with you, aren't I?" I ask.

"Did you expect anything less?"

BOOK PLAYLIST

"Lovely" by Billie Ellish & Khalid
"Let Me Hurt (Acoustic)" by Emily Rowed
"In The Stars" by Benson Boone
"Dark Times" by The Weeknd (feat. Ed Sheehan)
"Hostage" by Billie Ellish
"Oxygen" by Emeli Sande
"Are You Scared of Love" by Maya's Diary
"For Tonight" by GIVEON
"Hopeless Romantics" by James TW
"You Should See Me in a Crown" by Billie Ellish
"Take Me Home" by Jess Glynne
"Glitter" by Nicolina
"Scared" by Josh Nichols
"Pull Me Down" by Mikky Ekko

ALSO BY EMILY A. MYERS

The Truth About Unspeakable Things
Bound by the Unspeakable

ABOUT THE AUTHOR

Emily A. Myers is an award-winning author of romantic suspense. When not writing, Emily enjoys traveling, devouring the latest Netflix series, and scouring the shelves of Sephora. Connect with Emily via her website www.emilyamyers.com or on social media @emilymyersauthor

ACKNOWLEDGMENTS

I'd like to personally thank my cover designer, Vanessa Mendozzi and my editor, Beth Attwood. For business inquiries, you can reach both of them through Reedsy.

I'd also like to thank my beta readers, Marisa Sevenski and Monika Moreva.

Lastly, I'd like to thank the bookstagram community for keeping me excited and motivated to write. And, of course, all of you who have been with me from the beginning and who have given me constant encouragement.

Manufactured by Amazon.ca
Bolton, ON

39368000R00231